Thin Ice

Thin Ice

Crime Stories
by
New England Writers

Edited by

Mark Ammons

Kat Fast

Barbara Ross

Leslie Wheeler

Level Best Books
Somerville, Massachusetts 02144

Level Best Books
P.O. Box 371
Somerville, Massachusetts 02144
www.levelbestbooks.com

text composition/design by Kat Fast
Printed in the USA

ISBN 978-0-9700983-8-1

Library of Congress Catalog Card Data available.
First Edition
10 9 8 7 6 5 4 3 2 1

Thin Ice

Contents

Introduction   ix

The Bank Job
          Bev Vincent   1

A Good, Safe Place
          Judith Green   15

Double Take
          Mo Walsh   31

Duck Sandwich
          Mark Ammons   45

Key West
          Barbara Ross   52

The Kitchen Witch
          S.A. Daynard   67

Wall to Wall
          John R. Clark   81

A Perfect Landing
          Kat Fast   89

Closer
          Joe Ricker   96

Madame Blavatsky Takes a Lover
          Mary E. Stibal   111

Tribute
          Michael Nethercott   120

Gracie Walks the Plank
          Kate Flora   131

Reduction in Force

       Edith M. Maxwell   145

Size Matters

       Sheila Connolly   157

Changes

       Ruth M. McCarty   173

Unleashed

       Cheryl Marceau   179

Inside Out

       Virginia Young   192

Long Live the Queen

       Alan D. McWhirter   198

The Recumbent Cow

       Susan Oleksiw   213

Hard Fall

       Ben Hanstein   230

Ring of Fire

       Steve Liskow   242

Tag, You're Dead

       J.A. Hennrikus   248

Communion

       Ray Daniel   252

The Book Signing

       Kathy Chencharik   261

Dead Man's Shoes

       Leslie Wheeler   263

Introduction

When the editors at Level Best Books announced that the seventh anthology, *Quarry*, would be their last, like many in the New England writing community, we were disappointed but not surprised. Disappointed, because the Level Best collections have been such an important and integral part of the New England mystery writing scene. Not surprised, because we knew the anthologies were a labor of love, with emphasis on both the labor and the love.

The idea that we would take on Level Best started as a "could we?" and rapidly progressed to a "should we?" We were ardent fans of the collections, and, in fact, two of the four of us had our first fiction publication with Level Best. We had functioned together as a writers group for almost fifteen years. We knew each other's strengths and weaknesses; we had a lot of complementary skills and perspectives; but we had never run a business together. Incredibly, we found the more we talked about the prospect, and the more we talked to the former editors, the more enthusiastic we became. "Should we?" became "we must." The die was cast. We stood in a circle, held hands high, and vowed to do our "level best."

Kate Flora, Ruth M. McCarty and Susan Oleksiw have been generous in their support. We truly would not be here today without them—without their advice, without their patience in answering what must have seemed the most obvious questions, and, most of all, without the legacy they created by having published seven previous anthologies of the highest quality short fiction.

With this edition, we have tried to honor that legacy. Like the previous editors, we have included stories from debut authors and veterans, and from authors all around New England, telling every kind of tale that can be told with a crime at its center. We have aimed to do this the way that Kate, Ruth and Susan did, by using quality as our ultimate guidepost.

As always, we are proud to begin the anthology with this year's winner of the Al Blanchard Award. Bev Vincent's "The Bank Job" is a rich story about the power of loyalty and friendship. In counterpoint, Ray Daniel's "Communion" looks at the same themes from a different and darker angle.

We've also included a 2009 Al Blanchard honorable mention winner: Mo Walsh's "Double Take" explores the improbable connection between lederhosen and larceny.

Edith M. Maxwell's "Reduction in Force," about the dangers of layoffs, and J.A. Hennrikus' "Tag, You're Dead," about Facebook, tell tales that are particularly of the moment, while in Mary E. Stibal's "Madame Blavatsky Takes a Lover" and Michael Nethercott's "Tribute," the actions in the present spring from events buried in the past.

Cheryl Marceau has her first fiction publication with "Unleashed," a tale of a New England town meeting gone terribly wrong. John R. Clark's "Wall to Wall" also describes a uniquely New England crime revolving around a stone wall.

Judith Green is published for the eighth time by Level Best with the brilliant "A Good, Safe Place." While Woody Hanstein's stories have appeared in the anthologies in the past, this year, his son Ben makes his Level Best debut with the comic romp "Hard Fall."

In "The Book Signing," Kathy Chencharik flashes us with a grisly surprise in under four hundred words. Sheila Connolly's "Size Matters" and Alan D. McWhirter's "Long Live the Queen" weave satisfying whodunnits in a few thousand words. Steve Liskow's "Ring of Fire" and Joe Ricker's "Closer" tell stories of revenge. S.A. Daynard and Virginia Young challenge us to question everything we read in "The Kitchen Witch" and "Inside Out," respectively

This year, we are delighted to have wonderful submissions from all three former editors with Kate Flora's "Gracie Walks the Plank," Ruth M. McCarty's "Changes" and Susan Oleksiw's "The Recumbent Cow." And finally, we're pleased to offer our own stories with Mark Ammons' "Duck Sandwich," Kat Fast's "A Perfect Landing," Barbara Ross' Al Blanchard 2010 honorable mention story "Key West," and Leslie Wheeler's "Dead Man's Shoes."

Before we began work, the former editors warned us that the quality of the submissions had gone up in each of the previous seven years, and that the decisions would be challenging indeed. Seeing for the first time the rich variety we have to choose from, we now understand better the difficulty of the task. But, we think we've done Kate, Ruth and Susan proud, and we hope you enjoy reading the collection as much as we enjoyed putting it together.

Mark Ammons
Kat Fast
Barbara Ross
Leslie Wheeler

The Bank Job

Bev Vincent

I didn't even know that Joey DeStefano was out of the joint. Last I heard he was serving three to five in Walpole for roughing up a pregnant woman who fell behind on her payments. I figured I was free of him for at least another year.

"Frankie," he says when I answer the phone. My skin goes cold when I realize who it is. I briefly consider saying "Wrong number" and hanging up, but that would only delay the inevitable. It's not like I can go somewhere to get away from him. I don't even have enough money for caller ID.

"We have a little unfinished business," Joey says.

I don't know what to say, so I say nothing. He's probably used to that. Takes a guy with high self-esteem to do his job, since pretty much everyone hates him. It'd give me a complex. I want people to like me, which is one reason I get into so much trouble. Someone says to me, "Hey, Frankie, let's knock over that convenience store," and I say "Sure" just to be agreeable. Next thing you know the cops are on our tail, and I have to lay low for a while. One of these days I'm going to figure out how much of my life I've spent laying low. At least half, I bet.

"When did you get out?" I ask, not because I care, but because it's something to talk about besides the five grand I owe him that I don't have.

1

"Last week," Joey says. "Good behavior," which I think is pretty hilarious, but I keep that to myself and offer him my congratulations. He probably thinks I'm kissing up, which I kinda am. "I'm a little upset you didn't visit me," he says.

I can't tell if he's joking or not. "I'm allergic to prisons," I say, and he laughs like it's the funniest thing he's ever heard. Makes me laugh, too, though all of a sudden I feel like I need to go to the bathroom.

"Doesn't explain why you didn't write," he says, and just like that, I'm the only one laughing. I clear my throat. My palms are sweaty. Then Joey laughs again, but this time I don't join in. I'm too busy thinking about how I'm going to get out of this hole that suddenly dug itself around me. I've been pretty much keeping my nose clean lately. A few little things, but nothing major, nothing that can get me into big trouble . . . and yet trouble found me all the same.

"The way I see it, Frankie, old buddy, old pal," Joey says, not that we've ever been any more buddies than you're a buddy of the guy who mugs you in a back alley. Definitely not pals. "The way I see it, I've got fifteen grand coming my way."

"Five," I say before I can stop myself. That's another problem I have. Can't keep my damned trap shut. Talk first, think later—that's me. One day it will be the death of me. Seriously.

"Compound interest, Frankie. Plus a penalty, whatcha call a late fee. Just like the IRS. Like I said—you shoulda sent me a few letters while I was away. Kept up with your payments, you know?"

I only thought I was in a bad spot. Five gees is way beyond my means, let alone, what, two, three times as much. Might as well be a million. So I do the only thing a guy in my position can do: I lie. "I've got your money, Joey. Honest." Guys like Joey appreciate it when you tell them you're being honest. It reassures them. "It'll take me a few days to get at it, is all. Maybe a week." My mind is swimming. "Two, tops." Two years wouldn't be long enough for me to raise that kind of money.

Joey doesn't say anything. For a minute I think we've been disconnected, but no such luck. Me and luck, we ain't on a first-name basis, let me tell you. We're hardly even on speaking terms. I've been doing my best to stay away from racetracks and casinos, because that's what got me into this mess in the first place. Bad luck. Those places, they know what they're doing, with their free booze and pretty girls. They mess with your mind, make you take risks you wouldn't ordinarily.

"I don't wanna have to do something we'll both regret," Joey says finally. That's pretty funny, too, because Joey doesn't regret anything except lending money to deadbeats and getting busted by the cops. Everything else about his business he plain enjoys, including sending a few guys overdosed on steroids to beat someone into seeing the wisdom of getting back on the payment schedule. He absolutely loves that. Sometimes he rides along just to watch.

"Don't suppose you'd take a check," I say with a laugh that sounds hollow to my ears.

Joey chuckles. "Tell you what," he says. "Stop by and see me tomorrow afternoon . . . let me check here . . . around two. You know the place. Then you can tell me how you're gonna come up with that much money when you can't afford a Happy Meal. Then I'll explain your options." He doesn't say "Capice" at the end, because he's trying to get away from his ethnic roots, but I hear it all the same. He hangs up without saying goodbye. I guess he has other calls to make, other people to intimidate. Busy guy.

Joey's call ruins my day to say the least. Likely to spoil the rest of my pathetic life, too, unless I can come up with a plan, and fast. The only thing I can think to do is join my buddies down at Marty's at the end of Beacon Street in Chelsea, near the river. That's where some of my best thinking gets done. Some of my worst, too, to be honest, but I'm all out of options, and I don't look forward to hearing the ones Joey will have for me tomorrow.

The boys and me, we have a table near the back. It's next to the bathrooms, so it's almost always free. We have this thing we do whenever one of us arrives. Everyone who's already there calls out the guy's name, just like on TV with that big guy, Norm. It sounds a little lame when there's only one person there, but it picks up after that, and we always get a kick out of it. I like hearing my buddies calling out my name. I mean, there are probably people in the world who don't have two friends to do something like that for them, let alone four.

The guys figure out pretty fast that there's something on my mind, probably on account of the way I ask Holly for a shot with my beer. I don't usually splurge on liquor, but I'm willing to go a day without food for that warm burn and its afterglow. After all, if I don't come up with a plan, and soon, I'm not going to be eating anything that won't go through a straw—and that's only if Joey is feeling generous. Not a trait he's known for.

"What's up, Frankie?" Huey asks. His real name is Donald, but we call him Huey, you know, like in the cartoons. He doesn't seem to mind. We could have picked Duey, after all.

Holly delivers my drinks, and the others hold their questions while I take care of business. They all know I'm sweet on Holly, but she's out of my league. You can tell she's got class, in spite of the get-up Marty makes her wear. I think she looks sweet in her ripped T-shirt and skimpy shorts, but she'd look good in anything. She always has a smile for me, and today's no exception. I want to say something cheerful and witty, but I've got a lot on my mind, so all I manage is "Thanks," which is kind of lame, because just about everyone says that.

The scotch burns all the way down, like kerosene. The beer puts out the fire, which I guess is why you drink them in that order. I clear my throat and say, "Joey DeStefano called me a while ago. He's out of jail."

My friends all nod. Most of them have done business with Joey, so they know what that means. "How much you owe him?" Edgar asks. The others are probably wondering the same thing, but Edgar's the only one who would come right out and ask. He's about six-six, two-eighty, and thick as two short planks, whatever that means. It's one of those things my daddy used to say that sounds like it makes sense, but doesn't. Edgar's a solid guy, though. There's nothing he wouldn't do for a person—friend or stranger. Happy? Let me tell you, you'll never meet a happier guy this side of the looney bin.

"Fifteen," I say. There's no point in lying. If I make it less, the guys might not think it's so bad. I mean, most of them live in houses, and some of them even have regular jobs. Like I said, it might as well be a million bucks for me, but for the others maybe it's not very much.

"Whoa," Mikey says in that high-pitched girlie voice of his, and the others look equally shocked, so I guess it is a lot after all.

"Whatcha gonna do?" Vinnie asks. "I mean, you don't got that much, right?"

"Huh," I say. "I've never seen that much money in one place in my whole life. Supposed to be only five, but Joey said there's compound interest and late fees."

"Like the IRS," Edgar says. He had some bad dealings with them a few years back. Almost went to jail, but that didn't dampen his spirits one bit. At least the Feds weren't going to break his jaw, or chop off a finger, or kill him, nothing like that. I mean, that's not the sort of stuff they do, is it?

"Yeah, that's what he said."

We're all quiet for a while. Holly comes by often to see if we need anything. She takes good care of us. I wish I had more money, so I could tip her every now and then, but she doesn't seem to hold it against me. She must sense something's wrong, though, because the fourth time she passes our table she says, "It's happy hour. Next round is on the house." We all know it isn't, because Marty's never has happy hour, especially not one where the drinks are free, but it's kind of her to offer, and we pretty much have to play along or else it would be like we were calling her a liar, right?

After we finish this round of drinks, Vinnie comes up with a great idea. I mean, Einstein would have been proud of this one. The way he lays it out, it's like something you might see on TV or at the movies, it's that brilliant. All I have to do is tell Joey we're going to rob a bank, and that will be the end of my problems.

"He'll love it," Mikey says. "You'll see."

□   □   □

"You gotta be kiddin' me," Joey says the next afternoon when I meet him at the bowling alley on Saratoga where he hangs out. He has a big booth not far from the counter where they rent shoes that's within shouting distance of the bar.

Trying my best not to look too hurt by his reaction, I explain how we have the whole thing worked out. We sketched it all out on a napkin and transferred it to a sheet of paper Holly fetched for us from Marty's office. Edgar knows where to get ski masks, I tell him, and Huey says he can come up with a few guns.

"So, when is this great heist scheduled for?" Joey asks.

"Next week," I say, being careful not to spill all the beans. "We still have to case the joint and get our gear together. Pick up a getaway car. You know, stuff like that." Joey must have robbed his fair share of banks in his time. Where else would he get all the money that he lends people?

"Right," he says. "Right." I can tell he's thinking about something from the way he says it, like he's talking to himself. Then he looks me square in the eyes and says, "Do you know what assets are, Frankie?"

"Yeah," I say, though I have only a vague idea.

"Then you understand that I have to protect mine." Joey waves at the bartender and a few seconds later a buxom waitress on roller skates arrives with a glass of draft. I'm not offended that he didn't ask me if I wanted anything. Not much, anyway. He takes a sip, wipes his mouth on his sleeve and says, "Right now, Frankie, you're one of my assets. You're worth fifteen grand on the books. How you gonna pay me back if you get arrested during this crazy stick-up?"

"It's not crazy," I say, though probably not loud enough to be heard over the rumbling from the nearby bowling lanes.

"You ever hit a bank before?"

I contemplate lying again. All it would take is the word "Yeah," but then he'd probably ask me questions I couldn't answer, so I shake my head. "Convenience stores, though," I say. "And a liquor store once."

"Yeah, yeah, I remember that job. As I recall, the guy behind the counter tripped the alarm, and you had to high-tail it outta there with nothing."

"Mikey got a case of smokes."

"This is how it's gonna be, Frankie. You and me, we're gonna be partners. You don't do nothing without checking with me first." Again, no "Capice," but I can tell he wants to say it. "You're no good to me cooling your heels in Walpole."

I'm no good to him in traction, either, but I keep this thought to myself. Around Joey, I do a much better job of keeping my mouth shut than usual, because all he needs to do is nod at the right guy and my body would end up in a landfill with a bowling ball crammed down my throat.

"I hear you been doing stuff you're not telling me about, and we'll talk again, and it won't be in such posh surroundings. Clear?"

I nod without saying anything. Feels like the bowling ball is already wedged in my throat.

□   □   □

This bank job is complicated. Not penny ante stuff like we've done where we see a place, go in, stick our index fingers through our jacket pockets, and take what we can. Unless, of course, the guy behind the counter triggers the alarm, as Joey so kindly reminded me. None of us ever cased a place before, so we find some paperback novels with bank robberies in them and read those parts a few times until we know what to do. Edgar underlines all the important passages, so we can refer to them again.

Huey comes up with two starter pistols, two cap guns and a flare gun. They look pretty real to me. It's not like we're going to shoot anyone, after all. Edgar must have looted his grandmother's knitting basket for the ski masks. They have bright stripes and pom-poms on the top.

Mikey scouts a couple of banks in Chelsea, but when I tell Joey about this, he snorts and says something about not crapping in your own backyard, which I take to mean we shouldn't rob a bank in the neighborhood. Because Vinnie is the only one with a car, he scopes out a couple of places across the Mystic. He brings Mikey along to take pictures, something we learned from one of those paperbacks we skimmed.

Joey keeps calling me to find out what's going on, and I keep answering because I think it might be one of the guys. "Tick tock," he tells me during one of these calls to remind me he's not going to wait forever for us to pull off the gig, and the interest is mounting daily. "Pretty soon you're going to owe me twenty gees," he says, which boggles my mind.

The night before the bank job, we meet at Marty's, like always. Vinnie and Mikey are the last ones to arrive. "Vinnie," the three of us say, because he's a few steps ahead. We wait for him to sit down and then call out "Mikey." I catch sight of Holly picking up a drink-laden tray from the bartender. She's smiling. For a second, I almost forget about all that money.

Mikey pulls a bunch of pictures from his coat pocket. After Holly delivers our orders, he spreads them across the tabletop. "This is the place. It's not one of those chain banks. Vinnie thought they would probably have more experience getting robbed, so we eliminated them."

The rest of us nod. Makes perfect sense. From the outside, it looks like just about any other bank. A brick building with double doors in front. There's a parking lot to one side and meters on the street in front.

The bar gets quiet all of a sudden. When we look up, there's Joey looming over us with two thugs in tow. Joey might be trying to play down his ethnic origins, but he and his musclemen look exactly like what they are: Trouble with a capital T.

"Frankie, you neglected to invite me to this little rendezvous." He likes to throw around big words like that. He looks at my friends. "Gentlemen," he says, as if he's just stopping by to say hello. No such luck. He grabs an empty chair from a nearby table and pulls up next to me. One of his goons watches the main entrance, and the other keeps an eye on us.

"I was going to call you," I say. "Honest."

Joey grabs Mikey's pictures and looks them over. He holds one up to the guy staring at us the way a Rottweiler eyes a chunk of beef "Whatcha think?"

The goon squints at it and nods, which is hard for him to do since he doesn't have a neck. "Could be done," he says.

"When are you planning to hit it?" Joey asks me.

"Tomorrow."

"What time?"

That's a detail we haven't worked out yet. "Ten o'clock," I say, picking a number out of the air, because I'm on the spot.

"Right when they open. Good thinking," Joey says. "I'm coming witcha."

About twenty things leap into my mind. Fortunately, none of them make it past my lips. I nod.

Joey looks at the others. "I know what you're thinking," he says. I'm glad he does, because I sure as hell don't. "An extra mouth at the table." When no one picks up on this, he says, "I'm not looking for a cut of the money. Just what Frankie here owes me. I'm simply protecting my assets."

Edgar raises his hand like a schoolboy who needs to use the bathroom. Joey stares at him. "What?"

"Our car."

"What about it?"

"It only holds five people." Edgar points at each of us in turn, except for Joey and his thugs. "One, two, three, four, five." For Edgar, that's advanced math. Calculus, almost. The IRS guy must have had a ball explaining deductions and withholdings to him.

"My guys here will get a van. That way there'll be room for all those bags of money you'll be hauling out of the bank."

"Good idea," Huey says.

"Meet me here at nine," Joey says. He leaves us with our warm beer and our photographs and a plan that hadn't accounted for huge bags of money. I wonder what else we've overlooked. All I want is to get out of the hole for a while. I haven't thought about anything beyond that.

I seldom do.

□   □   □

The battered white van pulls up in front of Marty's right on schedule. Gus, the goon behind the wheel, gets out and Joey tells me to drive. He's traveling light—I've never seen him with only one bodyguard before. "Understand this," he tells me. "You get us lost or stuck in traffic, and the fish they serve at that new restaurant near the aquarium on Central Wharf are going to be of the well-fed variety, if you catch my drift."

I catch his drift. The van makes me nervous, because I've never driven anything where I have to use side mirrors to see behind, but I get us through the toll plaza and across the Mystic River Bridge without sideswiping some delivery truck crowding my lane.

We get to the block where the bank is located with thirty minutes to spare. Edgar volunteers to go to Dunkin' Donuts and get us all coffee and something to eat while we wait, which I think is pretty nice of him, but Joey tells him to stay put. So we sit in the van, seven guys all wearing baseball caps, all with eyes for only one thing— the bank across the street. Gus grunts when he sees our weapons.

"Watcha gonna do with that one?" Joey says, pointing at the flare gun. "Alert the Coast Guard?"

Huey's lower lip juts out a fraction of an inch.

"This is how it's going to work," Joey says, even though we went over everything during the drive. "Frankie is going to stay with the van. He's gonna keep the motor running and the side door ajar. The minute he sees us running out, he's gonna slide open the side door, jump back into his seat and be ready to go the minute I say so." Talking about me as if I'm not even here.

"Gus and me, we'll go in first. All of us go at once, the guards are gonna think something's hinky."

Edgar laughs. Joey gives him a look, not realizing that Edgar probably thinks "hinky" is a dirty word.

"Gus and me will wait at the place where you fill out deposit slips. Thirty seconds later, the rest of you cross the street. Look at the ground. There are cameras outside the bank, too. Talk to each other like you're good buddies, not four guys about to rob a bank."

"We are good buddies," Edgar says.

Joey glares at him, a look he probably practices in the mirror. "When you reach the door, pull on your masks. Forget about those toy guns. Gus and me, we'll show the guards our pieces and make sure they don't cause any trouble. You four move in on the tellers and get them to fill these." Joey hands around garbage bags from a roll. "Don't let them take anything off the bottom of the till or do nothing funny with their feet. We'll probably get a dye pack or two, but we'll let Edgar here open those. He'd probably enjoy it."

Edgar grins. I can imagine him engulfed by a cloud of purple dye wearing that same smile.

All the while, I'm watching the dashboard clock. A couple of people are hanging around outside the bank entrance, waiting for it to open. At ten o'clock, a teller appears at the door, turns the lock with her key, and pushes it open. "We're on," Joey says. "Remember— wait thirty seconds. One Mississippi, two Mississippi."

"Three Mississippi," Edgar says. "Four Mississippi."

"Not yet," Joey says. "Don't start until Gus and me are inside. And leave behind anything that could identify you. I don't want one of you dunderheads dropping your wallet on the way out and squirreling the whole deal." He and Gus remove their own wallets and put them on the bench seat. "Remember to put on your masks unless you want your faces plastered all over WBZ at six."

Even though it's a cool morning, I sweat behind the wheel of the stuffy old van. Gus pulls open the side door, and he and Joey climb out. Edgar starts counting Mississippis after Joey and Gus go inside. When he reaches thirty, he, Vinnie, Huey and Mikey cross the street, staring at the ground and waving their hands like they're discussing baseball or women. The moment they reach the steps, I start the engine, make a U-turn and pull into an empty spot in front of the bank. Then I reach back, open the sliding door a crack, and stare at the entrance.

It seems like they're inside forever, but it's only a few seconds. Then the front door swings open and they come tumbling down the steps toward the van. I push the side door open the rest of the way, check the mirrors for traffic and hit the street before the door slams shut.

"It worked?" I ask.

"Just drive," Vinnie says. "Go a few blocks, turn the corner and pull over." He takes his ski mask from his pocket and stuffs it into one of Joey's garbage bags. The others follow suit.

I park next to a fire hydrant on a side street. Everyone grabs the gear, and we get out and saunter along the sidewalk as if we're out for a leisurely stroll. A Boston PD squad car roars past on the main street, sirens blaring, lights flashing. Sooner or later the van will get towed, and that will be the end of that. A few blocks east, we encounter another Dunkin' Donuts. We toss the bag of masks into a Dumpster in the parking lot, along with the weapons and the gloves we've all been wearing so we wouldn't leave fingerprints inside the van. Those paperback novels are good for details like that, things we might have overlooked.

We go inside, order coffee and donuts, and sit around a big table near the window where we can watch the parade of blue-and-white cop cars heading toward the scene of the crime.

"Well?" I ask, impatient to hear what happened.

"Like clockwork," Huey says.

"Exactly like we planned it," Vinnie says.

"Tell me," I say.

"As soon as Joey and Gus see us coming through the door, they put on their masks and pull out their pistols. Then Mikey yells, 'Oh my God, they've got guns,' in his girliest girly voice and the guards are all over them faster than you can blink," Huey says, taking a big bite out of his donut. "In two seconds flat, they have them both on the ground crying uncle. No one figured out who yelled."

"They just let you go?"

"They were too busy taking care of Gus and Joey," Mikey says. "We just turned around and walked right back out."

"Armed robbery," I say. "Should be good for ten years, right?"

"At least," Vinnie says. "Looks like you don't have to worry about Joey DeStefano for a while."

"You're sure he won't rat us out?"

Vinnie shrugs. "If he thought we set him up, he might, but this way it just looks like the job went bad, and we vamoosed. The cops have him dead to rights—they'd have no reason to make any deals."

"You guys are the best," I say—and they are. They saved my bacon. Vinnie was the one who predicted that Joey would insist on taking over our robbery, and they all played their parts brilliantly. Even Edgar.

"Wait, there's more," Huey says. He reaches into his pocket and hands me two wallets, stuffed with cash. I glance inside one and see a bunch of brand new hundred-dollar bills. I don't want to count it sitting in front of the window with all those cops running around, but there must be a few thousand bucks in them. "Joey and Gus left them in the van," he says.

"What are we waiting for?" I say. "By the time we walk back to Marty's, it'll be time for a beer, dontcha think?" I hold up the thicker of the two wallets. "Joey's buying." And this time, Holly's going to get a nice tip, too. Maybe the biggest of her life. I've got a lot to make up for. Maybe I'll even take her out to dinner with my share of the money.

"I have a question," Edgar says as we head toward the bridge. The confused look on his face is familiar to the rest of us.

"What?" I ask.

"Whose name we gonna call out if we all get there at the same time?"

"We'll figure out something along the way," I tell him. "We're good at that."

$$\triangle \quad \triangle \quad \triangle$$

Bev Vincent *is the Edgar® and Bram Stoker Award-nominated author of* The Stephen King Illustrated Companion. *He's a contributing editor with* Cemetery Dance *magazine and has written over fifty short stories, appearing in places like* Ellery Queen's Mystery Magazine, *the MWA anthology* The Blue Religion, *and other anthologies including* When the Night Comes Down, Evolve *and* Who Died in Here? *His website is bevvincent.com.*

A Good, Safe Place

Judith Green

As Celeste hitched her walker into the living room, she stopped short. "Who are you?" she demanded.

The young woman looked up from the old rolltop desk where she had been rearranging stacks of papers, a feather duster tucked under one arm. She sighed, her shoulders drooping. "I'm *Lisa*, dear," she said with elaborate patience, as if she were talking to a child. "I'm here to help you while your daughter is away."

Watch your tone, young lady. Celeste pushed her walker across the floor and lowered herself into her armchair. "Is Margery at school? She teaches school, you know."

"No, Margery's in Wisconsin, dear," this Lisa person chirped. "They all went out for Melanie's graduation. Oh, aren't you just so proud of your granddaughter?" she added, with that false, bright smile. "Now, can I get you anything? A cup of tea? Are you warm enough, dear? Would you like a blanket over your legs?"

Celeste waved the questions away. She wished the woman would stop fussing. She looked at the desk, its top still rolled up to expose bundles of yellowed papers, a stack of leather-covered ledgers, a box of old Christmas cards. "What are you doing in there?" she asked. "What are you looking for?"

The woman looked at the desk, then at her. "Me? Why, nothing, dear. You were looking for something in the desk this morning. Shall

I close it?"

"No. Leave it." This morning? Had this woman been here already this morning? This person—What had she said her name was? Never mind.

At any rate, that had been Walter's desk. Ever since he'd been gone, she hadn't been able to bring herself to use it. She kept her important papers in—Hm. Well, they were in a good, safe place. Somewhere.

"What's that sound?" Celeste's head snapped around. "Who's in the kitchen?"

"My husband," the woman said. "I hope you don't mind if he—"

But Celeste hauled herself to her feet again and started hitching her walker toward the kitchen doorway. At the table by the window sat a beefy sort of man unwrapping a hamburger. He nodded curtly in Celeste's direction, and then laid the hamburger on the paper it had come in and reached a paw into a white paper bag for a fistful of french fries. Celeste could smell the hot grease.

She peered out the kitchen window. "Whose car is that out there?"

The woman had followed her into the kitchen. "Why, that's our car, dear."

"What's it doing in the back yard?" Celeste asked. "We've always parked in the driveway, right next to the front steps. There's plenty of room, now that they've taken my car away. He needn't go mucking up my back yard." She glared at the man, who kept his eyes fixed on his hamburger, holding it in both hands as if it might get away. He took a huge bite and chewed noisily.

"Oh, but," said the woman, "that's where Margery told us to put it."

"Why would she tell you *that*?" Celeste hitched herself around so that she could look at the woman again. "Who did you say you were?"

Again that sigh, the droop of the shoulders. "I'm *Lisa*, dear. Your *care*giver."

"Caregiver!" Celeste snorted. "That's a stupid word if I've ever heard one!"

But the girl *did* look familiar. Where had Celeste seen her before? In the grocery store? Yesterday, perhaps, at the hairdresser's. There'd been someone getting a trim, all swaddled up with that sheet thing around her neck, while she and Gladys had been under the hair dryers. Celeste had caught the person's eye in the mirror once, while Gladys had been going on the way she always did, shouting over the roar of the dryers about immigrants who can't speak English. Oh, and about banks failing all over the country. The two of them had been smart, Gladys said, to get their money out yesterday before their own town's bank failed.

Celeste shook her head. Whatever would she do without Gladys?

"Here's your lunch," the woman said, trotting over to the table with a sandwich of some sort, neatly cut in quarters, on a plate. "By the way, you're out of coffee."

"I couldn't be!" Celeste homed in on the table. The meaty husband had, mercifully, already choked down his hamburger and was just heading out the back door. "I'm sure there's at least half a jar of coffee left."

"Well—" The woman held up the jar, which held nothing except a dark crust around the bottom. "Empty!" she sang.

"Hmph!" Celeste snorted. This woman's husband must have drunk up quarts of Celeste's good instant coffee to wash down that nasty hamburger. She hmphed again as the man let the back door slam shut behind him so hard that a satchel stuffed full of folded brown-paper grocery bags jumped off the doorknob and fell to the floor.

"Let's just hang this over here, shall we?" The woman crossed the floor to hang the satchel on the cellar doorknob. "Now, what else do we need? We should start a list. Probably the usual. Bread, milk. Are we out of eggs?"

We? Celeste gripped the edge of the kitchen table and hoisted herself out of her chair, then grasped her walker and swung it smartly into position. She hitched her way back into the living room and lowered herself into her armchair. She always felt more—well, *collected* in her armchair. Smarter, with her calendar, and her box of Kleenex, and her magazines, and the TV remote, and a nice hundred-watt bulb in the lamp. She thought of her armchair as Headquarters.

But the woman had followed her, carrying the plate with the quartered sandwich, which she laid on Celeste's card table, right on top of the letters Celeste had been meaning to answer. Now she hovered, backlit by the early summer sunlight streaming in at the window so that her face was in shadow. "Would you like to go after you've finished your lunch?" she asked.

"Go where?"

"To the grocery store!"

"Oh, that." Ignoring the sandwich on its little plate, Celeste riffled through the magazines in the basket next to her chair and drew out a *Woman's Day*. "What did you say your name was?"

"I'm Lisa, dear. So we'll go to the grocery store right after lunch."

"Oh, no." Celeste peered at the magazine's brightly colored cover. Hm. *Easy Summer Barbecues Your Family Will Love*. "I always take a nap after lunch. Besides, I do my shopping with Gladys Whitman."

"Yes, but Gladys is in Millinocket, isn't she? She went to visit her sister for the Memorial Day weekend."

"Oh. Yes, I suppose."

"So we'll go right after lunch, okay?"

Oh, dear. Go where? The young woman seemed to expect an answer, so Celeste smiled her sweetest smile. "We'll see," she said.

She looked back down at the magazine in her lap. *Turn Your Deck Into An Outdoor Living Room*. That sounded interesting.

□   □   □

"My, my, look at you!" chirped the woman. "I came in to fix your supper, and here you are eating already!"

What was the woman's name? Priscilla? No, that didn't sound

right. Melissa? Celeste gave up and went back to her toast. She'd fixed it as she always did, buttered and then a thin skim of marmalade, with a cup of tea to which she'd added a half-teaspoon of sugar and a dite of milk from the plastic jug in the fridge.

Hm. The milk might have gone by. Perhaps this woman could make herself useful and get some more. Otherwise Celeste would have to call Brenda, next door. She hated to bother Brenda.

"What else would you like to eat this evening, dear?" The woman opened the cupboard door and began moving things about. In a matter of moments, she had the saltines next to a box of cereal, and the cans of soup where the sack of sugar ought to be.

"Leave that be!" Celeste snapped. "I've already made my supper!"

"Oh, yes, dear," the woman said. "But just a piece of toast won't be enough." She stood on tiptoe to survey the top shelf. "How about a can of Chef Boyardee spaghetti?"

"Thanks, but no."

The woman closed the cupboard door and looked at Celeste, her skinny blond eyebrows drawn together in a worried frown. "Well, then. I'll get a load of laundry started." She bustled into the back room, and Celeste could hear her opening the cupboard doors in there, too. "Just looking for the laundry soap," she called.

"Well, it's in there somewhere." Celeste took a sip of her tea. Yes, the milk was quite definitely off. She'd really have to see about sending that woman to the store in the morning for another pint.

Did she have any money in her pocketbook? No, she'd put her last dollar bill in the collection plate last Sunday. She glanced over at the satchel of shopping bags hanging from the cellar doorknob. She'd better give the woman at least ten dollars. There was bound to be something else they needed. Perhaps even a twenty.

But before she could begin the process of getting up, the washing machine started up with a slosh, and the woman reappeared beside her chair. "Can I get you more tea, dear?"

"No, thank you," Celeste said. "I always have one cup."

"You just enjoy it, then, and I'll go turn down your bed." And the woman scuttled toward Celeste's bedroom. Well, properly it was the dining room, but Margery had insisted that she sleep downstairs after she took that fall—was it last year? Two years ago?

Now, there'd been something she wanted that woman—Lisa! That was it! Lisa!—to get at the store. But what?

Celeste looked around the kitchen, hoping for inspiration. She took another sip of her tea. Hm. Was the milk a little off?

□   □   □

"Hey, Mom, how's it going? This is Ted."

Celeste sat up on the edge of her bed, where she'd been having a bit of a lie-down after supper, and smiled into the telephone. "Why, hello, sweetheart. How nice to hear your voice. How's Nellie?"

"She's great. Just great. So— Everything's okay? You're eating, and everything? Taking your meds?"

"Yes, yes. I presume that your sister asked you to check up on me while she's gone."

"Yeah, well—"

"She's always worrying about me. Silly girl, hiring someone to stay here with me while she's away. I've been perfectly used to living alone ever since your father died, but Margery stops in every day on her way home from school and—"

"Wait a minute, Mom. Did you say she hired someone?"

"Why, this woman Lisa, of course. Her husband, too, I suppose, though he's been mostly tidying the cellar and the attic. Just for something to do, he said."

"Mom, there's someone staying there with you?"

"I *told* you: this woman Lisa and her husband. She's very attentive—"

"Mom—"

"But I wish her husband would park in the driveway instead of behind the house."

"Mom! These people—"

"It's just while Margery's gone. She's in Wisconsin, you know."

"Yes, Mom. For Melanie's college graduation. But about these people— "

"What people?"

"Staying with you. How do you know them?"

"I *told* you. Margery got them to—"

"Crap! Mom, are you sure—"

"Language!"

"Sorry. Look, Mom, I've got to go. I've got to try to get hold of Margery."

"But, sweetie, we've hardly—"

"Bye, Mom."

Celeste sat glaring at the receiver before she replaced it in the cradle. "Boys!" she muttered. "They'll never tell you what's on their minds!"

"Who was that?" Lisa stood in the doorway. Her hair was tousled, and festooned with bits of cobweb. Helping her husband in the attic, most likely.

"Hm? Are you all right, dear? You seem awfully tired."

Lisa straightened up. Plastered that cheery smile on her face. "I was just wondering who you were talking to on the phone."

"The phone?" Celeste looked down at it, resting quietly on the bookcase beside the bed. "Oh, the phone. I was talking to my son in California. He just called to say hello, but he never stays on the line for very long." She sighed. "It gets lonesome sometimes." She looked up at Lisa. "Would you like to look at some pictures for a minute?"

"Uh—yes, sure."

Celeste patted the bedspread, signaling Lisa to sit next to her, and pulled a photograph album off the lowest shelf of the bookcase. She opened it, spreading it across both their laps. She pointed to a blurry snapshot of a tiny baby in a carriage, so bundled up that nothing showed but a button of a nose. "This is Ted. The one who called.

And here he is holding Billy, my other son," she added, pointing to another snapshot. "I remember when that picture was taken. He was so afraid he'd drop the baby and break him."

The page crumbled slightly at the edges as she turned it. Tiny fragments of black paper slid into her lap, and she brushed them off onto the floor. "And this is Margery. Here she is when she was four. Look at those fat little legs! This is her with her favorite doll. You know, I haven't had this album out for years! Now, here's Billy with his first bicycle. Doesn't he look—"

"Beautiful children." Lisa smiled brightly. "But, oh, my, look at the time! Shouldn't we be getting you ready for bed?"

"Oh, sit still, dear. You've been working far too hard, and we've got lots of pictures to look at still. Now, here's Margie with her 4-H calf. Didn't she love that calf! I swear—"

□   □   □

"I couldn't help noticing . . ." Lisa said as she brought Celeste a cup of tea the next morning. "There's a tax bill lying on your table."

"Oh, my. Is that due already?" Celeste stirred her tea, watching the sludge of milk slide into the amber liquid. Why wasn't she having coffee?

"Well, we should get it into the mail for you this morning. Just tell me where—"

Celeste looked up at her. "Where what?"

"Um—Where you keep your envelopes and stuff. And—um—we'll need a money order. I'll go to the post office."

"Oh, thank you, dear." Celeste looked around the kitchen. Her gaze wandered to the lighthouse salt-and-pepper set sitting on the counter, to the cupboard under the sink, to the knife rack beside the stove. "I've just got to think where I put—"

"Put what?"

"Hm?" Celeste looked up at Lisa. The poor girl's skin looked pasty in the early-morning sunlight.

"Put what?" Lisa asked again.

"Lisa, dear, I'm worried about you. Look, you've got dark circles under your eyes. I don't think you're getting enough sleep."

□   □   □

Cupboard doors slamming out in the kitchen. Drawers being yanked open and whacked shut. What on earth was Lisa looking for?

Celeste hoisted herself out of her armchair and hitched herself through the kitchen doorway. She found Lisa on her hands and knees, her blue-jeaned rear in the air, her head poked into the cupboard under the sink. "Heavens!" Celeste said. "Can I help you find something, dear?"

Lisa backed out of the cupboard and slammed the door shut. "No, thanks."

"Lisa, dear, I'm afraid you're just wearing yourself out. Why don't you sit down and rest, and I'll make us all some lunch." She parked her walker by the kitchen table and shuffled over to peer into the refrigerator. "I could do up some grilled cheese sandwiches— Well, perhaps not. This cheese has gone a bit green around the edges."

Lisa scrambled to her feet, stalked across the floor, and snapped open the cellar door so hard that the satchel of shopping bags flew off the doorknob and thumped against the wall. She stamped down the cellar stairs, and Celeste could hear her talking to her husband. Sounded like she was pinning his ears back. Oh, dear.

Well, a little lunch would be just the ticket. Celeste shuffled across the kitchen and bent slowly down to pick up the shopping bag satchel. She ought to send Lisa to do some grocery shopping— give her a bit extra and tell her to get whatever she wanted—but it didn't seem to be a good moment, if they were arguing down there. She hung the satchel back on the doorknob and poked about in the cupboard, looking for a candidate for lunch.

Ah. A can of Campbell's chicken noodle soup. If she added some water, it would serve the three of them. But Lisa's husband—Men always wanted more to eat. Hm. Maybe if she cut the edges off that cheese. Humming to herself, Celeste put a pot on the stove, then dug in the drawer for the can opener.

The phone rang. She laid down the can opener, hobbled over to the phone on the wall, and lifted the receiver, holding onto the doorframe for balance. "Hello?"

"Mom? It's me, Margery."

"Well, hello, sweetheart. How is everything in—Ohio, isn't it?"

"Wisconsin. Everything's fine. The graduation's this afternoon, and it looks as if the weather will hold. But listen—Ted just called from California. He'd been trying to reach me since last night. He says someone's in the house with you."

"Well, of course, dear. Your friend Lisa, and her husband, too. They've been keeping me company while you're gone. Of course, you really didn't need to arrange for—"

"But I didn't arrange for them to come, Mom. I don't even know them!"

"Of course you do, dear. Why, Lisa's known you for years! We've been looking at the old photo albums. She's a good girl. She tidied your father's desk, and all those boxes of papers in my bedroom closet. And her husband's been kind enough to go through all that old stuff in the attic and the cellar, and now he's working on the garage!"

"Mom—Mom—Listen, let me talk to Lisa."

"To Lisa? She's down cellar. No, wait, she must have gone out the bulkhead door—I hear them outside. I'll call her."

"No, wait. Um—look out the window. Are the Johnsons at home next door? Is their car in the driveway?"

"Why, no, dear, they haven't been home all weekend. I think—"

"Okay. Look, we'll be home tomorrow. We fly out first thing in the morning, and we'll come straight—"

"Oh, now. We're fine."

"Well— Oh, Lord. I've got to go, Mom. The graduates are lining up. I'll see you tomorrow. In the meantime, don't give them anything. Okay? Don't give them *any*thing. Good-bye."

Celeste sat looking at the dead receiver. Don't give them

anything? It wasn't as if they'd asked for anything! And after all that Lisa had done to help. Why, Margery had been promising to clean the attic for years!

She peeked out the window. Lisa stood in front of the garage door, hands on hips, looking weary. Perhaps some lunch . . .

Celeste yanked up on the window, then bent down to halloo through the crack. "Lisa? Come in for lunch. Oh, and Margery was on the telephone. She wanted to talk to you, but she had to go."

Celeste turned to face the kitchen again. Let's see . . .

The can opener lay on the counter. Oh, yes, soup.

Better hurry. The burner on the stove was already glowing red under the empty pot. She shuffled over to fetch the can.

□ □ □

She was dozing in her chair when a hammering sound woke her with a jolt. "There's someone at the door," she called. "Hello? Lisa? Lisa, dear, someone's knocking!"

Now the front door slowly opened, and a head poked through the gap: a man's head. As it pushed further into the house, Celeste saw that it was attached to shoulders clad in police blue. "Mrs. Laidlaw? Are you here?" rumbled a pleasant baritone voice. "Oh, hello, ma'am. Officer Theriault, ma'am."

The policeman came in and shut the door behind him. He was on the short side for a policeman, Celeste thought, but reassuringly clean-shaven and middle-aged. His eyes roved over the room's furnishings and stabbed through each of the doorways—into the kitchen, the dining-room-turned-bedroom, the study—and up the staircase, as if he were actually moving through the house, searching for . . . For what?

"Is everything all right?" Celeste asked. She wished Lisa would come in. The girl must be *still* out in the garage.

She and her husband hadn't yet touched the lunch Celeste had prepared for them. When she'd called them in, Lisa had promised just a minute. Then the car had pulled away—probably the husband going out for more trash bags or some such. But Lisa must be somewhere about. Lisa wouldn't leave her alone. Lisa was good like that.

"Well, ma'am," the policeman said, shifting uncomfortably from one foot to the other, "we had a call from your daughter."

"Margery?" Celeste's hands clutched at each other in her lap. "Is Margery—"

"No, no, ma'am, your daughter's fine. Fine. She was worried about *you*, is all. She called the station, and—She felt that there might be someone in the house who doesn't belong here."

"Well!" Celeste drew herself up in the chair. "There's no one here but me, and of course Lisa, who Margery hired to look after me—not that she need to have bothered, I'm perfectly capable of looking after myself, but Lisa *is* very good company—and there's her husband, whose name escapes me at the moment, but he's gone off somewhere just now in the car."

The policeman raised an eyebrow. "Your car?"

"No. My daughter Margery saw fit to take my car away from me. Though I always did just fine as long as I had my friend Gladys Whitman with me to watch the side streets and warn me if anything was coming."

The policeman winced. "Do you mind if I have a look around?'

"Suit yourself. But if you bump into Lisa, tell her that her soup is getting cold."

□   □   □

After the policeman left, Celeste sat for a long time with her hands clasped in her lap, listening for the slap of the screen door in the kitchen and the familiar clatter of Lisa's feet across the linoleum. What could be keeping that girl so long in the garage? Perhaps she'd gone with her husband to the store.

Celeste waited, listening for the car to pull into the driveway, passing under the living room windows to park out back, the thud of the car door.

Had something *happened?* A car accident? If they were both

hurt—Well, no one would know to call, would they?

Or—had the husband got annoyed with Celeste for not wanting him to park in the back yard? It was all right. Really. He hadn't hurt the grass. In fact, you couldn't tell where the car had been. Really. It was all right.

The sun dipped behind the ridgepole of the Johnsons' roof, and the living room grew shadowy around Celeste. In the kitchen, the refrigerator switched on and hummed companionably for a time. When it switched off, the silence was like a blow.

Out on the street, a car went by. Kept going.

Celeste leaned a little to the left so that she could see the clock on the kitchen wall. Quarter past six. Time for supper.

She didn't want to go into the kitchen. She didn't want to face the two bowls of soup on the table, each centered neatly between a folded paper napkin and a spoon. The soup would be no good any more, in this summer heat.

Celeste shivered. Her family seemed very far away. Both of her sons out there in California all these years—she hardly knew her grandchildren. And now Margery haring off to Wisconsin, and taking her whole family with her. Gladys was right. Things in this country were going to hell in a hand basket.

She'd *never* had a policeman come to the house! He'd poked his nose into every room, even the attic and the cellar and out in the garage. And then he'd gone away and left her all alone.

And her with all this money in the house! She wished she'd never let Gladys convince her into drawing her money out of the bank last Friday. All this talk, talk, talk about the bank failing—

Imagine! A policeman! In her house! Had there been break-ins in the neighborhood?

Celeste caught herself plucking at the legs of her trousers. Now, stop that.

Well, she couldn't do anything about being alone. But she could take care of the money. Celeste hauled herself to her feet and hitched herself into the kitchen. She took the satchel of folded paper shopping bags off the cellar doorknob and reached down to the bottom for the one bag that was just a little thicker than the others. She peeked into it. Yes, the money was still there. Everything she'd taken out of the bank, a neat block of hundred-dollar bills.

Abandoning her walker, she pushed open the screen door and lowered herself gingerly down the back steps, leaning heavily on the railing. She scuffed over to the garage—the big overhead door was standing open, for heaven's sake—and found a shovel. She leaned on the shovel as she made her way across the back yard to the old oak tree.

She picked out a spot where a big root twisted across the grass. She was pleased with how well she handled the shovel, considering. It was the work of a minute to pry up a chunk of sod under a curve in the root.

She bent down and tucked the block of bills into the hole, then patted the sod back into place. Perfect! No one would ever know the ground had been disturbed.

When Lisa got home, Celeste would explain about the money. Lisa's husband could go out and dig it up again, and take it back to the bank. In the meantime, it was safe.

Celeste pressed the switch to close the garage door. Then she shuffled toward the house and pulled herself slowly up the steps.

□   □   □

She wasn't hungry for supper. She sat in her chair for a while, trying to read. At last she just turned off the lights and went to bed.

Somehow she didn't want any breakfast either. Or perhaps it was lunch she didn't want.

She was sitting in her chair, looking out the window at the sun going down behind the Johnsons' house, when Margery came in.

"Mom—" She still had the front door key in her hand as she crossed the floor. Her husband and younger daughter hung in the doorway as if they were afraid to come in. "Mom," Margery asked, "are you okay?"

Celeste looked up at her. "Hello, sweetheart," she said. "How was Melanie's—thing?"

"The graduation went fine. But, Mom—Have you eaten today? Have you taken your pills? Mom, have you been sitting here like this all day?"

Celeste looked down at her hands. She watched them plucking, plucking at the folds of her nightgown. Her nightgown? At this time of day? "I don't know," she said. "It seemed awfully quiet in here."

"I'll get you something to eat so you can take your pills." Margery trotted into the kitchen. "Mom! What's with these bowls of soup? Yuck!" Celeste could hear water running in the sink, then the refrigerator opening. "Mom," Margery called, "there's nothing to eat in here! Didn't Gladys take you shopping?"

"She went away," Celeste said. "To—Up north somewhere."

Margery reappeared in the doorway, her face hollow with concern. "And what about those people?"

"Which people?"

"You said someone was here, someone named Lisa, and her husband."

Celeste stared down at her hands, plucking, plucking at the fabric of her nightgown. "I don't know," she said. "They—I don't know."

Margery sighed. "Okay. Let's get you dressed, and gather up your medicine, and some clean clothes. You're coming home with us for the time being. Oh, I know you don't want to live with us way out in the country, but you'll just have to make do until we can find you a place in assisted living here in town. You can't stay here alone any more."

Celeste allowed Margery to dress her, then waited while she went through the bathroom shelves for toiletries, and the kitchen cabinet for her pills. "Here's your pocketbook, Mom," she said. "But I don't see your checkbook. You didn't give it to Lisa, did you?"

"Mm? My checkbook? Oh, no. I threw it away after Gladys took me to close my checking account. The banks aren't safe any more, you know."

"But where's the money?"

"Mm?"

"Oh, my God, Mom, they took all your money?"

"Who?"

"Those people? That Lisa person?"

"Lisa?"

Margery sighed again. "Okay. First we get you home and fed. Then I'll talk to the police. See what we can do. I expect it's too late, though."

She and her husband helped Celeste negotiate the front steps and climb into the car parked where it ought to be, right next to the front porch. But Celeste kept thinking they should have gone out the back door.

There was something she needed in the back yard. What could it be?

Oh, well. She'd think of it later.

△   △   △

Judith Green is a sixth-generation resident of a village in Maine's western mountains, with the fifth, seventh, and eighth generations living nearby. She served for many years as director of adult education for her eleven-town school district, and has twenty-five high-interest, low-level books for adult new readers in print. She is currently branching out with a mystery novel starring her Maine high-school English teacher and sleuth as well as a wintry YA adventure.

Double Take

Mo Walsh

We were about five seconds away from being arrested, and all I could think about was how sexy Dillon looked in lederhosen. Not many men, not Americans anyway, could carry off those leather shorts with the embroidered suspenders and fancy strap across the chest, not to mention the knee socks, but my guy was one of them.

I was pretty stunning myself in a black-and-red dirndl cut low at the bodice and high at the hem with a bit of lace peeping out at each end. Together, me and Dillon had upped the sex appeal of the Green Mountain Tyrolean Inn about six thousand percent. We'd been here a month and made double in tips what we were getting, under the table, from Dillon's mother's second cousin Fred.

Him and Dillon were facing off over the cluttered desk in Fred's office, a tiny room with fake maple paneling and cheesy posters of families skiing, gaping at orange leaves, or hiking in a meadow. I was sitting in the only chair on our side of the desk, right where I had the best rear view of my guy in those leather pants. I could swear the desk photo of Fred's wife Cindy, aka Elsa, aka Frau Dumpling, was checking him out, too.

Friedrich, as he called himself at the resort, couldn't even wade in the same gene pool as Dillon. His lederhosen refused to stay put where his waist should have been, but hiked up to the top of his paunch, bunching up his suspenders and exposing way more than I needed to see of his pudgy thighs. He might have had a decent face about a hundred pounds ago, but right now he looked like the Man in the Moon choking on a hunk of bratwurst.

"Ingrates!" He slammed his fist on the desk. "Thieves!"

Well, duh. He knew me and Dillon had records in Massachusetts, even if he didn't know I'd jumped bail on attempted armed robbery charges. (Great-Aunt Minnie posted my bond when the parents turned me down. I guess she can kiss that investment good-bye.) Anyway, Fred knew we'd both done a little time, but he had no problem with us working at his third-rate resort, cheap and without benefits, even. But let a few little things turn up missing, and it was just like Dillon had predicted.

"The first ones he's gonna look at if something goes wrong is you and me, Bev," he'd warned when we moved into the old handyman's apartment over the equipment shed. "So I got a plan."

"Don't tell me I can't lift anything," I warned him. "I've got to." Already, I had my eye on a winking cow from Elsa's collection of souvenir cream pitchers. And what was the point of keeping a crystal maple leaf ashtray in a lounge where nobody was allowed to smoke?

"You can't lift anything from the resort, Bev." Dillon held me by the shoulders and looked right into my eyes. He didn't blink till I nodded, then he pulled me into his arms for a hug. "We can get into Stowe once a week, maybe Burlington now and then," he promised.

I hugged him back and started a little hip action, but Dillon said it wouldn't look good for me to be late for my first time serving tables. Neither one of us has got much "impulse control," as they'd called it in our court-ordered therapy group, but Dillon's our brakes.

"Slow down, Fred," he was saying now in that voice the TV dog guy uses on demonic Chihuahuas. "It wasn't us, I swear."

"I should call the cops right now!"

I stopped adjusting my cleavage, because Dillon wasn't looking anyway, and gave old Fred the same wide-eyed look that got the judge to grant me bail and squeezed the twenty grand out of Aunt Minnie.

"But we didn't take anything!" I put just a little quiver in my voice. "You took us into your home, Fred. We're family. We would never betray your trust."

"We don't spit in our own soup," said Dillon. "You can't tell me nothing ever went missing from this place before we showed up."

Fred shrugged. "Watches from swim bags. Sunglasses from the tennis court. A few dollars maybe left on a dresser, but who's to prove it? Until this week. Now it's cell phones and laptops and DVD players. And a wedding ring!"

"That was the guy's fault for pretending to be single," I said, "but we still didn't take it."

Fred flopped back in his desk chair and his lederhosen crept up another inch. "I can't tell when you two are lying, so I've got to figure you are. And I can't afford any blot on the resort right now. VIVA is coming next week."

"Who?" asked Dillon.

"Values In Vacation Accommodations. VIVA. It's a timeshare exchange service."

"Really?" I pretended to be impressed. "So, like, if you own a week at the converted Howard Johnson's on the Jersey Shore, you can come here instead?" I was pretty sure there was no VIVA Las Vegas, Aruba or Vail.

"We would be one of their Silver Suitcase resorts, for certain." Fred puffed out his chest. "Possibly a Gold Suitcase. But not if we're found to have—"

"Missing suitcases?" Dillon nodded like we'd been called in special just to help with a little pilfering problem. "Then you can't call the cops, Fred. We've got to tackle this another way."

"What 'we'? I want you out of here!" Fred's face turned purple like the bratwurst was stuck in his throat again. Lucky for him, he wasn't really choking. I never did memorize that chart in the kitchen on the Heineken Maneuver.

"I understand how you feel, Fred, but we can help you. You forget my dad's a cop."

It's true. Dillon has had a juvie record since he was twelve, but his old man was still pushing him into the Academy until he got himself busted on his eighteenth birthday. They don't get along.

"You can trust us on this, Fred. We owe you." No one does sincere better than Dillon.

I sat with my knees together, hands folded, and tried to channel Fraulein Maria, the nun one from *Sound of Music*, not the Trapp Lodge yodeling-in-Vermont innfrau.

I pictured all the tacky treasures I did *not* take from the resort— not even the Grandfather figure from the Heidi set made in Hong Kong, the one that looked like Confucius in lederhosen. I should've felt saintly, but when I thought about all the temptation I'd been resisting, I just got more steamed at Fred. So I kept my mouth shut, while Dillon tried to talk him out of calling the cops.

He was sitting on the edge of Fred's desk now, and I got all distracted by the rearrangement of his lederhosen till I heard him say, "You're doing the smart thing, Fred. In twenty-four hours, we'll have your thief for you, and VIVA will never know you had a problem. Come on, Bev."

He grabbed my hand and we beat it out of there before Fred wondered if he really wanted us starring in his remake of *It Takes a Thief.*

"Twenty-four hours?" I backed Dillon up against the wall of the empty dining room and plucked at his suspenders. "What are we going to do with the other twenty-three?"

"Easy, Bev." He was putting the brakes on again. "We've got to act natural, do our jobs, don't draw any special attention."

"But we know who it is."

"Yeah, but who do we want it to be?"

□   □   □

I can think of worse places to vacation than the Green Mountain Tyrolean Inn. The women's cellblock at MCI-Framingham, for instance, where I once did ninety days for larceny. Or anyplace in Nebraska.

The inn's "mountain chalets" were just twenty-three prefab A-frames squatting at the base of a hill with an inflated ego. The lodge was a converted barn with a beige stucco facelift. The pool held water, the tennis court had a net, the playground had swings, a slide and sand.

"Family-owned and operated" meant they relied on cheap help from Cindy's divorced sister and her perfect son, from Fred's Aunt Bab and Uncle Vinnie, and from their own kids, two sullen teenagers we called Hansel and Gretel (real names Ryan and Tammy). And from Dillon and me.

Easy for him to say we had to do our jobs like always. He was the pool boy and outdoor guide. I was the waitress and maid.

Dillon was going to scoop dead bugs off the water, then lead his harem of women on the daily Tyrolean Woodland Stroll. When Vinnie had the job, it was all middle-aged women and old couples tramping along a path so beaten down they could play shuffleboard on it. Most of them had been frightened off by the herd of giggling girls who suddenly had a thing for either nature or the hot guide in lederhosen. Did I mind? Well, yeah. Teenagers don't tip.

My workday started in the dining room, stocking the "authentic Tyrolean breakfast buffet" with tasteless muesli, watery yogurt, limp potato pancakes and "Elsa's Apfelstrudel." The kitchen work table held big canisters of flour and sugar and a basket of shiny red apples for show, but I knew the storeroom was stocked with buckets of Quikbiskit and gallon cans of pie filling.

A couple of the old geezers tipped me good for bringing their coffee right to the table and slipping them Pop-Tarts under it. Gretel, in a frumpy black dirndl with white polka dots, fluttered from one end of the buffet to the other, looking like someone who'd lived her sixteen years entirely on muesli and yogurt and not enough of it. Fourteen-year-old Hansel had a potato-pancakes-and-strudel figure and looked like a younger version of his father in outgrown lederhosen. He served water as if the cost was coming out of his allowance and bused tables like he was making a commission on new dishes.

Aunt Bab, as hostess and dining room supervisor, bleated her usual morning greeting to the guests and answered their questions about the day's activities, the weather forecast, and what overpriced items were available in the resort Alpenmarkt. At nine sharp, she trotted out the dining room doors and closed them behind her. Like everyone else, she was moving on to her next task, answering the same stupid questions and taking reservations and complaints at the Guest Services desk.

I waved good-bye to the last of my geezers, scooped a ten-dollar tip off their table, and breezed through the kitchen on my way to Housekeeping.

"Ciao!" I called to Elsa/Cindy who was wrestling a ham-shaped meat product onto the table.

"Aufweidersehn!" she corrected.

"Gesundheit!" I smiled as if she were the sister I'd never had and didn't like much. "Don't sneeze on lunch!"

I found the other sister I liked even less in the housekeeping supply room, carved out of a corner of the old barn where sheep must have been sent to die. That eau de disinfectant had to be covering up something.

"Bonjour, Liesl!" Her real name was Lisa, but I preferred the faux version that rhymed with weasel. Some names just fit.

"You're late." She tapped the face of a serviceable watch with a thick black band. Everything about her was functional, from the coveralls and gumboots she wore for cleaning, to the big ring of keys with their numbered tags. "Grab your cart and hop to it."

"Like a bunny, ma'am," I said, just to irritate her. Hop to it? Who says that? I zipped a housekeeping smock on over my dirndl, looking, I suspected, like a graduate from birthing class. "Any special orders today?"

She scanned a clipboard like she was reading it with her nose, the dark hairs on her upper lip quivering like they couldn't wait to grow into real whiskers. "One turnover today, Number 9. I'll take it." And any tip the departing guests left behind. She handed me a master key. "You've got towels and trash in the other chalets and some kind of carpet stain in Number 17."

"That's one of the Blucher Family Reunion units, right?"

"So?"

"Nice family." For a FOX cartoon show. Four dysfunctional generations swarmed over eight chalets, so I could be dealing with anything from glitter glue to pizza sauce to bodily fluids. No tip, for sure, but that suited our plans.

I lugged towels and trash bags and the atomic carpet cleaner out to the little trailer behind my assigned golf cart. I pulled out fast and steered into a fishtail just to hear Liesl growl as the cart swung from side to side. I do like to drive.

I did my job like normal, just like Dillon said. I dumped towels in the bathrooms and trash into the big bags I left outside for Vinnie to cart away. I made my mental lists. Twice I got a peek at Dillon, heading into the woods with a string of flirty girls in tank tops and flip-flops and then heading out again with a bunch of scratching, limping, whining brats. When in the country, girls, remember Frye makes a très stylish ankle boot.

I worked lunch at the poolside biergarten, where I could watch Dillon hosing down the deck and adjusting umbrellas for women who really shouldn't wear bikinis. The ham product showed up in sandwich form with German potato salad warm from the can and limp slices of dill pickle. Nobody seemed to mind as long as they had a Pilsner or Rhineland Red in hand and me and Dillon to check out. I was still in my dirndl, but I'd switched the Dorados for heels in red leather. Not many American women can balance a cocktail tray in four-inch spikes, but I'm one of them.

Dillon wore swim trunks and a tan.

I loaded two bottles of water on my tray, the second for Liesl's son Lance, standing guard at the deep end, wearing chunky sunglasses, trunks faded pink, and a Red Cross muscle shirt that exposed his long, stringy arms. He wore a tan, too, but even without the white goop on his nose, the effect wouldn't have been the same. Lance was twenty-two, working on a graduate degree in Hospitality and Hotel Management. He was trying to get a grant.

"How's the Perfect Son?" I pressed the cool water bottle into the middle of Dillon's chest.

"Concerned. Seems the pH was unbalanced this morning."

"Too much 'p'?"

"Mmmm." Dillon chugged the water, while I watched each gulp slide down his throat. He should do commercials. "Meet me in the woods after dinner. Wear your old slip, okay?"

I swallowed the mouthful of water he'd left for me. "Mmmm."

I took my time strolling from one end of the pool to the other. Lance's head never turned, but behind those dark glasses I'd bet his eyes were swiveling like Hula-Hoops.

"Are ya hot, Lance?" I dangled the water bottle from two fingers. I love to make gawky guys blush.

He grabbed the bottle at the bottom and tugged it away from me. No contact. Mr. Ironman. "Thanks." He twisted off the cap and managed to slurp water without taking his eyes from the pool.

"You do realize there's no one in the water, Lance? They're all eating."

"I'm still on duty. I shouldn't be talking to anyone." The empty bottle crackled. He unclenched his hand and thrust the bottle in my direction. I slid my fingers over his as I took it. I waited.

"Thanks for the water," he managed.

"Mmmm." I walked away.

□　　□　　□

The stolen goods were stashed in the woods in a fifty-foot section of ruined stone wall. Dillon always stopped his strolling group there for a water break and the story of farms abandoned to the wilderness when the farm boys went to war and discovered there was land in other parts of the country that didn't grow rocks. Not so dumb, those farm boys. This particular wall, he didn't say, was thrown together by Fred and Vinnie with stones they hauled away from a condo development. The plastic trunk buried under the end section came later. It was now empty.

"What could we get for this stuff? Five grand?" I scrolled through the photos on a pink digital camera and found six of Dillon at poolside skimming bugs. I took the memory card. "We could get to New York on that. Why don't we?"

Dillon closed the trunk and started piling rocks on it again. "I don't know, Bev. You're still pretty hot."

"With the cops and the bail bondsman, I know. How about you?" I don't worry about me and Dillon much, but a girl likes to hear she's worth more to her guy than her bounty. "Any of those tummy-tucked pool babes offer to take you away from all this?"

"You know better." Not much gets Dillon mad, but he does not like his honor questioned. He dropped another rock on the pile. "I was waiting outside the courthouse for you, wasn't I?"

In a boosted Ford Escape, I remembered. Dillon's got style. "You weren't afraid I'd roll on you? 'My big, bad boyfriend made me do it?'"

"Not a chance." He filled the gaps with smaller rocks. "And you know I'd never turn on you, right? You're just pushing my buttons?"

"Mm-hmm. See?" I picked up one of those cell phone computer things named for a fruit and tapped at the keyboard. "We should get a couple of these. I could make lists of the best stuff when I'm doing the chalets, take photos, too." I typed IMHOT4U. "Guess what I'm texting?"

"I prefer oral communication." Dillon plucked the cell thing from my hand and convinced me we did not need wireless technology. He dropped the phone in his daypack along with two laptops, a DVD player and three digital cameras. "These are mine. You got the rest?"

I slipped the last MP3 player into one of the dozen pockets in the slip I wore under my skirt and tried to walk as if I weren't wearing a small electronics department. "Do I rattle?"

"I was too busy looking to listen. Walk on ahead of me."

It took another ten minutes, with a couple of stops for Dillon to rearrange my components, before we reached the edge of the woods, a distance of maybe two city blocks. The brakes were holding, but just barely.

Gray shapes swarmed the central slope of the hill as guests wandered over to the weekly Family Alpenfest, held on the asphalt slab that passed by day as a tennis court. Vinnie and Bab, transformed into Jolly Otto, the One-Man Oompah Band, and his sidekick, Frau Hilda, organized polkas and waltzes and line dancing. The guests helped themselves to root beer and pretzel sticks, and the rest of the staff, in dirndls and lederhosen, tried to herd them onto the dance floor whenever the festivities flagged.

It was fairly simple for me and Dillon to grab Randall Blucher and twirl him across the slab and into the dark on the other side. He was the oldest grandson of the clan's one-hundred-year-old patriarch and the head of this misguided reunion of tightwads.

"Hey, what's up, guys?" he protested as we hustled him away toward the lodge. "Party's back there!"

"We're sorry to disturb your evening, sir," said Dillon, "but it's imperative that Herr Friederich speak with you about a matter concerning your family."

"It's not Grandpop, is it?" Randall stopped dead, apparently forgetting we'd just left the old terror gumming pretzels and leering at anything in a dirndl.

"No, sir, but there is a situation we need to clear up without creating any unwarranted talk or distress to your family." Dillon sounded just like those over-polite cops on TV. His dad would have been proud.

"What? What's going on?"

"Herr Friederich will explain, sir."

Randall was hustling now, and I was breathless when we reached the lodge. Fred was waiting in his office, his desk looking like a pawn shop display of used electronics. "Thank you for coming, Mr. Blucher." Like he'd had a choice. "Please sit down."

Clearly bewildered, Randall perched on the edge of the visitor's chair, while Fred swiveled nervously in his seat behind the desk. Me and Dillon backed away.

"Let me say first, that I just wish to put a stop to a difficult situation, Mr. Blucher. I have no wish to prosecute."

"What!" Randall jumped up from the chair. "What is this?"

Fred flinched, but kept his voice even. "Please sit. I'd like to settle this quickly."

Dillon touched Randall's shoulder and eased him back to the chair.

"These items were all reported missing this week by guests at the resort. They've all been recovered, so we can settle this very easily." Fred launched into the speech Dillon had drilled into him. "My security team"—that was us—"located these items in three separate stashes under chalets occupied by your family, sir. Acting on their information, I entered the three premises and retrieved one additional item." He held up the wedding ring. "I will return everything to the owners without disclosing where they were found. I want only your word that you will speak to the others in your party and your assurance that this will not happen again during your stay."

I thought Randall would explode. His beefy muscles bunched, ready for a leap across the desk and the pounding he thought Fred deserved. Then Dillon was there, talking him down, pleading with him not to complicate a simple situation with injuries that might lead to a 911 call, a police report, a lawsuit.

"It's probably just some of the kids, sir. One or two influencing some others. Parents not able to keep track in a big group like yours. I'm sure you don't even know them that well."

Randall grabbed at the excuse like the last in-stock voucher for the top new video game at Christmas. "There are some wild ones in the bunch, but it won't happen again," he promised. "I'll break heads, if I have to. Just don't let this get to Grandpop."

It took five more minutes to ease him out of the office and another ten to get rid of Fred. From the look he gave us, he wasn't totally convinced, but I flashed him the "V" for VIVA sign. Truth versus a Gold Suitcase? No contest.

□   □   □

The Alpenfest was breaking up with not a single Blucher in sight. Me and Dillon crept around the edge of the tennis court, grabbed an arm each and hauled our real thief away into the dark. We did it fast and quiet and kept going till we reached the woods, Dillon doing the muscle work and me hanging on to the towel we were using as a gag. When we got to the stone wall, we let her go.

The moonlight turned Gretel's face sickly pale and her arms and legs into thin white sticks. She was the kid nobody noticed much, always fluttering in the background. Great set-up.

The braid coiled around her head was coming undone, and she brushed the hair away from wide, bright eyes that showed no fear or distress. She knew she was caught, and she knew she was going to get away with it. It was like looking in a mirror.

"What's going on?" she demanded.

"Sit down." I pointed to the wall. "And by the way? Your stuff's gone. We found it and gave it all back for you."

"What stuff?"

The conversation, I could tell, was going to lack a certain originality. I won't go through it all, but we passed from "So what if I did?" to "I hate this place!" and ended up at "You two have got nerve."

"More than you'll ever have, *liebchen*." I smiled. "We've also got an empty trunk just your size under that pile of rocks. Don't tempt us."

"You don't understand!"

"Yeah, we do, which is why we're doing this in the woods and not in Herr Friedrich's office," said Dillon. "Because you are going about this all wrong."

That shut her up.

"Lesson One," I said. "You are working too hard, too cheap and too close to home." I lifted my skirt. "Lesson Two: Wardrobe."

Our little chat ended with Gretel trying on my slip and saying, "I know these great shops in Stowe" and "Swear you won't tell my dad."

"Afraid he'll have you arrested?" Dillon was leaning on the wall, tossing a rock from hand to hand.

"No." Gretel swiveled her skinny hips away from him. "Parents can't testify against their kids. It's the law."

"Wrong." Dillon should know. His old man had been called as a witness. Maybe he didn't have much choice, because Dillon stole his patrol car, but still. "That only goes for husbands and wives. Married couples can't be forced to testify against each other."

And there, in the moonlight, it hit us.

"What?" Gretel must have felt the tension in the air.

"Scram," I said. "Keep the slip."

"You two are so weird." She stalked off down the path.

"Bev?" Dillon boosted his leather-clad butt up on the wall and pulled me up next to him.

"Mmmm?" I'm not usually stuck for what to say, and Dillon and me don't need words anyway, but my throat closed up like the time I mistakenly ate clam dip.

"We don't have to live in Connecticut to get a marriage license there. And there's no wait period, so we could be on the road before it showed up on a records check."

I looked up at the moon shining through the treetops and the millions of stars you don't see in the city sky. It was so quiet I could hear the wind rustling the leaves and my own heart thumping. Scary.

"Would we come back here? To your family?" I thought of these past weeks with Herr Friederich and Frau Dumpling, Weasel and the

Perfect Son, Jolly Otto and Hilda, Glum Hansel and Greedy Gretel. All of Dillon's second something-or-others, far removed.

He was shaking his head. "Nope."

I dragged Dillon off the wall by his suspenders and kissed him till the brakes were smoking. "Let's pack."

We took the dirndl and the lederhosen. We also took the master list of guests, their home addresses and their credit card numbers. For a wedding gift, Dillon let me lift the winking cow pitcher. And I let him boost Randall Blucher's car.

△ . △ . △

Mo Walsh writes weekly newspaper features and is past coordinator of the South Shore Writers Club. Mo's stories have appeared in Mary Higgins Clark Mystery Magazine, Woman's World, Windchill, Still Waters *and* Deadfall. *She lives in Weymouth, Massachusetts, with four men, a dog and six novels in progress*

Duck Sandwich

Mark Ammons

Even the simplest murder needs a little story. So what should mine be? And how little?

Sure, there are plenty of big stories. Ooodles. Books, mags, movies, every third Oprah, just chock-full of heart-pounding tales of rage, lust, greed, betrayal, revenge, infidelity, even full-blown insanity, all leading to a grisly end. But I don't have the grand stuff. And I definitely don't have the energy. Forty years of marriage to that hambone was tiring enough. No, *War and Peace* isn't in me, even if matrimony is the purest Petri dish of motive and opportunity.

So filthy. A shower will be nice, maybe even a long, long bath.

Once upon a time, a little story might have been easy. Back in that first year when it all began innocently enough with "The Joke." What a mistake, laughing politely while he brayed like some demented jackass at his gross gag about a ship captain, a bunghole, and a horny first mate's day in the barrel. Yuggh.

Uhmmmm, hot water. Nice not having to pray anymore he'd accidentally leave me a thimbleful. When was the last time I'd really been able to soak till I puckered?

Nope, never should have laughed. Might as well have given him a license to kill. Can't blame myself too much, though. How could I know then that "The Joke" was his one and only joke? Umpteen ugly retellings later, always in the most embarrassing situations, and all I could manage was a stiff smile and a silent scream—*If he tells that joke one more time, I'm going to kill him!*

Meant it, too. Maybe should have. Simpler times and all that. At least my little story would've been really, really short.

But, after a few years and a hundred more trips around the captain's barrel, the whole thing somehow became a weary "so what?" Hey, just a stupid joke from a stupid man. A hangnail on my soul, but hardly grounds for murder.

Anyway, who am I kidding? I'm not so special. As far back as I can remember, every woman I've ever known has gone on endlessly about the things men do that drive them nuts. And they, too, inevitably capped their laments with "I'm going to kill him."

My girlfriends' catechism of male crazy-making was so universal they might as well have joined arms and sung it like my church choir cranking out some weird twelve-part harmony. Guys in their twenties? Too little commitment, too much sex, and no next-day calls. In their thirties, too much ambition, too little attention, and no memory of anniversaries. Their forties? Ambition kaput and too much yappity-yap. All together now, girls . . . *will-oh-will-that-man-never-shut-up! Aaaaaaaaamen.* As for the fifties, all bets off. A hint of ambition again. But most of it devoted to producing as many obnoxious noises and gasses as possible while simultaneously cultivating an amazing array of simian hair growth. In the nose, on the toes, out the ears, down the back. Double yuggh.

That was just for openers. Spanning the years was a mile-long list of constant complaints—he never listens, he hogs the remote, he always has "a better idea," he picks his nose with the pride of Little Jack Horner. On and on until, tying it up in one neat bow, came everyone's perennial favorite: the male species' inability to put down the toilet seat.

Their litanies were compelling, the indictments persuasive, their mates' collective guilt absolute. Yet, so far as I know, no man was dead. All their husbands were still walking too little, talking too much, and—despite leaving the seat up—still missing the bowl.

Big deal. My bonehead not only couldn't hit the porcelain, he couldn't drive ten feet without losing his way. To be sure, each and every woman also rated the perverse male refusal to stop for directions the hands-down toilet seat runner-up. But, I had them beat in spades. My personal idiot not only refused to stop, he would actually speed up, really speed up, killing any chance I might be able to yell out the window for guidance without getting my head knocked off by a telephone pole. He'd crash madly hither and thither like a rat in a maze, all the time bongo-beating on the steering wheel while barking, "KFM, KFM, KFM!" As in "Keep Fruckin' Movin'." Not friggin', not frickin'. Yes, "fruckin'." His one concession to my distaste for the "F" word. Real cute.

Wish I had a scratchy towel. I love a scratchy towel. It'll be good to be able to line-dry again without having to worry about Little Lord Tender-Rump.

KFM, KFM, KFM . . . Maddening. Yes. But still not enough, still not sufficient grounds.

Got to think. Well, there's always "I'm gettin' to it." Talk about a one-way ticket to the loony bin. Although a crack hunter-gatherer, Bongo Boy was one lousy accomplisher. Like so many men, his primary talent resided in demolition. He'd buy a bunch of supplies—sheetrock, tiling, pails of paint, miles of molding—and tear a room down to the studs. Then, dropping everything, he'd wander off in search of the next thing to rip apart. When I'd find him on Rape-and-Pillage Project #8 and gently ask when he might get back to Project #1 so I didn't have to continue peeing in a bucket while balancing a candle on my head, his answer was invariably "I'm gettin' to it." The only exception was when, in a fit of desperation, I'd decide to finish one of his messes on my own. Like clockwork, he'd magically appear midway through the job, snatch away my tools and announce, "I was gettin' to that, and now you're screwin' it up."

To be fair, there was that one time he oiled the squeaky chain on the back porch swing. Too bad. That squeak had been oddly comforting compared to listening to him beat his chest about his accomplishment for the next three months. At least the two drops of oil had been cheap.

Case in point, your honor: the fall-out fiasco. Like many old houses in our neighborhood, the backyard contained an ancient stone well easily forty feet deep and bone dry for over half a century. Once town water reached our street in the 1950s, most everyone capped or filled their wells with dirt. But the old man we bought our place from had never gotten around to it. Must have been related to you-know-who. Twenty years later and dealing with the well was still on my good ol' Gettin'-To-It's "gettin' to it" list. Probably not enough wholesale destruction involved.

But one bright May morning, the well suddenly became exhibit "A" for the wisdom of never rushing a project. Somehow Bongo Boy got it into his bonnet, probably from watching too much Fox News, that the next 9/11 was just around the corner, and this time it would be "so much bigger, oh yeah, you bet." The well provided perfect access for a fall-out shelter, he proclaimed. Install some rungs, do a little digging down below and, presto, we'd have ourselves a cozy little bunker. "Nothing to it, be done in a weekend, the terrorists can go suck sand."

He hunted. He gathered. He maxed-out both credit cards. Soon the driveway overflowed with steel reinforcing rods, concrete forms, winches, pulleys, picks, shovels, mason's tubs, a brand new jackhammer, a used generator—enough stuff for a small pharaoh's tomb. His crowning glory was a pallet of what he solemnly announced was "'Poly-Form 80' high-strength hydraulic cement: no-mixing-required-just-add-water-for-an-impenetrable-shield, capable of expanding to fill every nook and cranny" of our new Armageddon home.

His treasure trove sat untouched through the summer, then the fall, while he contemplated gettin' to it. No hurry, he said. Apparently Fox News had determined that the greatest threat to the American

Way was now a dubious sex scandal involving some third-string Democrat. Besides, he was too busy tearing up the front yard. Something about needing a carport because the driveway was full.

Then, a sleet storm hit in December. Without warning, he sprang into action. The flimsy plastic tarp over his prized Poly-Form 80 had shredded in the fierce winds. If he didn't get the sacks of concrete out of the weather quickly, they'd be drenched and harden into useless boulders. He rocketed into the jaws of the tempest. Like some odd blast from the past, it kind of turned me on seeing him move so fast.

It wasn't until spring and time for me to plant that I discovered what the jerk had done. To find shelter for his magic cement, he'd busted into my potting shed. Then, to make room, he took my precious collection of one-of-a-kind garden tools, lovingly passed down from my great grandmother, and heaved them out the back window where they landed in the compost heap. My beautiful hickory-handled hoes and rakes, my hand-wrought Victorian spades and trowels, everything, all utterly rotted, rusted and ruined by the brutal New England winter.

Good. Now I'm getting somewhere. But who kills someone over a bunch of old garden tools, heirlooms or not? Too weird, too complicated . . . and way, way too long a story. Second degree, twenty to life. At best.

I've learned to tolerate a lot over the years. "The Joke," KFM, the hunting-gathering-sitting. I should be able to tolerate this.

But, damn it all, that's my shed. I built it myself, no thanks to him. And those were my tools. Mine. This was unacceptable. This was personal. Funny, a marriage getting "personal."

Should have called him on it the moment I'd found them. But didn't. Why? Who knows, maybe age has a way of reducing everything to a simple Darwinian proposition: adapt or perish.

Besides, fat chance even trying to discuss it with him. Futile. No way to argue with that baboon.

Yes, that was the worst thing of all. He wouldn't argue. Wait.

Actually, he would argue. He just wouldn't have an argument. No matter what the issue, he always made sure to have his say first. Planting himself like the Pope, he'd pronounce "the facts of the matter" in excruciating detail. Then, as I'd start to have my say, he'd slap on his hat and head for the door.

My feeble "Where are you going?" was unfailingly met with the same response: "I have to see a man about a duck sandwich."

A bang of the screen door, and he was gone.

In the early years, he'd only disappear for hours. As time wore on, it became days. Now, it could be a week. That duck must have been in Peking.

Unfortunately, he always came back, waltzing in like nothing had happened, asking if I was making him his special spicy-spicy meatloaf for dinner. Though he never actually demanded it, I knew that somewhere deep in his testosterone-addled brain he somehow viewed spicy-spicy meatloaf as his right and proper reward for having deigned to return to me.

It was no different this last time.

So, I rewarded him. I placed the meatloaf on his plate. He wolfed it down. I leaned over and murmured sweetly in his ear, "Adapt or perish, my ass."

He wasn't listening. As usual. He just leered at me with his moronic, adolescent grin. "My ass" was all he'd heard.

In spite of what I've read in the papers, getting rid of a body was astonishingly easy. I tipped him out of his chair into my wheelbarrow and simply dumped his scrawny butt down the well, pitching the remaining meatloaf in after him. One of his few redeeming qualities was he'd always loved leftovers. One of the many redeeming qualities of a spicy-spicy meatloaf—it could hide a multitude of sins.

Then, in his now all too mortal words, I went about "gettin' to it." In fact, he'd set the table for me. His one true accomplishment. A few sacks of his stupid high-strength hydraulic cement, no-mixing-required-just-add-water-for-an-impenetrable-shield, a couple of barrows of compost, some leaves and branches as garnish, run the hose, job done in thirty minutes. The bottom of the well looked exactly like it always had.

As I sway on my back porch swing, the chain is squeaking again. A welcome return, like the night birds just beginning to tune up in the gathering dusk. But, still, what's my story? In our entire time together he'd never let me have any stories. With friends—when we still had friends—he always took up all the space. On the rare occasion where I somehow managed to wedge my way into one of his monologues, I'd barely get past my first sentence before he'd barge in to declare I was telling it "all wrong." Not only would he say I was telling the story—*my* story—wrong, he'd steal it right out of my mouth, claiming it as his own. And he hadn't even been there.

Well, now I have one little story he can't hijack.

When someone asks where he is, if anyone even bothers to, I'll keep it short.

"He had to see a man about a fruckin' duck sandwich."

△ △ △

Mark Ammons is a Medford, Massachusetts-based, former stage director, producer, and screenwriter/script doctor. He teaches contemporary drama and advises graduate thesis projects at the Boston Conservatory. His story, "The Catch" in Still Waters, *won the 2008 Robert L. Fish Memorial Award for best first mystery and was also nominated for an Edgar®, the first time a story has been simultaneously recognized in both arenas.*

Barbara Ross

Key West

Barbara Ross

Every night, after they unload the booze-filled tourists from the sunset cruise, wash down the decks, and put the *Morgana* to bed, they go to the Paradise to eat, drink and listen to music. It's Caroline's favorite part of the day, her reward for being at the markets in the early morning and carrying the heavy coolers up and down the steep cabin stairs.

Tonight, as always, the Captain sits at the head of the table. Caroline has known him for fifteen years now. He's as handsome as ever, though his sun-bleached hair shows some gray, as do his whiskers on the days he doesn't shave. For twelve hours or more each day, he and Caroline move around the *Morgana* without words, in perfect synchrony. Yet, when he leaves the Paradise, Caroline isn't exactly sure where he goes. She's never visited his home. He has come to hers only sometimes in her dreams.

But then, if he has things he chooses not to tell, so does she. What does he know about her, really? He knows she's an excellent cook. Over the past fifteen winters she's learned to make the most of the island's fresh ingredients. He knows he pays her no salary; she accepts only her share of the cash the tourists leave in tips. And he knows that, though he asks her every year, she firmly but politely refuses to sail north to Martha's Vineyard with them for the summer to feed the tourists as they sail the waters of Nantucket Sound. Caroline's been careful to give no other clues.

On Caroline's right, Ortiz, the first mate, is telling a story in his soft Dominican accent. It's a tale he has told over and over, until it's burnished smooth. "So I say to her," he winds up, "lady, if there is a shark in there with you, you have nothing to fear. Because I have never, in all my years, seen a shark go after a whale!"

Ortiz came to Key West as a boy. He has many relatives both here and back there. Caroline doesn't know his immigration status, though she can guess. He's never told the story of his arrival, and here at the southernmost point in the continental U. S., no one asks for information that isn't volunteered.

Wade isn't at the bar yet. He only goes out on the *Morgana*'s daytime runs when there are snorkelers to guide, but he often joins the crew for dinner. Unlike the rest of them, he is an open book. Half his family runs the town. They own bars, fight fires, arrest miscreants. The rest make regular appearances in the local paper's Crime Report. Wade's older brother, Bart, Police Lieutenant Stoddard, checks on the *Morgana* and her crew whenever business brings him to the waterfront. When he appears, Caroline's stomach clenches and her palms sweat. She's afraid someone will notice, but no one ever does. Bart is funny and cute and calls her Ms. Taylor, a surname she uses only when one is absolutely required, a rarity in Key West.

Their table at the Paradise is long, covered with platters of colorful food and pitchers of beer to wash the salt from their throats. The rest of the seats are filled by the *Morgana*'s seasonal hires, mostly college-age kids taking a semester off. When the band takes a break, Caroline closes her eyes, exhales, and then opens them again. This is my family now, she thinks. This as close to happy as I can ever be.

Wade comes in with a new girl in tow just as the band is starting up again. He shouts the girl's name over the music, but Caroline doesn't catch it. The girl can't be more than sixteen, maybe younger. She's petite and dark like Caroline, but curly-haired and blue-eyed.

The girl falls on the food, ravenous. The waiter brings another pitcher and the girl pours herself one beer and then another.

The band takes another short break, then returns and starts up raucously. The girl drinks a third beer and a fourth.

"You should slow her down!" Caroline calls to Wade, but he pretends not to hear. Does he realize how young she is?

The girl stands as if to go to the restroom, and then bolts for the front door. Caroline finds her outside, puking and crying. Caroline holds back her hair. "Do you have a place to stay?" she asks her. The girl shakes her head miserably, no.

□   □   □

Caroline appears at the top of the stairs dressed in blue jeans and a sweatshirt. She is nine and her mother wants to take her to some awful doll tea party given by the daughter of a friend. Caroline isn't interested in tea parties, dolls or the girls who play with them. She isn't interested in the daughters of her mother's friends, and she knows they aren't interested in her. Her outfit has the desired effect. Her mother is furious.

"You cannot go dressed like that," her mother barks. "Change immediately." Then, under her breath, she mutters, "Dungarees to a tea party. No one would do such a thing."

Even at nine, Caroline has figured out that when her mother says, "No one would do such a thing," she means no one she knows would do such a thing, and the people she knows all share the same New England roots, intertwined tentacles of money, ancestry and education. These people would never do such things, and the people who would, don't matter. Caroline has also figured out that her mother has an uncanny ability not to see or hear things that don't fit into her version of the world. When Caroline tells her mother she hears Daddy weeping in his study every day, her mother snaps, "Don't be silly."

Five years later, by the time Caroline starts her private high school, she and her mother are in a state of permanent, though uneven, war. "You need to try, especially now," her mother commands. "Try being nice to people. Smile and say hello. Show an interest. It's not so hard." Of course, by "people," her mother means the people who matter, the children of her friends, and by "especially now," she means now that Caroline's father is dead.

Caroline ignores her. At lunch, she sits at the last table, the one with the misfits and rebels—the girls with crazy hair who push their uniforms to the edge of the dress code. Every day, when they leave school together in the afternoon, Caroline sees her mother parked across the street, hands clamped tightly on the steering wheel, shaking her head.

□   □   □

The girl from the bar says her name is Emily. Caroline brings her home to spend the night. She's never had an overnight guest in the little pool house she rents for cash from a couple happy to keep the IRS out of the transaction. But, Emily needs to be somewhere safe. The town has changed since Caroline arrived in the Keys. The police no longer allow sleeping on the beach, and the vagrants who gather under the palms on Stock Island are more typical of big city homeless than the generous, loose crowd Caroline encountered.

Still woozy from the alcohol, Emily falls instantly asleep on the couch.

In the morning, she's still there, deeply unconscious when Caroline hurries off to work. Caroline looks for Emily in the Paradise that night, but she never turns up. When Caroline asks Wade about the girl, he shrugs his shoulders. Emily is already barely a memory.

When Caroline awakens the next morning, Emily is there again, asleep on the couch. They go on like this for three days—Emily coming in when Caroline is sleeping, Caroline leaving while Emily sleeps.

On the fourth day, there is a storm and the *Morgana* doesn't go out. Caroline spends the day quietly in the pool house, waiting for Emily to wake up. Caroline's goal is to find out Emily's full name, and then convince her to tell her family where she is. Emily refuses.

"They must be looking for you," Caroline insists.

"They're not. My stepmother, she's a witch, and she's turned *him* against me. They're happy I'm gone."

"Then just let them know you're okay," Caroline counters, but Emily ignores her.

□   □   □

Caoline is still new at the gallery in Boston when Ben wanders in. She and college weren't a good match. Her studio art courses taught her she had the eye, but not the hand, of an artist. She left for good after her sophomore year. She and her mother are both deeply disappointed at her failure, though for different reasons.

Ben returns to the gallery three times to see the current show, an installation of beat-up bureaus sawed in half to show their contents. Caroline is inexperienced enough to think he might be a buyer. He has so many questions.

"Do you like one of them in particular?" she asks on his fourth visit.

Ben blushes to the roots of his hair. "What I'd like is to ask you out."

What makes being with Ben so easy is that he's instantly acceptable to her mother. Caroline is so tired of fighting with her mother. Ben is a lawyer, and even though he works for the U.S. Attorney's office instead of a real firm, he graduated from Dartmouth. And, Caroline's mother knows his freshman-year roommate's mother. When they discover this, it seals her approval. Ben also possesses the dark hair and deep blue eyes that Caroline thinks are the nicest combination in a man.

Their courtship is smooth. Ben is respectful of the seven-year difference in their ages. He doesn't push her. In the spring, much to Caroline's mother's elation, Ben proposes.

Once the wedding juggernaut is in motion, there isn't much time to think, and it's only in the final days that Caroline begins to have doubts. Not about Ben, who is a solid, kind man, but about the choice to marry at all, how young she really is, and what other paths there might have been.

A half-hour before her wedding, Caroline confides to her mother that she doesn't think she can go through with it. Her mother rises up to her full height in heels, towering several inches above Caroline. "What do you think you're doing?" she hisses through clenched teeth. "The church is full of my friends!"

In the chaos of the moment, as Caroline and Ben dash from the reception chased by good wishes and flying rice, Caroline leaves her purse with her birth control pills swinging on the knob of her old bedroom door. Nine months later, Claire is born.

□ □ □

As the months go on, Caroline and Emily develop the rhythms of people living together. Emily goes through spurts when she desperately craves Caroline's approval. She tidies the pool house, listens attentively to Caroline's stories about the tourists, and makes popcorn to accompany their TV movies, which they watch with Emily sprawled across the couch, head on Caroline's shoulder.

During these periods, the only thing Caroline can't do is ask Emily's full name or urge her to call her parents. If she does, the peace is shattered. Emily's story changes constantly. Now she can't go home because her stepfather is abusing her.

"I thought you said the problem was with your stepmother?" Caroline says.

"My stepmother hates me, so I can't live with my Dad, and my stepfather is always going after me, so I can't live at Mom's, get it?" Emily spits back, then storms out.

But she always returns, sleeping while Caroline is working and then slipping out before Caroline comes home. Caroline gives up her evenings at the Paradise to spend time with Emily, but Emily catches on and starts going out earlier. When Caroline leaves for the markets in the morning, she smells the alcohol oozing from Emily's sleeping form.

□   □   □

Caroline is aware the moment it begins—the feeling rushes in with her milk. She is awake most of the night, mind twirling. At 2:00 a.m., when the nurse realizes Caroline's light is still on, she comes in and wheels the plastic cot holding the infant Claire out of the room. "So· you can get some sleep."

Toward daylight, Caroline plummets. She is so disappointed in herself. How could she, of all people, healthy and young, have required a caesarian to deliver Claire? Why couldn't she do what untold billions of women have done through the ages?

Caroline smiles when her mother comes to see the baby. She smiles the entire time Ben is there. When she's alone, or just with Claire, silent tears run down Caroline's cheeks. The fine hair on her newborn's head is almost always damp with tears.

After she's been home for a while, the old Caroline, the Caroline who can analyze and accept, returns long enough for her to understand she is depressed. Whenever the despair comes, she tries to reason it away, to make her thoughts drive her emotions instead of the other way around, but her mind is like a car careening down a curving, rain-slicked road. No matter what she does, she cannot gain control.

She expects the depression to burn off like a morning fog, to feel a little less sad every day, but it doesn't work that way. Over the next two months, the periods of equilibrium grow longer, so a whole hour goes by without the hopeless feeling, and then a whole day, and then a week. But when the feeling floods back, even for a minute, Caroline feels it as intensely as she did every hour of every day at the beginning.

Caroline knows what is happening to her is chemical, and she realizes she has never been depressed before. In the past, when she's said, "I'm depressed," what she meant was "I'm angry at myself," or "I'm feeling lazy," or "I'm bored." All these years, she's blamed her father for leaving the way he did. She couldn't understand why he didn't love her enough to will himself to be well. Now she understands and forgives.

□   □   □

Caroline is certain Emily is using drugs. Sometimes during their brief encounters, Emily is nervous as a cat, a thin line of perspiration across her upper lip. Other times she is slow-moving and sleepy, drifting off in the middle of sentences. The drugs and the people who sell the drugs make Caroline frantic with worry. She considers asking Wade or Ortiz for advice, but she hasn't told anyone Emily is living with her.

Caroline doesn't want to think about where Emily is getting the money for the drugs. She knows Emily has been searching the pool house. Caroline has lived alone for so long, she can tell when something has been moved. She takes her wallet with her whenever she leaves. She moves her savings, fifteen years of accumulated cash, from the crawl space above her closet to the laundry room of the empty main house.

I cannot, I cannot, I cannot lose another child. Though the thought is too painful to bring fully into consciousness, it pulses at the edges of her brain like a prayer.

Talking to Emily about the danger of the alcohol and drugs is impossible.

"Relax!" Emily demands, aggrieved. "I know what I'm doing."

"You couldn't possibly."

"What're you going to do, call the cops?"

Caroline tries to control her face, but she knows the old fear always shows itself in response to this threat. Emily is triumphant. "I didn't think so," she sneers.

The weather has been dazzling, and the *Morgana* is going out every day. Caroline begins to take days off, something she has never done. The Captain is concerned, then annoyed. Ortiz does his best to cover for her, but they are all feeling the strain.

One morning when Caroline rises early, determined to go to work, she notices something odd in Emily's breathing. When Caroline tries to rouse her, there is no response.

□   □   □

The twins, Lily and Emma, are born eleven months after Claire.

"Don't believe the old wives' tale that you can't conceive when you're nursing!" Caroline jokes at the shower her mother's friends host. It's the third, counting her wedding shower, she's had in two years. Caroline is embarrassed by the attention, but her mother insists. "It's what we do."

When the babies are born, the depression that nipped at her after Claire's birth smothers Caroline. Her life is a blur. Somewhere, someone is always crying. Even Claire, who had become such a little person before the twins were born, is absorbed into the featureless, howling blob that is her children.

Ben tries to help. He takes a nighttime feeding as soon as bottles are a possibility. But he is working longer and longer hours. When they found out Caroline was pregnant again, he gave up his government job and joined that "real" firm, to Caroline's mother's delight. In two years he's gone from carefree bachelor to breadwinner with five mouths to feed, adding debt from a house and a car and all the major appliances to his mountain of law school loans. Caroline can't go back to her gallery job. She could never earn enough to cover daycare for three children.

Caroline's father left her the little bit of family money that was his own, but it's in a trust until she's thirty. How could anyone have known she'd need it when she was so young? And now, it doesn't occur to her mother, or to Caroline for that matter, that money could be used to solve any problem that should be addressable by self-discipline and hard work.

So Caroline drags herself through each day, unshowered, smelling of sour milk from the stains on her clothes.

When her high-school friends come to see the children, they are clearly horrified—by Caroline's appearance and the house, the overflowing diaper pail and Claire's cereal hardening on the counter where it spilled. No longer misfits or rebels, they are starting their adult lives, and this specter of what might come is too much for them.

"But you knew you were having twins," they point out, as if foreknowledge should make all the difference.

"Not," Caroline answers, "at conception."

The day Ben comes home and finds all four of them sobbing, he calls Caroline's mother. Though she lives thirty minutes away, she arrives with a suitcase and clean sheets for her own bed.

"Caroline, dear, you need to anticipate," she says. "Try not to let anyone be hungry or tired, because if you wait until the first one cries to feed her, the third will be starving and hysterical by the time you get there. Think ahead, dear. Get everyone on a schedule."

Under her mother's program, the babies thrive. The house is clean, and there are dinners at the end of the day. Ben comes home earlier. Her mother manages it all. Caroline sits in the rocker in the living room and nurses. She feels like the family cow.

Claire begins to walk. Emma figures out how to roll over. Caroline's mother packs her bag and goes home. Caroline, following the meticulous schedule her mother leaves for her, keeps it all together until Lily develops a croupy cough, and then they all come down with it, fevered and wailing. The meals fall by the wayside, and the house smells again. When Caroline gets the flu and can't move from her bed, Ben calls her mother back.

□   □   □

The police find Emily's full name and contact her parents in a matter of hours, something Caroline has been unable to do in all these months. Emily, it turns out, is not Emily at all. She is Lauren Crocker from Buckhead, Atlanta. Her parents are Karen and Alan. They are married to each other. There is no stepmother or stepfather.

Caroline is sitting on a hard chair across from the ICU nurses' station when Emily's parents arrive. They rush the desk, both talking at once, battering the head nurse with demands. It's as if, now that they've been released from all the months of helpless waiting, they need to take charge, to feel they're in control.

"Here's what we're going to do," the nurse responds softly, but firmly. She's dealt with frantic families before. "I'm going to take you to your daughter. As soon as I see you in, I'm going to page her doctor and call the police lieutenant." Emily's parents deflate, as if the nurse's calm authority is a slap at their already suspect parenting. They both nod assent and follow the nurse out.

When the Crockers return from Emily's bedside, the sight of their daughter filled with tubes and IVs has shrunk them even further. Mrs. Crocker has been crying, though she brushes her tears aside and straightens up as the doctor approaches. From her chair, Caroline strains to hear. Over and over, the doctors have asked her what Emily took, but because she's not a parent or guardian, they won't tell her anything, won't let her into the ICU. The doctor, trained in patient privacy, keeps his voice low. Caroline catches the words, "blood pressure," "breathing tube," "brain," but they don't help her understand.

□　□　□

She holds Emma under her tiny arms. Mother and child are face to face, and both are screaming and crying. Caroline is yelling, "Damn you! Damn you to hell!" as tears stream down her face. Caroline's screams heighten Emma's hysteria, and she howls at such a high pitch that at times no sound comes out. Her face is bright red and screwed up with the torment of her screams.

Claire and Lily awaken in their cribs, startled from sleep and crying now, too. Caroline shrieks at the three-month-old in front of her, "Damn you! Now look what you've done!"

Her mother went home for the second time four days ago. She and Ben have come to some sort of agreement that Caroline can handle the babies now, but when Ben and her mother are together, they talk in low voices and glance at Caroline as if she is a ticking bomb.

Ben is like a ghost in the house. He leaves in darkness and returns

after ten. He can't look at Caroline. He's afraid of her. And why not?
Every time he's touched her, she's become pregnant. Caroline can't
help him and he can't help her. They stagger around the house too
tired to talk or see or even sleep at night.

On good days, on the best days, the girls all nap. Caroline puts
the babies down and then is asleep before her head hits the back of
the couch. She hasn't had a dream since she brought Claire home.

On this day, Emma, the one who has already staked out the role
of the troublemaker, will not sleep, no matter how much Caroline
wants her to, needs her to. Three times she's picked Emma up and
nursed and put her back down, then fallen into the blackness, only to
be pulled back to consciousness as if yanked by a leash.

They are all crying now. Emma shrieking, staring into the
murderous rage on Caroline's face, while Caroline screams, "Damn
you. Damn you. Damn you."

□   □   □

Wade's brother, Lieutenant Stoddard, arrives just after the doctor
leaves. He acknowledges Caroline, but goes straight to the Crockers.
He speaks in his normal voice, a rolling baritone with traces of good-
ol'-boy. When the Crockers ask, "Where did you find her?" Bart
gestures to Caroline. "This lady called the EMTs."

Caroline rises and advances toward the Crockers, hand
outstretched. She knows this will interrupt their conversation with
the lieutenant, but to sit and ignore them now that they are looking at
her would be worse. "I'm Caroline," she says.

Alan Crocker takes her hand. "Thank you." His voice is hoarse
with emotion. "Thank you. Thank you." He clears his throat. "Where
did you find her?"

"This morning? On my couch."

Crocker looks confused, so Caroline says it all, very quickly.
"She's been staying with me. For several months. Since she arrived."

Alan Crocker looks around wildly. His wife and Lieutenant
Stoddard are attentive now as well, though Bart has heard this story

already today. "I don't understand." Crocker's voice is loud. "Did she know you from before? Is that why she came here?"

My God, he thinks I am one of those internet pedophiles. Caroline rushes to clarify. "I met her through someone I work with. She didn't have a place to stay, so I offered . . . I tried to get her to call home." Caroline's voice is failing her. "She told me her name was Emily."

Caroline forgets to breathe as she waits for the Crockers' reaction. The fear has been sitting in her chest all day, next to the fear that Emily will die. The police have accepted Caroline's identity and story at face value, but if Emily's parents press, surely there will be a more complete investigation.

Crocker looks like he is about to have a stroke. "Why in the name of God, would anyone—"

"Ms. Taylor has lived and worked in the community for many years," Bart reassures him. "She has no record. She called the EMTs this morning and saved your daughter's life."

Why is Bart protecting her? Is it because he thinks he knows her? Caroline suspects he wouldn't be so helpful if he hadn't, with her permission, searched her little house from top to bottom looking for what Emily took and found nothing—no pornography, or drugs, not even a computer.

"Alan, this woman found our little girl," Karen Crocker says with certainty, "and cared for her when we couldn't. So we are grateful to her."

Crocker hesitates, but acquiesces. "Thank you," he says for the fourth time.

Karen Crocker moves in for a hug, eyes filling with tears. She asks, "Are you a mother, too?"

□   □   □

Claire hoists herself on the rails of her crib, staring at her mother holding Emma out in front of her. "Maaa!"

Caroline glances at Claire's teary face, the snot running freely down her upper lip. Claire knows. She sees straight through to

Caroline's heart.

Caroline puts Emma down. "It's okay," she says, wiping Emma's tiny face with her hand. "It's okay," she says to Lily and Claire as she closes the door.

She locks the house from the outside. She is calm, even though it pierces her through to know her babies are safer alone than with her there.

She leaves her car at Logan Airport. Maybe Ben and her mother will think she's flown away. Or waded into the cold water of Boston Harbor. Either will do.

She takes the T to South Station and boards a bus, going south, her breasts already tender from the milk she will not use.

□   □   □

Caroline goes to the hospital everyday. Lauren is more responsive as time goes on. She opens her eyes and squeezes a hand if someone asks a question. The doctors monitoring her brainwaves are optimistic. Karen and Alan arrange to take her home. The talk turns to airline policies and health insurance coverage, topics so far outside Caroline's experience that she can only nod with sympathy when the conversation comes her way.

On the day they are to leave, Caroline rises early. She's planned all along to go to the airport to say good-bye, but before she's finished dressing, she knows she will not. Karen, Alan and Lauren are a unit now. Caroline is already part of their past.

There never was an Emily. Whatever fantasy Caroline may have held about Emily's age, her petite size, her Ben-blue eyes, the fabulous coincidence of her name—the elision of Emma and Lily— was just that. Karen Crocker was always Lauren's mother.

So, instead of going to the airport, when she steps outside her gate onto the sidewalk, Caroline turns toward the docks. She arrives at the *Morgana* just as the last tourist is climbing aboard. Ortiz whoops when he sees her. The Captain turns to her, smiling. He helps her across the gangway and hugs her tight, for the first time ever.

That afternoon, in a moment that leaves her shaking with both excitement and terror, Caroline tells him she will go north with the ship to New England this summer.

△ △ △

Barbara Ross' *story "Key West" received an honorable mention for the 2010 Al Blanchard Award, a contest jointly sponsored by the New England Chapters of Sisters in Crime and Mystery Writers of America. Her mystery novel,* The Death of an Ambitious Woman *was published in August 2010. Barbara and her husband divide their time between Somerville, Massachusetts and Boothbay Harbor, Maine.*

The Kitchen Witch

S.A. Daynard

A iden Tucker stared at the blank computer screen in the tiny kitchen alcove he called an office, waiting for her to remind him novels didn't write themselves. He took a long, hard swallow from his mug, feeling the liquid burn down into his gut. He tried to remember when he'd stopped adding the Folgers to his Irish coffee—probably around the same time he'd brought her home. He took another sip, wondering how long it was going to take, even with her bound, gagged, and shoved inside the closet, for her to let him know she smelled whiskey on his breath. She wasn't happy unless she was harping on him about something; his writer's block, his transgressions, the rats and roaches.

A brooding groan escaped him as the gathering cobwebs screensaver took over his computer. His chest tightened as he positioned his fingertips along the keyboard. Sweat gathered on his upper lip and brow and trickled down the back of his neck. His breath quickened and his pulse raced on the verge of a full-blown panic attack. He looked down at his bruised and bloodied knuckles and heard a voice badger from deep inside his head. *Write something. For the love of God, just write something.*

His index finger jabbed a key, sending a jolt of electricity racing through his body, setting every hair on end. He pounded another and another in rapid-fire procession. A bitter sneer crept across his face as one word begot the next in her suicide note.

□   □   □

Aiden Tucker looked out the diner's grime-and-soot-smeared window, watching his on-again, off-again soul mate cross Elm Street. One hand clutched a designer handbag to her chest, the other, a brown paper shopping bag. Her full crimson lips were drawn into a tight, angry red line. The sole intent of her gaze was the pavement at her feet, ever vigilant should she step in shit or something worse.

Her flawless ivory skin paled just that much more stepping inside the crowded diner, as if she'd somehow found herself lost within the confines of a minimum security facility for the mentally and criminally insane, and the one door marked EXIT had opened into a circus freak show. If even a flicker of fondness flashed across her bottle-green eyes upon spotting him, he hadn't seen it. Apparently, there wasn't any need to rush out and update his relationship status on Facebook to "on-again." Claire Butler's visit was strictly on the business end of their agent/author relationship.

Three years ago, when he ruled the bestseller lists, she couldn't wait to climb into his bed. Twenty-four months later, she couldn't get out of it fast enough. Funny how something as trivial as a court-mandated stay at the local loony bin can sour a romance.

"So this is Manchester, New Hampshire," she sneered, covering the ruptured red vinyl seat across from him with a section of the morning paper before parking her ass on it. "I can see why you couldn't wait to be evicted from your Back Bay brownstone and take an efficiency here. Between the multicultural graffiti, the al fresco drug deals, the ho couture, and that precious homeless person I found peeing in the parking garage elevator, it's got to be a smorgasbord for that quirky little mind of yours. I can't imagine why they call it ManchVegas."

Sure she could. All that was missing from her travelogue were the white tigers, the pirates, and Elvis. Then again, it was only two in the afternoon. "Stick around 'til dark and the vampires will be out."

"Save it for one of your books, Aiden. Since we're on the subject . . ." She forced a smile and held her hand out.

He slid a grease-stained menu across the once-white, cigarette-scarred Formica tabletop. "I thought we'd have coffee first, something to eat, and maybe a piece of pie—your treat of course." He watched her face harden. "Catch up on the old neighborhood, chitchat about friends and family. You know, act like real people for a change."

"I don't have time for this, Aiden."

"This?" He made a sweeping gesture, intimating the diner and its patrons. "Or us?"

"All of this," she lowered her voice to a whisper, "is your choosing."

"Really? Because I seem to remember, you were the one that signed me up for an extra three months at the spa." He curled his fingers into air quotes around "the spa" as he spoke. "Trust me, Claire, there's nothing tranquil about Tranquility House. Sure, they've got those 1000-thread-count luxury linen straightjackets, but a heated bedpan would have gone a long way on those cold February mornings."

"Why do you have to make this so difficult?"

"Because difficult's all I've got left," he said, motioning to a waitress for two coffees. "You're in for a treat, Claire." He offered the waitress a smile as she deposited two well-worn mugs and topped them off with black-as-hell coffee from a glass pot that looked as if it hadn't seen the business end of a soap pad in decades. "None of that macchiato crap you've been swilling in those fancy espresso bars. This is the real stuff—the burn-a-hole-clear-through-your-gut-if-you-don't-cut-it-with-cream stuff. And as an added bonus, after you drink down the very last drop, you can tell how old your mug is by counting the number of rings inside it. Am I right, Delores?" he asked, reading the waitress' nametag.

Delores, like Claire, wasn't in the mood. She shifted the bulk of her weight to one hip, tapped a pen to her notepad, and waited for him to order.

"Seeing that today's such a special day for my ex-fiancée and me—" he batted his eyes at Claire "—we'll each have the blue-plate special, and for dessert, the lady will have the Jell-O du jour, and I, a sinful slice of warmed apple pie topped with a decadent wedge of your very best aged cheddar. Is there perhaps a wine list I could look at?"

The waitress gave Claire a roll of her eyes before walking away.

"Isn't this exciting, Claire?" he asked loud enough for everyone in the diner to hear. "Who knows what's on the blue-plate special? I don't know about you, but I've got my heart set on sloppy joes and creamed corn. Yum."

"Please, Aiden, enough. I knew it was a mistake coming here."

"Sorry," he sighed. "I tried getting reservations at the Third Street Shelter, but they were booked. Or so they claimed. I would have slipped the maître d' a twenty, but that would have necessitated—"

"Just give me the manuscript, Aiden."

His face twisted into a venomous knot, triggering a quake of tremors through her. Silent and slow, he counted to ten before relinquishing his glare. "Don't poke the bear," he warned.

As quickly as his mood had shifted from condescending to malevolent, it swung back. With a *ta-da!* he placed an old shoebox on the tabletop, tapped its lid three times, and returned it to the seat next to him. "Not before we have a civil conversation. Tell you what. I'll go first. Gee, Claire, you look great. Love the bangs. How long's it been since you threw me under the bus? Your turn."

She bit down on her lower lip, as if formulating her thoughts into something that wouldn't set him off. It was useless. "Look at yourself, Aiden. Look at the way you're living. What are you doing for money?"

"For your information, Claire, I'm making a killing in the commodities market." It wasn't so much a lie, as it was a half-truth. Over the last few months he'd become a pro at spotting that certain something in someone's trash that would garner a few bucks at the local pawn and consignment shops. Not that it was beneath him to rummage through the dumpsters behind the downtown restaurants for take-out.

"Are you still taking your medication?"

He'd wondered how long it was going to take for her to bring up his current state of mental health. He nodded his head and smiled. *No. The Clozapine fairy stopped leaving pills under my pillow when I ran out of cash.*

"The last thing your career needs is another incident."

"You are so right-a-roonie on that one," he mocked. He'd given up both meds and booze when the "incident" took place. "I'm a lot smarter than I was a year ago." *I'm still drinking.*

"And you don't have to refer to it as an incident, Claire. I've learned to take responsibility and accept my actions." He leaned toward a table with three elderly women intent on eavesdropping. "I know what you're thinking, ladies, and yes, I am Aiden Tucker, international bestselling author of the critically acclaimed Damian Noir series. I do hope Claire and I were enunciating every syllable and speaking clearly enough for you to catch every caustic word."

Each of the women offered a sheepish nod as their faces flushed in varying shades of red.

"Wonderful. Just to get all of you up to speed on my so-called descent into madness—which to be honest, I think was more of tumble than a full-fledged free-fall as Claire maintains—I was doing a book signing in Harvard Square when I lost my frigging mind." He lowered his eyes and waggled his head in mock melancholy before scrunching up his nose in a terse giggle.

"I was autographing a copy of my novel, when my hand slipped into the book—literally, into the book. Before I knew it, I was being pulled inside. The very words I'd written turned on me, biting, slashing, tearing at my flesh." He paused a second or two, letting the imagery sink in, waiting for the biddies to place hands to their mouths in horror.

"What did you do?" one managed in a squeak.

"I did what anyone of you would have done under the same circumstances. I screamed like a banshee. I kicked and thrashed. I threw punches and bit back. I found a gun in my hand and I— Nope, nope, nope. You'll have to forgive me, ladies, that wasn't quite right." He held his palms up and shrugged. "I didn't lose my frigging mind, I misplaced it. After a longer than expected stay with the good folks at Tranquility House, I got it back. Well, at least most of it. And hell, all those sessions must have worked. I haven't seen the wallpaper come to life in weeks."

"The DTs," one of the women murmured to her companions.

"The delirium tremens," he concurred, "a.k.a. the sweats, the shakes, the heebie-jeebies, and my personal favorite, the staggers and jags."

"Stop it, Aiden," Claire snapped, drawing his attention back to her. "You're a relapse away from ending up like this." The red lacquered nail of her index finger stabbed the front page of the morning paper.

He picked it up and read the headlines aloud: "Homeless Rate Reaches Record Numbers in the Queen City"; "Drunk Driver Slams Into Police Station"; "Resident Wanders Away From Nursing Home"; "Distraught Gunman Takes Own Life in Standoff"; "Third Case of EEE Confirmed in Hunts Falls." He offered the biddies a grimace and returned the paper to the table.

"You drove all the way up here to bitch at me about Triple E, Claire? So what's in the goody bag, mosquito netting?" He motioned to the brown paper shopping bag.

"A house warming gift," she answered, pulling a small stuffed doll from the bag—a grinning witch decked out in a frilly pink party dress and a white feather boa, riding a broomstick with a rhinestone-studded wand in her hand. "It's a kitchen witch."

"Wow." He turned to the old women and rolled his eyes, looping his index finger around his temple before turning back to Claire with an exaggerated smile. "You shouldn't have." *Especially when what I could really use is a side of beef.*

"They're muses." One of the old women felt the need to join the conversation. "They ward off cooking disasters and provide inspiration in the kitchen."

"Hang her over your kitchen sink and food won't burn, pots won't boil over, and sauces won't spoil," another added.

"She'll bring good fortune and keep your demons at bay," the third chimed in. "You look like someone who could use a little help in that department."

He slammed the palm of his hand off his forehead. "Deino, Pemphredo, and Enyo! I hardly recognized the three of you without the black cloaks and the caldron. So tell me, what brings the Stygian Witches all the way to Manchester, New Hampshire? No, let me guess . . . Your annual eye exam and tooth cleaning."

"Aiden," Claire coaxed him back to the here and now. "I really have to be getting back. The manuscript . . . Please, Aiden."

"Whatever, Claire." He held the shoebox at eye level and let it drop on the tabletop. "It's all yours. Enjoy." He shoved it in her direction and grinned. "Go ahead, you might as well read the first few pages. Make sure I haven't forgotten any commas or left any modifiers dangling for dear life. Lunch is here anyway and it looks like . . . Dammit! Shepherd's pie and green beans."

She waited until the waitress deposited their silverware and plates before opening the lid on the shoebox. A smile of relief spread across her face as she read the cover page. "*Neither Noir*, I love the title, Aiden. I can't wait to read the rest." Her smile slumped as she flipped through one blank page after another. "Is this a joke, Aiden? Where's your manuscript?"

He tapped his temple three times and scooped a forkful of shepherd's pie into his mouth. "I've gone green, Claire. No sense in wasting paper."

"Thirty days, Aiden." She rose from her seat, snatching up her handbag and the kitchen witch. "You have thirty days to put what's in your head on paper, or, God help me, Aiden, you'll be spending the rest of your life in a five-by-eight shithole with padded walls." She tossed a fifty down on the table and walked out of the diner.

He shrugged his shoulders, dumped the contents of her plate onto his, balled his left hand into a fist, raised it above his head, and flipped off anyone looking his way.

□   □   □

The thirty dollars and change left after paying for lunch with Claire's fifty seemed to evaporate overnight. A few bottles of booze and *poof!* it was gone. It made him wonder how the drunks camped out in Victory Park managed to make ends meet.

He'd been scouring trash cans by the light of a full moon for hours, for something other than garbage. If morons cleaning out attics and storage rooms could stumble upon an authentic Van Gogh or Cézanne, you'd think he could at least find a diamond ring, a first edition Dickens, or an old leather briefcase stuffed with treasury bills. Even a warm pair of long johns would have been a welcome find on a night so raw his breath lingered in his wake like an apparition.

He was exhausted, hungry, and ready to drag himself home, when he spotted it nearly hidden beneath a mountain of black trash bags, cloaked in a torn and tattered vinyl Christmas tablecloth. It wasn't a priceless painting, a diamond ring, or even a pair of long johns, but he knew a payday when he saw one.

"Cha-ching," he whispered to the night as he pulled the life-sized, soft sculpture mannequin from the heap.

She reeked of cat piss and rotting food. Like the Van Gogh, some idiot probably found her covered in cobwebs and rat turds, tucked away in a forgotten corner of dear old dead grandma's attic and tossed her as fast as they could. Sure she was old and dirty, but hardly ready for a landfill. He stood there speculating how much mannequins sold for. A hundred dollars? Five hundred, maybe? Not to mention, this one was special. It wasn't every day you saw a mannequin made to look like an elderly woman. Somebody ordered her special.

He looked at the rumpled housecoat she was wearing and the filthy pink scuffs wondering how long it'd been since she'd graced a showroom window. He turned back the collar of her housecoat hoping to find the name of a manufacturer or department store. "PROPERTY OF THE BIRCHES" was written in laundry marker. The Birches might not have any use for her anymore, but he did.

The longer he stared at her, the more amazing she seemed. She was a quality piece of work all right. Everything about her was incredible. From the thinning grey hair on her head to the liver spots on her shins, she was the real thing. All he had to do was spruce "Mrs. Birch" up a bit, and he could easily take in a grand.

There was a Goodwill bin in the 7-Eleven parking lot over on Central. Every now and then he'd haul home the trash bags that poked out from its top or spilled out onto the pavement. A few dollars worth of washing and drying usually netted him a three-figure return on his investment. If there was anywhere he was going to find a dress and a pair of decent shoes in his price range, it would be there.

He ran his hand through his hair trying to decide what to do with Mrs. Birch in the meantime. There was no telling if she'd still be there in a couple of hours, should he leave her. He could bury her back beneath the trash bags, but even that couldn't guarantee one of the shopping cart zombies—as he referred to the homeless people that wandered the city with their stolen grocery carts—wouldn't find her. He scanned the alley from left to right, listening for the sound of their wheels on the pavement and heard the muffled squawk of a police radio. In a panic, he dove deep into the pile, taking Mrs. Birch down with him.

He held his breath, watching the patrol car's spotlight scour the alleyway. The last thing he needed was the cops getting in his face, asking questions, and giving him a hard time just for the hell of it. He couldn't remember how much he'd drunk or what he might have used to take away the sting from Claire's visit. Not enough to kill him, but more than enough to land him before a judge. He'd lose what was left of his frail mind if he had to spend another night locked in a cell. Sweat seeped from every inch of him as the cruiser's doors opened and slammed shut. Beams from their flashlights flickered along the walls of the buildings on either side of him and ricocheted off the pavement. His breath quickened as his heart and temples pounded in a deafening unison, making it impossible to hear what the cops were shouting.

He had no idea how long he lay there trembling, shrouded in refuse and filth after they left, or how long it took before his hands stopped shaking. Like a discarded child seeking comfort from a nightmare in a careworn ragdoll, he drew Mrs. Birch to him and wept wondering what he had done in this life or another to deserve the lot he had been handed. In a bone-chilling drizzle, he wrapped her in the tablecloth and carried her home. He propped her delicate body in a kitchen chair and journeyed back into the night.

□   □   □

It was the most beautiful dress he had ever seen. Why anyone would toss it into a Goodwill bin was beyond him. Billowed in layer after layer of beaded lavender tulle, it reminded him of the 50's prom gowns he'd seen in grandmother's photo albums. The shoes he'd found were a different story. The best he could manage were a pair of flip-flops. He hoped the white chiffon scarf he draped around her neck made up for them.

He wiped her face and hands clean with a damp dishcloth, combed her matted hair into something a bit more presentable, and sprayed her from top to bottom with enough Lysol to disinfect a small third world country. When he stepped back to admire his handiwork, he couldn't help but notice how much Mrs. Birch resembled Claire's kitchen witch. All she was missing was a smile and a rhinestone wand, which he remedied with a thick red marker and wooden ruler.

Mrs. Birch looked so content sitting in his kitchen, he wondered what his hurry was in getting rid of her. Tomorrow or next week, she'd still bring in enough cash to pay the rent. He opened the empty cabinet above the hotplate on the counter and slammed it shut. He reached his hand deep into the filthy water filling the kitchen sink and pulled out a plate. He held it up to the light, made a face and tossed it back.

He drew a half-eaten burger wrapped in foil from his pocket and took a seat across from her. "Come here often?" he asked, taking a bite. "The service sucks, but the prices are great." He pulled a handful of fries from his other pocket and laid them on the foil. "Can you believe all this cost me was my dignity?"

He shoved the last of the burger and a few fries in front of her before heading to his bed. "Good night, Mrs. Birch," he said, shutting off the lights.

When he woke in the morning, rats had taken the last of the burger and fries, Mrs. Birch was still at the table, and a fresh pot of coffee was waiting for him. He couldn't remember starting it the night before, but there were a lot of things he couldn't remember lately. With his head pounding from a hangover, he staggered over to the sink to hunt through the stagnant dishwater for a coffee mug and shrugged. Apparently he'd done the dishes in his sleep.

He poured a cup of coffee and turned on his computer. He pulled up a file named *Neither Noir* and opened it. He scrolled past the cover page and stared at the blank page. When the screen saver kicked in, he shut it down.

"Just three hundred and fifteen more pages and I'm done," he toasted Mrs. Birch with his mug. He looked around the one room apartment and wondered when he'd found the time between making coffee and doing dishes to vacuum the rug and take out the trash. He looked back to Mrs. Birch and heard the three old bats from the diner cackling in his head. *She's a kitchen witch.*

And what if she was? A muse by any other name was still a muse. If she could inspire him to clean, she could inspire him to write. All he had to do was ask. And ask he did. He spilled his guts to her. He told her about Claire, about his breakdown, and his stay at Tranquility House. He told her about the book he hadn't written, about Claire's ultimatum, and his writer's block. He told her everything.

He turned on the computer, opened the file, positioned his fingers on the keyboard, and closed his eyes, waiting for sweet inspiration. He swore for just a second, just an instant, he heard the crinkling of her tulle gown right before he felt something slam down along his knuckles. His eyes shot open as he screamed, looking at the blood trailing down his fingers onto the keyboard. He looked up to see Mrs. Birch standing next to him, holding the wooden ruler above her head, poised to strike.

"It's all in your head," she hissed, bringing the ruler down again. "Write something, Aiden. Type, type, type," she demanded, punctuating each word with a blow from her ruler.

□   □   □

"She's not real," he'd told himself again and again. "She's a mannequin." He only wished he could believe it. He wasn't losing his mind; she was taking a tiny bit of it at a time.

The last two weeks with her had been a living hell. She wouldn't let him sleep. She was inside his head, taunting him. *Novels don't write themselves.* She wielded that damn ruler like an iron fist. *It's all in your head, Aiden. Write something.* It'd come to the point where he welcomed Claire's ultimatum to put him back in a straightjacket. He'd go anywhere just as long as Mrs. Birch didn't tag along with him. He'd take his meds, go on the wagon, and do his penance, anything just to get her out of his head.

All he had to do was get rid of Mrs. Birch to get his life back. She wasn't real. She was a kitchen witch. All he had to do was dump her in the canal and let her sink to bottom. What was the worst that could happen to him—pay a fine for littering?

He tried not to giggle, watching his fingers fly across the keyboard, typing her suicide note tell-all. It was nothing personal, just a little joke between the two of them. It was also a warning should the Merrimack River carry her away and some unsuspecting fool fish her from her grave. Had the person who put her out with the trash the night he found her shown the same consideration, he wouldn't be teetering on the brink of madness.

He pulled the note from his printer and sealed it in a plastic baggie. "Ready to go, Mrs. Birch?" he asked, opening the closet door. "Time to go bye-bye."

He secured the baggie to her dress with a strip of duct tape, and rolled her in the Christmas tablecloth. He hoisted her up over one shoulder, walked out of his apartment under the veil of night, and made his way to a footbridge over the canal.

It was almost too easy. He waived hello to the shopping cart zombies, the streetwalkers, and addicts with Mrs. Birch slumped over his shoulder snug inside the vinyl tablecloth. He stood on the footbridge and dropped her into the rushing water of the Merrimack and watched it carry her back to hell. He closed his eyes and took in a deep breath of freedom.

□   □   □

For the first time in months he'd slept through the night. He checked every nook and cranny of his tiny one room apartment for her, just in case she'd found her way back to him. She was gone. He poured himself a cup of coffee minus the Jameson's, turned on the TV, and felt the wind knocked from him. A photograph of Mrs. Birch, taken in better days, was plastered in the background of the screen. He turned up the volume to hear what the reporter was saying.

"Manchester Police are investigating the murder of Vivian Wilmont, the 83-year-old Alzheimer's patient who wandered away from The Birches nursing home two weeks ago. Wilmont's body was found along the Merrimack River early this morning. Anyone who might have seen Vivian Wilmont since her disappearance is asked to contact the Manchester Police Department."

"She wasn't real," he told himself as knuckles pounded on his door. "She was a kitchen witch." He rocked back and forth repeating the mantra.

"Manchester Police, Mr. Tucker. Open the door."

△　△　△

S.A. Daynard *is a member of the New England chapter of Sisters in Crime. Her short stories have appeared in magazines and anthologies in the U.S. and Canada. "Widow's Peak" earned her a Derringer Award nomination for Best Flash of 2004. www.sadaynard.com*

Wall to Wall

John R. Clark

It's not often my sister Kylin is at a loss for words. She was standing in the driveway at Simonton Hill Farm when I pulled in, twenty minutes late.

"Sorry, I got stuck in construction on Route 17. Why in heck they're working on a Saturday, I'll . . ."

The stricken look on her face brought my apology to a sudden halt. She pointed toward the house and started to cry.

I looked at the front door that a drunken friend of our late mother had kicked in the previous October when he forgot she was dead and wanted to present her with the first partridge of the season. Nope, the repair work I had done was intact. I started for the steps bisecting the stone wall Dad had so lovingly built almost forty years ago and stopped dead in my tracks.

"Jesus in overalls," I said, pointing helplessly at raw earth where flat stones had lain in perfect order since Kylin and I were little. "How could somebody steal fifty feet of stone wall right in front of God and everybody?"

It was gone, every last stone. I wanted to cry too, but settled for the comforting numbness of shock instead. Granted, my father and I hadn't had the greatest of relationships, but I could still remember that summer in 1959 when he toiled day after day in one of his ragged "Wirthmore Feeds" sweatshirts, hauling rocks from the old barn foundation in a steel-wheeled barrow, laying them in, sizing up their pitch and level before adding just the right amount of sandy loam to set them firmly in place. I had no idea how many hours Dad had invested in the wall, but now some son of a bitch had destroyed it in a single act of greed.

"When did you come over last?" Kylin had managed to compose herself while I was recreating Dad's summer-long effort in my mind.

"Well, I couldn't get over last weekend, because I needed to get the rest of the garden planted, so it's been two weeks." I picked at the dirt beside the front steps where we were sitting.

The sad fact was, that after having made endless trips for the nearly three years our mother lived alone following her first stroke, we were both burned out. Kylin had made weekly pilgrimages from central Massachusetts, and I had come in a roundabout circuit from my job in Augusta or down the disaster known as Route 7 from my small farm in Somerset County. In the seven months since she had passed on, both of us felt the need to face the daunting task of figuring out what to do with more than fifty years of accumulated stuff less and less often. We were both convinced that a ghost looked on in disapproval, while we sorted through things which had great meaning to Mom, but were for the most part, just things we had to get rid of.

After giving the inside a quick check and finding nothing obvious out of place, we sat in Kylin's SUV while she called the sheriff's office. Both of us had to grin when she reported a stolen wall, and there was a long pause before a familiar voice boomed out of the dashboard speaker.

"Sissy, you and that wiseass brother of yours hadn't better be trying out some new plot theme on the local constabulary." Deputy Sheriff Waldo Parkins knew both of us from high school days. He had tried unsuccessfully to convince Kylin to go watch submarine races off the Rockland Breakwater half a dozen times when they were juniors. Wally and I had been in our share of scrapes as well. Fortunately, his father had been county sheriff back then, and one four-hour session in a cell next to the drunk tank after we were nabbed setting up a fake pay toilet at the town beach cured us of further misadventures, or at least made us better at not getting caught.

We waited under the giant locust trees, watching loons swimming in the cove that ended near the property line. Neither of us said a word, wrapping ourselves up in private memories sparked by loss of the wall.

Wally handled the call himself, a courtesy both of us appreciated. His handshake was still rock solid, even though his hairline was receding and his gut threatened to hide his belt buckle. We waited while he took photos and studied the crime scene. He hunched down and took a sample of something in the driveway before rejoining us in the shade.

"I bet you think this is an unusual crime, eh Bubby. I can tell you different. I bet we've fielded a dozen calls the last few years from irate landowners who discovered parts of rock walls missing. Remember Lonnie Deener up on Clary Ridge? He caught a couple rocket scientists stripping flat rocks outta the walls around his blueberry field last July when he went to add a couple extra hives for better pollination. He took out their radiator and windshield with one load of #4 buck. I bet those two are still running. We traced the truck to one of those overnight pop-up landscapers down on the coast. Fella claimed someone had hot-wired it the night before. Funny how he neglected to file a stolen vehicle report."

I brushed an ant off my pants leg. "Stealing rocks sounds loopy to me. Heck, I remember how Dad used to say rocks were the number one crop because the frost kept pushing up new ones every year."

"T'ain't the same thing, Bubby. With all due respect to Sissy, 'cuz I know she has one of them fancy away places down the coast a bit, the damn flatlanders have taken over most of the high end property between Bucksport and Brunswick. I swear, the first thing they do is hire someone local to build them a stone wall. Well, maybe that's second on the list, after making sure they post no trespassing signs every fifty feet." Wally spat over the edge of the bank, a bitter look clouding his face.

I looked at Kylin to see how she was handling our old friend's diatribe. Oddly enough, she seemed more composed than she had when we were sitting in her SUV waiting for someone from the sheriff's office to arrive.

She smiled at Wally. "Guilty, your honor. We have a rock wall, but it was built when we had the ledge under the camp removed, so we didn't have to swim in the hallway after a heavy rain." She looked away for a second before asking the question that was on both our minds. "How could someone steal Dad's wall when it's no more than fifty feet from the road? Somebody must have seen something going on."

Wally grimaced. "I'm trying to tell you, Sissy. It isn't like when we were growing up. The economy tanked years ago. You remember how it was when your dad was raising chickens. There wasn't any money in it, but you ate on a regular basis."

I remembered our poultry farm days and shuddered. I hadn't been able to eat eggs or chickens for three years after going away to college. Too bad Dad's sweatshirt didn't say "Wirthless." It would have been more accurate.

"Well, then we lost the quarry, the casket factory and most of the fish packing plants in Belfast and Rockland. That didn't leave much besides commuting to the VA hospital or a state job in Augusta. Couple that with the influx of flatlanders with money dripping out of their backsides, and you had a situation where things you and I took for granted when we were kids suddenly acquired value, and people who used to be satisfied scraping by, got tempted awful easy. Of course, there's also some of those kids we used to look down on when we were at Simonton High who grew up and quickly boarded the Tommytown Shuttle. As soon as they get released from prison, they're right back at it, thinking some of the tricks they learned from other losers on the inside are gonna work for them, because they're smarter than the average bear. It hardly ever plays out the way they imagine, but it keeps us County Mounties hopping." Wally got to his feet and Kylin and I walked with him back to the front yard.

"Any chance you'll find out who stole it?" I gestured at the ragged row of holes resembling some poor soul's mouth after a tooth-yanking session.

Wally shrugged, "Maybe, if we get lucky, or whoever did it screws the wrong person or messes up a stolen goods buy. I'll keep both of you posted." He shook hands with me and gave Kylin a half-bashful hug before getting in his cruiser and heading toward town.

As I watched his cruiser go up the hill past our elderly neighbor's house, one of the loons in the cove began its insane laughter. That pretty much summed up how I was feeling at the moment.

Kylin and I spent a couple of aimless hours sorting things in the attic before the sense that Mom's ghost was looking on unnerved us and we left, she back to Massachusetts and I to the relative seclusion of rural Somerset County.

Wally checked in on a weekly basis for a while, sharing some of the leads and tips he received. While three led to arrests, none were connected to Dad's missing wall. By mid-July he had to put the case on the back burner. Drug busts, assaults on tourists and the impending lobster festival were consuming most of his time.

On Labor Day, Kylin and I held a memorial picnic down at the family swimming hole in honor of the wall. Over red hot dogs and burned s'mores, we rehashed old memories and even staged an impromptu funeral by creating a miniature wall on the beach before scooping up handfuls of sand to bury it. I figured that would bring closure to the whole bizarre experience.

Columbus Day morning I went out to do some partridge hunting. It was one of those perfect fall days, frosty at sunrise, followed by a cloudless sky and warmth that made me sweat as I walked through our neighbor's abandoned orchard. When I returned shortly after noon, the light on my answering machine was blinking.

"Bubby, better haul tail as soon as you get this. I want you to see the oddest thing before I bring in anyone from the department. I'm up on Blackberry Ridge across the pond from your place. It shouldn't be hard to spot my cruiser."

I beat feet, barely keeping to the speed limit as I sped down Route 7 until I hit the turnoff that would take me to Route 131. Half an hour later, I was jouncing up the steep climb to Blackberry Ridge Road, steering wheel shuddering as I went from ledge to pothole and back.

Wally's cruiser was parked at the end of a long driveway leading to one of the new mini-estates dotting the ridge's skyline. He was leaning against it with an unreadable expression when I pulled up behind him.

"You made good time. Hope you didn't have to bend too many traffic laws in the process. I got a call around ten this morning from a woman who was some hysterical. I had to holler at her before she settled down enough to tell me what had happened. You'll see for yourself, Bubby."

I followed his car up the driveway where an ashen-faced woman stood on a wrap-around porch. Wally didn't bother making introductions before leading me around to the back where a recently built stone wall held a small hill at bay.

"Hope you have a strong stomach, cuz this won't be pretty." Wally pointed to the far end of the wall where a body lay half under a pile of rocks that had come off the top of the wall. "Lady said she hired this guy to build her a wall last spring. He hemmed and hawed until she threatened to find someone else. Seems everything went fine until he started topping off the far end. She had to call him back twice, because something kept knocking down his handiwork. Today was the third time he came to get it right, and it looks like it was unlucky for him."

We approached the corpse. A crimson trickle was seeping out of the pile near the spot where his head must be. I bent down to move a rock.

"Hold it, Bubby, possible crime scene. I wanted you to be here when the medical examiner and the Staties showed up. I have a sneaking suspicion we found your dad's wall."

Wally called for assistance and we sat in his cruiser sharing lukewarm coffee from his thermos.

"Any idea who's under the pile?" I asked.

"Ayup, an old acquaintance of ours, Ervin Nowell. He was in Kylin's class. I bet you remember his performance at the graduation party your folks let us throw down by the lake. Poor booger came staggering out of the outhouse and passed out head first in a trashcan. We had to drag him out and peel burnt marshmallows and ketchup-covered napkins off his face, so he wouldn't smother. Life never did get much better for him: three OUIs and a couple breaking and entering raps in between scut jobs. I heard he was involved in some other stuff, but never had enough to pursue any charges. The lady who owns the place never heard a thing. She said she came out to see if he wanted something to drink and found him like that."

We watched as three cars with flashing blue lights came up the driveway. I hung back slightly as the medical examiner and two burly state troopers surveyed the scene and took pictures. One of the troopers grunted and leaned closer to a rock near the remains of the wall. He took some close-up photos and waited for the M.E. and his fellow trooper to examine what he'd found. He took a pair of tongs from his crime scene case and teased something out from under the rock. I felt a prickling sensation run down my spine as he put the tattered cloth fragment in an evidence pack, but not before I caught the faded "Wir" across it.

Ervin, or what was left of him, was recognizable although hard living and some serious substance abuse had, as Dad would have observed, fried a piston or two. The back of his head was caved in by a large flat stone that must have weighed as much as he did. I watched as the coroner finished examining his corpse and called for a hearse. No need for further investigation. Carelessness and shoddy workmanship had come back to bite the deceased. Case closed.

I hung around until the body had been removed and everyone but Wally was gone. He was eying me speculatively as I turned to verify my suspicions. Sure enough, the fallen section of the wall was in direct line of sight from Simonton Hill Farm and the blueberry-covered knoll where we had buried Dad's ashes twelve years before.

"Was that fragment what I think it was?"

I avoided his question. "Come here and take a look," I said, pointing down at the family farm. "See the knoll down by the swimming hole? If a person believed in ghosts, they might wonder if Ervin had made the mistake of building a wall out of Dad's rocks where the old man could watch. If I were to take that line of thought a bit further, who's to say that maybe Dad's ghost might have tested his mettle by dumping part of the wall in preparation for the main event."

"You and Kylin want to pursue getting your wall back? I bet we could match half a dozen rocks in this one to holes in your Mom's front yard."

I stared down at my father's resting place before replying. "I guess not. As long as Dad can admire his handiwork, I think I'll let sleeping rocks lie."

△ △ △

John R. Clark is a public librarian in Hartland, Maine. In addition to trading every sort of library material online, he writes young adult fantasy novels as well as weekly newspaper columns on librarianship and slightly left-wing politics. His spare time is filled with gardening and providing consulting services for other Maine libraries.

A Perfect Landing

Kat Fast

I excused myself from the party early, claiming the onset of a migraine, but I didn't fool anyone. I just couldn't bear watching the sweet young things—for surely they weren't formed yet—fawn over my husband Bart as he and his buddy flyboys told stories of high spirits and derring-do from their days in the service.

He was still handsome with the unfair advantage of white sideburns, dashing one would say, and a charmer, God knows. But I'd heard the stories enough times that I could emulate his hand motions on final approach as he lined up his fighter with the deck of the aircraft carrier. Would he "catch a wire" or "bolter" and go around for another try?

I caught his eye, waved, and mouthed, "'Night, Ace."

He smiled, threw me a kiss, and swooped back into his story.

Rick, the host, walked me to the door. "'Night, Corporal. Drive careful now, y'hear?"

"'Night, Sir." I offered Rick a mock salute and a smile. "Corporal" hearkened to the early years when Rick served as operations officer in my husband's squadron. When I'd left messages for Bart at the air station from Coral Morse, my maiden name, the dispatch wrote "Corporal Morse," and so I became.

"Nah, I want a hug." Rick set a Coke bottle aside and gathered me into his arms.

"You on the wagon?" I asked.

"Just tonight, sweetie. I got the call this afternoon. I have to take the morning run across the Pond at oh-dark-hundred. The captain who was scheduled for the flight has the flu." After two tours of duty in the Marines, Rick had traded in his military wings to become a commercial pilot. Now, with years of seniority, he flew the plum route between Boston and London a few times a month for big bucks.

"OK, you two. Break it up!" Vickie, Rick's wife and my best friend, tapped Rick on the shoulder as if she were cutting in at a dance.

Rick released me for my goodnight hug from Vicki. "Hope you feel better soon, hon," she said.

"I'll be fine." I sniffed the air. "Ooooooh, delicious! New perfume?"

"Like it? Rick got it for our anniversary. It's called 'Poison.' Made by Christian Dior."

"Perfect name, 'Poison.' It's to die for."

"That's what I said, but one of Rick's English mates corrected me. Evidently, the Brits say, 'It's to die for,' while we bloodthirsty Yanks say, 'It's to kill for.'"

As I drove toward home, I longed for the days when I was the sweet one, still young and supple and new, listening to Bart's stories for the first time. Now, I'm the older toy, a little beat up and worn at the edges, set aside for the new, unopened packages under the tree. I wondered which of the sweet nothings he'd select tonight.

The first years had been the best, but I suspect that's true of most marriages. Ours was so volatile—first romance, sex, and marriage, then the war, the birth of our children, and all the moving about. I remember looking forward to more settled, mature times. Fat chance. With a fighter pilot, adolescence is forever.

Last month, I screwed up my courage and broached the topic of divorce. "Oh no," he'd said, "Mama hasn't kicked yet." He laughed to show he was kidding, but the more I think on it, the more truth there was in his saying. My Mama was plantation rich, and I was an only child.

Truth be known, I'd rather see him six feet under than cavorting with a trophy financed by Mama's money. What I'd said at the time was he'd never see a red cent of her money, or something more dramatic like "Over my dead body." Must have been that, because he said, "Your choice. But let's wait until Mama succumbs."

We buried Mama last Sunday afternoon. Half of Charleston turned out. Even my charming husband, Colonel Bartelby Jameson came all fitted out in military dress to pay respects to her money.

I think the party tonight was his way of celebrating her passing. He'd hated Mama for her tightfisted control over her purse strings and the way she made us grovel if we needed money.

To be honest, I was rather relieved myself after she'd teased us with promises of dying for over a year, threatening at every perceived slight to revise her will. But forget about all of that, girl. It's over. She's under.

Tonight I'd driven my own car from work to the party, so I wouldn't have to fight Bart for the keys when it was time to leave. Now, part of me worried because he was already half in the bag, and he still had to drive home. The other part pictured a car wreck with sirens screaming, and a sobbing, very rich and fine looking (if I do say so) widow looking on.

As I turned into the long driveway to our house the tears began. How could I daydream about killing off the man I love? Why did I love him so? Why did he have to live life on the edge?

Even this driveway was a stupid contest. He'd stop at the end, shift his flashy new sports car into neutral, rev the engine, and then jam it into gear while pressing the garage door opener. Halfway up the drive, he'd slip back into neutral and hit the garage door button again. The challenge was to glide to a stop inside without braking before the garage door pancaked the car. A perfect landing.

I pushed the garage door opener on the visor, parked, and entered the house through the door that connected to the kitchen.

Inside, I flicked on the light switch. Nothing. Damn. The bulb must have blown. In the dark, I waited until my eyes became accustomed to the shadows and felt my way to the dining room. I flicked the switch. Nothing. Double damn. The power must be out. But, no, the garage door had opened and closed. Had to be a fuse.

The fuse box hung on the right hand side of the stairwell that led down to the cellar. I finger felt my way back to the kitchen, following the wall until I felt the doorjamb to the cellar. As I opened the door, cool musty air washed up from below. I reached out and touched the wall to keep my bearings in the total darkness.

I bent low and explored the area around my feet until my hand brushed against metal. Phew. The flashlight. I hadn't realized I'd been holding my breath. Get a grip, girl. Your imagination's getting the better of you. I heard Mama's drawl in my mental scold, and smiled despite myself. But when I pressed the button on the flashlight, nothing happened.

No matter. There were only three or four steps down to the fuse box. All I had to do was locate the right circuit breaker and flip it back on.

Problem was, I was scared of the dark. Childish, I know, but true. I could hear Bart laughing at me, taunting me, as I stood paralyzed, afraid to descend three baby steps in the dark.

I could do this. I pictured the fuse box and mentally opened it. I'd carefully written out labels for each area and major appliance. The kitchen/dining room circuit breaker would be the top left switch; next to it, the utility room with washer and dryer; and then . . . but all I needed was the top left.

I lowered my right foot ever so slowly until my toe touched the wood below. Suddenly, I froze and backed away. There was no reason to check the fuses, because the garage door was on the kitchen circuit. Just some crazy fluke that the kitchen and dining room bulbs had burned out at the same time. Probably because I'd replaced the old bulbs with new ones on the same day.

Relieved, I fumbled my way to the hutch in the corner of the kitchen and opened the bottom drawer where I stored light bulbs and vacuum bags. Holding a new packet of bulbs, I walked, hands outstretched, until I bumped into a chair tucked under the counter of the island in the center of the room. Placing the bulbs on the counter, I climbed onto the chair, and from it, to the surface of the island.

The light should be directly above. I waved my hands overhead to connect with the globe that protected the light. Carefully, I removed the screws that held the globe in place, lowered it to the counter, and picked up a new bulb.

As I touched the blown light bulb, a blazing flash of light blinded me. When I regained my breath and eyesight, I realized that the light hadn't burned out. The bulb was just loose.

I screwed the bulb tight, replaced the globe, and climbed down. While I was at it, I decided to replace the light in the dining room. I carried the kitchen chair into the dining room and stood on it to reach the light. Just in case, I turned my head to the side when I touched the bulb. To my surprise, it lit up, too.

Now, what were the chances that both bulbs would loosen and a flashlight battery would fail at the very same time? I walked to the kitchen and reopened the cellar door. On the third step two bottles lay on their sides, a sure invitation to a rollercoaster ride to the cement floor below.

Well planned, Ace. Perfect. You wouldn't even be here when I landed.

I hauled the chair back into the dining room, loosened the bulb and flicked off the switch. Returning to the kitchen, I rummaged around in the top drawer of the hutch, found two new batteries, and reloaded the flashlight. I turned it on and laid it on the island countertop before remounting and loosening the bulb. It wasn't easy to replace the globe with the dim light of the flash, but finally I tightened the last screw with my fingers. Satisfied, I climbed down and turned off the kitchen light switch. I left the door to the cellar stairs open.

Now what? I'd wait behind the door. He'd come in. The lights, of course, wouldn't work. "Coral?" he'd call in the dark. No answer. He'd walk to the cellar door and call down louder, "Coral?"

I'd creep up behind him. "Yes, dear," I'd answer. He'd whirl about, and I'd blind him with the flashlight and give him a gentle push backwards.

Then I'd tighten the bulbs once more, return the flashlight to the stairwell and be off to bed.

My story? He'd been drinking heavily. He kept his booze in the cellar. He must have gone down for one more bottle. Of course, I couldn't hear anything. When I get a migraine, I plug my ears and cover my eyes to shut out all sensation.

I kept my vigil as long as I could but must have dozed off, because I awoke with a start to the loud clunk and whirr of the garage door opening. The sports car engine revved at the end of the drive. One last game, Colonel? Enjoy, sweetheart.

Gravel popped as the car approached, slowing halfway down the drive. Clunk, whirr. The mechanical door began its descent.

I ran to the kitchen window. Didn't look like he was going to make it. "Come on!" I urged. "Faster!" I heaved a sigh of relief as the taillights slid through just before the door clamped down.

What was I saying? I was rooting for the man who tried to kill me to make it into the garage safely? I knew then that I couldn't go through with it. I replaced the flashlight and closed the cellar door. Maybe we could still make it work. I sank into the chair and waited for him to come in.

But he didn't. I could hear the soft purr of the engine through the door. Was something wrong? I flung open the door and ran to the car. His window was open, and he sat, eyes closed, with a flask in his right hand.

"Perfect landing, Ace," I said, shaking his shoulder to rouse him.

His eyes opened in surprise, and then he slumped forward.

I'll never know if it was the shock of seeing me upright or the alcohol that caused him to pass out. What I do know was that he'd had himself a right party while thinking I'd taken a tumble into the cellar. He reeked of alcohol, and sex, and, damn his soul, Poison perfume.

I watched him until the exhaust fumes got too bad and then backed away, closed the kitchen door behind me, and locked it. I poured a glass of Chardonnay and carried it outside to a lounge chair on the patio where I could daydream in the clean night air.

△   △   △

Kat Fast is on her eighth or ninth life focusing on fiction writing, watercolor and handwriting analysis. Her story "The List" was published in Level Best's Deadfall *anthology. "The Bonus" won NEWN's Flash Fiction contest in 2007. She's now doing her level best as an editor. She lives with her husband, big Boss dog, and two cats in Weston, Massachusetts.*

Closer

Joe Ricker

The frays of blood vessels broke the old man's bulging eyes into jagged yellow-white fragments. Audrey thought that any jarring or even a sneeze would force them to shatter like the bones in the boy he had killed. It was almost winter, a season she loved, because even in the cold pages of the books she surrounded herself with, she found warmth on Maine winter nights. But in those eyes that stared back at her impatiently, she felt a chill writhe through her bones.

Hobbs, the old man, was small. His shoulders drooped and he breathed heavily as if the walk from the shelves to the front desk with the one book was a lifetime of work. He was an old man when she'd seen him last, when she was a girl. His short index fingers tapped the edge of the book waiting for her to scan the barcode and his card.

"I'd like to read this before I turn to dust." Hobbs muffled a hack in his throat. He smelled of sweat and dirt and wet ashtrays.

The other librarians snickered behind her. She'd been holding the heavy, metal scanning pen like a dagger and she quickly relaxed her hand. She dragged the tip of the device across his card and then over the barcode on the back of the book. He took the book without another word, and the librarians watched him shamble through the exit.

Audrey excused herself to the other women and went to the ladies' room. She wanted to be away from the smell he left in the air—the smell that man had carried on the day he killed her little brother Jack. She remembered Jack stepping from the sidewalk to reach for a penny in the gutter on their way to the park, and then Jack was gone, like some prehistoric beast had gobbled him up, leaving a small Velcro shoe propped against the sidewalk. He had been so close; it didn't seem real. She heard the sirens and the quiet voices of people gathering at the edges of the sidewalk. The whine and chug of Hobbs' truck engine and the skipping beats of her own heart. Hobbs shuffled to his truck and returned with a paper sack with the open neck of a bottle poking out. The police arrived first, and when they approached Hobbs, he lifted the bottle and gulped down whatever was inside it. When he took the bottle from his lips, he smirked at his own delightful cleverness.

She wondered how many days she'd thought of her little brother while that man shuffled through the library—that smirk he wore on his face when the prosecution couldn't prove he was drunk when he'd hit Jack, and the jury convicted him of negligent homicide. For years, she'd harbored some relief in the hope the man had died, but no. All the pain he had caused her had never been redeemed—Hobbs moved through the world wafting his miserable odor into the faces of the people he made to suffer. She squeezed the porcelain of the sink until cramps invaded the space between the bones of her hands. When she left the bathroom, she could still smell him, heavy in the air like something dead and rotten in the wall. The rest of the day she grew anxious to be home, in her bed after a long bath, to have Chance close to her.

When Chance got home from work, Audrey was in bed propped against the headboard with the faint light from the table lamp on the nightstand lighting the pages of a book of poetry. All the poetry she read was in French, undiluted, she'd told him once, by translation. The room smelled of vanilla, the candles she'd lit on the dresser. The edges of her lips were burgundy from the wine she'd been drinking— nothing but swill left in the stemless glass and a few drops left in the bottle. He sat down on the ottoman at the foot of her bed and looked at her in the mirror.

"Rough day?" he asked her reflection in the mirror. He pulled his shirt over his head and leaned over his knees to untie his boots. The scars on his back between his ribs from shivs and other makeshift prison weapons warped and slipped closer to his stomach.

"I saw him today."

"Who?"

"The man who killed Jack."

"Oh." He turned to face her. "Are you okay?"

Audrey closed her book and traded it for the wine glass on the nightstand. "I'll be fine."

"Talk about it?"

"No." She placed the wine glass on the book and pulled the comforter tighter around her waist.

He turned back to the mirror and toed his boots from his heels letting them thump on the floor.

"What's it like to kill a man?" she asked.

He rubbed his palms over his face. "We've talked about that."

"I know. I'm sorry. I'm drunk. I don't really know why I asked. I guess I just wanted to know."

She pulled the comforter off her legs and crawled to the end of the bed. She wrapped her arms around his shoulder and nuzzled into his neck, taking in a deep breath of sawdust and sweat—the musk of his labor.

"I need a shower, babe. Join me?"

"I took a bath earlier. Hurry, and come lie down with me for a while."

She let her arms fall from his shoulders. She lay against her pillows waiting for him.

The next day at the library, Audrey shelved books in the mystery section while the other women sipped on their coffee and talked about their book club meeting the night before. When Audrey first started at the library, her first summer out of college, she poured herself through narratives. It was a relief to be able to lose herself in a story and not the dull, monotone of nonfiction and critical assessment. Audrey found comfort in the agenda of their characters, how simple they made primal desire seem with the most complex of motives. Sex and murder were about taking control—easing the searing burn placed against the soul like the blue flame of an acetylene torch. She enjoyed the older novels best, the hardboiled stuff. The newer novels about gunshot residue and microfibers—the elimination of hardboiled detectives replaced by dorky lab rats with clean white robes and delicate fingers—killed her interest in the genre.

When Wendy and the other girls went to get their lunch, she pulled Hobbs' information up on the computer. She stopped herself from writing the information down, deciding it was a bad idea for one reason or another. She scoured through the information and repeated the address to herself. When the girls returned, she went about her day filing books, and organizing the magazine and periodical racks.

At the end of the day she drove to Acton. The address Hobbs had on file brought her to a large garage on Route 109. There was a camper beside the garage, tilted, and the roof was covered with a blue tarp. There was a picnic table in front of the camper that Hobbs lay over. A half empty bottle was cradled in the crook of his elbow. Just past the garage was a small dirt road where she pulled on and stopped her car, unseen from the road. A wind flexed through the trees scattering dead leaves, and the smell of him came to her.

□   □   □

Audrey drove to the Kittery Trading Post and made her way through the clothing and camping sections to the upstairs where they sold guns. She walked along the glass display, admiring the difference in elegance and the brutishness of weapons. The first person to help her was a man about her age in his mid twenties; his round face, the scatter of facial hair made him much younger, boyish. She stopped at a rack of small revolvers, clutching the straps of her purse and keeping it tucked closely to her body with her elbow.

"Can I help you find something?" he asked.

"I don't know. I don't know very much about guns."

"I do. My dad and I have forty-three altogether. Seventeen of those are handguns."

"That's a lot."

"Yeah. You can never have too many guns. So what are you interested in a gun for? Personal protection? Target shooting?"

"Personal protection, I suppose."

"I carry a forty-five in my truck. Most people nowadays think a nine millimeter is the way to go, but that won't stop shit. I even put a laser sight on it, too, and a hi-cap magazine."

"A laser sight?"

"Yeah. It shoots a red laser out, and wherever you see a red dot is where your bullet is going. You know, like the movies."

"Oh. And what's a hi-cap magazine?" She felt she should be writing things down. She felt foolish, discouraged she hadn't done any research before she went there. She even began to wonder why she'd driven there in the first place. Surely there were places closer to her home where she could have bought a gun.

"High capacity. A hi-cap magazine is just like a regular magazine except it holds more rounds. A regular clip, that's a magazine, will hold about ten rounds, but with a hi-cap, it holds about fourteen."

"Why so many bullets?"

"Well, you know, just in case you miss your target."

"But what about the laser sight?"

The boy pushed his hands in his pockets and craned his head back. He began to move his chin from side to side in bewilderment or annoyance, she couldn't tell. Before the boy had a chance to respond, another man approached and asked the boy to help in a different section of the store. When the boy left, she waited for the older man to speak. "What kind of gun are you looking for, dear?" He was less enthusiastic when he asked her, which made her feel more comfortable though she didn't know why.

"Personal protection. We got about that far." She waved her finger from her chest to the boy who had helped her. "I don't know anything about these things, really."

"You know they're not toys, right?"

"Yes sir. In all honesty, they scare me."

"Well, that's good. That means you'll respect them. If you're looking for personal protection," he motioned her to follow him down to another display case—to the revolvers that she had initially found. He unlocked the sliding glass door behind the case and pulled out a snub nose revolver. "This little beauty is probably going to be the best option for you." He checked the round cylinder and the barrel and handed it to her. She placed her purse on the glass and took the gun from him. It was heavier than she'd anticipated, and it seemed anxious to do harm, but there was a comfort about it that she admired. It reminded her of Chance.

"Now, that is a .357 magnum. It's hammerless with a two-inch barrel and it will hold five rounds. I recommend this to all female customers looking for a weapon for personal protection, because you can shoot it from your pocket or your purse, and you don't have to worry about the hammer getting caught on anything."

"I'll take it."

"That was easy. I'll need to see your driver's license."

The man gave her a form to fill out. She paused over some of the questions because of Chance, but finished the paperwork and waited for the man to make his phone call. When the phone call was over, and after the man had run her credit card, he handed her the weapon in a box and two boxes of ammunition. Before he let go of them he told her: "Make sure you have someone teach you about handling and shooting this. I'd highly recommend a handgun safety course. There are two types of rounds there. The .38s you can use to practice with, and the .357s you should use for protection. I hope it never comes to that."

She smiled and kept smiling until she got into her car. She rested the box on the passenger seat, and it was then that she realized, not that she had forgotten exactly, why she had bought the gun. She became conscious of the events that were now in motion, and a brief panic came over her as if she had already committed the crime. For the first time in her life, as many times as she tried to think of something other than the day she wailed over the crumpled body of her brother, she forced herself to think of it—his small body heaped in a sack of tattered bloody clothes, and Hobbs leaning against the bed of his truck gazing around at everything but what he'd done.

She waited at the kitchen table for Chance to come home, and in the time that she waited she brushed her fingers over the steel. Like Chance, the gun looked brutal. But she knew that brutality would protect her as much as it could hurt her—the gamble women suffer every day, she thought. When she met Chance, it was in the library. He was looking for a book he said wasn't in his other library. She found out later that he was referring to the prison library where he'd been for three years. The official charge was manslaughter, but Wendy had told her murder. Chance walked with his elbows close to his body; he moved fluidly. When he spoke to her, he kept his gaze over her shoulders or at the windows for their reflection of what stood behind him. She led him to the fiction section and pulled a copy of *Desolation Angels* from the shelf.

"Let me know if you need help finding anything else," she told him.

"I don't have a card."

"That's not a problem as long as you have your ID. I'll get you set up when you're ready to check out."

He'd simply nodded to her while cradling the book in his hands.

When Chance approached the front desk, Audrey listened to Wendy stir and whisper to the other librarians. Chance smiled to Audrey and gave her his ID. Before she could fill in Chance's information Wendy stepped beside her and spoke.

"I'm sorry, but we're no longer offering cards."

"I don't understand."

"We've reached our quota for the month. I'm sorry, sir."

"I see." He held his hand out for Audrey to return his ID. She handed it back to him confused and embarrassed, hoping Wendy would explain further, which she did only after Chance had left.

After work that day, Audrey hurried home and took her copy of the book from her shelf. She drove to the address she'd remembered from Chance's ID. He came to the door of the apartment and stood expressionless behind the screen. She fumbled for something to say, realizing her impulsivity then, and she wondered how foolish he thought she was.

"I'm sorry about what happened today, at the library," she finally said. "Wendy is a—"

"Cunt."

She pursed her lips and nodded. He opened the door and stepped outside. She gripped the book tighter.

"Anyway, I brought this for you." She handed him the book, but he kept his arms at his side.

"Why?"

"I felt bad, and I don't know. This is stupid. I'm sorry."

"Wait." Chance extended his arm and caught her wrist with the tips of his fingers as she turned. His grip was gentle with the firm immediacy of a child's. "Thank you. It's very sweet, but you don't know me. It's pretty dangerous to do what you've done—come to a stranger's house like this."

"I wasn't really thinking."

"No shit. You do this often?"

"Only when I want to get laid." She laughed desperately, again realizing she'd probably said the wrong thing. "Sorry. I was joking."

"You're funny. You want to come in? I'll keep in mind that you're joking about the getting laid thing."

She sat with Chance in his small apartment for hours talking about the books that he'd read. She suggested books to him and laughed at the ones he'd been reluctant to read but did so because there were no other choices. He offered her an explanation for his crime before she could ask. And when he explained it, she found a comfort in his honesty despite the facts of his confession—that it was a bar fight, a horrifying accident.

☐   ☐   ☐

Chance got home and stared at her, bewildered. She sat at the table holding the gun.

"I bought a gun," she said.

"I see that. What for?"

"To shoot. Can we go shooting?"

He put his lunch cooler on the table across from her. "Let's go, it'll be dark soon."

Chance took her to a sandpit on the outskirts of town where townies gathered on Saturday nights to drink cheap beer on the tailgates of their trucks. The target he set up was an empty jug full of sand so she could see when she hit the target. He explained the basics to her—breathing, squeezing the trigger and not pulling, pointing the bullet to where she wanted it to go. Chance stood behind her involved in thoughts he wouldn't reveal if she had asked. The first shot startled her. She almost dropped the gun. It was the sound that bothered her more than the pistol bucking in her hand. All the death she knew had been silent, without shouting or anger. The gun was all of that— vicious, barking.

She made him fire the gun while she sat against the hood of her car. When he finished, she motioned him to her with her finger. She smelled the gunpowder on his hand when she took it and pushed her cheek into his palm.

"Why did you ask me about killing the other day?"

"I was drunk, I told you."

"What's the gun for, Audrey?"

"I want to feel protected. I know it's silly, but seeing that guy made me feel unsafe."

"Do you still want to know?"

She paused for a moment then nodded and pushed her cheek against his chest.

"Killing a man makes you feel like you can dig your fingers into the ground and lift the earth over your head. But that only lasts for a moment and then—" He held his breath.

"Then?"

"Then the blood is sucked from your veins and it crushes you."

She slipped her hand beneath his shirt and rubbed her fingers against his body, over the ragged scars on his back. Because of his past, she felt a world apart.

◻︎   ◻︎   ◻︎

Audrey called out of work the next day. She left a message for Wendy on the machine, and drove to Hobbs' camper in Acton. She parked the car where she had the day before and moved slowly through the woods to the back of the camper. The air had become cool, and swirls of rogue snowflakes slipped through the bare branches of the trees. Before Audrey could see the camper, she could smell it. She heard his fumbling and hacking. When she could see him, he was sitting on the picnic table. She waited for a while, until he stumbled inside, and she watched his movement to the end of the camper.

She walked quickly across the driveway and stepped inside where the putrid smell of moldy wet towels and urine crawled over her skin. Cigarette burns marred the carpet in a small area near the couch. Empty bottles of booze were scattered everywhere—on counters, cushions, in the open cabinets and on the stove. She saw his legs in the doorway of a small room at the end of the camper and made her way toward him.

He sat in a small chair and looked up at her when she came to the doorway. She had been displaced for so long, no more alive in the world than the books she shelved daily. She'd embraced them because she could leave the tragedy and sorrow within the guts of their pages. If she wanted to experience it, she needed only to grab them by the spine. She was in control there. And it was a control that had comforted her until she pulled the gun from her pocket. Except for Chance, until that day, she had been a woman of little action, moving through her life the way she did through the library—a steady, somber gait up and down the rows of torment. Until then, she had not forced herself to act on the rage she felt tremble her fingers each morning she awoke.

Hobbs stared at her through the glasses that rode crooked on his nose, and she pointed the gun. She heard more the sound of his desperate, blinking eyes than the gunshot. The bullet ripped through his neck and through the pane of glass behind him. Blood chased the bullet only to be cut short by the glass and paneling behind him where it hung for a moment before sliding down the wall, and his hacking gurgle was more like the laughter of a small boy in the distance—a sound that required nothing of her emotions for remorse.

She moved back to the car, her ears ringing in alternating tones. She set her cruise control and pushed her heels into the floorboard in an attempt to stop her knees from shaking. He'd reached for her when she shot him, his fingers grabbing clumsily at the air while the fingers of his other hand folded and he dug his knuckles into his cheek. Blood had bubbled thick from the wound on his neck and he flung his arm toward her, knocking the glasses from his face. She'd felt drops of his blood hit her hairline. He'd arched his back, his calves flexing until the chair he was sitting in toppled over and he fell to the floor. His movement had stopped, and a surge of fecal odor pulsed through the room. She'd squatted and reached for his glasses on the floor, but stopped herself before she touched them.

Chance was washing out his cereal bowl when she entered the house. She had driven the entire way home still gripping the pistol and entered the kitchen with it at her side. He stopped moving his hands, and the water splurged from the bowl showering the counter and the front of his shirt.

"What the hell?"

"I killed him."

Chance tightened his jaw and placed the bowl in the dish rack on the counter. He stopped the water and dried his hands. "You killed who?"

She tried to say his name first. "H-H-him."

Chance gripped the edge of the counter and pushed himself up so his shoulders rose toward his ears. "You shot him?"

She nodded.

"With the gun you just bought?"

She nodded again adding a quiet groan.

"Did anyone see you?"

She shook her head.

"Did you call out of work?"

Nodding.

He breathed deeply and looked away from her. In a blur of movement he grabbed the bowl from the rack and threw it against the cabinet doors. It shattered and fell in pieces. His movements then were quick, and his speech was low and controlled—indifferent and lacking the deepness in pitch she was used to.

"Take off your clothes," he told her.

"What?"

He charged at her. "Give me the gun and take your fucking clothes off." He checked the cylinder. "Good, you used the hollow points." He went to a cabinet first and took out a trash bag and threw it at her feet. "Put them in there." He slid the junk drawer open and pulled out a small round file that he slid into the end of the barrel and worked against the metal.

"What are you doing?" she asked, standing in her panties and bra.

"Those, too." He pointed at her underwear with the file. He took the bullets from the gun and placed them in a trash bag with her clothes. "If they recover a fragment from the hollow point they can run a ballistics test on, they won't be able to match it to this gun. The file changes the rifling marks. I'm going to vacuum your car out and get rid of this bag. Go get in the shower, and stay there. Use the Lava soap I have under the sink and go over yourself at least three times." She held her hands against the small of her stomach and moved slowly through the house.

When she came out of the shower, all but a corner of the mattress hung off the bed. The sheets and comforter were strewn over the bedposts. Her candles had been swept from the top of the dresser. She moved into the living room. Couch cushions were flipped up on the couch. DVDs and CDs were scattered across the floor. In the kitchen, a chair lay on its side. Chance dropped a stack of plates on the floor as she entered.

"Do you know how much I love you, Audrey?"

"What are you doing?"

Chance bit his bottom lip to cease its quivering. He took her by her hand and positioned her in front of the sink. A tear struck the corner of his eye and slid down edge of his nose.

"Audrey, you fucked up."

"Chance—"

His fist smashed into her cheekbone and she flailed backwards into the sink. She tried to hold herself steady, but her knees gave out. She crumbled to floor. Often, she'd wondered how he could have killed someone, what rage he'd embraced to exude that kind of power. She had only ever known his hands to be gentle, despite the abuse he put them through. In that instance she knew just how powerful he was—how crushing and absolute his violence could be if he chose. He stepped closer to her and knelt.

"Audrey, the cops are going to come here and ask you questions. They're going to want to know why you bought a gun, and why the man who killed your brother was killed with the same caliber only days after you bought it. They're going to want to know why you called out of work the day he was killed. You have to have answers to these questions."

She felt her pulse throb through the warmth in her face.

"Listen to me very carefully. With my record, they're not going to doubt your story. You bought the gun because you were scared—because I had gotten violent. I've been violent for months. You called out of work today because of what I did to your eye. Now repeat it back to me."

The puffiness in her face was aching. She'd never been hit. The eye was beginning to swell. "I bought the gun, because I was afraid. You hit me."

"Good." He reached past her and opened the sink cabinet. "Get the gun."

She pulled the gun out and looked back at him.

"Okay. After you do this, call 911. Tell them you were in a fight with your boyfriend and he came after you and you shot him."

"What?"

"Listen to me. It'll be okay, I promise. I put .38's in it. I'll have to go away for a little while, but not long. Just do what I told you to do, and you stick to the story no matter what. I mean it, no matter what the cops tell you, you stick to the story. I got violent. You got the gun for protection. Got it?"

Audrey nodded. Chance gripped her hand and moved the muzzle of the gun to his chest. He pushed it into the soft part of his flesh just inside his shoulder below his collarbone. She felt the tension in his hand keeping her grip on the gun.

"This is important. If the cops ask you about anything else besides what we talked about, you lawyer up."

She was crying, and Chance kissed her cheek.

"This will bring us closer."

He pushed her index finger against the trigger with his thumb.

△ △ △

Joe Ricker *is a former bartender, innkeeper, and cab driver currently teaching English.* Esquire *referred to him as "a man of letters who's gentle in the way that only the toughest hard-asses can be." His fiction has appeared in* Deadfall: Crime Stories by New England Writers, The Hangover, Rose & Thorn Journal *and* Thuglit.

Madame Blavatsky Takes a Lover

Mary E. Stibal

I never paid much attention to the neighbors in our building in Boston's Kenmore Square, until eight months ago. I remember the first time I saw the heavy-set woman lumbering up the stairs to the fourth floor apartment just above us. She had a broad, Slavic face and piercing, wide-set gray eyes with a stare that went right through you. I thought she looked exactly like Madame Blavatsky, the nineteenth-century mystic.

My kind of century.

I told Newton about her and he teased me about spying on the neighbors. As if I had nothing better to do. The deadline for my master's thesis on Britain's General Gordon and the 1884-1885 Siege of Khartoum was three months away, and I had no time to think about an upstairs neighbor who looked like a seer.

Until she was murdered.

I called Newton in his cubicle at M.I.T right after the ambulance blared away. (I do have to say his parents, both physicists, had a lame sense of humor when it came to his name, but that's another story.)

He thought I was joking.

"Funny? You think I'm being funny?" I repeated.

"Well," he began, and I could just see him running his hand through his thick red hair, which he did whenever there was a problem that couldn't be solved with an algorithm. "There was a . . . murder? The woman right above us? They think someone killed her?"

"A woman isn't likely to drop dead with a knife in her back unless someone put it there," I said.

"Oh, of course. A knife?"

That's what the paramedic had told me as he followed the gurney out the front door, and he should know, although I did ask him twice. Newton wanted to know if I was all right, and if our front door was locked, and I said yes to both. And no, I didn't want to go work in the library because my notes and books were scattered all over the living room.

A cop showed up twenty minutes later, a polite, handsome man in his mid-twenties with a Marine haircut, the usual questions, and a blue spiral notebook. I told Detective Lammers that I knew who the murdered woman was, of course, and that we'd say hello on the stairs or picking up the mail, but that was it. I asked him about a suspect, but all he said was, "We are proceeding with the investigation." I also wanted to know the specifics of the blade, but because my knowledge on that subject was pretty much limited to the armory of the British Expeditionary Forces, I didn't bring it up. There was that, and the fact I was in total shock.

It wasn't until that night I remembered the short, dark-haired man in a gray overcoat I'd seen on the stairs a couple of times, usually about 9:00 p.m. He could only have been going to Madame Blavatsky's apartment on the top floor. It hadn't occurred to me before, but once I thought about it, he could have been her lover. In fact, I was sure of it.

And I did wonder if maybe he killed her.

The next morning the police were back, and I told the detective about the dark-haired man, but I didn't mention the lover or the killer parts. However, because I'd only seen him from behind, my description more than bordered on the sketchy. There were probably thousands of men in Boston about five feet, nine inches tall with a gray overcoat and black hair. The detective asked if I'd seen the man the day of the murder, and I had to say no.

Her obituary was in the paper two days later, if you could call the five sentences that ran in *The Boston Globe* an obit. She was from the Ukraine, and her first name was Helena, just like Madame Blavatsky, I told Newton with a certain degree of satisfaction. Helena had a Ph.D. in Russian literature and was an adjunct professor at Harvard. That's the kind of position where you're technically a faculty member, but professionally regarded as itinerant labor. I was getting to know my way around academia.

Newton didn't look up from his computer in the living room when I'd finished reading the obituary aloud. He didn't say anything either, so I added, "How do you feel living underneath a murdered clairvoyant?"

That got him to look at me.

"She was a clairvoyant?"

I said, "Possibly." I didn't point out that if she was, she hadn't been that good, or she wouldn't be dead.

At least it showed he had been listening.

There was a contentious tenant meeting in our building that night, with a lot of loud talk about strangers and security and buzzing in people we didn't know. Paul the building superintendant thought it was a robbery gone bad, probably drug related he said, but he thought all roads led to drugs. He told us that Helena's laptop was missing, but no other valuables seemed to have been taken.

At the meeting, Paul and Newton argued about security cameras and Christopher and Steve, who live across the hall from each other, came close to a fistfight over resident parking. Other than that, not much happened. Just before the meeting ended I proposed a "Resident Task Force on Security" that everyone thought was a great idea, and I ended up as the head. Christopher was the only volunteer; so much for a murder bringing neighbors together. He and I adjourned to a bar across the street to hammer out a preliminary set of rules and regulations, but all he wanted to talk about was having titanium locks installed on all the doors. Christopher has expensive taste even in hardware.

The next day I was back at work on my "Chinese" Gordon thesis. (The general picked up that nickname in China's Second Opium War, which sounds exotic, but was decidedly not.) I was at the critical part where a rebel army in the Sudan was gaining strength under the fundamentalist Al Mahdi, so Britain pulled out of the Sudan, and the Prime Minister sent General Gordon to evacuate Khartoum. But once he arrived my general ignored his orders and decided to defend Khartoum instead.

It was a heroic decision, which, by the way, would not end well.

While I was struggling through my source texts, I heard someone on the stairs. I got up and cracked open the front door and saw the man in the gray overcoat on his way up to the fourth floor, a key in his hand. Maybe he had an extra knife strapped somewhere on his body, too. He looked down and saw me, so I had to say something. I thought he looked a little like Trotsky, although that might have been the rimless glasses.

"She died," I said, and then added, "abruptly." That was clumsy, I thought, but better than the rather bald, "She's been murdered."

"I know," he said, with a thick Russian accent. "It was a tragedy."

Bingo on the Trotsky part.

The man continued up the stairs.

I went back to my desk, but I could hear footsteps as he walked back and forth from room to room. Like security, the acoustics in our building were second-rate. What was he doing? The man had a key, so he had not broken in. Why did he have a key? I called Detective Lammers and left a description of the man on his voicemail. Then I called Newton.

"He's in her apartment right now," I whispered, "Madame Blavatsky's lover. He has a key. I think maybe he killed her."

Newton said, "Are you crazy? Leave it alone! Who do you think you are, Nancy Drew?"

That last part stung.

Half an hour later I heard someone come down the stairs, and, after a couple of minutes, I looked out the window and saw Madame Blavatsky's lover on the front steps. He wasn't carrying anything bulky or suspicious. So what had he been doing up there for an hour? I wanted to call Newton again, but I knew better, so I went down to get the mail and ran into Christopher in the lobby. I asked if he just saw a man leave.

"Yes. Why?"

"Have you seen him here before?"

"Yes."

"He doesn't live here," I said.

"Oh. Well, he has a key to the mailbox."

"He's Madame Blavatsky's lover, I mean Helena's. I think he was her lover."

"Whatever," said Christopher. "I thought he did—live here I mean. I've seen him a couple of times in Harvard Square with a woman, a blonde woman. I remember his glasses. They were having drinks at the Harvest."

A blonde I thought. Why is it always a blonde? I tried not to be interested; this kind of conversation was beneath a scholar. But maybe not.

I had to ask, "Were they together-together or just together?"

Christopher sighed. "Now you're beginning to sound like a cop. He was just a guy in a bar with a woman. And no, I don't know what they were talking about. And also no, I don't know if they were sleeping with each other."

I didn't think Christopher was all that helpful, and I would have fired him from the Task Force except he was all I had.

Late that night, not long after Newton fell asleep, I thought I heard someone in Madame Blavatsky's apartment. I slid out of bed and waited by the front door until 3:00 a.m., but no one came down the stairs. When I crawled back into bed, Newton turned and asked where I'd been, and I told him I was having an affair with one of the neighbors.

After Newton left for classes the next morning, I thought about calling the police again. But because I didn't know for sure that anyone had been in her apartment, I went back to my thesis.

After Britain abandoned the Sudan, to no one's surprise, including mine, the army of Al Mahdi made straight for Khartoum and General Gordon, laying siege to the city. Within ten months the general's food stores were all but gone, and a cholera outbreak had decimated his garrison. The good news was that Prime Minister Gladstone finally decided to rescue him, and the British Relief Expedition was just two days away. But my hopes were not raised, because, like I said, the general was about to have a very bad day.

Still, I couldn't stop thinking about Madame Blavatsky and her lover. She had been my neighbor after all.

Then late the next day, he showed up again. I was in the lobby when I saw him walk through the front door. I turned back to the mailboxes, hoping he hadn't seen me, and I waited until he went up the stairs. What was he doing here? I decided to call the cops, but when I got to the third floor landing, there was her lover standing right in front of my door. Up close he didn't look much like Trotsky, more like Lenin. I do know my revolutionaries.

"Perhaps you could help?" he asked.

"Help?"

He told me his name was Felix, and he taught with Helena at Harvard. A "close colleague" was how he described their relationship. Yeah right, I thought.

"I have a favor to ask," he began. "It's about your mail."

"Mail?" I seemed able to reply only in one-word questions. Then I asked, "Why do you have a set of keys?" I was not the head of the resident Task Force on Security for nothing.

"Actually, Helena and I were . . ." he hesitated, "lovers."

I knew it, I thought, I was right! My God was I good! But that also meant that he . . . The man continued, "Your mailbox is next to hers, and she was expecting an important letter last week, and it never came, and I thought maybe it was put in your mailbox. By mistake. It was addressed to her, but it was meant for me."

Granted, I had been rather absorbed of late, what with my stubborn general under siege and starving and a murderer stalking the hall right outside my front door, but a letter from Moscow would have caught my eye.

"No, I didn't get any of her mail," I said.

I thought back. There had been a day last week when I'd scooped a lot of mail out of our box, mostly Newton's physics magazines. I had sorted through it, but not carefully, and dumped the pile on his desk. Sometimes it would take him weeks to go through his magazines, if at all.

I backed up a couple of steps. Felix saw me hesitate, and his eyes flickered. He moved toward me, and alarm bells went off in my head.

The walls of Khartoum were breached at dawn that last day of the siege by 30,000 troops of Al Mahdi. There was a fierce battle, but General Gordon and his soldiers were outnumbered five to one. Khartoum was taken, and my general killed in a bloody sword fight on the staircase of his headquarters. Queen Victoria and all of Britain went into mourning, and Prime Minister Gladstone was ousted.

As far as I was concerned, I didn't want to die in the first place, and in the second place most definitely not on a damn staircase. I tried to keep my face blank as I stepped back down a stair. Then I whirled around and flew down the steps to the lobby and out the front door. Felix came down a couple of minutes later, white-faced and in a hurry, jumped in his car, a Toyota I noticed, and roared away.

I didn't go back into our apartment until an hour later, and only then because Detective Lammers was with me. Because he was in plain clothes, I did ask if he had a gun, and he opened his jacket and showed me his shoulder holster with a nasty-looking revolver tucked inside.

"Very nice," I said and took him to Newton's desk.

And yes, there was a letter addressed to Helena from Moscow, stuck in the latest issue of the *American Journal of Physics* that I'd told Newton before had looked like a real page-turner. The detective told me later it was from Moscow State University, and included Felix's official transcript. Turns out he had not earned a Ph.D. in nineteenth-century Tsarist literature as he'd claimed in his resume, but a B.S. in chemical engineering. The cover note thanked Helena for her contribution, probably a bribe was the detective's take, and the writer ended with a P.S. that a copy would also be emailed to her. No wonder Helena's laptop was missing.

For whatever reason (I suspect the blonde had a role), Helena had tracked down enough ammunition to blow her ersatz lover's career in the U.S. sky high, and so he stopped her. Permanently.

Detective Lammers told me that Felix was regarded as a "person of interest" by the police, but they had no evidence, and his alibi—that he had been at Harvard's Widener Library—was difficult to confirm. However, Helena's letter was enough for a search warrant to be issued and cause to haul him into headquarters.

Newton told me that night I was brave and heroic, so the Nancy Drew dig was forgiven.

Felix was charged with Helena's murder three months ago, and the case was in the headlines of *The Boston Globe* for weeks. His trial starts in April, and Detective Lammers said I will need to testify, so I'll be going to my first, and with any luck, my last murder trial.

As for me, I've just started work on my Ph.D. thesis, "Madame Blavatsky and the Impact of 19th Century Colonialism on the Rise of Theosophy." It is my century, and after everything that's happened, I feel as if I know her.

It was Newton's idea that we move to a different apartment a couple of months ago, and I was glad to leave our old building. We live in a bigger place in Cambridge now. I have my own office and a picture of Chinese Gordon hangs over my desk, right next to a photo of Madame Blavatsky.

Too bad they never met. She could have warned him about the stairs.

△   △   △

***Mary E. Stibal** lives in Boston's Seaport District and has published fiction in* Yankee Magazine *as well as Level Best Book's* Seasmoke *(2006). She is a partnership marketing consultant and is also learning to ride English (harrowing, yet thrilling). She is working on her second mystery novel,* A Socialite in Pearls, *a sequel set in Boston, that features Madeline Lane, a gemologist in the high-end jewelry gem business. In the book, Madeline is also (what a coincidence) learning to ride.*

Tribute

Michael Nethercott

It had taken Alan too long to find the old trail. As he pressed on through the snow-laden woods, he cursed himself for starting out as late as he had. Assuming he could even locate the cabin, he'd be lucky to make it back to the car before dark. The light of day had taken on a lonely silver sheen, making the world seem brittle, unsubstantial, adding to the man's sense of unreality. He moved slowly and silently, a phantom in a dreamscape.

How long had it been since he'd last walked these Vermont woods? Twenty-five years? Thirty? Probably he'd not been much out of his teens. Uncle Dewey, his mother's brother, had been fit and sound in those days, narrow in overalls, a Lucky Strike forever dangling from his grin. He and Aunt Paula never had their own children; so, from a small tribe of nieces and nephews, Dewey had handpicked Alan as his sidekick and heir to his various wisdoms. While Alan's home was Connecticut, and his uncle's New Hampshire, the remote Vermont cabin became their place of shared adventure. Though the property actually belonged to Aunt Paula's side of the family, in Alan's recollection she only made the trip there two or three times.

Most of his cabin memories whirled around his uncle: trail blazing together as Dewey sang out "*Davy, Davy Crockett, king of the wild frontier*" stridently in his cracked tenor; fishing side-by-side for largemouth bass at Big Pond, a fifteen-minute walk from

120

the cabin; taking turns reading aloud at night from a mildewed old volume of ghost stories by the quivering amber of a kerosene lamp.

Alan paused for a moment to fix his bearings, resting his hand against the rough hide of a large maple. One of these trees out here had once cradled a tree house that he and Dewey built out of boards hauled in from a collapsed barn. Another had served as the perch for that big, imposing owl that they'd dubbed Fat Frank. Once, every other tree may have held some childhood tale, but now the forest had become an indifferent army of winter sentinels, and he himself unrecognizable as the boy who had played here.

And Dewey was gone. Though only weeks in his grave, in a way he'd been gone for almost twenty years. Following the accident back in '91—Dewey at the wheel, left alive, barely scratched; Aunt Paula dead on impact—the man began to slide downwards, quickly and irreparably. Two months after Paula's funeral, Dewey marked his sixty-second birthday with a whiskey binge that led to the mistake of his life. Afterwards, Alan had gone a couple of times to visit him, but seeing Dewey like that—dressed in prison grays, his skin becoming gray itself among other gray men—was more than he could stand. He stopped visiting and, after a while, stopped writing.

Last month when he got the call that the cancer was closing in on Dewey, Alan relented and went to see him. Reduced to an ancient scarecrow, the old man whispered in his nephew's ear one last wisdom. Three days later, he smiled at an attendant nurse, called her Paula, and died.

Relocating the trail, Alan continued on, his boots crunching through the crust of snow, his nostrils stinging a little with each intake of crisp air. It wasn't even a certainty that the cabin still stood. Upon Paula's death, the acreage here had reverted to some second cousin who, reportedly, never once came to view it. When Alan had first heard that news, he was up in arms. How could this place of simple marvels and memories fall into the hands of someone who didn't give a damn? The world was an unfair place—but then he knew that. It was a place of unfaithful wives and disinterested children. It was a place where you could break your back at a job for twenty-six years—twenty-six goddamned years—and they'd demote you in a heartbeat.

Then he glimpsed it, there at a distance through the tangle of branches. He hurried forward, an almost painful nostalgia gripping him. Inside that small hidden structure dwelt a good chunk of his childhood. As Alan entered the clearing, the cabin came into full view, but, in the way of childhood revisited, seemed much smaller than he remembered it. Though he had prepared himself to find only ruins, the building had survived, apparently still solid and serviceable beneath its thick quilt of snow. But it wasn't anything to be found within the cabin that had drawn him here; it was what lay behind it.

On his deathbed, Uncle Dewey, with few words left in him, had whispered into Alan's ear: "Under Bunyan's marble." Indecipherable to any other listener, the meaning of the phrase was more than clear to Alan. It referred to the large rock—a small boulder really—that lay just behind the cabin. The rock was almost perfectly round. Dewey had always claimed it was one of the giant Paul Bunyan's marbles that had rolled astray. Just one of the old joker's many fancies.

As Alan started to circle the cabin, something he hadn't noticed before stopped him in his tracks—smoke was issuing from the roof stovepipe. He had no time to digest this unfeasible fact before his attention was summoned by a movement to his left. Someone had appeared on the edge of the wood and now stood watching him.

Frozen in place, Alan called out, "Hello?"

Half-hidden among the trees, the watcher made no movement, gave no response. Alan could not tell if it was a man or woman.

Again, more firmly now, he called out, "Hello! Who's there?"

The figure approached without haste, not so much cautiously as languidly. Alan saw now that it was a young man, somewhere in his early twenties. His long straw-colored hair was tied to one side by a ribbon from which hung several peacock feathers, and a wispy beard barely overcame his look of boyishness. The fellow was very slender, which was evident even through the long black overcoat, worn and patched, that hung to his boots.

When he had come within a few feet of Alan, he spoke: "No one's been out here before." His voice was airy, almost singsong. "I thought maybe I'd see some hunters in the fall, but I never did. You're not a hunter. You've got no rifle."

"No," Alan agreed. "I'm not a hunter." Not having considered the possibility that he might encounter someone, he had no explanation to offer as to his presence here. Quickly, he turned the inquiry on his companion. "Are you one of the Robinsons?" These were the cousins who had taken over the property.

The bearded boy shook his head. "I am not."

"Then what are you doing here?"

The youth shifted on his feet and cocked his head. "Are you friends of the owners?"

"Yes, that's right." Alan hoped he sounded convincing. "What's your story? Are you squatting here?"

"Squatting?" The young man began to giggle in a way that took Alan aback. "Only when I relieve myself." Then his grin shifted abruptly to something like a frown. "It's good that I'm here. The land *wants* me here."

"Oh?" was all Alan could muster.

"Yes, the land. The trees and creatures are glad I'm here, too. Even the snow." Here the young man leaned forward, lowering his voice conspiratorially. "Though, to be honest, I think the snow would like to kill me if it could." Then he let loose a loud, high laugh as if he'd just shared a wonderful joke that anyone would appreciate. "But, I'm sorry—please come on in. You're my guest. As you can probably ascertain, I don't get many out here." Without waiting for a reply, he scurried over to the cabin, flung open the door and disappeared inside.

His game plan now thrown off, Alan felt he had no choice but to follow. Inside, he found a bewildering blend of the remembered and the unanticipated. The old deer antlers, fixed above the south window, still remained, as did the blue floral curtains with which Aunt Paula had tried unsuccessfully to spruce the place up. The table and chairs seemed to be the ones that were here decades ago, and the wood stove, presently filling the room with modest warmth, was the same that Dewey had cooked their oatmeal and hot dogs atop.

But mixed with these familiar things were other objects, strange in every sense of the word. In one corner of the cabin, a sizable pile of pebbles and acorns supported a yellowed cow skull. From the hollow sockets sprouted what looked to be plastic doll arms. In another corner, jumbled in with a pair of skis and several tools, leaned three street signs, still on their poles. The original locations obscured by painted red letters, all bore the same word: *nowhere.* The bookshelf, which had once held paperbacks and sports digests, now hosted a small army of statuettes—little clowns, children with umbrellas, animals, saints—all cracked or damaged in some way; many were headless. Most disconcerting, one wall had been pasted over with a collection of magazine photos, jagged-edged and off-kilter, presenting a single theme: women's eyes. Apparently torn from cosmetics ads and celebrity spreads, the eyes reached from roof to floor and must have numbered in the hundreds.

Alan felt a surge of discomfort. "Are you some kind of artist?"

The youth closed the door behind them. "I don't think so. What's your name?"

"Alan." Once he'd said it, he wished he hadn't. It was better perhaps not to be so forthright with this stranger.

"Alan . . . Like Alan-a-Dale, Robin Hood's minstrel." The young man knelt beside the stove and fed in a log. "Me, I'm Orcus."

"Orcus?"

The youth began to speak very rapidly. "It's the name of a minor Roman god. I chose it because I didn't think it was right to take a major deity's name. *Hubris.* The Greeks would have called that hubris, but we're talking about the Romans right now. Orcus lived in the underworld. He was the punisher of broken oaths."

"I see."

"Rural god. They didn't worship him in the big cities, but it's better that way. Means that even when all the urban gods faded out, he still survived out there in the boonies. Off the map, just like me. Mythology. Mythology's what it's about. I came into these woods last summer because I wanted to follow my myths and they led me here. I was just wandering when I stumbled on this cabin. Took it as a sign. No electricity. No neighbors. Nothing but a stove, four walls and a roof. I had to put some new boards in, but all in all, things were pretty intact."

"So you came alone?"

"Well, there was this girl . . ." The young man's voice dropped to a whisper. "I'm sure she would have come." He slammed the stove door shut. "But she died."

"I'm sorry to—"

"Don't!" Orcus shot to his feet. "It wasn't my fault, really. We don't need to talk about her. Just because I invited you in, doesn't give you the right to pry."

"I wasn't trying to." Alan began edging away from the youth.

Orcus was becoming more agitated. "There are certain rules of etiquette! This is my home, Alan. I don't care who has a bill of sale. There are greater laws, make no mistake. I'm wanted here. Needed. Do you have a purpose? A true purpose? Well, *I* do. I give names to everything."

Alan found himself wondering where the line lay between eccentricity and madness. He decided he didn't want to find out.

Orcus began to pace the room, no longer looking at his guest. "The trees around us are the Old Sons. The swarm of black flies that comes in summer is Darkus Mistus. The beam of sunlight that slips through the door in the morning is Goldena. I name them all and I compose praise songs for them. If I wasn't here, who would do that?" He stopped and rested his hand upon the cow skull. "And this is Bronwin of the Sorrows."

Alan seized on the pause. "I just need to check on something outside, then I'll be going."

Orcus turned to him, distress evident on his face. "But I was going to make you hibiscus tea."

"That's all right."

"And I have some peanut brittle that I've been saving."

"Maybe another time."

The young man's eyes narrowed. "Don't lie to me. There won't ever be another time, will there?"

Thinking it best not to answer, Alan opened the door and stepped out into the gathering dusk.

He hurried behind the cabin and found his objective right away. With its covering of winter white, the boulder looked more like a half-constructed snowman than a giant's marble. But here it was. Last month, upon hearing his uncle's dying words, Alan had figured it all out. Nearly two decades before, in those few days between the robbery and his capture, the fugitive must have traveled up here and hidden the stolen jewelry under the rock. Dewey no doubt figured he'd return here one day to reap the harvest of his crime. His arrest, and then the cancer, had derailed that plan. Now Alan was the beneficiary by default. Now, at last, maybe things would turn around for him.

He dug his gloved fingers beneath the boulder and, with groaning effort, rolled it aside. There in the black earth, free of snow, an oblong imprint suggested that a box had once rested here—but had been removed. Alan swore under his breath as he noticed an object peeking up from the soil. A peacock feather.

He stood and turned around. Orcus had followed him out.

"You took it," Alan said.

The young man stared back, his face unreadable.

"You took it," Alan repeated, sliding his right hand into his jacket pocket.

Orcus' eyes widened as the older man extracted a revolver and aimed it at his heart.

"Don't deny it." Alan heard the growl in his voice and felt the weight of the gun in his hand.

This was the same weapon with which Dewey, almost twenty years before, had committed his robbery. It was the same weapon that had shattered the chest of the jewelry store clerk—a West Indian immigrant with four children—who had died instantly. Alan always needed to believe that his uncle's finger had twitched at that fatal moment, that he never meant to kill the man. But kill him he had. Dewey had been the most inept of holdup men, and his image on the store surveillance camera was soon in police hands. Dewey vanished for several days—to where, he refused to say—before a barkeeper in Boston recognized him from a newspaper photo. Like the jewelry, the handgun was never located. That is, until a few years back when Alan discovered it with a boxful of bullets in an old trunk that Dewey had left behind. He was not sure when he started out this morning just why he chose to bring it along. But now he knew.

"This wouldn't be the first time this gun has killed a man." To Alan's ears, his own voice seemed to come from some faraway place, each word possessing the resonance of an echo.

"No," Orcus said quietly to him.

Alan blinked at this response. No? No *what*? Did the squatter mean no he didn't think Alan would fire? Or no he didn't wish to die? Or perhaps no he did not believe that he himself could perish. Had the boy's unsteady mind convinced him that he was invincible?

"Tell me what happened to the things you found here. Did you sell them?"

Orcus stood very still, his eyes fixed on the gun. "Sell them?"

"Is that what you did?"

"I don't like to sell. I don't like to buy. I prefer to just accept. Like when the wind comes down and—"

"Enough!" Alan now aimed the revolver at the youth's face.

"You crazy little bastard! I want what was in that box."

He hadn't noticed that Orcus had been hiding something in his right hand. With a swift, fluid motion, the youth drew back his arm and let fly a baseball-sized stone. It struck Alan squarely in the chest, the impact causing him to drop his weapon. In the few seconds it took him to retrieve it, his prisoner vanished around the side of the building. Alan lumbered after him. Upon reaching the cabin door and finding it barred, he hurled himself wildly against it. On his second attempt, the door gave way and he stumbled into the room.

Orcus stood with his back pressed to the wall of eyes, a hatchet now in his hand. "You get the hell away from me!"

"You throw anything again at me and I'll shoot you where you stand," Alan hissed. "You won't surprise me a second time. Even *you* can't be insane enough to think that an ax can stop a bullet."

Orcus scrutinized him for a long moment before letting the hatchet fall from his grip. As it clanked on the floor, the youth let out a sob and slid down to a sitting position, encircled by the gaze of a hundred women.

"If you kill me, maybe I'll see Annie again." A mist rose in his eyes. "But I don't even know if I believe in heaven."

Alan drew in a long breath to clear away a chaos of emotions. "You don't need to die. Just tell me where the jewelry is."

"I gave it all to Vasella."

"To who?"

"I don't even remember why I moved that big rock. But when I did, I found all those beautiful things made of gold. And all those gems. It took me a long time to decide what to do, but in the end I realized I should give it all to her—to Vasella. Shall I bring you to her?"

Without waiting for an answer, Orcus rose and led Alan out of the cabin. As they moved through the thick of the woods, the armed man kept his captive well in sight, but the youth seemed to have lost the desire for escape. After fifteen minutes of walking, Alan found himself at another place of old memories—Big Pond. For a moment, he could almost see Uncle Dewey sitting there on the edge of the small lake, a curl of cigarette smoke rising from his lips, a fishing rod arching in his hands.

"Now what?"

Orcus gestured across the frozen surface of the water. "I named her Queen Vasella."

Alan felt his stomach tighten. "The pond?"

"She's a great silent monarch." The young man spoke in a tone of reverence. "Queen Vasella, She Who Reflects. I swam out into her heart and gave it all to her as a tribute."

In his mind's eye, Alan saw the glinting gold and diamonds sinking down, down, past the bass and the algae, to disappear into the thick silt below. He seemed unable to move, unable to think; he could only stare across the pond and feel the heaving of his chest. After a long minute or two, he raised the handgun and fired into the ice. Then again. And again. The bullets, spaced closely together, created a sizable hole from which a thin web of fissures stretched out slowly in all directions.

How will this end? Alan wondered, darkly reviewing the possibilities. He had no doubts as to the unlikeliness of ever retrieving the jewelry—the unlikeliness of buying himself out of the desperation that had enveloped him as of late. Why not simply plunge himself into the gap in the ice, diving so deep as to never return? Or, instead, he could empty the gun into the young interloper who had robbed him of his legacy. Orcus might die instantly, releasing his mad soul before he struck the ground. Or perhaps the youth would not perish right away, but would linger just long enough to offer Alan some terrible words of forgiveness.

None of this came to pass. Instead, Alan lobbed the gun into the hole in the ice and watched it disappear. Then he turned to meet Orcus' eyes for a few hollow seconds before heading back in the direction he had originally come. As he moved through the woods, he heard a high chanting behind him and knew that Orcus must be serenading his gods.

The sky was quickly darkening, but Alan pressed on, telling himself he would not stop until he found his way back to the road. As he proceeded, a question filled his heart, one that his uncle and all other gray men who'd gone astray must have asked themselves more than once: *How did I come to this?*

△ △ △

Michael Nethercott *has published tales in* Alfred Hitchcock Mystery Magazine, The Magazine of Fantasy and Science Fiction; Crimestalkers Casebook; Plays, the Drama Magazine for Young People; *and various anthologies including* Best Crime and Mystery Stories of the Year 2009, Dead Promises, *and* Gods and Monsters. *He is a recent recipient of the Black Orchid Novella Award for traditional mystery writing.*

Gracie Walks the Plank

Kate Flora

The sound of a car door slamming brought Grace to the window. The car that had crunched up her gravel drive and now sat in a cloud of settling golden dust was new. Clean and dark and, until the dust finished coating it, shiny. It fit in this neighborhood of rust-blossomed double wides like feathers on a turtle. The man who got out didn't fit either. He was as clean and dark and shiny as the car. Wearing a suit, for shit's sake, on a ninety-five degree day.

She stubbed out her breakfast cigarette in the butt-choked ashtray and checked to see if she was fit for company. Exiled to this crap job, she paid little attention to her appearance. The ratty housecoat was held together with a rusting safety pin, its once tropical colors as faded as her childhood dreams. Bare toes on the grubby brown carpet still wore traces of girlish pink polish, a color the little Vietnamese girl at the salon had called Blushing Dawn. Her unbrushed mahogany hair was wrapped with the twist tie from a bread bag. She hadn't yet put on a bra and her breasts bobbled gently under the thin cotton. The only touch of elegance was a diamond necklace, grand enough for a queen, heavy on her throat as the hand of God.

As the Suit's demanding fist rose and fell against the tin can's flimsy door, Grace wrapped a colorful Indian scarf—dots, not feathers—around her neck and padded across the room.

"Who's there and what do you want?" Her voice, unused yet

today, poured like honey over gravel. Billy used to say she had a big voice for such a small woman. Big enough to fill clubs, that much she knew. Big enough to make complete strangers cry. She wouldn't mind making this man cry.

"Dirkk Postman, from the Marshall's service, Ms. Gillespie. We need to talk."

Grace didn't open the door. She wanted him out there sweating in the already too-hot sun a little longer. She wanted him to feel how pissed off she was about this visit.

After a pause, Mister Impatience banged again. "Open it up, Gracie. This is important." Postman always rang twice.

Like he'd travel ninety-five miles to the backass of beyond if it weren't? Sighing, she undid the locks. The door creaked in protest as she pulled it open, as though it, too, wanted to remain undisturbed.

Postman filled the opening, so tall he had to bend his head to enter, blotting out her view of scrub and gravel and her neighbor's collection of eviscerated sofas and abandoned appliances. He straightened, and his trained eyes took in his surroundings. "Are we alone?" he asked.

Grace plucked at the housedress. "You think I entertain dressed like this?"

He shrugged, the big gesture throwing off some of the hot air he'd carried in. "Gracie, you're living like a pig. How should I know what to think?"

"You know what to think," she blazed, startling the opaqueness right off his face. "Billy's freaking dead is what we both know, and we both know that means nothing else matters." She flipped a hand toward the world outside her door. "You think there's anyone out there in tin can land can interest me, after Billy?"

"He died robbing a bank, Gracie," Postman said. "It's not like the guy was a candidate for sainthood."

"Yeah, I always did have a soft spot for bad guys. But Billy . . ." She knocked a fist against her chest. "He got me right here."

She snagged a cigarette from the pack and lit it, blowing smoke at the polished man across the table. "And to what do I owe the pleasure of your company on this fine day?"

"Road trip," Postman said. "Assistant U.S. Attorney wants to see you. She thinks you've forgotten about her."

"As if she wasn't getting my messages? I told her I'd let her know when things were firmed up," Gracie said. "If I'd known you were coming, I would have baked a cake."

Postman loosened his tie. "Hot enough in here without you baking, Gracie."

"Tell me about it." She tipped her head up and blew smoke rings at the dingy ceiling. "Hotter than the hinges of hell, as they say. I'd almost rather get dead myself, if this is the alternative."

The Suit let himself bend a bubble off plumb. "Seriously," he said, "how's it going?"

She nodded at the overflowing ashtray. "I've started smoking. I'm dressed like a slattern. I can't remember when I last combed my hair. And there's so little action in this trailer park that if a dog farts, it's news."

Postman raised an eyebrow, and she didn't miss the slight twitch of his nose. "The truth, Dirkk with two k's?" She let it go a beat, until he deigned to show some interest. "I'm on the cusp of something. Unless you've just blown it wide open by coming up here with city clothes and a fancy car and knocking on my door, when there's no logical reason this side of hell for someone dressed like you to come calling. If I'm lucky, my felonious neighbors are sleeping. They tend to be nocturnal."

She stubbed out the cigarette. "If her Highness the AUSA would read my messages, instead of checking off a box and throwing 'em in a file, you'd have known enough to stay away." She squinted at the clock. "Okay. You've been here ten minutes, which is about how long it oughta take for me to give you the blowjob you came out here to get. Least, that's how my neighbors think I make my money, since there's been kind of a trail of you guys through here lately—"

"A trail?" he interrupted. "What does that mean?" This time, his nose twitched for real.

"Just pulling your leg, darlin'," she said, dropping her voice a range.

Man. It worked every time. He actually licked him lips before he spoke. "Weren't you just complaining about being isolated, Gracie?"

"Am isolated. Look out the window. No. Don't. It's time for me to throw you out and chase you down the path, hollering about how you didn't fuckin' pay me enough. You ready?"

A whisper of a nod. He didn't like it when she talked dirty. "Where are we meeting?"

"Truck stop. Twenty miles down the highway. And don't get impatient. I've gotta get spiffed up a little. I don't really wanna look like trailer trash next to Miz Laura Assistant U.S. Attorney Bower, now, do I?"

She chased him down the walk, hollering to high heaven and the citizens of the surrounding tins about him stiffing her one when he wasn't no longer stiff. She even threw an empty beer can at his rear window, though she was careful to miss. Mustn't damage government property.

Then she stripped off the weary Goodwill housecoat and stepped in the shower, wondering how the fuck she was going to handle this.

□   □   □

AUSA Laura Bower was too thin, too blonde, and looked too sweet to be the mean-assed SOB that she was. Maybe that's how she got away with it. Anyone else acting like she did would be decked twice before noon. At least, that's what Gracie thought. She didn't know what Postman thought. He'd never deigned to enlighten her. And Billy, her poor, departed Billy, had thought Bower had nice legs and liked to imagine them—well, never mind, Gracie wasn't going there. Billy said that was what men were always thinking when they said a woman had nice legs.

Bower should have known better than to put temptation in Billy's path. Bank robbers were like snapping turtles. They had this one synaptic reaction when they saw vulnerable banks. Not that Gracie really held it against Bower. Not much, anyway. Bower's job was to catch bad guys and put them away. When she got a bad guy—or bad gal—she thought she could turn, she tried to do that. And it was just, in Bower's words, "an unfortunate accident" that Billy went into that bank to scope it out so he and Gracie could help Bower catch a more seriously bad bank robber, and got a little carried away with play acting.

Only then, a teller had gotten carried away, a security guard had gotten carried away, a cop had gotten carried away, and after the gun party ended and the smoke cleared, Billy got carried away in a black, zipped-up body bag. And now, to do penance for her role in things which mostly consisted of a failure to read minds or the future, and some overconfidence about handling Billy, Gracie was stuck in the middle of freakin' nowhere, trying to get the goods on a bunch of toothless, inbred meth cookers who might have blown up their last neighbors, and she was too depressed to even wash her hair.

But a chance to get out of Tinville, however briefly, energized her. She washed and conditioned her Pre-Raphaelite hair into a russet glory, put on a nice black pencil skirt and an ivory silk top, pulled a candy pink muumuu on over it, tucked her Bruno Magli's into a canvas bag and scuffed out to her rusty jeep in pink flip flops. Her nearest neighbor Randy, who had more teeth than brains, and only a handful of those, was out at the mailboxes, holding his elastic-sprung track pants with one hand and a cigarette in the other. He waved her down and leaned into the Jeep, blasting her with leftover beer breath.

"See you had you a visitor, Gracie," he said.

God, she couldn't wait to get back to big city anonymity. Around here, they practically counted how many times she flushed.

"The Suit? Yeah, Randy. Some a-hole from the IRS, would you believe it? Looking for my cousin's husband, the one that ran off with his company's payroll? I think I told you about him? I dunno why he'd be coming to me, the way I live. Maybe he thinks I've got the money hid in that butt-busting sofa of mine?" She narrowed her eyes at Randy. "So I asked him did he think I'd live like this if I had money? And you know what he said?"

Randy shook his head, leaning in closer so she could share his lack of hygiene.

"He said the government has a long memory."

"In your dreams, Gracie," Randy said. "That's a good story." He punctuated his comment with a bobble-head nod. "Only, I heard you goin' after him. Guy's got all that money, and he can't even pay a poor girl for her services?"

He stared down the empty road. "Where you headed?"

"The VA," she said. "Then I gotta get some groceries and cigarettes."

"You sick?"

She cocked her head at him. "Dunno. Guess I'm gonna let them tell me, aren't I?"

He backed up, then, like maybe she had something he might catch, and wiped the hand that had been curled around the window frame on the side of his pants, causing them to descend further and treat her to a swatch of hairy purple belly. "You take care," he said.

"I try, Randy." She cranked up the window and gunned the Jeep. Already running late, and now running later. Dirkk didn't like to be kept waiting and neither did his boss.

At the roadhouse, she slipped off the muumuu, dumped the flip flops, and dug the black slingbacks out of her tote. She pulled the bandanna off and walked over to the shiny black car. The wave of cold air that welcomed her was heavenly. She clicked her seatbelt and leaned back, closing her eyes and drinking in the scent of new car, of leather and luxury and Dirkk's spicy aftershave.

He had the car rolling before she'd shut the door. "What took you so long?"

"Making miracles and placating nosy neighbors." She got out her brush and began tugging it through her now dry hair. She might not be as tall or as skinny, but in the hair department, she had the AUSA beat all to hell. "Wake me when we're close."

"You okay?"

"Beat," she said. "When's the last time you were up for ten nights straight with night vision glasses, Dirkk, lying belly down in gravel, trying to get license numbers and faces? Hoping nothing crawls over you or bites you and that you don't have to sneeze? It's a whole hell of a lot of fun." She wasn't letting him think all she did was drink and smoke and sit around in that hot tin box, waiting for the reprieve that would get her out of this piece of hell.

She couldn't picture Dirkk sitting ten nights in the dirt—he was always too polished, too prissy. But he must have put in his time.

"Tarantulas," he said. "One walked across my face once."

Surprise, surprise. "Yuck," she said. She closed her eyes, practicing the well-developed art of catnapping. Eat when you can. Sleep when you can. Pee when you can. True in the army and true for investigations. When she woke, they were almost there.

"What time are we meeting Laura?"

"Four. Five. Whenever she gets free."

At her beck and call, in other words. "And I'm staying?"

"At the hotel next to the office."

"Nice place," she said, checking her watch. "So we'll have at least two hours."

His hands shifted on the wheel. He didn't say anything as he steered them off the highway, through city streets where everyone was buttoned up tight in their air-conditioned cars, and into the underground parking.

When they were waiting for the elevator, he said, "Two hours," very softly, and nothing more. He didn't look at her.

They took the elevator to the tenth floor, and she followed him down a quiet, carpeted corridor. Watched him stick the key in. The light flashed green, and they were inside. A giant bed. A big TV. The drapes closed. Nothing smelled hot or dusty or tired. Gracie slipped off her shoes.

Barefoot, she hardly reached his armpit. She watched as his nimble fingers took off his gun and undid his crisp blue shirt. Watched him carefully hang it over the desk chair. No undershirt. She slid her hands up his chest, her pale skin lovely against his café au lait, resting her fingertips on his shoulders.

She'd been alone too long, and this would keep her from thinking. "Rock my world," she said.

□   □   □

In her dream, they were all kids again. She and Patrick and their foster brothers, holed up in the tree house in the back yard, refusing to come down for supper. Her foster brothers—the real kids of the family, Irish twins only eleven months apart—were always the instigators. She and Pat the bad seeds, convenient fall guys for the blame.

The dream shifts, and this time, when they're in the tree house, they're playing pirates. Billy and Jack the pirates, she and Pat captives, Billy making them walk the plank. Pat small and scared and clinging to her leg. Gracie agreeing to walk the plank, if he'll spare Pat. Billy, grinning hugely, tying the bandanna blindfold over her eyes and making her walk out on the tree limb, both of them knowing what will happen. Gracie will walk. Gracie will fall. Then she'll get the belt for being so stupid. Only that time, she broke her arm and for once, Billy got the belt.

Billy was the scourge of her life. No way she could have imagined that twelve years later, she'd be ex-military working for the Marshal's Service and Billy would be a bank robber turned informant to save his handsome ass, and there would be insane chemistry between them. That the pain of that fall would be nothing to the pain of watching her foster brother's head blow apart—a scene she relived at least twice a night, which was the real reason she didn't sleep. Her dreams were always interrupted by that sudden shower of gore. Or that she'd lose it, a woman who prided herself on her cool. Pull her own gun, threaten everyone in sight as she tried to save a mission gone horribly wrong, and get banished to a tin can in the desert to redeem herself.

No way to imagine that out there in the desert, far from being redeeming, the goddamned thing would come full circle, what she was watching every night suddenly pulling her guts out. People who casually said it was a small world didn't know the freaking half of it. She had to wonder if Laura knew what she'd find out there, and that was why she was sent. She'd seen how Laura looked at Billy, the way all women looked at blue-eyed, black-haired piratical Billy.

She moaned and Dirkk's big arm snaked over her and pulled her tight against him. "Easy, Grace. Easy." He was so fit, it was like being up against a warm, breathing wall.

But now she was awake. She rolled onto her back and opened her eyes. "You rock."

"You sound surprised." He propped himself up on his elbow. "You shouldn't wear clothes, Grace. Ever," he said. "You're just so goddamned perfect."

"Hard to work undercover naked." She thought about how dumb that sounded.

He ran a finger down her body, from her chin to just below her navel. "So you've got something for us?"

"You bet. Isn't that why you brought me in?" She gave it a beat. "Who else knows about this?"

"No one. Laura's playing this one close to the vest."

She shoved back the sheet and stood. "We'd better hit the shower and make the bed. We don't want her getting jealous now, do we?"

He blinked at her.

"What?" she said, her voice low and honey smooth. "You thought I didn't know?"

"You're a strange woman."

Grace shook her head. "Perfect woman," she said. "Remember."

□ □ □

The AUSA stared at the images on Grace's screen, her small white teeth biting into her lower lip as the slide show progressed: The trailers, the cars and motorcycles, people's backs as they came and went. Close-ups of license plates.

"There are no faces," she complained.

Grace held up a warning hand. "Wait."

A slender man with a long black ponytail was backing out of a van. In the next shots, he was turning toward the camera. Turning. Turning. As he turned, Grace watched the other woman's face, waiting for the shock of recognition, for the frisson of disbelief. The gotcha. Laura's tight jaw actually dropped. For a moment, as she held her breath and stared at the small screen, she gaped like a landed fish.

Then she turned angrily on Grace. "This isn't new stuff," she said. "That's Billy, goddamn it, and we both know what happened to Billy. What are you trying to pull here?"

Your pointy little nose, Grace thought. She hit pause, stopping the show. She let it go a beat, then another, while Laura glared and blew through her nose like a bull. "*I* know what happened to Billy," Grace said. "I'm the one who got covered in his blood and brains, remember? So why the fuck would I try to sell you pictures of a dead guy?"

"Why don't you tell me?" Laura stalked to the end of the room, pale white pencil legs moving like chopsticks, and swiveled, hands on her hips. "Well?"

"Because that isn't Billy. That's his brother. That's Jack."

She'd seen how this would go from the moment, two days ago, when he turned and faced her scope, her e-mail that she was on to something already sent. Too late to take it back. She'd seen the arguing, disbelief, the back and forth. Laura prowling around in a self-important frenzy. The revelation that Grace had known Billy before, and Jack. And all the rest of the gut-wrenching crap that was coming. She wasn't ready to have the remnants of her life dragged out and inspected by a bunch of Feds without a heart among them.

They wouldn't understand anything.

She hit the play button and turned her back, letting the slide show go on without her, screening their voices, comments and questions through a haze of indifference, letting her mind float. It went the one place she didn't want it to. Back to the tree branch. The blindfold. She was walking the plank again and she knew it was going to hurt. Big time.

□ □ □

Finally, it was over, Laura and Dirkk both pumped with satisfaction. Clean. Neat and smug, like they'd been out on *their* bellies in the dirt and had arisen unscathed. They wouldn't, though. Not from this. This was about Billy and Jack. About family. About where past and present collided. It was going to get messy.

"Can we go eat somewhere?" she said. "Somewhere decent?"

The AUSA was willing; Dirkk, appetite whetted from rocking her world, eager.

"Give me a minute," she said, carrying her bag into the bathroom. She put on a bit of lip-gloss, a touch of shadow. Wound her hair into a discreet chignon. Attended to business.

She was slipping the laptop into her bag, when Dirkk said, "Why do that?"

"Because I don't want to leave it here. Because we could have been followed. Because these guys aren't just amateur meth cookers; this is a big operation with La Famiglia connections. I feel safer when I've got it with me." She jerked her chin at his briefcase; at the AUSA's. "Wouldn't you?"

He held out his hand. "You've got everything on a memory stick for us, right?"

Nodding, she crossed his palm with a small bit of silver.

Laura wasn't paying attention. She was standing by the bed, her thin nose sniffing, patches of red blooming on her cheeks. The look was about as flattering as Grace's housecoat. Women walked such a fine line. All Dirkk had to do was be. Be, and puff out his chest.

Then the AUSA turned on Dirkk. "You bastard! You two-timing, whoredog bastard."

"She's been out in the desert. She needed it." A graceful shrug of his shoulders. "It doesn't mean anything."

Grace hid her smile behind her hand. It was so satisfying to see icy Laura being unladylike. To see Dirkk's confident indifference, thinking he'd had her, and that it didn't matter. Gracie thought she'd had him. She felt her lingering fragment of guilt, like a bit of popcorn husk caught between teeth, loosen and be gone.

"We'll take my car," Dirkk said. He was the guy. Of course he'd want to drive.

Grace was hungry. She was thinking about food not eaten at a battered Formica table. About food smells that didn't have to war with dust and old grease. She was also thinking about her instinct that all hell was about to break loose. How underground parking garages always gave her creeps. How silk blouses and bulletproof vests didn't mix. How carrying her gun in her bag made her feel vulnerable. She liked it in the small of her back, like the weight and feel of it. Envied Dirkk's easy access.

The elevator spilled them out like pebbles, rolling from too bright light out across the greasy garage floor into patchy light and the scent of dusty cement, her heels and Laura's chattery and sharp in the silence. She heard the rubber squeal of tires, the confined roar of an engine. Felt Dirkk stiffen beside her, Laura still indifferent.

Two cars. Coming from opposite directions.

She tugged on Dirkk's arm. "Something feels wrong. Let's go back."

He shook her off as he pulled his gun. She was reaching for hers when the cars sandwiched them in beams of blinding blue-white light. She was backing toward darkness, toward the greater safety of parked cars, when shots exploded.

Laura gasping, staggering, falling. Screaming. Dirkk toppling like a felled tree. She had her gun up, firing at the bright blue lights, when she felt the hot stab in her chest. Suddenly she couldn't breathe.

Gracie walks the plank.

It wasn't supposed to happen like this.

Was it?

□   □   □

She knew where she was before she opened her eyes. Hospitals have a distinctive smell and the beds are always miserably uncomfortable, never mind the poor quality of the bedding. Not much better than her trailer.

A tired-looking man sat in the chair beside her bed. Only his eyes moved when she opened hers. The same russet hair and eyes like hers. Patrick was three years younger. Looked hard worn.

"Gracie," he said. Same honey over gravel voice, too. They could have sung duets.

"I walked the plank," she said. Today her voice was only gravel. No honey. She felt old as Methuselah. It hurt to breathe. It hurt to move. Her chest was swathed in the sticky discomfort of bandages and tape and she felt the tight beginnings of scars. No more perfect body.

"You do too much for me," he said. "You always did."

"Big sister," she said, still surprised she wasn't dead.

"Billy says to tell you he's sorry. He says he didn't have a choice."

Billy. The big brother who'd screwed up, sending Jack into the bank in his place, when he should have known what Jack would do. He hadn't saved *his* little brother. She saw herself gesturing for Dirkk, the fist against her chest. *Billy gets me right here.* Right here was almost where the bullet had entered. She wondered if the hole had let Billy out? Would he be gone from her now? She was beyond freakin' pathetic.

She closed her eyes.

"Does it hurt?" Patrick asked.

She didn't answer.

"You got nothing to worry about. Everything's gone," he

said. "The trailers. Your car. Computers. Memory sticks. Blown to kingdom come. It's a clean sweep."

"Clean?" she said. "People are dead."

"It was necessary, Gracie." He rose to go. "What are you going to do now?"

"Try to quit smoking. Get a grip." She started a laugh, but it hurt, so she stopped. "Buy a new housecoat. Tell a lot of lies. Hope I still have a job. I think."

He nodded, heading for the door. "Billy says goodbye."

"Patrick?"

He turned back, pivoting on his foot in that funny, boneless way, like he did when he was four. Gracie felt tears start. "Be nice if you could find someone new to play with."

"I'll try, sis."

She listened to his footsteps until they faded away, her hand over the hole near her heart

△   △   △

Kate Flora's eleven books include seven Thea Kozak mysteries, two gritty Joe Burgess police procedurals, a suspense thriller and a true crime. Finding Amy *was a 2007 Edgar® nominee, has been filmed for TV and is being considered for a movie. Flora's short stories have appeared in numerous anthologies, including the Sara Paretsky edited collection,* Sisters on the Case. *This ninth generation Mainer divides her time between Massachusetts and the Maine coast.*

Edith M Maxwell

Reduction in Force

Edith M. Maxwell

My phone rings. Patricia, my manager, says she needs to see me. Now. I am instantly numb: talk of layoffs has been buzzing in the halls for an hour. Pressing my lips together, I begin the long walk down through the blue-gray cubicles. Patricia has an office with a door.

I huddle half an hour later with my now-former coworkers. For years we've worked together, writing and debugging software to further the prospects of the company. It's all over. I feel like there's a knife behind my eyes and a scarf wrapped too tightly around my throat.

"So, Jackie, what'd Patricia say?" George asks, the furrows in his forehead deeper than usual.

"My position has been eliminated. Said she was sorry to have to do it. But that Corporate mandated a reduction in force. Ha." My mouth tastes bitter, and the knot in my stomach is a clump of lead.

"Where's Art?" I ask, looking around. Nobody knows.

"Well, I have packing to do." I fight to keep my voice from trembling. I march my five-foot self around the corner of the five-foot high cubicle wall and slam into Art's considerable bulk.

"Whoa, that was almost fun." This is one of Art's stock phrases, but his tone is not his usual. He puts out his arms to steady us both.

I look up and sigh. "You, too?"

"That's me, lovely lady. Out of a job after thirteen years."

His face is so drawn I almost hug him. I pat his arm instead. "Damn, Art. This place . . ."

"Well, hey, now I can go work at the wine store and get the employee discount, right?" Art's voice shakes and his eyes look vacant.

"Buy some for me, OK? I'm canned, too," Raymond says as he walks up to us. "I can't believe it! What are they thinking?" He blinks hard.

"Not you, too?"

"Oh, yeah, and I'm steamed! The company stock is doing fine, I do the work of three people, and this is the thanks I get from those jerks? Why me?" He clenches his large hands into fists and starts beating the right fist against his leg. "Why me?"

"I heard they're going to outsource our work to the Ukraine. Good freaking luck, that's what I say." Art hikes up his pants around an oversized midsection.

George escorts me out an hour later. "I'm really sorry about this. I know what you're going through."

I stare at him. "Listen. You're the team leader. You selected me out of everybody to be fired. You can't be that sorry." I head for the exit.

"But I am! Patricia told me I had to pick somebody, and I didn't want to lose any of you."

"Does she even know all the things I do? Does she have any idea about my areas of expertise?" I increase my pace.

"I'm sure you'll get another job soon."

"Yeah, maybe. It's not exactly the best economy out there."

"Listen, I . . ."

"Have a great life, George." I open the door to a blast of July heat.

□   □   □

The gin and tonic tastes perfect in the late-afternoon New England sun. My former group is probably headed out for the weekly drink session. Without me. I watch my cat, Athena, reposing in the shade, while I gaze at the dark purple clusters on the butterfly bush next to the showy bells of an angel's trumpet plant. I decide to do some pruning. Now that I have time.

It's been a month since I was canned. I've applied for over two dozen positions, but applications either enter a void or companies say hiring is frozen. Art's worse off. He has four children and a wife with MS to support. Raymond went on a hunting trip with his buddies right after the layoff. Said he needed time to think about his future.

"You'd think somebody in the group might care enough to check in and see how we're doing," I address Athena. I glare at my silent cell phone. "Nobody even asks. They don't write, they don't call." I finish my drink and get back to weeding the vegetable patch.

My phone rings after all. I dust my hands on my shorts as I walk to the picnic table to retrieve it. "Art! How're you doing?"

Art says he's fine, and that Patricia wants him to come back on a contract basis.

"Do you think she needs anyone else?"

"I don't know. Give her a call. How have you been, anyway?"

"You know how it is. I can't really relax and enjoy being home, because I'm supposed to be finding a job. Except there aren't any." I switch the phone to my other ear. "I guess this is what retirement is like, if I were twenty-five years older and had a lot of money in the bank. Which I'm not, and which I don't."

"I'm worried about Raymond, you know. He's a sensitive kid under all that bluster."

"I know. He hasn't answered my emails lately."

We chat a few more minutes. Art says that using developers in the Ukraine wasn't quite working out for several reasons, not the least of which were the language barrier and the seven-hour lag between Eastern Daylight Time and Eastern European Summer Time. Surprise, surprise.

□　□　□

A chill washes over me as I sit in Patricia's office. I remember the last time I took this chair.

"Would you like some tea?" Patricia says. "I'm having a cup." She's florid and looks stuffed into her blue knit jacket and skirt. Brown hair straggles back from a round face, and her finger is puffed up around the ring on her right hand. With a bare left hand she pulls out a tissue and blows a reddened nose.

I take a surreptitious deep breath. "Yes, thank you." I take a sip. It's bitter. Patricia actually likes this?

"Excuse my allergies. Fall, you know." Patricia swallows a small yellow pill. "So, we'd like to offer you a three-month contract. George will be your team lead again. The contract might be extended if things work out."

Oh, fun. "The same work I did before I left?"

"Yes. The, uh, outsourcing was not as successful as we'd hoped."

"I'd like a day to think about it." I set my mug down.

"Certainly." Patricia stands. "We'd like you to start Monday if you can."

"I'll let you know by tomorrow. Are Art and Raymond back, too?"

"Art is. Raymond seems to have decided to follow a new career path." Patricia avoids my eyes as we shake hands.

□　□　□

I sit on my couch and peruse the offer letter. The hourly pay is good, as it should be for a top engineer, but the contract doesn't include benefits.

"Can I bring myself to work with people who now seem to think I'm some kind of pariah?" I ask Athena. She turns her eyes up to gaze at me, giving that you-never-pet-me-enough look. My eyes fall on the mortgage bill. I can't risk losing the house. The severance package runs out next week, and I was lucky to get even that much. Unemployment checks won't cover my expenses. The whole situation sucks.

Curious, I dial Raymond's number, a bit surprised when he picks up. Twenty minutes later I hang up and rub my ear. Raymond ranted about Patricia, working in hi-tech, the job market, the President, and firearms laws. Whew. Said he was working at a friend's bakery and had no plans to return to programming anytime soon.

So, Raymond won't be back in the group. That's a shame—he was one of our most creative programmers, if a little unstable. Maybe baking will do him good.

I spend the afternoon deadheading flowers in my garden, imagining each is Patricia, and collecting seedpods for varieties I want to propagate next spring. I remove the diseased tomato vines and plant spinach in the cold frame. I pull several other plants and spread them in the shed to dry.

After I clean up, I call Patricia and accept the offer, then send Art an email. He replies immediately, saying that, yes, he's there on a three-month contract. Says it isn't much fun to be back alongside former coworkers, and while it's great to be earning money again, it's hard not to hold a grudge.

I still feel like I was stabbed in the back, too. Did they think I was in the "Eccentric and Deadwood" category? Before I lost my job, that's what I tended to assume about people who were laid off— either they were too weird to keep around, or they'd stopped being productive. I sigh, and call my friend Elise to arrange a hike.

☐   ☐   ☐

Art and I sit alone with sandwiches at an outdoor table on Monday. A maple tree nearby is reddening with the cool weather and a vee of geese honk southward.

"Welcome back, my sweet desert flower," Art says before he bites into his lunch. "What do you think of this contract business?"

"Haven't been back long enough to think anything." I push windy hair off my brow. "What do you think? You've been back, what, three weeks?"

"It's definitely strange. Patricia seems to want to be very friendly. But I haven't gotten over being angry yet. You know?" Art picks at the edge of his Styrofoam cup with a fingernail bitten to the quick.

"I don't think I'm as angry at Patricia as Raymond is, but I still feel that combination of hurt, confusion, and just plain pissed off."

Art leans across the table. "Speak of the devil . . ."

Patricia stumps across the parking lot toward us. Her heavy thighs strain at a brown tweed skirt and the low heels she wears do not bring out the best in her calves.

"Oh, I'm glad I caught both of you!" She approaches our table. "We're ramping up for the next release, and I'm going to need extra hours from you. I'm sure you can use the money, right?" She's wheezing after her short walk from the other building where the executive offices are.

"Beyond forty hours, you mean?" I ask.

"Yes. We'll need some overtime, if we're going to fix all the priority-1 bugs before RTM. You're part of the team again!" She smiles, but the tension lines between her eyebrows remain.

RTM, release to manufacturing, is in three weeks, and the first customer shipment, FCS, follows by a week. I examine the plastic wrap from my sandwich, saying nothing. Part of the team, my ass.

"Whatever you say, boss," Art says, looking at me.

"That's settled then. Ta-ta." Patricia pulls her ID badge out of a pocket and heads for the building.

"I'm not working any weekends."

"I, for one, need the extra money," Art says. "She's absolutely right."

"Sure she is, that's the problem. Or one of them." I jab at my sandwich. "The good thing about being a contractor is supposed to be that you don't have to be part of the damn team. Just do the work and get out."

"Remember, my friend, it's a paycheck."

"I know, Art. When I was part of the company, when I felt like they wanted me, I was willing to work weekends, do the whole corporate thing. But now? Never."

□   □   □

Over the next several weeks, I program, debug, and attend code reviews. I spend little time schmoozing in the halls. Our former team members treat us like we're contagious, anyway. Art's the only colleague I want to socialize with, and he's busy, too. Things aren't going well for the release. FCS is pushed out a fortnight.

Occasionally Patricia stops by and invites me for a cup of tea. It feels like an order. I always accept, forcing myself to make small talk and take at least several sips of the awful brew.

"I noticed that you weren't in this weekend," Patricia says one day.

I peer at her in the faint light. Why she keeps her office so dark is a mystery. The small lamp on her desk and the light from her monitor provide the only illumination.

"We really need you to put in some extra hours. We have revenue recognition that depends on it."

"I had a family emergency and couldn't make it."

"Oh, what's wrong?"

"It's personal, Patricia." I'm not about to tell her anything, particularly when the emergency was a critical attack of not feeling like working on a Saturday for the benefit of a company that doesn't even want me as a regular employee. "I've been doing ten-hour days during the week, though."

□   □   □

"What's up?" I ask Art when he stops by my cube late one afternoon.

He says he called Raymond, asked him to meet us for a drink. "I feel guilty, you know? We're working and he's not. At least not for real money."

I agree and grab my coat. Drinks are always a good idea.

Raymond is waiting for us outside and we walk to the pub. Raymond talks, fast, about how he likes working with his hands kneading bread, although he doesn't earn even half of what software development pays. His voice is bitter when he refers to our being rehired. He repeatedly adjusts his leather jacket and taps his fingers on his leg.

We return to the side door of the building just as the sun sets. We're saying goodbye when Raymond announces, "I need to come in and use the head. It's a long drive home."

Although Security often reminds employees to make sure visitors are cleared through the front desk, this is Raymond. I look at Art. "We'll walk you down there. You know, it's kind of against policy for you to even be in here without a Visitor's badge."

Art says, "Say 'hi' to the old gang if you want."

"I'd rather never see that bitch, Patricia, again." Raymond gives a short barking laugh, but the look on his face is grim.

We walk down the central hallway, passing model spacecraft hung from the ceiling above an ubergeeks's cubicle and a whiteboard scrawled with algorithms.

Raymond takes a sudden turn to the right. Toward Patricia's office. I guess he wants to say "hi," after all, and we follow him.

Patricia looks up from her desk, annoyed. "Yes?" From behind Raymond, I see her eyebrows lift. Her mouth opens in horror.

Raymond is pointing a pistol at her.

I try to back away to call Security, but Raymond grabs my arm with his left hand as he glares at his former boss. Am I going to be shot, too? My hands are cold, and my face is hot. My heart is beating so hard it feels like a sledgehammer.

"You can't jerk people's lives around, bitch," Raymond snarls. "You almost ruined Art's family. You screwed around with Jackie, think you have her where you want her, and me, well, you don't care about me, do you?"

"Raymond, just calm down!" Patricia says in a fast, high voice. "It wasn't my decision, you know."

"Screw that, lady." He chops the air with the gun with every word. "Even if they told you to 'reduce the force' by three people, it was still you who decided who got it!"

Suddenly, Art has Raymond prone on the floor pinning his gun wrist with one hand. Art grasps a handful of Raymond's hair with the other. Raymond isn't going anywhere with Art on top of him.

"Drop the gun, young man, and be quiet," Art commands as Raymond struggles. "You just ruined your own life all by yourself."

"Art, you're amazing," I say, leaning against the wall so my rubbery legs don't betray me.

"I may be a fat guy, but you never forget Marine training. Now go get Security."

◻   ◻   ◻

I sit in the dark on the floor in front of my French doors that evening, swirling bourbon on a couple of melting ice cubes. Raymond and his crazy bravery. Definitely crazy, but brave, too, to try to achieve a kind of justice not only in his own life but also on behalf of me and Art.

I walk to the kitchen and turn on the light. It's time to start work on that project.

◻   ◻   ◻

The next day dawns cold and windy. I tuck a box of tea into my bag before I leave the house. After I arrive at work, I walk straight to Patricia's office. The door is closed, as usual, so I knock on the strip of glass next to it. The blinds behind it are also closed, as usual.

I hear Patricia's voice and open the door.

"Good morning." I lean on the doorjamb. "Are you OK after yesterday? That was quite a shock."

Patricia looks up from the computer. "If you and Art hadn't let him in the building, it wouldn't have happened." Her voice is terse. Tense lines pull at her eyes and mouth, and her hands shake on the keyboard. "But yes, thanks for asking. I am fine."

"That's good. I just wanted to bring you some of your favorite tea, since I've been drinking half of it."

Patricia raises her eyebrows and tilts her head, and then smiles, looking pleased and surprised. "Thank you. Stop by this afternoon for a cup, will you?"

"If I get today's bugs resolved, I will."

I walk to my cubicle and pull off my coat and gloves. I settle into my chair but don't open my email or start to work. Around me are sounds of keyboarding, office chairs creaking, two deep voices discussing the latest Patriots game, and always in the background, the hum of thousands of motors and fans powering the brainwork of software creation. I open the list of bugs assigned to me for fixing. It's unlikely I'll have them done in time to have tea with Patricia.

□   □   □

On Monday morning, I stare at an email message. Dated Friday morning, it's from Patricia, with a copy to the VP of Engineering. Patricia praises my design skills and work ethic, and recommends I be rehired on a salaried basis. I feel a sudden cold queasiness.

I'm reading a message from Corporate—"Third quarter revenues were up"—when a knock at my cubicle opening makes me whirl my chair around.

"Relax, lovely lady," Art sinks into the spare chair. "Just fat boy here. Any idea where the boss is?"

I shake my head. "Am I my manager's keeper?"

"I'm supposed to have a progress review with her. She hinted that she might be recommending me for rehire. On salary. But she didn't answer when I knocked."

My queasiness increases, but I lift my shoulders and eyebrows, then drop them. "No idea. Did you send her an email?"

"Yeah. No reply."

"Is her car here? You know she always parks in the same spot."

"Didn't she say something about it being in the shop for a while?"

"Oh, yeah." I turn back to my monitor and the familiar lines of code. "Listen, I have a review after lunch, so I need to get this finished up."

"Sure, I'll leave you to it." A siren pulses outside, getting closer.

"Hope it isn't another damn fire drill."

The vice-president of Engineering sends an email to the department an hour later. Patricia Demers, senior manager of the User Interface group, has been found dead in her office that morning of unknown causes. More information, including details about the wake, will be passed along as it becomes available.

I drop by Art's cubicle on my way out of the building.

"Going home early, are we?" Art leans back in his chair.

"Why not? Some news." My quavering voice reveals how I feel: shaky, bad.

"That lady never looked very healthy. Think it was her heart, or maybe a stroke?"

"I don't know. Too bad Raymond is in jail for something that was about to happen anyway."

"Did she have family? Hubby?"

"No idea. She didn't wear a wedding ring, and the only picture in her office was of two little dogs." I shrug. "I wonder who's going to manage us now?"

"Maybe they'll promote George."

"Maybe. See you tomorrow." Whew. I need to get out of there.

□   □   □

I put the unused stems, seeds, and leaves from the angel's trumpet plants I had dried down my seldom-used garbage disposal and run it with the water on full for twice as long as it needs. I wipe down the counter with disinfectant spray and scrub my hands. I feed the extra papers and wrapping from the Press-N-Brew tea bag kit through my paper shredder. I also shred the information I'd printed out about the toxic, often deadly effects of Datura tea, particularly on people with respiratory and circulatory issues, and then put away my iron. In the long autumn gloaming, I take the paper shreddings out to my compost pile and thoroughly mix them in with the vegetable waste and rotting garden refuse, watering the pile several times.

I sit on the garden bench and watch while the sky becomes

completely dark. Funny, isn't it, how death can be arranged when it's least expected and most deserved? Patricia's email from Friday made me feel slightly nauseous, however. And Art's comments about Patricia's hints to him—had I ruined his chances at regaining his job? Several diehard leaves rustle and a cold breeze runs its fingers over my scalp.

Inside the house, the doorbell rings. Damn. My heart races and a tic beats under my eye. So there's no perfect crime, after all. I gaze at my living room through the glass doors. Light pushes out onto the dark deck. My house looks like it belongs to someone else: a safe, comfortable, unconflicted refuge.

I walk like a zombie to the door. I wait a moment, steeling myself, rehearsing my confession.

I open the door and just stand there.

Elise stares. "Jackie, what's wrong? Come on! We're late for the meeting."

I stare back. Right. Monday. Hiking club.

△　△　△

Edith M. Maxwell, a software technical writer, lives on the Massachusetts North Shore. "Obake for Lance" appeared in Riptide *(2004); she has two other published short stories, as well.* Speaking of Murder, *a mystery featuring linguistics professor and Quaker Lauren Rousseau, is in search of an agent. Edith, mother, world traveler, and Ph.D. in Linguistics, also gardens and tends cats.*

Size Matters

Sheila Connolly

"She's a medium."

"What?" I tried to focus on Jani's voice. It beat throwing up, which was what I really wanted to do. "Well, if she was, she sure didn't see this coming."

"No, I mean, she's a medium. Size. You know?"

"Oh." I forced myself to look at the blood-soaked body that lay crumpled on the floor of the dressing room. The harsh fluorescent lighting made her look awful. But then, even healthy people looked awful in that light. "And why are you telling me this?"

Jani looked more excited than upset. "Think about it. Look at what she's wearing."

"I don't want to." But as manager, I was responsible for taking care of messes at the store, and this qualified as the biggest mess in my seventeen-and-a-half months at Sharp. So I had to look, if only so I could tell the police about it. Her. Short answer: body, female, twentyish, bloody. Ick. "All right, I'm looking. She's dead. What else am I supposed to notice?"

Jani gave me a pitying look. "Her shirt."

I squinted. Yes, Jani was right: she was wearing a shirt. Duh. "So?"

"It's the wrong size."

"Huh?" I definitely was not following.

Luckily, Jani was patient, for a teenager. "She's a medium. She's got on an XL."

I felt a stab of annoyance. "Jani, so what? Maybe that's her fashion thing."

Even before I finished, Jani was shaking her head. "No, no, no. Look, I know her. She buys medium, sometimes even small. Size four jeans. She likes to flash her body, you know?"

I was still processing what Jani had said first. "You know her? Who is she?"

Jani hesitated. "Well, I know what she buys, see? I don't know her name." Then she brightened. "But I betcha we can check credit card receipts. I know she never paid cash."

"So she's—she was—a regular customer? Then that's what we'll tell the police." She didn't look familiar to me. But then, people usually look different when they're dead, don't they? "Time to call them."

I swear, Jani looked disappointed. "Can I stick around? Maybe they'll let me help."

"Sure, Jani. Okay, here's the deal: I'll make the call, and you clear out any customers and pull down the grill in front until the police get here. Go!"

Jani went. Me, I sat down on the plastic bench along the wall opposite the dressing rooms and took several deep breaths. So far I had kept my cool: when I saw the feet sticking out of the cubicle, I had hoped that it was the usual—a mallrat who had passed out from the drug du jour. It wouldn't be the first time that had happened. When I had opened the door, the blood had convinced me otherwise, fast. Luckily, there had been no customers in the store, because we had been open only a few minutes, and it was a Tuesday morning. I had forgotten to warn Jani to make up a story for any unfortunate person out front. Saying, "Sorry, one of our customers has just been murdered" would not exactly encourage business. As manager, I was supposed to think about things like that.

Murdered. No doubt about that. Not that I'd examined the body that closely. But there was a lot of blood, and it still looked pretty sticky. How long had the girl been dead?

And where had the killer gone?

When I hit that thought, I jumped up from the bench, then dropped to my knees and peered up and down the hallway. Nope, nobody in any of the other cubicles. Or at least, nobody with feet on the ground. No way was I brave enough to open each and every door and check.

I backed away to the employee phone in the alcove at the entrance to the dressing rooms, grabbed it and hit 911. Keeping an eye on the row of cubicles, I gave the operator the bare bones. "There's a body in the dressing room at Sharp, at the Heritage Place Mall. Yes, she's dead." Nobody turns that color and lives. A very unflattering color. "I don't know how she died. I haven't touched her." I don't want to touch her, not now, not ever. "But there's lots of blood. It's just me and one clerk here now. We'll keep anyone else out. Yes, we'll wait here. Thank you."

I laid the phone down to keep the line open, and turned to see Jani hovering at the entrance to the dressing rooms. "They're on their way," I said. "You cleared the place?"

"Yup, no problem. There were only a couple of customers."

"What did you tell them?"

"That the last shipment of T-shirts came from China and might be toxic."

Great short-term solution; lousy long-term solution. I sighed. "And you shut the gate?"

"Yes, ma'am. So, do we need to get our stories straight?"

"What stories? I opened up, I came in here, I found a body. What else is there?"

Jani bounced on the balls of her feet. "But I told you, I knew her, at least sort of. So I can help the cops to ID her. But what about evidence?"

"Jani, what are you talking about?" Jani was bright. She was working at Sharp as part of a work-study program at her high school, and she planned to go to design school. She was eager and didn't complain about boring tasks like shelving new stock or picking up the clothes that her peer group left crumpled on the dressing room floor. She was a good employee, but I didn't recall seeing "detective" on her brief resume. "What evidence?"

Jani grinned at me, relieved that I was willing to play along. "Okay, how long do you think she's been there?"

"How should I know?"

"Was the blood wet or dry?"

I was beginning to see where she was going with this. "Halfway in between?"

"You closed last night at nine-thirty, right? Was she here then? Did she hide out somewhere overnight? Or did she come in sometime after we closed?"

Any of the choices made me look like a lousy manager. I certainly should have been aware of anyone loitering near closing. I tried to remember what I had done the evening before. It had been a slow night. I'd locked up as usual, and all locks had been in place when I opened up this morning, not that anybody with the slightest criminal intent couldn't have gotten in if they really wanted to. And I knew I had cleared the dressing rooms and made sure there weren't any discarded clothes there. I like to leave things neat. That makes me feel better.

"I'm pretty sure she wasn't here last night when I closed."

"So, somebody probably sneaked in her body overnight. Wow."

"She wasn't killed here," I said firmly. "There would have been a lot more blood, all over the place."

Jani's brow wrinkled. "Good point. Hmmm. Puddle of blood, but did you see any wounds?"

Reluctantly I dredged up the image of the dead girl, and realized what Jani was saying. "No," I said slowly, "I didn't. Her shirt was bloody, but I didn't see any visible stab wounds or bullet holes. And I don't think her throat was cut, or she slit her wrists, or anything like that."

"I'll check." Jani bounded off down the row, her pink Converse high-tops flashing.

"Jani, don't touch anything! Fingerprints!" I yelled after her.

She skidded to a stop. "Oh, right." She darted back and found a wad of discarded plastic, covered her hand carefully and opened the door to the Cubicle of Death. After staring into it for several seconds, she shut the door gently with her still-covered hand and made her way back to where I waited. She was distinctly paler than she had been.

"No, no visible wounds," she said in a shaky voice. "But you know what that means?"

"Uh, no."

"It means she wasn't killed in that shirt! Somebody put it on her after they'd stabbed or shot or whatevered her! I told you it was the wrong size!"

"Why would anyone do that?"

Jani looked crestfallen. "I don't know. Did you see if she was wearing a bra? Maybe somebody had a thing against naked corpses."

"I most certainly did not check out her underwear! But you're saying that someone killed her and dressed her afterward?"

"Exactly. This girl was into what was new. That's why I remember her. No way she would hang at the mall wearing the wrong size shirt. It was *not* her shirt. And it's not one of ours."

"If you say so," I said dubiously. Maybe I was losing my eye for style, or maybe I just couldn't see past all that blood. "So, if it wasn't her shirt, and it wasn't from here, where did the shirt come from?"

"From the crime scene, of course." Jani, unconcerned, moved on to another question. "There was blood on the floor, right? So she was still bleeding when whoever it was dumped her there. Maybe she wasn't even dead."

"Jani!" For a moment I felt a flash of horror at the thought of that poor girl dying on the floor of my store.

Jani had the grace to look ashamed. "Okay, not cool. But still, it's got to mean something, right? So say he slashed her or whatever, and panicked, and decided this was a great place to dump her—like, her favorite store. So wherever he did it, there's got to be spatter and all that stuff . . ."

"You've been watching too many television shows," I said sternly, although I probably watched the same ones. "Anyway, that's not our problem. Let the police sort it out."

"I'm just thinking out loud, right? It beats thinking about *her*, lying in there. You think he hung around until he was sure she was dead?"

I shook my head. I didn't even want to think about that. We both fell silent, in tribute to the late Ms. Medium.

The police arrived ten minutes later, and I wrestled with the security grill to let them in. They were a mismatched pair, one mid-size, thirtyish, probably a 38 long; the other painfully young, his neck barely filling his uniform collar. Older Guy gave Younger Guy a nudge, and Younger Guy spoke. "What seems to be the problem, ma'am?"

When did I become a "ma'am"? The officer couldn't be more than five years younger than me. Well, maybe eight. I *think* he had to shave every day.

"When I came in this morning, I found a body in the dressing room."

The officer had pulled out a small notebook and was busy scribbling. "When you say body, ma'am, you mean a dead person?"

It's not easy to talk between clenched teeth. "Yes, Officer, there is a dead person in the dressing room."

"Are you sure this person is dead, ma'am?"

What was it with the "ma'am"? "She is not breathing, and there is blood all over the place."

The officer jotted something else, then looked around. "What is this place?"

Earth, you dummy. "This is Sharp. It's a clothing store, part of a regional chain."

"The body was here when you arrived?"

I nodded.

"What time did you close last night?"

"Nine-thirty. I tidied up and left around ten."

"And the body wasn't here when you left?"

"No. I think I would have noticed."

The juvenile officer was spared any more of my sarcasm when Jani emerged from the back of the store. "Teddy!" she squealed.

Officer Teddy fought a smile, but the smile won. "Hey, Jani. You work here?"

"I do. And you're investigating our murder? How cool is that?"

Hello? I was still standing here. "Would you like to see the body, Officer?"

Officer Teddy tore his eyes away from Jani. It did not take a detective to deduce that they knew each other, but there were more serious matters at hand. Like a murder.

But Officer Teddy was on the job. He squared his shoulders, looked me in the eye, and said, "Show me the body."

I led the way to the entrance to the dressing rooms, stopped, and pointed. Even from where we stood, the poor girl's feet were visible. "There she is."

I wasn't about to go any further, but Junior strode forward manfully to investigate. Older Guy stayed behind. He leaned against the doorjamb and sighed. "Damn, I hate training the new ones."

"Hey, officer sir, you have a name?"

He nodded. "Detective Richard Jarvis. I assume you do too, although Junior didn't bother to ask for it."

"Kristin Foster. Kris." Hmmm . . . Richard. Detective Dick. *No, don't go there, Kris.* This dead body stuff was making me light-headed.

"With a K?" The detective had pulled out a notebook of his own and dutifully wrote it down.

"Right." At this rate the investigation would take a month, and in the meantime I was losing sales. "Listen, you sure Teddy is up to the job?"

"Got me. It's his first murder. But we've all got to start somewhere." He lapsed into silence, and we waited.

But not for long. Officer Teddy backed out of the cubicle, his face an interesting shade of bilious green, or maybe it was pale lime. "Presence of a dead person confirmed, sir," he said in a strangled voice, swallowing several times.

"And what do you do next, officer?" Detective Jarvis said patiently.

"Uh . . . call in the forensic team?" Junior recovered quickly: his ears pricked up like an eager puppy's.

"Very good, officer. Why don't you do that? Oh, and also the Medical Examiner."

"Yes, sir! I think I should go out there to make those calls, sir." Without waiting for permission, he bolted toward the front of the store. *Please don't barf on the displays, Junior,* I prayed.

I turned to Detective Dick. Oops—Jarvis. "Do you think we could pick up the pace a little here? Because I've got a store to run."

The detective looked down at me. "Obviously you haven't been involved in a murder investigation before, Ms. Foster. This is going to take some time. But I think Teddy there has his hands full, so why don't I take your statement? Is there someplace we can sit?"

There was my office, which was really a corner of the storeroom with a chair, a telephone, and a countertop that I had to shovel clear whenever I needed to do paperwork. There had to be another chair around somewhere, maybe under all the returns. "This way."

Because I didn't know anything, it took no more than five minutes to spill it all. The second repetition took even less time. By the time Detective Jarvis had dotted the i's and crossed the t's, the first wave of forensic people had arrived, and we went out to watch the show. Apparently Officer Teddy had pulled himself together enough to take Jani's statement: we found them standing in the front, Jani gesticulating, Teddy scribbling. We arrived for the tail end of it.

"So, you see, it's like, she couldn't have been wearing that shirt. It was all wrong."

Officer Teddy stopped writing. I watched as he and Detective Dick exchanged a glance. Jani and I swapped looks of our own: *Men! Clueless!*

The senior detective turned to us. "Ladies, why don't you go and get a cup of coffee somewhere? There's nothing you can do here until the team is done. We'll call you back if we need anything else."

I was torn. This was my territory, and I was responsible for what went on. At the same time, I really didn't want to see them haul the bloody body out. Easy choice. I smiled up at Detective Dick. "Why, certainly, Detective. Jani, why don't we go right over there?" There was a fast food place across the wide corridor. "Then you can find us easily. Right?"

Detective Dick responded absently, "Fine." Apparently we were dismissed for now.

I smiled at him. "Oh, and please try not to get that fingerprint powder stuff all over the merchandise?" I had a feeling it would never come out, and I didn't think corporate headquarters would let me write off the loss.

"I'll see what I can do," the detective said. "Now go."

I grabbed Jani's arm, and we fled across the corridor.

We bought coffee and plunked ourselves down at a table with a clear view of Sharp. When Detective Dick looked our way, I waggled my fingers at him. He nodded without smiling, then turned his attention to the crew of people bustling around the store.

"What now, boss?" Jani said.

"How do you know Teddy?" I asked.

"I've gone out with his younger brother. Teddy's not a real bright bulb, if you know what I mean, but he's a nice guy."

"Is he a good cop?"

Jani shrugged. "No idea. I think he just joined the force a couple of months ago. I was surprised to see him here. I didn't think they let the rookies do much of anything for a while."

"You told him about your T-shirt theory?"

Jani looked disgusted. "Yeah, and I can tell he thought it was *really* important."

I considered. I should call Sharp corporate HQ and tell them what was going on, let them get the PR team cranked up to handle any negative publicity that might crop up. Might? That *would* appear, especially if it was a slow news day. And that meant sales would fall off at my store, and I didn't need that. The current lousy economy had cut way into our profits, and somehow I'd end up being blamed, and I couldn't afford to lose this job. That made me mad. I wasn't about to watch my career in retail go down the tubes, because the police were going to take their own sweet time in solving this crime.

I looked at my watch; I looked across at the store. No news crews in sight yet, but I'd bet my paycheck that they would show up in time for the mid-day broadcast, if there was nothing else more urgent. So I didn't have much time to figure out what had happened, which, if I did, would make me look like a real heroine and maybe even clinch my promotion. Now all I had to do was find out who killed the girl, whoever she was. In the next hour.

I sat up straighter. "Okay, Jani. Tell me everything you can remember about the dead girl."

Jani frowned. "I thought I did."

"Humor me."

Jani sat back in her chair and stared at the ceiling. "Okay. Twenty, twenty-one, maybe. Five foot six, about 140 pounds. Blonde hair, not natural, maybe some extensions. Deluding herself about what size she wears, but lots of people do that."

Wow, Jani really did have a good eye. "How often did she come in?"

"Maybe twice a week?"

"She check the sale racks or new stuff?"

Jani was beginning to get into this. She leaned forward, elbows on the table. "Always new. She could spot a new shipment from across the mall."

"She a looker or a buyer?"

"Looked at a lot, tried on a lot, usually bought something, but one, two pieces at a time. Not a big spender, but steady."

"When was the last time she was in?"

Jani shut her eyes to concentrate. "Not yesterday. Sunday, I think. Yeah, Sunday afternoon. We were kind of busy, but she picked up a couple of shirts."

"Jani, this is great! Now we need to figure out why she ended up in our store last night. Oh, was she with anyone? Sunday, or ever?"

Jani shook her head. "I don't remember seeing her with anyone, male or female. Real loner—or maybe she just took her shopping seriously and didn't want to be distracted."

I thought harder. "Okay, if she was dumped in our store, why? And how? The doors were locked when I came in."

Jani snorted. "Like that makes a difference. You do know that all the managers have a master key to get in the back?"

I wanted to hit myself on the head. Of course I knew that. I had one. And I had to fill out a whole batch of paperwork, and go through a criminal records check, before the mall administration would give me one. "Oh, right. So, if we assume that someone came in the back door and dumped her, that narrows down the suspects, right? To store managers?"

"Sure. Or somebody who has access to the manager's key."

I couldn't just sit still and let some unknown creep trash my career. "Well, if somebody managed to transport the body, then, like you said, it would take someone big to carry her, because we know she wasn't dragged. Right? We know any beefy managers?"

Jani looked at me with a gleam in her eye. "The guy at the sports store. He isn't big, but he works out, and he lets everyone know it."

"But why would he kill our girl?"

"How should I know?"

I stood up. "Well, why don't we go talk to him? Maybe something will pop out." I looked across at Sharp, but nobody was paying any attention to us. "Let's go."

When we walked into the sports store, Jani pointed silently: Beefy Guy was behind the register. I recognized him in a vague kind of way, but I didn't remember ever talking to him. As I walked toward him, I tried to think of something to say.

He solved the problem for me. "Oh, hey, hi! You work over at Sharp, right? What's goin' on?"

"Um, I found a body there this morning." A girl sure doesn't get to say that very often.

He looked impressed. "No way! Dead?"

"Very dead."

"You know her?" Beefy asked.

My radar pinged. How did he know it was a "her"? We sold both men's and women's clothes. "No, but Jani says she's seen her in the store."

"That sucks. Hate to lose a customer, right?"

Beefy didn't appear too broken up about it. To my uneducated eye, it looked like Beefy had been helping himself to some handy steroids. Still, it was a big jump from XL shirts and steroids to murder. And why would he do it?

The answer walked out of the storeroom. Willowy blonde, skin-tight jeans, ridiculously high heels. She sashayed up to Beefy and laid a proprietary hand on a bulging bicep. "What's going on?"

Beefy looked at me to explain, but I was too busy goggling at Blondie's chest to answer. No, not her boobs, although, given their symmetrical immobility, they had to be fake. But the T-shirt stretched across them read "Babe." One of ours, from the shipment that we had unpacked yesterday morning to inventory but hadn't put out on the shelves yet. I could feel Jani beside me, quivering like a teacup Chihuahua. I jabbed her with my elbow.

"Hey, nice shirt," I said. Luckily Jani kept her mouth shut.

Blondie beamed. "Yeah, Sid here just gave it to me this morning. Wasn't that sweet? He thought it would make my new additions look good." She shoved out her chest even further, which I wouldn't have thought possible. The Babe logo bulged right along with her.

I thought furiously. What did I have? A guy big enough—and apparently stupid enough—to do the deed, and a T-shirt that shouldn't be where it was. Not exactly an airtight case. But if Beefy—er, Sid— had killed our girl, there must be blood somewhere, and close. Not in the sales area. Blood was hard to get out of carpets, and he couldn't have had much time to clean up. The storeroom? But what excuse could I give him to check out the storeroom right now?

A wild thought slammed me. I took at look at Blondie and decided she might buy it. I leaned in close. "Hey, you know, I'm thinking of having mine done, too. Could you show me what your surgeon did? Maybe I'll go to him."

I held my breath while she processed my lame request. Her eyes fell to my chest, and a look of pity flashed across her face. "Hey, sure. I'm real happy with mine. Gee, maybe he'll give me a finder's fee or something. Come on, let's go into the back room, and I'll show you." Bingo!

Jani looked at me as though I had lost my mind, and I shot her a warning glance. I followed Blondie into the storeroom, admiring the tramp stamp peeking over her low-rise jeans. Inside, she peeled up her T-shirt, revealing . . . Heck, I didn't really care what she revealed: I was busy scanning the entire room for anything that looked like blood.

And I found it. If you weren't looking for it, you wouldn't have noticed, but once you knew it was there, there were little droplets everywhere. Beefy Sid wasn't a great housekeeper, but he'd probably been in a hurry. I dragged my attention back to Blondie, who was prattling on happily about her 36Ds. I tried to make admiring noises. Luckily, we were interrupted by a bellow from Beefy.

"Hey, you better get out here. There's something goin' on at your store—TV cameras and stuff."

"Nice work," I tossed back at Blondie, as I hurried toward the front of the store. Sid was right: the news vultures had arrived and were setting up lights and doing sound checks and whatever news people do. I checked my watch: 11:47. I nodded at Jani. "We'd better get back there." Then I turned to Beefy. "Want to come watch?"

Beefy wavered for a moment, but there were no customers in the store. He followed us across the corridor, with Blondie in tow. I leaned close to Jani and whispered, "You saw her shirt?"

"Yeah! Sid?" she hissed. The girl was smart. I nodded, and then I shoved my way to the front of the gathering crowd and motioned to Detective Dick. He ignored me. Jani sidled up to Officer Junior and whispered in his ear, and I saw his eyes swivel to Beefy, now standing beside me. Junior started moving slowly toward us.

The TV lights flashed on and focused on the storefront. Newscasters ran through their lead-ins, and then all microphones swiveled toward Detective Dick, who launched into his statement. "At approximately nine o'clock this morning, the body of an unidentified woman was found in . . ."

Before he could go further, I elbowed my way to his side, then turned to face the cameras. "I'm Kris Foster, manager of Sharp, and I found the body. And I know who killed her: him." I pointed at Beefy, who looked startled. And then his face turned bright red, and he let out the closest thing to a roar that I had ever heard come from a human throat. "Where'd you get that T-shirt? It's one of ours!" I yelled, over the increasing din, pointing at Blondie's chest.

Blondie looked down at her shirt, then up at her now-magenta boyfriend. You could almost see the light bulb going on over her head. In one swift motion, she peeled the T-shirt over her head and threw it at Beefy. "You! You! . . ." she shrieked.

Oh yes, we were going to get news coverage today.

Later, Detective Dick and I found ourselves back at the fast-food place. "All right, one more time. How did you figure out he did it?" he said wearily.

"Elementary, my dear, uh, Jarvis. The dead girl had the wrong shirt on. Only a guy would have put that shirt on her, and it had to be a guy to move the body without leaving a bloody mess along the way. And then, when I saw his girlfriend wearing our shirt, and she said he had just given it to her, it all came together. That shirt isn't available for sale yet. It came in yesterday." Note to self: Make sure the Babe shirts were out on the racks when curious people showed up after seeing the broadcasts. "You did find the blood in the storeroom?"

He nodded. "We did. And the weapon—a box-cutter. And Sid confessed. The woman was in the mall late last night, and they started talking. He came on to the victim, and he thought she was into him, or so he says, at least long enough to take her shirt off, but then she had second thoughts or something, and he went nuts, grabbed the first thing he laid hands on. Classic 'roid rage, I guess."

"And he dumped the body in our store, because we were close but not right next door. A real Einstein, isn't he? And while he was there he decided that our T-shirt would make a nice present for his lady love?" Guilt over betraying Blondie? We'd probably never know. I shook my head. The stupidity of men never ceased to amaze me.

"Looks that way. Anyway, thanks for the help."

"No problem," I said smugly. I'd taken what could have been a PR nightmare and turned it into some great publicity for Sharp, and I'd make sure headquarters noticed. "By the way, he got the right size Babe shirt."

△ △ △

Sheila Connolly *writes the Orchard Mysteries for Berkley Prime Crime. As Sarah Atwell, she also writes the Glassblowing Mysteries, whose debut book,* Through a Glass, Deadly, *was nominated for an Agatha Award for Best First Novel. Sheila's new series, the Museum Mysteries, opened in October 2010 with* Fundraising the Dead. *"Size Matters" is her first published short story.*

Changes

Ruth M. McCarty

Alice McDermott sighed and rolled over. Her daughter Elaine's words were the first thing on her mind. "Mom, you have to make your decision by Tuesday!"

She kept her eyes tightly shut in defiance against the bright sunlight sneaking past the heavy brocade curtains that graced her bedroom windows. *Easy for her to say.* Today was Tuesday, and Alice still hadn't made up her mind.

"Maybe I'll sleep straight through 'til Wednesday," she said aloud, her voice cracking at the first words of the day. Sighing again, she opened her left eye long enough to catch the two-inch tall, bright red numbers that glowed from the clock across the room. Only 5:47 and already, the room was stifling hot. She'd been awake since 3:23 a.m., when she'd heard the banging noise above the whirr of the fan. Alice was sure someone was breaking in. Hadn't someone nearly scared the life out of her closest neighbor, Mary Thompson, just three weeks ago? Broke the windowpane on her back door and would have turned the lock to get in if Mary hadn't grabbed the cast iron frying pan and whacked him right in the knuckles.

Alice had truly believed it was the same man at her back door, and now he was coming after her. She'd lain perfectly still for what seemed like hours, barely breathing, sweat seeping from every pore, sheets sticking to her too fragile body, too frightened even to get up and shut off the fan that cooled her wet nightgown. Now, in the light of day, she ached all over and worse, she'd almost called the police again!

Oh, they were very polite the first time she'd called. They'd checked her house, cellar, and attic and even pointed out that the bushes in the front of the house needed trimming. "Blocks the view from the street," they'd said. "Now don't you worry, Mrs. McDermott. We'll send a squad car around to keep an eye on you."

They weren't so nice the third time. "Mrs. McDermott, we've searched your house twice this week, and once last week," the baby-faced officer who knew her daughter, shouted at her as if she were deaf. "There's no sign of anyone trying to break in."

Then that darned baby-faced officer had gone and called Elaine.

"Mom, why didn't you call us?" she'd yelled into the phone. "I have to hear this from the kid who used to deliver my newspapers?"

"I didn't want to bother you," Alice had answered.

"'Not bother me,' Mom? That's crazy. And what about Mrs. Thompson? When were you going to tell me about her?"

"I told you, Elaine. I know I did. The day you had to bring Amy to dance class." Elaine, Alice had thought then, was always so busy with the children that sometimes she just didn't listen.

"You didn't, Mom. I would have remembered something like that. Mom, you can't stay there anymore. You have to sell your house."

"I couldn't sell this house. I raised all you kids here. Your father and I—"

"There's an opening at the Senior Housing on Main Street," Elaine had interrupted. "I called there this morning. You can move in with us, or you can move there. But you have to make your decision by Tuesday, or they'll give the apartment to someone else."

"I'm fine, Elaine. I can stay here."

"You're not fine, Mom. Your neighborhood isn't safe anymore. You called the police three times in the last three weeks."

"I won't call them again, Elaine. I promise."

Alice had promised and now she'd almost called them again. Elaine would be so mad. Finally, at 6:00 a.m. Alice started the slow process of getting out of bed, washing up and getting dressed. Elaine would be here by ten and she wanted to be ready.

□ □ □

Elaine stood in the front entryway, sizing her up. "Mom, that dress needs to go to the cleaners."

"I checked it before I put it on, Elaine. It's fine."

"Mother, it's filthy! Come over here and look at it in the light. There's a spot here, and what's this? It looks like spaghetti sauce. And it hangs on you!"

Alice looked for the spots Elaine pointed out, but she just couldn't see them. "I'll go change, Elaine. It won't take me long."

Alice sighed. They were going to lunch, and now she had no idea what to wear. Elaine always looked like she'd just stepped out of the pages of *Town and Country* magazine. Always cleaned and pressed, as if she hadn't sat in the car on the way over here. Alice tugged on her closet door stuck tight by humidity. It wouldn't budge, so she kicked the bottom right corner, pulled on the handle at the same time, and was nearly knocked over when her strategy worked.

"Mother, are you all right?" Elaine stood in the doorway. "It's so dark in here, no wonder you couldn't see the stains on your dress. Let me open the curtains."

Alice looked into her closet. The first thing she saw was the maroon pantsuit that she'd worn on the day she surprised her youngest daughter Diane with a baby shower. But that was ten years ago. Diane lived in San Francisco now and had been there for at least seven years. Maybe Elaine would think it was out of style.

"It's too hot in here," Elaine said. "Let me open the window."

"Please don't, Elaine. We're going out to lunch, and no one will be here."

"You can't live like this, Mom." Elaine's voice softened as if she was talking to a baby.

"What do you think of this?" Alice said, holding up the pantsuit, hiding her anger.

"Oh Ma, not that old thing, let's see what else you have." Elaine pushed and pulled at the clothes. "I can't believe you kept this," she said holding up an outfit that looked like a navy blue blazer and a pleated white skirt, but was really a one-piece dress.

"Elaine, that's the dress I wore when Ronnie graduated from college." She smiled at the dress. Ronnie was her change-of-life baby. Alice had been sure that something terrible was wrong, with her cycle stopping and feeling sick all the time. She was relieved and scared when Dr. Caruthers told her she was going to have an addition to the family.

"What will the neighbors think?" she'd asked Harry the moment he'd walked in the door.

"They'll think we're very lucky!" Harry had twirled her around the room.

"How will I tell the girls? They're teenagers! They'll be so embarrassed. *"*

"Mom, what about this?" Elaine interrupted her thoughts. She was holding the dress she'd bought her for her seventieth birthday party. Alice smiled. She'd felt like Princess Diana in that dress. Pale blue with darker blue roses. It seemed to move by itself. *If only Harry was alive to see it.*

"Too fancy for lunch, Elaine." Alice sat on the bed. "But remember my party? Why, you transformed the back yard into a palace. The blue and white striped tent and the tables set with real china and silver . . . and your sister came all the way from California, and Ronnie from New York."

"Yeah, Mom. I remember. You looked like a princess." Elaine

pulled out the plain gray pantsuit that Alice had worn to lunch last month. Elaine had bought it for her last Christmas. Alice thought it made her look like a concrete column. Gray hair, gray suit, gray skin, no Alice. Well, she'd wear it for Elaine.

At lunch, they talked about everything except the Senior Housing. "Aaron passed his driving exam," Elaine said. "Maybe now he can drive his sister around."

"That'll be good, Elaine. It will give you more free time." Alice thought Elaine had plenty of free time, but she didn't say so.

"I called Aunt Mary, Mom."

Here it comes, Alice thought.

"She's happy living at the Senior Housing."

"I know, Elaine. I'm just not ready yet. I don't want to give up my memories. I really don't like changes."

"You'd just be giving up the house, Mom, not the memories."

"You don't understand."

"No, Ma, you don't understand. You have to get out of that neighborhood!"

"I'm not leaving, Elaine, and that's final."

Alice pushed her food around on her plate so it would look like she was eating. She didn't want Elaine to start about how much weight she'd lost. Alice knew what she looked like. Her eyesight might be getting worse, but she could still look in a mirror.

Elaine barely spoke on the way home. She walked Alice to the door then said, "Make sure you lock your doors. I'll send Aaron by to check on you this week."

□   □   □

A strange noise woke Alice from a restless sleep. It sounded like it came from the front of the house. She looked at the digital clock. Only ten-thirty. It felt like the middle of the night. She sat up in bed and tried to remain calm. Another sound. Alice turned her head to the side and strained to hear where the noises were coming from.

The backyard. That's where it came from. Someone must be in the backyard! Sweat dripped down Alice's arms, and her hair stuck to her head. She'd taken the fan out of the window three nights ago, on the day that Elaine had taken her to lunch, sure that she'd feel safer with the bedroom window locked, too. She didn't, but she wouldn't call the police this time. No, this time she'd take care of things herself.

The nightlight cast enough light for Alice to get to the wardrobe across the room. She pulled the silk flowers out of the vase on top of it and spilled out the key to open the wardrobe door. With shaking hands, she pulled out Harry's gun. It wasn't loaded. She knew Harry had kept the bullets in an old hatbox on the top shelf of the closet, and she'd never taken them out of it after he died. Alice laid the gun on the bed, then yanked the closet door open. The hatbox was heavier than she thought and she almost dropped it. She dumped the contents on the bed and picked up the box of bullets. She tried to remember what Harry had told her about loading it.

Alice tiptoed down the hall to the kitchen. She heard heavy footsteps on the porch. She thought she would faint when she heard a key slip into the lock. *They found the key I hid under the flowerpot!*

Alice raised the gun. The door flew open.

"Grandma," Aaron called as the gun went off.

Alice slumped to the floor. It was time to leave the house and this awful memory. She put the gun to her head and pulled the trigger.

△   △   △

Ruth M. McCarty's *short mysteries have appeared in all of the Level Best anthologies. She received honorable mentions in* Alfred Hitchcock Mystery Magazine, NEWN, *and mysteryauthors.com for her flash fiction, and won the 2009 Derringer award for Best Flash Story for "No Flowers for Stacey," published in* Deadfall: Crime Stories by New England Writers.

Unleashed

Cheryl Marceau

Jill took in the scene around her—the wood paneled Town Hall auditorium, with a stage in front and a balcony that ran around three sides, old-fashioned schoolhouse light fixtures hanging from the ceiling. Clusters of people gathered, greeting each other like old friends, while others kept to themselves. *What could I have been thinking?* Jill asked herself. *How the hell do I get out of this now?*

At first she had been excited. Then the reality began to sink in—weekly meetings for weeks, late sessions on work nights, hours of preparation between meetings, e-mails from constituents. With growing reservations, she sat on one of the dozens of metal folding chairs placed in rows on the main floor of the hall. Her first session as an elected representative member of Town Meeting for the town of Belville, Massachusetts was about to begin.

There were, it was said, two kinds of people in Belville—doughnut eaters and scone eaters. "Doughnuts" were townies, born and raised in Belville, proud of their working-class roots. "Scones" were exiles from nearby Cambridge and Boston's Back Bay, driven to Belville by its lower real estate prices and their desire for houses with yards and driveways. Jill was definitely a "scone," a transplant whose roots did not grow deeply in town soil. She'd worked hard to fit in to her adopted community, volunteering for library fundraisers and park cleanup events. At thirty-four, she was a brand new homeowner, and she wanted desperately to put down roots in this town she had carefully chosen. Still, her townie neighbors made sure she never forgot she came from away.

"This better not go as many weeks as last year."

Jill looked up from her marked-up copy of the Town Meeting warrant to see her next door neighbor, Nancy MacLeod, the other member representing their precinct. Nancy was in her fifties and made no effort to hide it. "How long have you been doing this?" Jill asked.

"Fifth term, fourteen years in all so far." Nancy pulled off her windbreaker and sat down. "Last year was the worst. Went on forever. Some horse's ass got an article in the warrant to rezone for a burger chain in that spot where the car dealership used to be. You'd think they were talking about tearing down the high school and building a bordello. It's just a burger place, for heaven's sake."

"Well, I imagine people were worried about trash and traffic."

Nancy sighed. "If folks don't want traffic, maybe they oughtta move to apple country out in Stow. Heaven's sake, we're not talking about the backup on game days down by Gillette Stadium. Just a little fast food place."

Jill was tempted to answer with arguments against the fast food joint—she'd circulated one of the petitions herself—but let it pass. For now.

The loud buzz in the room softened to a faint hum as a man in a charcoal suit and red bow tie took the podium. Chairs scraped along the wooden floor. Jill could sense speeches being readied and battle lines being drawn.

Nancy leaned over to Jill and pointed at the man standing at the podium. "Name's Fitch. Town Meeting moderator since Hector was a pup. Not for nothing, but you couldn't pay me to do his job!" she whispered.

Jill missed the moderator's opening remarks as she rummaged through her leather tote for her cell phone, which chimed as she turned it off. The man to her left glared and shushed her, and she felt like the newbie she was.

Metal chairs squeaked as butts wiggled. Jill settled in.

Belville had a representative Town Meeting with elected Members from each precinct. It was an adaptation of the oldest form of government in New England, where townspeople met to govern their town. The evening sessions in Belville always began in April, as New England finally shook off winter, and lasted for weeks. As important as Town Meeting was, it could also tax the patience of the most civic-minded, and Member seats often went vacant.

So on a fateful October evening, when Jill learned that there were no candidates for one of her precinct's Town Meeting seats, she decided to prove she really did belong.

Two hours and thirteen minutes after the first session was gaveled open, following lengthy debates on whether the town horn should continue to sound at noon, and whether to install bike racks in front of the library, the moderator announced the last item of business for that evening.

"The item reads as follows," Moderator Fitch read from the warrant document, "'Resolved, that all open spaces shall be available for the common enjoyment of domestic pets without restraint by leash during the hours of four o'clock p.m. to six o'clock p.m. every weekday and twelve noon to six p.m. on weekends. Pets shall be defined to include dogs, cats, rabbits, and all other animals permitted by state law for domestic use, other than service dogs. Pet owners will be required to ensure that any waste created by their pets in the parks shall be disposed of properly. Failure to comply with such requirement will result in a $25 fine.'"

"Hmphh." Someone behind Jill grunted. She turned to see a man who looked to be in his forties, wearing a cashmere pullover if she was any judge of clothing, with a good haircut. She couldn't divine his position on the warrant from his blank expression but that grunt sounded a little . . . disgruntled.

Nancy MacLeod followed Jill's gaze. "Works in mutual funds. Lives in the Heights. Third year as a Member," she whispered. The Heights was a neighborhood of large houses with spacious yards and views of the Boston skyline. Jill guessed that part of town might include a fair number of dog owners. It seemed to fit with having more space for kids and pets.

"I open the floor for discussion," the moderator said.

A man in the balcony shouted as he stood. "I want to say something."

"The moderator recognizes the member who is standing. State your name and precinct."

The man in the balcony tugged on his orange down vest. "Joe Miller, Precinct Two. I just want to say this. I'm tired of the jerks who act like they own this town. I pay taxes too. I got rights. Since when does someone got a right to let their dog jump all over my kid when she's at the park, huh?" He looked around, enlisting support. "Now she's scared to death to go there. And not only that, she steps in dog crap all the time that they don't even pick up!"

Heads nodded all over the room. There were choruses of "Yeah, that's right!"

Jill had skipped that item when she reviewed the warrant. There were so many other items—eighty-three in all—that she'd focused on those she thought were most important. This issue had seemed like a no-brainer. Didn't everyone let their dogs run off-leash in the parks? They certainly did in Boston's Public Garden, near where she'd lived before moving to Belville.

"This should be fun," Nancy said, rolling her eyes.

A tiny woman on the far side of the auditorium stood to speak. "Mr. Moderator," she called out.

"The moderator recognizes Alice Reeves."

Someone shouted, "Not her again!"

Reeves seemed to be in her late sixties or even older, a tiny wren in a brown sweater and trousers. "Thank you. As you know, I'm a member of Belville's Citizens for Social Justice." Jill heard a burst of applause, which drew a pounded gavel from the podium. "We pride ourselves in Belville on our commitment to diversity and inclusion. Are we really inclusive after all? Pets are family. They need to exercise and spend time with their little friends. They must be able to run free."

Jill heard snickers from the man in cashmere behind her.

"Pet owners are taxpayers," Reeves continued. "Surely we have a right to use the parks with our pets just as much as the gentleman in the balcony does with his children."

A faint yapping punctuated her speech.

"She even brought her dog here!" The woman seated next to Reeves shouted as she pointed, and heads craned.

Any decorum the moderator had maintained was gone. Some members of the assembly applauded loudly, a few even standing for the ovation. Others groaned, jeered, or hissed.

Jill started when she heard the man in cashmere call out, "My problem is the dog shit." He stood and continued, "You dog activists just don't pick up after your dogs. You keep bringing this up every year, Alice, and you don't listen to why anyone complains. I get tired of cleaning up after other people's dogs in my yard, let alone watching where I step in public. If you want a damn dog, keep it in your own yard. And keep your damn dog shit away from other people."

"We don't all leave our dog messes everywhere! Some of us even clean up after others." A woman in front of Jill, with long straight hair and wire-rimmed glasses, seemed agitated as she put down her knitting and rose to speak. "When I walk Barkminster Fuller—my husband calls him Barky—I usually end up picking up other people's trash. Do you know how many cigarette butts get tossed on the sidewalk around here? Why don't we ban public smoking?"

Nancy leaned forward and waved her rolled up copy of the warrant. "You self-righteous twit!" The knitting woman turned, and Nancy proceeded to poke the woman's shoulder with the warrant.

"If you had your way, this town would ban everything but tofu and organic water."

"Watch how you talk to my wife!" The man next to Barky's owner lunged at Nancy. Jill shrank from all of them.

The moderator banged his gavel on the podium. "Out of order! None of you are recognized to speak."

From a corner of the hall, someone called out, "Let the voice of the people be heard. You're the one that's out of order!"

Chaos erupted. People all over the room thrust their hands in the air, waving frantically for attention.

Jill shuddered. *What'll happen when we get to the really hard stuff in a couple of weeks, like property taxes?* She turned to Nancy. "Does this always happen in these meetings?" she asked.

"It gets a little hot sometimes. Not usually like this." Nancy chuckled. "You'd think we were talking about jailing their kids, wouldn't you? To think I gave up *Dancing With the Stars* for this."

Loud arguments verging on fights erupted on all sides of the room. Shouts of "your freakin' dog" and "crap all over the soccer field" and "I pay taxes so Barky can go for his walkies!" resounded through the hall.

Suddenly a different sort of pounding began and almost at once the din broke. There was the moderator, hammering on the podium as before. But this time he was pounding with his shoe. His face was crimson. He seemed prepared to throw the shoe at the first person who spoke.

As the noise evaporated and taut stillness filled the room, the moderator stood back. After a pause he leaned in to the microphone. Waving the shoe for emphasis, he announced, "I'm calling a break. We will return in fifteen minutes. When we get back, I will personally ask the Chief of Police to remove any one of you who so much as sneezes without permission. Do I make myself clear?"

The silence was broken only by Alice Reeves' dog yipping as the two of them walked out of the auditorium.

Jill had been in Town Hall only once before. The nineteen-twenties-style lettering on the signs and the dark varnished woodwork took her back to a different era. She had no idea where the restrooms were, and her neighbor Nancy had vanished as soon as the break was announced. She leaned over the row of chairs to talk to the knitter in front of her. "You've been here before, right?" she said. "How do I find the ladies' room?"

The woman nodded and pointed to a side door where several people were coming back into the auditorium. "You'll be better off going to the one downstairs. There's always a line at the one on this floor." Jill worked her way past the folding chairs to a corridor with a staircase leading to the basement.

As she reached the bottom step and rounded the corner, she nearly bumped into the man from the balcony who had identified himself as Joe Miller. She would never have remembered him without the orange down vest that seemed so out of place in the overheated building. "Sorry," she said. He grunted something at her in return.

This is going to be one long spring if I have to spend every Monday night like this, she thought. Then she spotted the ladies' room. Like the rest of the building, it was a relic of the nineteen-twenties. The panels between the two stalls were marble and the doors were the same heavy varnished wood as the trim throughout the building. They cleared the floor by just a few inches, barely enough to see feet on the floor. She bent down to check for shoes. In the first stall she spied a small pair of feet clad in mud-caked walking shoes.

She went into the next stall and pushed the door closed. The heavy door slipped from her hand and slammed against the frame, bouncing back open. Jill heard the creak of the other door as the frame shuddered, and apologized mentally for disturbing the woman in the next stall. She did what she had come to do. Her only thought was that she needed to hurry so she wouldn't return late and risk the moderator's wrath. She pulled open her door and dashed to the sink, then stopped short.

The door to the other stall stood open. Alice Reeves, the tiny woman who had advocated for dog rights, was slumped against the wall, not moving.

Jill rushed to help, standing next to Alice and trying to find a way to ease the woman into a prone position. She could tell Alice was breathing, but seemed to be unconscious. She grabbed a fistful of paper towels and stretched Alice on the floor with her head resting on the towels. The dog's leash was wrapped around Alice's right hand. Jill tried to release it from Alice's grip but soon gave up in favor of going in search of help.

Only in hindsight did she realize that Alice's dog should have been attached to the leash.

Jill ran upstairs and told Morris Fitch about finding Reeves, apparently ill, in the ladies' room.

Fitch announced to the assembly that Alice appeared to be ailing and asked the police to summon the EMTs. He continued, "The vote on the dog leash item will be tabled for tonight."

The announcement was greeted with groans. "Dammit!" Nancy said under her voice. She stood and waved her hand.

"The moderator recognizes Nancy MacLeod."

"Morris, for heaven's sake, can't we get this over with? Alice had her say. Everybody knows how they want to vote by now. Why do we have to wait?"

"Ms. Reeves was responsible for putting this item on the warrant. The way I see it, she ought to have the chance to vote on it. No further discussion." He banged the gavel. "Tonight's session is adjourned. We reconvene next Monday night at 7:30."

Jill gathered up her jacket and tote, only too happy to head home. She yawned deeply as she worked her way toward the exit.

Nancy MacLeod had been even faster to head out, and stood near the door leading out of the auditorium to the front of Town Hall. Jill approached Nancy and the two men talking with her. One was the man from the row behind, wearing the cashmere sweater. The other was Joe Miller, who she'd nearly knocked down on her way to the ladies' room.

"Mike Vendetti," the guy in cashmere said, extending his hand. "Sorry we had to be introduced this way."

"Jill Howard. I just moved here last summer, next door to Nancy. How do you three know each other?"

Vendetti shrugged, "You know how it goes. It's a small town. My mom and Nancy's mom were friends for years."

"Still are," Nancy said. "Bought themselves condos next door to each other in St. Pete."

You mean this guy's a "doughnut," too? Jill thought. She pulled on her fleece jacket and threw her tote over her shoulder. "I need to get out of here and get some fresh air. I parked out back. Does anyone need a lift?"

They all shook their heads.

"Then I'll see you all next week I guess. You don't suppose the dog issue will be postponed any longer, do you?"

"Why?" said Vendetti. "Wait till you've been here a while. Nothing stops us from getting the job done. We're a tough breed."

Jill followed the corridor to the back door of the building. The streetlight in the parking lot cycled off as she stepped out of the building. The dark seemed especially thick. *Can't see a damn thing out here. Good thing I have this.* Her car alarm system chirped as she clicked on the remote to unlock the driver's door, then held her key out in front as she'd learned to do in a self-defense class.

As she pulled open her driver's side door, an unexpected noise nearby made her jump. She stopped and listened for a moment, willing herself to hold her breath so she could hear whatever it was.

Then she heard it again. Muffled yapping, coming from near her car. She shoved her door shut and followed the sound to a sedan a few spaces away. The car looked a lot like Nancy MacLeod's Taurus although it was hard to be sure, seeing it only with the tiny beam from her penlight. Jill didn't see anything out of the ordinary, and was about to leave when the barking resumed. She came closer to the car and crouched low, listening harder. It sounded like the animal was in the back of the car. It was definitely Nancy's car—Jill recognized the Old Orchard Beach bumper sticker. *That's strange. Nancy doesn't have a dog.* She tried to remember if Nancy's kids or grandkids had pets.

The penlight didn't penetrate the car's dark interior. Jill tried several different angles, but nothing. The yipping continued. She put her ear to a back window and the sound grew louder. *Definitely a dog. Sure sounds like it's in the car.* She crept around, listening, until she realized the sound was coming from the trunk. The thought of Nancy putting an animal in the trunk of her car unsettled her.

As she returned to her car and slipped into the driver's seat, the back door of Town Hall clanged open. Voices floated out on the night air. Jill heard Nancy MacLeod and at least one male voice. Very carefully, she turned the ignition key one click to turn on the electrical system, and pushed the button to lower her window just a crack so she could hear the voices more clearly. She slid down in her seat to hide from sight.

"You get the dog?" *That man sounds familiar. Miller?*

"Yep." *That was Nancy.* "Brought it out here already."

"How'd you manage to get it to your car without being seen?" *That was definitely Vendetti.*

"There's more than one way to get around this building," Nancy said.

"So how did you do it, anyway?" Miller asked.

"She never saw what hit her. I found one of the janitor's big metal dustpans. Worked like a charm. Didn't break the skin. She'll be good as new in a couple days."

Nancy!? Jill clamped her hand over her mouth, afraid she might have said that aloud. She couldn't believe what she was hearing. Alice Reeves hadn't taken ill—she'd been knocked out.

"What're you gonna do with the dog? I can take it up to the camp in Maine this weekend if you want," Miller said. "Nobody'll notice it if I give it to somebody up there."

Jill strained to hear what they were saying.

"My sister's grandson's been wanting a new dog since they had to put theirs down. He might like that little guy," Nancy offered.

"Too risky. Somebody'll see it and recognize it. Alice'll have descriptions and pictures out everywhere," Mike Vendetti said. He seemed to have thought this through.

"All's I can say is it's about time we stopped that woman," Miller said. "She's gonna wreck this town if we let her. She's put this stupid item in every Town Meeting warrant since she moved here seven years ago. It's criminal."

"No kidding. I get sick of hearing our neighbor's dog run up and down the street yapping all the time, especially now it's getting nice and the windows are open," Vendetti said. "Sunday mornings, we'll be reading the papers and having a nice breakfast, and that animal won't shut up."

Jill turned in her seat to look at them, trying desperately at the same time to avoid being spotted. She was congratulating herself on her cleverness when the streetlight cycled back on. *Shit!* She slunk down, but not before giving herself away.

"What just moved?" Vendetti asked.

"I know that car," Nancy answered. "Hey Jill, is that you?"

Jill ducked, hoping they would go away. A second later she heard tapping on her driver's side window and peered up. It was Nancy.

"You taking in the night air?" Nancy laughed.

Jill straightened. "I couldn't get poor Alice out of my mind. I guess I lost track of time."

"Come out, be sociable, why don't you?"

"I'm tired. I should go home." She started to turn the key in the ignition when the two men walked around to the front of her car, blocking her only way out. She shoved the button to lock her doors, feeling increasingly nervous.

"Hey Jill, do you want a dog?" Nancy asked. "We found one, looks like someone lost it."

"I don't need a dog. I'd better just leave. You know how it goes. Gotta get up in the morning. This has been a long night. I didn't realize how late it was." Jill knew she was babbling. She reached for her tote on the passenger seat and slid out her cell phone.

"You can't leave yet. We need to talk." Joe Miller walked around to the passenger side of the car. "Nancy says you're regular people."

"Yeah, Jill, you don't want to rock the boat." Nancy said. "You're practically one of us, aren't you?"

Vendetti spoke. "Nancy just found a dog is all, and we didn't want Animal Control to take it. Is that a problem?"

Jill hesitated. It would be her word against theirs, with no proof of anything. Maybe she didn't even hear them right. She would feel like a fool if she overreacted. "No problem," she said, slowly starting to tuck her cell phone back in the tote.

"That's right, hon, just put the phone away." Nancy pulled on the door handle. "Come on, let's leave our cars here and walk over to the Dunkin's on Mass. Ave. for some coffee and crullers. They'll still be open for a while."

Jill's self-doubts were getting the best of her. She felt stupid. *I must not have heard them right.* Then the dog in the trunk started yapping again, this time louder than before. Jill remembered Alice Reeves on the ladies' room floor, gripping the leash. She looked at the three people surrounding her car and felt sick. She swallowed hard to push back the nausea that was rising to her throat. Her hands felt sweaty.

"Nancy was right, you're OK," Miller said.

"Is that Alice's dog?" Jill asked.

The voices assailed her at once. "What?" "You can't be serious." "Jeez, lighten up!"

Joe Miller walked to the passenger side of the car and tried the door handle.

"I thought you were one of us," Nancy said, shaking her head. "You wanna get along here, you gotta go with the flow."

Jill finally grabbed her cell phone. "Operator? Belville Police. Please," she said, her voice coming out as a croak. "Hurry!"

      □   □   □

Hours later Jill sat in the living room of a good friend on the back side of Beacon Hill, where she'd fled after the police responded to her call. She was afraid to go back to her little house in Belville. Sooner or later she would have to return, but she knew it would only be in daylight from now on, and never by herself. That chapter of her life was closed.

As she sat on the sofa gazing out the window at the Boston street below, she craved the comfort of a nice hot cup of tea. And maybe a scone.

△   △   △

Cheryl Marceau: *Having grown up moving from Newfoundland to the Marshall Islands, and (almost) everywhere in between, I cannot be called a native New Englander. However, I am an enthusiastic transplant to a nice town just outside Cambridge. I have never once considered running for Town Meeting.*

Inside Out

Virginia Young

Outside –
The near hurricane winds argued with the huge weeping willow in the front yard, with the twin sugar maples, the resistant and tall oaks and supple pines, and tested the bravery of the one ancient chestnut.

Puddles from saturating rain gathered at the feet of all that stood still, the granite bench, and the cast iron birdbath. Metal chairs toppled and slid gratingly across the patio flagstones, wet and glistening with strands of light from the log cabin's windows.

Twigs and freed leaves flew helplessly through the night sky, pinging at the roof, the doors, the windows. *Let me in, let me in.*

It was a fearsome night. No one in his right mind would want to be out in it.

Inside –
The lights flickered, and only the glow from the hearth lent a consistency to the room. Mia lit a candle just in case, and then carried it with her to the kitchen where the flashlight waited in a drawer. She walked back to the hearth, placed another log on the fire and noted that there were only two logs left inside. The woodpile in the shed would be dry when she needed more fuel, although she did not look forward to going out in the storm.

It was both comforting and sad to be in that old cabin by the lake, with so many memories of summers there, and even some Thanksgivings. She recalled the sweet aroma of her mother's caramelized onions and hot dogs served with a zesty potato salad on a bed of homegrown lettuce. Mia smiled recalling her dad's old straw hat on the top of a small gold lampshade, creating a featureless face when the light was turned on, which earned a scowl from his wife. They bickered, they teased, and sometimes they were genuinely angry at one another, but they loved each other and Mia.

She walked to the left side of the hearth near a large window and sat down in her father's barrel-back chair. A flash of lightening projected itself into the room, the lights flickered again, and Mia drew her legs up and under her body, curling herself into the protective curved back and arms of the old recliner. The mechanism to lift the footrest no longer worked, but the chair was too comfortable for her father to have cast it out for a new one. She wanted them back. Ridiculously stubborn, she looked toward the fury-filled sky and told God that if he was really there, she wanted them back, *now.*

Outside –

From the cluster of swaying pines and resilient rhododendrons, the cabin was the essence of refuge. Golden beams reached out beyond the windows and spilled carelessly and invitingly onto evergreens and more rhododendrons, all rustling against the taunting wind. The windows were muted with streams of rain and leaves plastered against the glass. Inside, it would be warm and dry, *inside.*

Inside –

Mia braced herself against the sounds of the storm, the crackling of light and the shrieking wind. Her eyes sought the comfort of the hearth and grew heavy with the desire to sleep. She closed her eyes, her lips parted slightly as she tucked herself deeper into the chair's curve and slept. When she opened her eyes, it was because of the loud crash she'd heard. Startled, she didn't move for a few moments, and then she slowly eased her legs to the floor and stood. With the flashlight in her hands, she moved from room to room, looking for what could have made that sound. She found nothing. Feeling a little edgy, Mia walked back to the living room's hearth and sat down again, this time on the sofa, facing the window. The fire was glowing but fading. Mia stood and walked to the two remaining logs and placed them on the fire. She tucked a few pieces of kindling into the embers, and then waited as the flames leaped and grew. She moved back to the sofa and wondered why she'd come up here alone.

Outside –

The rain was harsh, almost stinging to whatever it touched. The wind was unreasonably determined to have no direction, to toss and hurl, to tug and torture each victim in its way. Eyes blinked against the twirling pine needles and bits of twigs and grit. The lights from that cabin were intriguing.

Inside –

Just as the lights went out, Mia felt her heart twist as she saw what looked to be a face at the window. She froze, her eyes riveted to the blotch of yellow against the glass. She had not planned on any of this, not the storm, not being here alone, and the fear.

The lights came back within moments, then were lost again, but not before she could see that the yellow face at the window was really a clump of leaves clinging to the glass in desperation, fluttering like a giant moth pleading for help.

Now there was only the light from the small candle and the hearth. The whole place looked different. She'd never been there in a storm before, and especially not at night and not alone. She thought about making a cup of tea, but decided not to move. Maybe the lights would come back. Mia didn't like the shadows in the darkened room. They seemed to take the life from it, just as the accident had taken life from her parents.

She was tired. It was after midnight now and she rested her head against the soft cushions. Then she looked to her right where the needlepoint pillow her mother had made as a gift to her father sat propped in the sofa's corner. On a black background piped in moss green, a cluster of pinecones and acorns formed the intricate design. She touched it with her right hand, then lowered herself down on the sofa, drawing her legs up and allowing her head to rest on the pillow, the way, as a child, she had rested her head in her mother's lap before sleep.

Mia woke up one hour later believing she'd heard a knock at the door. But who could possibly be out on a night such as this? She listened, her head raised now from the pillow, and then she sat up straight. She was cold. The late September air had prepared itself for the coming season and the dampness from the storm was penetrating. The fire was nearly gone, only little pops of sound came from the simmering logs, now aging into cinders.

She stood. The lights were still out and the candle was low. She lit another candle and placed it on the mantle, then reached her arms into a jacket that had once belonged to her father. With the flashlight in her hand, she walked toward the door. Then again, the sound of a knock. Mia felt the adrenalin rush through her chest and she took a step back into the room and listened. Then again, a knock, but this time, softer. She went to the window and switched the flashlight on, shining it toward the path that led to the front door. At first she was stunned by seeing something different, but then she realized that a large branch had been urged to the ground and was resting and bumping against the cabin and the door. With a sense of relief, she unlocked the door and braced herself for the strong winds and rain.

Outside –

She wanted to run the thirty or forty feet to the shed, but branches and other debris were scattered in such a way that she needed to watch her every step. When she reached the shed, she heard hinges squeak, and, with the flashlight shining on the usually stubborn old door, she saw that it was open and yielding to the storm. Mia had been teased over the years about the shed, always fearful that spiders or some other crawly thing might be waiting for her inside. She thought of that now, but she needed the wood for the fire. She stepped inside, put the flashlight down to rest as she began to gather as many logs as she could hold in her arms, and then the flashlight went dark. Motionless, she stood and listened, then backed out of the shed and made her way as best she could back toward the cabin. Within ten feet of the door, Mia saw that it was open. Had she not closed it properly? *Had someone gone inside?*

The wind and rain tossed her shoulder-length hair and blew strands of it across her face and eyes. She dropped the logs to the ground, brushed her hair away from her face, and slowly stepped inside the cabin. She picked up her purse and car keys, blew out the candle on the mantle, and terrified, walked to her car. Seeing the light go on inside when she opened the door was a relief. She glanced in the back seat and on the floor, and then she sat behind the wheel and locked herself in. She pictured herself not being able to start the car, but it started fine, and the headlights provided an added comfort. Avoiding fallen branches as she drove, Mia felt sad that this wonderful cabin had at least temporarily lost its appeal.

Inside –

It was quiet in the cabin. The embers from the fire were smoking and some were still red. The front door was closed but not tight. Crackers and apples, and a still-wrapped meatball sub sat on the little round table in the kitchen next to a bottle of soda. He looked at the available food then tore open the white paper from the sub and ate most of it. He drank water from a half-filled glass in the sink. He looked around as best he could in the dark of that place, then made his way to the barrel-back chair where he curled his ringed tail over his eyes and went to sleep.

△   △   △

Virginia Young *wrote for* The South Shore News *and contributed articles to* The Patriot Ledger. *A painter, sculptor and writer, Virginia's main interest is fiction. She received honorable mention through a* Writer's Digest Magazine *contest, and has been published in literary journals,* Hoi Polloi *and* Shore Voices. *Her novel,* Out of the Blue, *was published and released August 1, 2010.*

Long Live the Queen

Alan D. McWhirter

There are more queens of romantic fiction than heavyweight champions of the world. But only one queen of romance was an ex-con with a rap sheet that included homicide. Just my luck to run into the One.

☐ ☐ ☐

At nine fifteen, give or take a few lost minutes, I stepped off from the Saturday night Bridgeport local to the glass and concrete half-roofed commuter platform that long ago took the place of Waterbury's old train depot. Across the street in Library Park, misdemeanor miscreants were out in force.

The flock of taxis that once nested at the depot on Meadow Street now take up weekend residence at The Palace, the refurbished theater on East Main, waiting for Cinderella. So, facing acid rain and a foul wind, I prepared to hike the quarter mile to Murphy's, the watering hole across from The Horse at the far end of Waterbury's green.

I stepped off and a lost yellow warbler pulled to the curb. A rubber rain slicker climbed out and made a run for the local. I bailed on the hero stuff and commandeered the cab. Royalty, cloaked against the elements, was right behind me. I wasn't about to leave a well-turned pair of ankles stranded in a cold Saturday night rain.

"Need a lift?"

"Thanks," she said. "I could use one."

"Where you headed?"

She pulled a scrap of lavender paper from a coat pocket.

"1302 East Main," she replied.

Not the best section of town; not an address on the hill either.

"Visiting?" I asked.

"For a few days."

"Family?"

"You might say that."

I also gathered you might not. She pulled off a knit cap and shook out a blonde mane. She was a knockout.

"Any place where I can grab a nightcap?" she asked. "My... relatives . . . don't allow booze in the house."

"Murphy's," I said. "I'm headed there myself."

She drew a crisp fifty and passed it forward. "Drop us at Murphy's and pick me up in an hour," she said.

The hack glanced in the rear-view mirror. "Any time, lady."

He dropped us across from The Horse, at the east end of the Waterbury green.

□   □   □

I bought the first round. Generous of me; I used the dough I saved on cab fare. She bought the next.

Cassandra York was a writer, a bestselling writer of romance novels set in the Victorian era. I asked how she knew so much about the Victorians. She didn't say. I asked what she did before she became a famous writer. She changed the subject and asked about me. I guess she was collecting failures for her next novel.

There's not much about my present to talk about, so I talked about my past. I'm a bona fide member of Generation-X; ex-New Haven cop; ex-husband three times; ex-Boy Scout. I'm sure the BSA has revoked my merit badges by now. More than once she asked me who I *really* was. I assured her I was a nobody. She insisted I was a somebody. I didn't make a big deal about it. Blondes are entitled to a wrong opinion now and then.

After the fourth round Cassandra York reminded me of my first wife, without the pretense of superiority. My first was a Fairfield County teacher before she graduated to Fairfield County housewife. She used to complain that in Darien, ninety per cent of the kids were expected to be in the top ten per cent of the class; and, if they weren't, it was the teacher's fault. I was sympathetic to her plight until she went "gold coast" on me. Now she shares the expectations.

Our marriage broke down "irretrievably" when I found out she was having an affair with a Greenwich software CEO who earned seven figures. I was having my own with a girl who worked the late shift at Dunkin' Donuts. My ex insisted we were "moving in different directions." She was right.

After the fifth shot, and without being read my rights, I confessed I was once a homicide detective. Cassandra bought another round, and I kept talking.

I left the New Haven force under duress, though I didn't tell the Queen why. She asked why I hadn't gotten into private investigative work. I told her I didn't have enough to pay the first year's fees or the bond the state required. She said that was a poor excuse. I didn't read her the rest of the list. The night was blossoming when the damn cabbie showed up, on time, as promised. You can't trust cab drivers these days.

The Queen of Victorian Romance wrote my address and phone number on the lavender scrap, and said she'd get in touch the next time she was in town. I filed the prospect with a lot of other maybes and walked her to the door. I never saw her again. But she did get in touch with me . . . in a manner of speaking.

□   □   □

A month after the cab ride, I got a phone call from St. Angelo, an attorney on State Street. My "presence"—I didn't know I had one—was requested at two to discuss the last will and testament of a Cynthia Walcott. I didn't know any Cynthia Walcott; so naturally I showed up.

I'm allergic to lawyer's digs and funeral homes. The last time I sat in a lawyer's den, my three ex wives were aligned and allied on the opposite side of the table. I emptied my wallet of the twenty-nine dollars I had to my name and went fishing. I assume they fought over my fortune a while.

St. Angelo's secretary showed me to the boardroom. At the near end of the mahogany table were Attorney Lucas St. Angelo and another lawyer-looking guy. At the far end was Lt. Brad Gooch of Waterbury PD. I should have guessed there was more to the invite than a mistake.

St. Angelo extended his hand. His wire-rimmed bifocals hung dangerously low. His rudimentary nose provided less than ample support.

"Mr. Joseph Chandler?"

"That's right," I said after a pause. I had to think about it. Couldn't remember the last time anybody called me "Joseph."

"Please have a seat. This is Attorney Wilson Baumgartner from New York. You know Lieutenant Gooch, do you not?"

I nodded at Gooch and sat down.

"Mr. Chandler, a Ms. Cynthia Walcott passed away a week ago outside her Manhattan apartment. In her last will and testament, rewritten not more than three weeks ago, she left you a sum of $10,000 . . . with a request."

St. Angelo waited for a response. So did Gooch. I sat out the inquisition and waited for the punch line.

"Ms. Walcott, the deceased Ms. Walcott, wants you to investigate her death."

"Was her death suspicious?" I asked.

Gooch couldn't resist. "Not until she asked *you* to investigate it."

"Cause of death?" I prodded.

Baumgartner answered, "She fell to her death from the balcony of her tenth floor apartment."

"Elderly lady?" I asked.

"You don't know her?"

"Am I supposed to?"

"She left you $10,000 in her will."

"I must be a nice guy."

Gooch turned over a photo that had been lying face down on the table. I expected a corpse, an M.E.'s special. It was a publicity shot of Cassandra York.

"Oh that Cynthia Walcott," I said. "I met her once. We shared a cab and a few drinks at Murphy's. Don't remember where she went from there."

"Why'd she leave you ten grand?" Gooch asked.

"Like I said, I must be a nice guy."

"Bull!" Gooch was a man of few words.

"Maybe she had a premonition or something," I suggested. "I guess I did tell her I used to work homicide."

Cynthia Walcott, a.k.a. Cassandra York, left me ten grand with the request that I investigate her early demise, should there be one. The rest of her healthy bank account she left to Robert Lawson Junior, a twelve-year-old living with his grandmother in New Haven. Inheritances are sometimes motive for murder. Gooch didn't suspect the twelve-year-old. I guess that left me.

Gooch got what he could from me, which wasn't much, then told me to stay out of the case. "You don't have a PI license. I'll run you in for taking a retainer."

"It's not a retainer," I said. "It's my inheritance."

In accordance with the directive of the deceased, St. Angelo gave me the lavender scrap Cassandra had when she left Murphy's. My address and phone number were of no use. "1302 East Main" was all I had to go on.

"By the way," Gooch added, "NYPD wants to make your acquaintance." Until I knew more about the suspicious death of Cynthia Walcott, I decided not to venture west of Bridgeport.

I lifted the check from the table and stopped at Murphy's for a drink.

"What'll it be, Joe?" Max, the barkeep, asked.

"A Cassandra York."

"Never heard of it."

I hadn't either until a month earlier.

"Just make it a double scotch."

□   □   □

An hour later, and well fueled, I set off for East Main by way of the back side of the Brass Mill Mall. It didn't take much to lose the tail Gooch sicced on me. No self-respecting snoop takes the bus; just those who can't afford an alternative.

The left door of a two-story side-by-side bore the number 1302. A middle-aged African-American woman of generous endowments answered my ring. If the plastic plate on the door could be taken at its word, her name was Gwen Ridley. Whoever she expected, it wasn't me.

"Can I help you?" she asked.

"Maybe," I said. "I need to ask you about Cassandra York."

"You the cops again?"

Figured. Gooch had visited before the meeting with St. Angelo.

"No. I'm a . . . friend."

The woman's eyes narrowed, and her lips hardened.

"What about this . . . Cassandra York?" she asked.

"You know her?"

"She writes stories."

I expected more from a relative-of-sorts.

"She's dead," I said.

"I know that," the woman said. "Who are you?"

"Like I said, I'm a friend of Cassie's." I got a cold stare. So maybe no one called her Cassie. "I'm checking out her murder."

"Murder!" I guess I said the magic word. Might not be true, but it got me in the door. "Cassandra was murdered? Oh, my God!"

A matched pair of ten-year-old urchins stared from a perch on the stairs. "Auntie York was murdered?"

Gwen Ridley anticipated my next question.

"They're my sister's kids," she said. "She's been . . . away."

The woman waved her hand and the pair retreated to the second floor. I told Gwen I'd been hired to investigate Cassandra's death. I didn't say by whom. She fixed strangely on my face.

"That's a dimple, isn't it?" she said pointing to my chin.

I'd denied it a hundred times without success.

"Wait here," she said, bustled off up the stairs and returned with a used nine-by-twelve mailing envelope. "Cassandra's letter said if anything happened and she didn't come back for these papers, I was to give them to the man with the dimple."

Damn dimple finally came in handy.

The letter inside was barren save the instructions. But three half-page scraps told me more. One message read: "i no ur secrit call my cell." Mrs. Purdy, my eighth grade English teacher, would have been appalled. Below the message was a phone number.

A second message said: "don b greedy thers enuf for all."

The third was ominous: "last chans bitch call me or els."

Maybe Cassandra never called, and the author followed through on his promise. Given the grammar and the spelling, I dropped Mrs. Purdy from the list of suspects.

"Blackmail," I muttered. Gwen didn't blink. "What was Cassandra's secret?" I asked.

"That's for Cassandra to say."

"She isn't here to tell me."

Gwen ushered me to the door.

An enemy did in the Queen. Her relatives-of-a-sort were too loyal to help me find her killer.

□　□　□

I didn't have much; just motive and a phone number.

I called Verizon and said my name was Lieutenant Gooch of Waterbury PD. I told them the phone had been found on the

Waterbury Green by a Good Samaritan who wanted to see it got back to its rightful owner. Verizon said it wasn't one of their numbers. So did Sprint. AT&T told me it was a phone that had been reported lost; wouldn't tell me whose it was without a warrant.

I called Gooch, thanked him for the backup and offered to trade my findings for his. Gooch got half what I promised. I got better. I didn't tell him about the phone calls he made.

In addition to a real name, Cynthia Walcott had a real record. She'd done eight years at York Correctional in Niantic, for manslaughter, and had been released a year before she set the romance world on fire. For a while she'd had a real and abusive boyfriend, the father of her twelve-year-old son, until she shot Robert Lawson Senior while he slept.

□   □   □

I had a longtime "in" at York—an inmate kind of "in." A decade ago, when I was still on the force in New Haven, Tammy Rogers got a ten-year bid for bank robbery. She would have gotten more for killing her boyfriend, if I hadn't gone to bat for her.

Niantic's an hour and a half drive from Waterbury as long as the Q Bridge in New Haven is passable; but I had no wheels. I forget which wife got my eleven-year-old Trans-Am. I used part of my inheritance to borrow an eight-year-old Dodge Intrepid from Pete, the desk clerk at the Ebony, drove to Niantic and called on Tammy. I figured she'd be in.

She was glad to see me. She didn't get much in the way of visits these days. When I asked about Cassandra York, Tammy clammed up. Maybe prison does change you. Tammy always loved to talk, which is what got her ten years in the first place. But she wasn't talking now. I drove home convinced Cassandra's secret lay within the walls of York Correctional. Every now and then I'm right.

A day later, I retrieved a message on my voice recorder. "Joe, it's Tammy. Come see me again. You need to talk to Mouse."

□   □   □

Even if you're just visiting, you leave your identity at the door of a correctional facility. I checked my wallet, car keys, and foil chewing gum wrappers in one of the lockers; passed the metal detector despite the pin in my left arm; and waved to Tammy who was waiting at a long table in the cinderblock room. As I approached, Tammy beckoned to a black matron, about five-ten and close to two-fifty.

"He's here to see Mouse," Tammy said.

Everyone at York has a street name, even those who never hung on the street. Everyone also has a real name. Mouse was Abigail Jennings.

Matron escorted me beyond the visitors' room to a garden surrounded on all sides by cinder block buildings. Kneeling was an elfish woman in her late sixties, a bandanna wrapped about her head to absorb the sweat of her labors.

"Ms. Jennings?" Matron spoke in a hushed and respectful tone. The elf woman's pale blue eyes were vacant, as if she were blind and staring past me. She wasn't.

"Why, Lillian," Mouse said, "This is a good looking man."

"He's here about Cynthia."

"Oh dear," she said. "I've been expecting you." She didn't ask my name. I gathered she knew. Mouse shook the rooted dirt from the plant she was repositioning. Matron waited patiently. I did, too.

"How did you know our Cynthia?" Mouse asked without looking up.

"She asked me to investigate her death," I replied, "posthumously."

"Post what?" Matron asked.

"Posthumously, my dear," Mouse explained, "It means an action taken after one's death. Lillian, could you leave us alone for a few minutes? I know it's against regulations but . . ."

"Of course, Ms. Jennings," Matron replied. "I'll watch from the visitors' room. Just wave when you're done." Matron walked away.

"You have clout here," I noted.

Mouse had four transplants to go.

"Can I do anything for you?" I asked.

She smiled a peculiar smile and rolled her eyes. "I'm afraid it's a bit too late for that," she said. I gathered she wasn't referring to her seedlings.

"I meant the plants."

"That's kind of you, but I always tend the darlings myself." Then without looking up from her labors she asked, "Are you trustworthy, Mr. Chandler?"

"Not usually," I admitted.

"At least honest, then," she noted. "Cynthia must have trusted you?"

I'd known Cynthia Walcott, a.k.a. Cassandra York, for little more than an hour. Not much trust-building time.

Mouse studied the root ball in her hand. "Who killed our Cynthia?" she asked.

"I don't know."

"Why was she killed?" Mouse inquired.

"Someone was trying to shake her down for a cut of the pie," I said. "Someone was trying to blackmail her."

Mouse nodded.

"Young man," Mouse said, "do you know what it's like to have purpose to your life?" She answered before I could make something up. "Helping others to a better life redeems the spirit as well as the soul. You can pay down the debt for the bad things you've done. You might think about it."

I promised I would. Then Mouse talked and I listened. She put her trust in me, I guess for the same reason Cassandra did. Wish I understood why. The damn thing about letting someone put trust in you is . . . then you have to keep it.

Mouse was more grandmother than murderess; but I guess she was both. She'd poisoned her abusive husband with garden herbs. Proud of it. The authorities thought her husband had a heart attack. Mouse never would have been charged if honesty hadn't undone her. He got death. She got forty. Now she ran the York Correctional Botanical Garden.

Tammy Rogers had used a knife. I'd known that a while. Cassandra, or rather Cynthia, had shot her son's son-of-a-bitch father in his sleep. Gwen Ridley's sister used a lead pipe and left her abuser with even less of a brain than he was born with. They were all part of a York Correctional sorority of which Mouse was president.

And Cassandra York was no author, which was why she couldn't tell me about Victorian times. Mouse was the ghostwriter and Cassandra the ghost of an author. The partnership funneled advances and royalties to the families of the York chapter of the sisterhood of the abused. Cassandra's mission the night she came to Waterbury was to pass on proceeds from the books for the benefit of Gwen Ridley's sister's kids, the two urchins on the stairs.

Someone found out that Cassie was no author. If word got out, Cassandra York would be dethroned in a heartbeat, demoted to scullery maid or worse. The Queen would lose her crown, her agent, her publisher and her contract. And those depending on her, the families and kids of the York estate, would lose even more. Cassandra wouldn't succumb to blackmail. She died protecting her secret.

I needed to find out who helped her from her tenth floor balcony, a promise to Cassandra; and how much he or she knew, a promise to Mouse.

□   □   □

Cassandra's killer had left a number to a lost or stolen cell, the kind you pick up cheap on the streets from a drug dealer, use for day or so, and then pass on down the food chain for a modest reimbursement. It had been more than a few days since Cassandra's murder. But maybe I'd get lucky. Maybe the cell hadn't been peddled yet. And maybe self-interest would entice Cassandra's blackmailer to renew the game.

I enlisted Maggie at the bar to place a call while I listened in.

"Who the hell's this?" A man's voice: gruff, crude, African-American.

Maggie went fishing and claimed she was Cassandra's agent. It was the right fish. He jumped on the hook and Maggie reeled him in. Maggie ought to play The Palace. The ghost agent for a ghost author said she needed the blackmailer's silence to keep the royalties flowing. The fish agreed to meet Maggie at the KFC on East Main in Meriden to discuss matters. Maggie wasn't going. I was.

☐   ☐ . ☐

The spelling champ showed wearing the "Ho" sweatshirt he said he would. He was five-eight, broad shoulders despite a narrow mind, and he was ugly. Across the street at Boston Market, I munched a chicken carver while Mr. Ugly paced the KFC lot for an hour. He left angry, in a late model Honda. I got his plate.

My former New Haven partner ran the registration. It came back a Thaddeus Walker, Seaview Road in New London.

I made New London in two hours, even with a mandatory pit stop at the Madison rest stop for a Big Mac, fries and a quart of oil.

You can't see Long Island Sound from Seaview Road. It's in a lower middle-class neighborhood inhabited by lower middle-class climbers on their way to middle-middle class. The Honda wasn't in the driveway. I found a scenic spot the other side of a dumpster, munched a few fries and waited.

An hour after parking and thirty minutes after the fries ran out, the Honda pulled in. A heated discussion was warming the front seat. I was too removed to hear, even with the windows down, but I didn't miss the whack the guy in the driver's seat dealt his passenger. She made a run for the front door of the apartment. He intercepted her, slapped her twice, shoved her to the concrete drive and said a few things that hurt more than his hands. She was big, which didn't help her at all. It was Matron!

☐   ☐   ☐

The next day, I reported to Mouse.

"Oh dear me! Dear me! None of us ever knew about *her* husband. She didn't talk about him. You never know until it's too

late. Sometimes Lillian drinks too much and talks too much. She'll
be horrified when she finds out."

"What can I do?" I asked.

"Nothing," Mouse replied. "I know how to take care of such
things."

Mouse asked me to sit on things a few days. I don't much like
sitting, but it was the least I could do. She said she'd get back to me.
I asked when. She didn't say. She asked me to send Lillian to see her
on my way out, turned away and went back to her gardening.

I lingered in the parking lot and thought about going back in. I
didn't. But I stayed long enough to watch Matron leave her shift at five
and head home. She wasn't holding things together well. Corrections
Officers aren't supposed to cry. Just like cops aren't supposed to cry.
What a bunch of bull! We just have advanced degrees in denial. I
thought about following Matron home; then thought poorer of it.

□   □   □

I don't much like staying out of things. I don't much like following
orders. Mouse had made a request, not issued an order. But it still felt
bad in the pit of my stomach. Following my gut instincts is what got
me canned in New Haven. NHPD couldn't fire me again. Maybe this
wasn't the time to turn over a new leaf.

I was almost to Waterbury before I turned around and headed
for Seaview Road. Matron had a weight advantage on Mr. Ugly, but
I didn't like the odds. I had a sick feeling when I turned into the
neighborhood and saw the crowd gathered at the end of the street. I
was too late. Two squad cars had the area in front of the townhouse
off-limits. An ambulance was parked in the driveway.

I didn't want to be the one to tell Mouse that Matron was gone.
I didn't have to. The EMTs came out the front door wheeling the
gurney. A white sheet covered the body. Matron followed supported
by two of the locals. She looked distraught. Her escorts must have
bought it. It turns out the bout between Matron and Mr. Ugly was a
tag team match. Mr. Ugly was badly outnumbered.

□ □ □

The following week I got an envelope from the Victorian Ladies Benevolent Society. Inside was an obit. I guess they thought I should know. Thaddeus Walker died unexpectedly from an undiagnosed heart ailment.

A day later when Gooch called to ask how I was doing, I confessed complete failure. So, Cassandra York's death went unsolved. So did Mr. Ugly's. One was an *accident;* the other *natural causes.*

Gooch asked if I was going to return my inheritance. I said I thought I'd keep it. He asked what I was going to do with it. I gave it half-a-minute's thought. Saving or investing it was out of the question. If word leaked out my three exes would drop by.

"Think I'll spend it," I said. "Buy me a new old set of wheels; get myself launched as a PI."

Gooch didn't say a word. I guess he wasn't looking forward to the prospect.

I dropped in at Drescher's and treated myself to the best dinner I've had in a while. I left a chair for the blonde. She didn't show.

□ □ □

A year later I glanced at the romance novels on the shelf at Walgreens. Some of Cassandra's were still there. There was a new book as well, *A Deadly Shade of Night*, by a new author. I scanned the notes version. "Deadly plotters discover the next in line to the throne is a pretender. Can Cass survive those who plot to reveal her secret and take her life?" I already knew Cass wouldn't make it.

I put the book back, but not before scanning the picture on the back cover. Tammy Rogers had been released and Tamara Chandler was "A new contender for the title of Queen of Romantic Fiction."

There was a new surrogate queen soon to ascend the throne. Mouse had written another bestseller and made another payment on her past. And the children of the sorority of abused women serving time for their crimes, would keep getting royalties to improve their lives and maybe . . . maybe . . . avoid the pit of horrors their mothers had fallen into.

Maybe Mouse was right. Maybe there was something to this redemption bit. Long live the Queen.

△   △   △

Alan D. McWhirter *has been a criminal defense trial attorney for over thirty years. His first work of short fiction, "Don't Call Me Simon," appeared in* Quarry, *Level Best Books' 2009 anthology. He is a member of the Connecticut Soccer Hall of Fame and is an avid model train enthusiast. He lives with his wife, Barbara, in Cheshire, Connecticut.*

Susan Oleksiw *(signature)*

The Recumbent Cow

Susan Oleksiw

If a cow decides the center of a dirt road, in the shade of a lacy pipal tree, is the coolest place to rest at midday, then an approaching autorickshaw can either go around the animal, if the shoulder is wide enough, or wait until the cow decides to move on. This was the situation facing Anita Ray and her taxi driver in the village of Perumachan, in the hills of Kerala, South India.

Anita climbed out of the taxi and approached the cow. When she was within four feet of the animal, she squatted down. The cow raised its head and gazed at her with a drunken, regarding look before lowering its head to the ground. Anita wasn't much of a nature fanatic—she agreed with the divinity that decreed people should be inside and animals outside. As a result, she was perfectly happy to leave the cow undisturbed, and take another route. The driver, however, was tired and wanted to deliver his passenger as soon as possible; he grumbled as he calculated the odds of riding clear of the animal. The shoulders of the lane were soft, falling down into paddy fields on both sides.

"I suppose there is another way," Anita said.

"It should be moving soon." The driver glanced up at the sky, where the sun sprinkled heat and light through the tree branches. "Foolish for it to remain here." But the cow seemed content where it was. After glaring at the animal, he gave the cow a good swift kick in the behind, sacred or not, then turned the autorickshaw in a circle, reversing direction.

The taxi whined its way along a lane skirting the paddy fields until it turned in among the trees. The taxi passed through a village defined by a cluster of houses and a row of shops carrying sweets, bottled drinks, cigarettes, and sundry items. Nearby was a whitewashed post office with a bright red post box hanging by the door.

"Here it is," Anita said, pointing to a modest house. A woman in her forties hurried down the cement steps to greet her.

□   □   □

Anita Ray followed her relative into the house, dabbing at her damp forehead with the cotton shawl of her salwar khameez. "It is very hard to reach you, Chitra Elayamma. Did you know that? It didn't used to be like that," Anita said. "You're getting farther from civilization rather than closer."

"It is the cow," Chitra said. "It occupies the road and no one can make it move." She snorted in disapproval. "But never mind. A cool drink will soothe you after your journey." She left the room. Anita walked to the window and peered out; she could just see the cow in the distance, still idling happily beneath the tree. Odd, she thought. It should have wandered off by now in search of fodder.

"Why is the cow willing to sit there for so long?" Anita asked Chitra when she returned.

"Ah, it is a mystery." Chitra handed her a glass of lime juice. "The priests have spent days talking about it, and now they are thinking of building a temple there. After all, the bull Nandi is Shiva's vehicle, so Shiva would be pleased with a temple there."

"Days?" Anita said. "Just how long has the cow been there?"

"Days." Chitra settled herself in a chair and gave Anita a bland look. "You have been away far too long. You have forgotten such things happen."

"I suppose so. Well, what about your daughter? After all, she is the reason I have come."

□   □   □

Ambala, Chitra's daughter and a few years younger than Anita, looked up from her desk when her mother entered the bedroom. Ambala tidied up her desk, sliding stationery and envelopes under a large book. Anita complimented Ambala on how lovely she looked, and Ambala did her mother proud by asking all the right questions and displaying a suitable interest in Anita's travel troubles in reaching the remote village. Anita answered these with only half her attention; the rest of her mind kept drifting to the atlas spread open on Ambala's desk.

"You haven't told her," Ambala said at last.

"Haven't told me what, Chitra Elayamma?" Anita said.

"Oh, dear." Chitra plunked herself down on the bed. "All our plans have fallen apart." She sighed. "It is shameful this is happening to you, Ambala, shameful. That family will pay. I vow to Shiva that family will pay."

"What family?" Anita asked. This sounded like a right juicy scandal, and considering how proper her family insisted on being, a good scandal was a rare treat.

"The marriage is off, I think," Chitra said.

"Off? But this marriage has been planned since childhood," Anita said. "You and the Pillais have talked about this for years. Ambala and Sunil would grow up and get married—and you both seemed such good friends."

"It's the groom's father. A cheap, mean-spirited man if ever there was one," Chitra said. "But Ambala is forgiving," she said, giving her daughter's arm an affectionate pat. "Please, let us not talk about it now." Chitra rose. "It is time for Ambala to collect the post." Ambala smiled warmly as she headed off to the village center.

□   □   □

That night, Ambala's father, Dilip Nayar, scurried off to his library, muttering to himself. Anita waited before following him. He glanced up at her as she entered the room, then returned to his papers.

The library was an old room designed in the 1930s to accommodate a new intellectual interest in the family; shelves reached chest high and held books published from around the world on a myriad of topics. The stone floor was covered with a tattered carpet, and the heavy wooden furniture had long since lost its luster.

"Chitra Elayamma told me the news. It must certainly be a disappointment to have the marriage called off so late in the planning."

"Murderer, that's what he is."

"Who?"

"Old Pillai, Sunil's father. A rotten, evil man."

Anita was taken aback by his venom. "But he was your friend, yes?"

"He wants me dead."

"Why do you say that?" Anita leaned closer. He was angry but still calm enough to know what he was saying.

"I have taken care of it," he said.

"Is that why the marriage fell apart?"

"Ah, that was greed. Pure greed." His lip began to twitch. "I would give all my wealth, such as it is, to make Ambala happy, but do I dare give her to a family that refuses even the modest sum she deserves for appearances' sake?"

"So it is a financial question?"

He nodded. "I have asked for the proper amount considering the Pillais' situation, and he has refused. Refused! Think of it! A man of his stature, with the understanding we have had all these years!"

"I thought this sort of thing happened all the time," Anita said. Indeed, arranged marriages hinged on a successful business negotiation. What reason did Dilip have for being upset? This eventuality couldn't be a surprise to him. The young man and woman might accept each other, but Nayar tradition required that the groom provide certain gifts—gold bracelets and necklaces, gold-bordered saris, and other items.

"He has become mean-spirited. And he thinks if I die, he'll have the marriage and no dowry to pay." His lip curled and he pounded the desk with his fist.

"Now why would he think you're going to die?" Anita asked, more to herself than to him.

□   □   □

Anita's relations lived in one of the tiniest villages in this part of Kerala, and she set out to explore the village on foot.

A row of children met her as she entered the packed ground of the village center. With the blank stare Westerners reserve for television, the children watched her pass through the compound and then fell into step behind her, following her through the village and along the lane until she came upon the cow, still sleeping in the middle of the path.

"It's sleeping," one of the children said.

"Sleeping," said another. This established, the children watched Anita as she circumnavigated the animal. She backed away, stepping down into a paddy field, and then clambered back up the embankment and approached the cow from the other side. The cow raised its head, studied her, then lowered its big snout and resumed sleeping.

"Sleeping," another child said.

"It seems to do a lot of that," Anita said.

"Six days," one of them said.

"Six days lying here in this spot?" Anita said.

Half a dozen heads nodded in reply.

□   □   □

Anita walked along until she came to a tea stall, where she ordered a tall glass of coffee. She drank her coffee beneath a stand of palms, eavesdropping on women waiting for the midmorning bus and men who came for a cigarette or a few bananas. A short man dressed in the usual plaid lungi, carrying a bundle of umbrella skeletons, stood off to one side while he drank his coffee. Anita could feel his eyes on her, but when she glanced at him, he looked away. When only the tea wallah remained, Anita moved forward.

"You are here for Ambala's engagement ceremony?" the tea wallah said. His name was Pran, and he sat inside his closet-sized shop with complete serenity. "I am learning all this from Sunil Pillai, the groom."

"I haven't seen Sunil yet."

"No matter. The wedding is off, you know. Disagreements."

"So I've heard. It's too bad. The families have been looking forward to this wedding since Ambala and Sunil were both children."

"Not so long ago," Pran said. "Not so long ago."

"What went wrong?"

"What always goes wrong. Money. They are not agreeing on the dowry. Mr. Nayar wants more than Mr. Pillai will give." Pran leaned forward to whisper. "It is said Mr. Nayar has asked for an exorbitant sum, and Mr. Pillai has countered with a tiny sum. It is a strange disagreement."

"It sounds perfectly normal to me," said Anita, who had listened for years to the tales of families trying to find a happy middle ground for the desired dowry.

"It is not," Pran declared. "They are of equal wealth, yet their expectations suddenly diverge. What has made it so?"

"There's something else I don't understand. That cow on the path," Anita said. "Whose is it?"

"Ah! Another mystery." Pran let a smile spread over his face as he rested his forearm on his thigh and leaned forward, warming to his subject. "One day we are walking along the path like any other part of Kerala, and the next it is barred by a cow. We are pulling and poking and pushing and tempting and yelling and nothing is happening. The cow is not moving. The priest comes and he cannot make it move. No one can make it budge."

"Whose cow is it?"

"It is Mr. Pillai's. It is the family cow, an old one ready to be sold, but a cow nonetheless."

"And he can't make it move?"

Pran shook his head. "No one can make it move. So the priest thinks it is an omen, and we should build a temple there. So another paddy field will be filled in for building. We will soon be a city like Trivandrum." He shook his head in dismay as Anita looked out upon an ocean of greens, with not a single building taller than the lowest palm tree.

□   □   □

Mr. Raman Pillai lived in a one-story house with a flat roof and a large compound on the other side of the village. Anita found Raman Pillai in his office, a small two-room building, with three tables crowded together in one room, and Mr. Pillai's desk and stacks of papers filling the other. Through a gate in the compound wall, Anita could see another building, where, Anita assumed, Mr. Pillai's workers manufactured the fertilizers that were the main product of his company.

"Ah, Anita!" Raman rose to greet her, his hands pressed together in anjali. "I am hearing you are coming all this way for the ceremony." His voice caught on the last word.

"It is a lovely journey nonetheless," Anita said. "I have seen the cow in the lane." Mr. Pillai immediately grew restless, shifting in his seat. "You must be upset. It is your cow."

"Yes, yes, yes." He began to mumble about how old the animal was and how little it would fetch on the market.

"Is it true the priest wants to build a Shiva temple there?" Anita asked. There was no mistaking the shudder that ran through him.

"Yes, we have discussed this. It is a difficult decision—I am to lose a cow."

"It's sort of an honor, though, isn't it?"

"I do not need honor. I have too many problems to worry about."

"Is business pulling hard?"

"I am not finding success in my new organic fertilizers. There is much suspicion among farmers."

"Perhaps a new temple will give people something to get excited about," Anita said.

"The priest should find more important things to talk about. Look at the village! Do you see the line of women at the public spigot in the morning and evening? Let the priest dig wells for us and forget about building a temple." He began to shove papers back and forth across his desk in a futile effort to relieve his anger.

□   □   □

On her way back to her cousin's house, Anita decided to take one more look at the cow, eyeball to eyeball, so to speak. She sauntered up to the animal, knelt down, tapped its muzzle to awaken it, and looked deep into its dark brown eyes. Anita felt the soft brush of the cow's breath against her face. The ground seemed uneven here, so she tugged at the cow's foreleg and the animal shifted to get comfortable again. Dark brown earth clung to its chest before it lowered its head once again, giving a gentle snort of relief. That cow, Anita thought, is not going to move on its own accord.

□   □   □

The evening meal was a disjointed affair, with Chitra transporting dishes from kitchen to table, hovering, fussing, and generally looking unhappy. Ambala chatted amiably about her studies, using a single perfunctory question from her father to wander the byways of geography and art history and any other topic that came to mind. She alone of the household seemed unperturbed by the changes in her marital fortunes. At ten o'clock, Anita admitted to a daylong weariness and withdrew to her room.

Instead of closing the windows and turning on the fan, however, Anita relaxed in a chaise longue and listened to the night animals prowling the compound. Off and on through the night, she awoke, found herself arranged uncomfortably, and repositioned herself. At two o'clock she heard what she thought was the sound of the gate latch, and leaned out the window to catch a glimpse of whom it might be. Seeing only an indistinct shadow, she crept from her room and out the front door, following the moving shadow at a distance. The shadow slipped into a paddy field. A few minutes later, the shadow, in the form of Dilip Nayar, climbed out of the paddy field beside the cow.

"Ah, Nandi, how you rest," Dilip said.

The cow raised its head and began to yawn; just as it did so, Dilip popped a large packet into its mouth. The cow gulped, began to chew, and after a while swallowed. With a contented sigh, it lowered its head again. Dilip stroked the cow's muzzle. Then, he crawled across the lane and slipped into the paddy field. Anita watched him turn into a shadow melding with the darkness.

□   □   □

The following morning, Anita announced she was going to visit the local priest.

"I'm interested in this temple idea," she said over breakfast.

"You shouldn't meddle." Dilip stopped spooning chutney over his idlies long enough to glare at her. "This is a matter for careful scrutiny."

"You are quite right, but I am thinking that perhaps I have neglected my roots, my family tradition. You know that roots and all that sort of thing are important to Americans," Anita said.

"That's right, Acchan," Ambala said. "Americans are always looking at their roots." She made Anita feel like a boat uncertain of its moorings.

"You seem to know a lot about what Americans are like," Anita said to Ambala.

"I read a lot," Ambala said, blushing. "Amma, would you like more coffee?" She retrieved her mother's cup and rose from the table with celerity.

□   □   □

By the time Anita reached the temple, the morning puja was long over and the temple compound almost empty. Through the open door she could see a man in a white dhoti, his tonsured head leaning over a small wooden desk. She climbed the two steep steps and stood on the sill, waiting to be acknowledged. The priest glared at her, then waved her in. She pulled a rickety wooden chair forward and sat down. "It's about the cow on the road."

"Ah, our own Nandi," he said. "A very grave problem." He nodded. "Why are you interested in this? You are the relations from America? Isn't it?"

"I like animals. All Americans like animals. We have lots of pets," Anita said, hoping he didn't know anything about her and wondering if a cow could come under the category of a household pet. "And I'm sort of wondering if the cow is comfortable there."

"It is a cow, is it not?"

"Yes, it's a cow, but cows have their standards, too."

"Ah, you are one of those. Hippie?"

Anita started, but refrained from telling him hippies had gone the way of the dodo bird. "Certainly not. I'm just concerned about the animal."

He glowered at her. "It is a cow in the road, nothing more."

"But it has been there for some time."

"A cow is a cow."

"Suppose you decide to build a temple there. What will happen then?"

"Ahha," he said with a broad smile. "Yes, a new temple."

"What happens to the cow?"

"She may stay. We shall create a fine pen for her, and feed her exceedingly well."

"So then she may never leave."

"Why would she leave?"

"Was this your idea?"

"Whose idea would it be? I am speaking to you, yes?"

"I was just wondering if people have been talking about it and this idea was in the wind, so to speak."

"It is an idea acceptable to others, if that is what you want to know."

"Does my family like the idea? Dilip and Chitra Nayar, for instance?"

"He has expressed support, yes. He has even pledged one lakh rupees." The priest was obviously impressed. "Of course, there are restrictions."

"Of course."

"About the cow." He sighed. "It is old, but on request we can find it a more congenial spot if necessary."

"And Ram Pillai?"

The priest frowned. "He is not so agreeable—it is, after all, his cow that is to be sacrificed for the temple. It will not return to him. It is now a gift to Shiva."

"So he is not donating any money?"

"Yes, he is donating, but a smaller amount." Again he sighed. "He, too, has restrictions."

"Of course. And you agreed to them?" Anita asked. The priest glared at her.

"A temple is a great undertaking."

"Did he agree to donate the money before or after you promised to keep the cow happy in its current location?"

"After. It is great work making such a promise, but we have done it."

"So the cow will be moved. And the cow will not be moved."

"Exactly," the priest said. He looked like a man tired of life, of the squabbles and bickerings that came with life in a small village.

"Interesting," said Anita, and made her departure.

□ □ □

All this walking around the village made her thirsty, so Anita headed for the tea stall and a chat with her new friend Pran. Tea wallahs seemed such sensible people, perhaps because they sat behind their wooden counter and watched the follies of their friends unfold before them like stage dramas.

"You have been making a round of the village," Pran said as he set a tall glass of coffee in front of her.

"I was just visiting the priest, the one who wants to build a Shiva temple around the cow. What do you think of the idea?" She reached for her coffee, glad for the refreshment.

"Another temple cannot go amiss, but we will now have to come up with more money to run it."

"I heard that Dilip Nayar has pledged a lakh to fund it."

"I too have heard this," Pran said.

"And you think it is strange?"

"I think he does not believe the temple will be built, so what does it matter if he promises a thousand lakhs? No money will ever leave his pocket."

"His pledge adds to the impression that he is a much richer man than we thought."

"Much, much richer."

"And it makes it look like he is richer, far richer, than the Pillais."

Pran leaned forward with a mischievous grin on his face. "Money is at the root of the dissolution of the wedding plans. Mr. Nayar has asked for an outrageous sum, and Mr. Pillai has refused." He leaned back. "How did such a state come about?"

"That," Anita said, "is the question to be answered."

"Now where are you going?" Pran asked.

"To the post office," Anita called back.

□ □ □

It had occurred to Anita earlier in the morning that she had not seen Sunil Pillai yet, Ambala's intended. And since there apparently was not going to be a wedding, she had better visit now or she might never have the chance.

Sunil Pillai was a young man of noticeable grace. His skin was shiny mocha, and his large brown eyes warm and unsuspecting. Anita wondered how he would make his way in the world without a coarser protective covering.

"It must be devastating to have your marriage plans ruined at the last minute," she said.

"It is what happens," he said with a shrug.

"That's very philosophical." He was relaxed and almost uninterested in her conversation, but not wanting to seem rude, she concluded, he was willing to chat. "Aren't you surprised that Ambala could not talk her father into taking a smaller dowry? After all, he won't have to worry about her moving away after the wedding. You are staying here, aren't you?"

"Me?" He sat up in his chair. "Yes, I am staying here. But it's not up to Ambala to talk her father into changing his mind."

That's a peculiar answer, Anita thought. "Would you like her to?"

"I don't think my opinion enters into it."

"And your father?"

"He's furious," Sunil said, more relaxed. "He's been trying to find a way to get even, but fate thwarts him."

"What has he tried?"

"I don't know for sure, but I think he has consulted people."

"There is someone other than the priest?"

"I think the old pariah still performs rites and such for people," he said.

"I don't think I know who that is."

"He mends umbrellas for a living," Sunil said. "You see him about the village."

"So your father went to some sort of shaman?"

Sunil shrugged. "But who believes in curses these days? And now, for all his evil thinking, look at what has happened to his cow?"

"Yes, indeed. Why doesn't he take it home?"

"He can't get the fool animal to move. It will not budge."

□   □   □

Dilip came home for a meal around one o'clock, and the family shook itself out of its lethargy to eat and talk about the passing day. After a while Anita said, "I went into the village today, to see what I could learn about the cow and the temple."

"Well, quite the idea, isn't it?" Dilip said.

"Yes, they're going to keep the cow there and build around it."

"No, no," Dilip said. "They're going to move the cow."

"No," Anita said. "It's staying where it is. The priest promised Ram Pillai. After all, it's his cow."

"But he promised me," Dilip said.

"Why would he promise you?" Chitra said. "Why do you care?"

"Yes, Uncle. Why do you care?"

Dilip looked around at three female faces, two staring at him in dismay.

"I think it's time for you and Ram to come clean," Anita said.

"What does that mean?" he said.

"The whole truth," Anita said. "You too, Ambala."

"Me?"

"Her?" her parents said in unison.

Anita's challenge momentarily silenced the three of them, but soon all three broke into loud exclamations of innocence and ignorance. "Fine, fine," Anita said. "Let me tell you what I think. This has been an interesting visit, that's all I can say."

"We are sorry you have wasted your trip," Chitra said, "but we can still have a nice visit."

"I don't think that's what she's talking about," Dilip said.

"What are you talking about?" Ambala said.

"You know the answer to that, I think," Anita said. "You were due to marry this summer, but you decided you wanted to do something else with your life. I stopped at the post office this morning, and the mailman told me you get lots of letters from universities in Europe and America."

"Is that true?" Chitra asked.

"America?" Dilip's voice cracked.

"Ambala knew you wouldn't want to hear about her plans, but a wedding would ruin them before she even had a chance to try, so she came up with the perfect scheme. She asked Sunil, her good friend since childhood, to tell his father that her family was secretly poor and would settle for a small dowry. Meanwhile, Ambala told you, Uncle, that Sunil's father was secretly rich and could afford a huge dowry."

"You said he made a fortune when he sold a parcel of land," Dilip said. "Is it not true, Ambala?" Ambala had the grace to look away.

"Oh, my child!" he said, then turned to Anita. "I thought he was rich and holding out on me, that he didn't value my Ambala and wouldn't give her the dowry she deserved. We have been friends all our lives, and I was devastated."

Chitra patted his hand.

"But I was right about his character," Dilip said.

"Why do you say that?" Anita asked. "It seems you both tried to get the better of each other."

"Because when I didn't agree to the paltry sum he was offering, he tried to have me murdered by a curse."

"Oh, husband! Such a thing to say!" Chitra said.

"It's the truth," he said. "I saw that umbrella mender coming out of Ram's house—you know he is a dangerous sorcerer—and later that night, on my way home from a visit to Ram's house—he especially asked me to come—I came to a spot on the lane where the ground had been turned up. It was quite noticeable—soft brown earth where normally there would be hard-packed light brown dirt. I found a stick and dug down and uncovered a metal plaque." He shivered at the memory.

"What was on the plaque?" Chitra said.

"It was an image of me with my name and a curse and symbols. It is the old curse that you bury in the ground and the intended victim walks over the spot and dies there," Dilip said. "That is what my old friend was trying to do to me." Chitra gasped.

"I'm sure it's a mistake," Ambala said.

Anita looked at Ambala. "Not quite the result you intended." Ambala shook her head.

"Where is it now?" Chitra asked.

"I put it back in the ground, but face downward, so it couldn't do me any harm, and then I thought I would get even."

"Oh, no! What did you do?" Chitra sat bolt upright, her hands clasped at her chest.

"I sneaked back to Ram's house and took his cow and led it down to the spot on the lane and left it tethered there."

"But why doesn't Ram Pillai just take it home?" Chitra asked.

"Because every night he feeds it," Anita said. "And he mixes in a healthy dose of, what?"

"Ram is experimenting with asafetida and other things to make organic fertilizers," Dilip said. "I am using the asafetida—it is a sedative, you know."

"So that's why the animal will not leave the spot," Chitra said.

"You drugged the cow?" Ambala said.

"Every night," Anita said.

"How did you guess?" Dilip asked.

"When I got a good look at the cow earlier in the day, the animal seemed too lethargic even for a cow. I figured someone had to be doing something to it, so I followed you last night and saw you feed it."

"So the mystery is solved?" Chitra said. "The Pillais are not poor and we are not rich. The marriage can go forward? We can settle the dowry?" Ambala gave a little yelp, and her parents turned to her. "What is the matter with you, child?"

"But you and Mr. Pillai are enemies now," Ambala said.

"Enemies?" Chitra said. "Don't be foolish. It's all a misunderstanding. Isn't it, Dilip?"

"Look at the trouble you have caused, child," Dilip said. "My old friend and I are not speaking. I must donate money I cannot afford to build a new temple that will destroy our one good road, and all the village will laugh at us for what has happened."

"It's Anita's fault," Ambala said.

"What?" the other three said in unison.

"It's her karma to find evil around her," Ambala said. "Look at all the deaths in Trivandrum that have been turned into murders." Chitra frowned at this unconventional defense.

"She does have a point, Chitra," Dilip said. "We wouldn't have to explain as much. And think how grateful Ram Pillai would be to have it all tidied up."

"You can't be serious," Anita said.

"But she is my cousin-sister's niece!" Chitra said.

"Anita," Dilip said, with a deep sigh. "You must admit that it would help us save face in the village."

"I won't allow it," Chitra said.

"Never mind," Anita said. "I think I have a plan."

△   △   △

Susan Oleksiw is the author of the Mellingham series featuring Chief of Police Joe Silva (A Murderous Innocence) *and a second series featuring Anita Ray* (Under the Eye of Kali). *Oleksiw compiled* A Reader's Guide to the Classic British Mystery, *and was consulting editor for* The Oxford Companion to Crime and Mystery Writing. *Oleksiw was a co-founder of Level Best Books.*

Hard Fall

Ben Hanstein

Hardboiled?" I tell the girl behind the desk. "Sweetheart, I'm so hardboiled that if I knock an egg off the counter, it sits back up and makes a wisecrack."

She smiles. Brilliant.

I cough discreetly and stub out the cigarette like I smoke the ugly cancer-sticks all the time. I am smoking, no more than ten feet away from a sign forbidding the same. I am talking like Humphrey Bogart, and I'm wearing a trench coat. The part is as good as mine.

"So your job references," the girl says, chewing on the side of her mouth and making her adorable mole dance. "Little thin, yeah? Extra, extra, mattress commercial down in Langdon. After that, most of these are . . ."

"Role preparation," I say, cutting off the litany of failures. "Short order cook, security guard, store clerk. I find that too many of my fellows cut themselves off from society, from the real world. I've got my finger—"

This line is pure gold.

"—on the pulse of humanity."

I'm surprised they don't just give me the part right now.

"In Greenly Falls?" she asks, arching an eyebrow.

"You are still human up here, right?"

She smiles, using her free hand to push an errant lock of dusky hair aside. I'm seeing possibilities beyond the part and the fifteen hundred bucks.

The advertisement had been a little odd: "Seeking new talent for 'tough guy' in small-town edition of a popular true crime series." The ad had been printed on a rather slipshod flier tucked into the local rag. I'd found a free copy jammed beneath the door of my dingy apartment.

Since I blew into town with my Ford Pinto (a mass of dents and rust given horrible sentience and purpose), my Macintosh trench coat (freakin' perfection personified), and my drama degree (completely useless), I had been drifting. This had been my usual status since Boston College: on the drift. But in Greenly Falls the feeling had intensified, and I was beginning to have a recurring nightmare where I actually blew away while behind the counter at the Greenly Falls Hardtack Diner, leaving behind a spatula and a faint sense of unrealized potential.

Then came the flier. And I'll be damned if I didn't find my degree, polish the frame and hang it back on the wall. This was my chance.

"Will you be conducting the interview?" I ask the girl. "I'm sorry, I just realized I don't even know your—"

"Molly. Molly Radcliff," she says with another smile, burying the mole in a dimple. "No, I'm afraid I'm just the vetter. Mr. Pratt will be conducting the interview, which we need to speak about first."

I look around the room. Clearly a rental, one of the innumerable unused rooms in the sprawling district court complex. Newly furnished too, the photographs and papers haven't had a chance to pick up a layer of dust, and the sign on the door, "Pratt Talent Agency," had been printed recently.

"He's down the hall," Molly says, nodding to the exit. "Not enough room in here for the whole works. We're still tossing everything together. Getting to fill spots for this special 'rural Maine' episode of *Hard Fall* is a real coup for us."

"Very exciting. It's good they're finally getting the *Hard Fall* guy out of Boston. You know, I had some ideas for that show, back when—"

"We're looking for a local slant on your typical vicious leg breaker," Molly says, scribbling something in the margin of a file. "We've had two guys in here who would fit in perfectly in Chicago or New York, but that's not what we want."

"You want local," I say. "Lobsters and moose and chewing tobacco."

She winces. "We like to think there's a bit more to Greenly Falls than what you see on the license plates," she says. "Maybe this is a bad—"

"No," I say. "No, I've got it. Acting's a hundred and ten percent role immersion."

The truth was, if I immersed myself any more out here I was going to burn the diner down. Between the looming rent payment, corned beef hash out of the can for three nights straight, and my Pinto's busted suspension, with the damn Greenly Falls potholes eating car axles like breadsticks, I was near the end of the proverbial rope.

"Fine," Molly says, after a moment. "Can't be worse than the others. Jack Pratt likes to run an organic interview."

"Brilliant. So, uh—"

"That means you go in and run through the scene without a script," Molly says. "We want actors, not readers. You go in and stay in character until you leave, then Jack and I put our heads together and call you back for a look at the actual script. Follow me?"

"So just . . . act?"

"Yeah," she says, closing her eyes for a moment. "That'd be super."

I wait a moment. From the street I hear the hiss of a pulp truck's brakes, as it slows on Main Street to turn onto Route 16. The trucks roll by my apartment nonstop; mechanical dragons venting exhaust, whose hunting cry is the shriek of engine brakes, hauling peeling pulpwood to lairs hidden among the surviving mills along the

Androscoggin. I have come to closely associate my own poverty with the rumble of those trucks.

"Okay, sweetheart," I say, pulling up the collar on the trench coat, my ace in the hole. "Pratt won't know what hit him."

She shakes her head and turns a page in the file.

"Here we go," she says, then rattles off the part: "You're a small-town drug dealer, fence and part-time thug, hired to tell the victim from scene three, Chad Taylor, to lay off your boss. He's been putting the squeeze on Ms. Woodbury, introduced in scene five, with a recording from a sleazy motel. Taylor is a lawyer, and his part will be played by Jack, for today's interview."

"Dirt bag is going to pay," I say, feeling pure character ooze out of my pores and coat my skin like sweat. I smack a fist into my hand and try not to wince. My part-time thug is not a wincer.

"Right," Molly says. "You want the recording burnt, and you want him to know you mean business. We're talking a minute-twenty bit to lead the episode, and the audience has to hate you. So lay it on thick and heavy."

"Heavy?" I say, wishing I hadn't put out the cigarette so I could take a drag. "I'll come down heavier than a double order of fried dough at the Hardtack Diner. With powdered sugar."

My word. If I wasn't used to the phenomenon, I'd be dazzling myself right now. I'm like a freakin' changeling.

"Very . . . apt," Molly says, clearly aroused by the magic of drama. This is a slam dunk. "His office is just down the hall. It's another rental, so look for the sign on the door. And whatever you do, don't break character."

"Brilliant, sweetheart," I say, tossing her a smile and tipping an invisible hat. "See you in the funny pages."

She sighs, exhaling pure adoration, and I smash open the door like it owes me money. Jack doesn't realize what a treat he's in for.

The building is home to a number of offices, with the hallway behind me forking off toward the district court and clerk's windows.

I pass the Inland Fish and Wildlife headquarters for the county, a bail bondsman's office and another empty rental. Two men, clearly lawyers in their dark suits and neat haircuts, nod hello and I sneer back. A deputy, skin nearly as wrinkled as his brown uniform, frowns at my upturned collar and I look away, as if nervous.

Sometimes I scare even myself.

The office has another sign with the same title: "Pratt Talent Agency." A note's been attached to the printout, indicating that anyone interested in the *Hard Fall* part should apply at Room 112 with Molly Radcliff. I pull the door open and hear a tone back inside the office somewhere.

I pass through a receptionist's office, abandoned except for a note saying "Back at two." Lunch break, probably at the Hardtack, God help her. I flex beneath the coat, feeling particularly villainous. I round the office corner, teeth grinding away like millstones.

"My job don't take no lunch break, Mr. Taylor," I announce, focusing on the man behind the desk. Freakin' perfect impact line. My Down East accent, needless to say, could easily fool a native.

"What?" he asks, phone in hand and a pad in front of him.

Jack Pratt, or rather Chad Taylor, is a couple inches shorter than me, but broader. His skin is the pink of a man who spends the right amount of time outdoors, out of the wind, and his hands are free of calluses. Black hair is greasy with gel, and the price of his suit could put me in corned beef hash for a year.

"No reason this has to be difficult," I say, stepping aside to kick over a wastebasket. "Be a shame to mess up your pretty office."

Balled-up papers roll everywhere. Taylor turns pinker and waves a hand at me.

"I'm busy until three," he says, returning the phone to his ear. "Pick up that mess and make an appointment. Sorry, Roger? Yeah, I'm here and—"

Ho ho! Upstage me will you?

I step over the wastebasket, seize the receiver and, after a brief and dangerously well-contested wrestling match, slam the phone down onto the cradle. Then I plant my fists on his blotter and stare right into his wet, cow eyes.

"Look, buddy," I say through gritted teeth. "This can go ugly real fast. Wicked ugly."

He stares down at his phone, then back up at me. I reach into my coat, pulling out the cigarettes and sticking one between my teeth.

"Look," he says. Rather hammy, but not awful. "I don't know who . . . Sir, there's no smoking in this building."

"Ain't it a shame?" I ask, admiring the burning cigarette without letting the horrid smoke enter my lungs. "That's what they call progress, eh, Chad?"

I'm wracking my brains, seeking a derisive nickname for "Chad," and coming up empty. Maybe they can change it on rewrites.

"I don't know who you are," Taylor says, glancing down at his phone. "But this isn't helping you. Let's sit down and talk about—"

This guy isn't bad, for a casting director.

"You sit," I say, the cigarette bouncing between my lips. "I'll talk. The boss lady wants the recording, Chad. Which means I want the recording. Which means you want to give me the recording. Or else."

"Are you nuts?" he asks. "Do you know how many laws you're breaking, right now?"

"Better laws than, say," I drawl out, letting the suspense build until it's causing me physical pain to withhold such a brutally amazing line, "your fingers."

Maybe I shouldn't be an actor, although I'm clearly a natural. Maybe I should be a writer.

"Look—"

"No, you look," I say, jabbing my fingers into his blotter and watching him jump. "This ain't difficult. You give me the recording of Woodbury, and I don't leave your bloated corpse for the lobstahs."

Greenly Falls is more than a hundred miles from the coast, but I have to assume there's a freshwater variant of the iconic crustaceans. Goddamn, could I be any more regionally appropriate?

"The what? Woodbury?" he gapes at me. "She sent you?"

"The boss lady's business ain't mine, and it sure as shit ain't yours," I say. "Where's the tape? Or should I ask again with this cigarette?"

He's gone all wobbly, pale and perspiring beneath a pompadour that seems to have lost all of its pomp. What was this guy doing working for a no-name talent agency, in Maine of all places? I'm going to have to crank it up a notch or three just to make separation between the two of us.

"Too late, buddy," I say, seizing the phone and yanking it off the desk. "I'm losing interest here."

I hurl it against the wall and watch glass shards rain down from a framed picture of Jack Pratt with his cute wife and kids. Damn, unfortunately aimed. Oh well, he'll thank me for it after riding my wake all the way to Hollywood.

"Please, sir," the man says, his voice as shrill as a pulp truck's e-brake. "Stop. This isn't right. We need to—"

"Where's the tape?" I ask, shoving a stack of files onto the floor. "Where's the tape, Taylor? This can all stop right now."

He stands up and yells something, reaching over the table to grapple me. Damn, this is bad. I didn't know there would be choreography for the part. What had that ex-gym teacher told me at the fight scene seminar? Grasp the forearm and pull while . . . something . . . something . . . true actors can do it on the fly?

Yeah, "Dramatic Weekend: How to be an Amazing Method Actor" had ended something like that. True actors can do it on the fly. Best hundred and sixty dollars I'd ever spent.

I seize his forearm and yank him toward me, pulling with his momentum and forcing him off his feet. He must have expected that, because he falls neatly enough, awkwardly sprawled across the table and sending pens and paperclips into full retreat. Two professionals at the height of their game. It's a goddamn crime that there isn't a camera rolling.

He gasps like a fish and tries to roll himself back to his feet, but I latch onto the lapels of his suit and position him on the table. I bring the lit end of my cigarette right up to his eyes and he goes quiet.

"That's right, Chad," I say. "No more games. I want the tape. You watching this cig, buddy?"

"Uh," he grunts. "Uh-huh."

"Good, Chaddy-wick, that's good." A little forced, but not awful on the spur of the moment. "I've got your eyes right here. And I want that tape. Because you know what, little Chaddy-wick?"

"W . . . what?"

"One way or another," I hiss into his ear. "Something's going to burn."

They're going to give me a role. Not a bit part, not a throwaway tough guy, but a recurring role. It's like I've walked out of a freakin' Bogart flick. To hell with the role, they might just hand me the lead.

After that last line, it's pretty clear that Pratt's made up his mind. He whimpers his acquiescence to my dramatic dominance and flips through a cardboard box until he comes up with the goods. A cassette tape, and when he places it carefully on the desk, I realize he's handing me more than a prop.

He's handing me a career. Goodbye diner, goodbye apartment, goodbye pulp trucks.

I look up and he glances away.

"Do you want—?" I whisper at him, leery of breaking character but uncertain as to protocol. "Should I actually—you know?"

He frowns at me. Shit, shit, shit! Never, never break character. No matter what, until a director says cut.

"I mean, shut up, buddy," I say, yanking the black tongue of the cassette out and bringing up my lighter. "I call the shots around here."

The tape goes up pretty quickly, leaving a stench of burning plastic and no lasting flames. Guess my concerns about setting Pratt's office on fire were unfounded. Time to close. And you better believe I'm going to close hard.

"Alright, buddy," I say, putting my cigarette out on his varnished desk. "Lean on the boss lady again, and it'll be more than a little pushing next time. It'll be those sweet wheels outside, or that pretty wife."

His face tightens up and I grin, flicking my thumb and forefinger up to point at his face.

"Up here, in Greenly Falls, there's two things that are always true," I say, hoping he remembers to write this down for the *Hard Fall* folks to look at. "Moose always drop their antlers in March—"

Or whenever.

"—and," I finish, dropping my thumb on top of my forefinger, "anything can burn."

I turn, trench coat morphing every step into a malevolent glide, and stride into the receptionist's office. I pump my fist out of sight, then turn to stick my head back into Pratt's office. The talent scout, stooping over with the remains of his phone, freezes with eyes locked on mine.

"I just wanted to say," I whisper, "thanks so much for this opportunity. I'd be happy to come back for another take, if you folks want, and have a great day."

He's still standing with his mouth open amid the stink of burnt cassette tape when I leave his office for good.

Molly is out, with a sign on the door saying she'll be back at four. I've got a shift at the diner, so I head for home with visions of fifteen-hundred-dollar checks dancing in my head. Then comes the waiting, the terrible waiting. The shift crawls by, followed by a night spent tossing and turning on the spring-infested mattress and then the whole lousy weekend. Why won't they call?

Finally it's Monday, and I just can't take it anymore. The landlady is breathing down my neck for the rent, and I break into a cold sweat whenever a pulp truck rolls by the apartment, carrying the stench of exhaust and failure. It may shatter every rule in the book, but I need to go visit Molly and Jack.

The district court building has a Greenly Falls police officer out front, which is a change. I nod politely to him, and he turns to stare at me as I open the door. I hear the squawk of his radio as I stride up to Molly's office in Room 112.

It's empty. Completely empty. There is a small card on the desk advising me that the office is available for rentals, with prices listed by the month, week and even by the day. Perhaps Pratt Talent Agency has found permanent digs? Setting up in unused portions of the district court was a trifle amateurish, after all.

Of course, that's it. Clearly, Jack Pratt is moving to a nicer office, well away from Main Street and the damn pulp trucks, and Molly has simply lost me in the shuffle. She'll owe me dinner for that one.

Jack's office no longer bears the handwritten sign either. It's been replaced by something painted on the glass, but whatever it says goes by the wayside when I see the man himself inside. Brilliant, he hasn't moved the whole operation yet.

"Jack!" I say with a wide smile as I shove the door open. "Just thought I'd drop in—"

"Jesus," the receptionist, a pretty thing with a bob of flaxen-colored hair, gasps. "Chad, is that—?"

"Dial the cops, Peggy," Jack says, the old kidder. "It's him."

"Damn straight," I say, striding up and slapping the agent on the back. "Thought you could get rid of me, huh? Not that easy, I'm afraid. Peggy?"

"Yes," she says into the phone, eyes darting back to me when I say her name. "Yes, *now*, Tim. Right now."

"Dead sexy and a talented actress," I whisper to Jack, nudging his ribs, "you old dog. Peggy, I'll take cream and two sugars. Thanks, you're a doll. Now Jack, about this part . . ."

Then I'm face down on Peggy's desk, with something cold snapping around my wrists, and wondering what the hell just happened. I twist my neck around to see the cop from out front talking with Jack.

"Yes, it's him," Jack's saying. "No, no doubt at all. He burned the DEA tape of Woodbury's meth deal. That whole case is probably dead in the water. Charge him with—"

"Jack?" I say, a little confused.

"—and criminal threatening with a dangerous weapon," he's saying. "If I can't take Molly Woodbury's head, I'm taking his."

"Molly?" I say. My face peels away from Peggy's desk as the officer lifts me away. "Jack, wait, Jack, I need to talk to you. Jack!"

We're almost to the door, and I can feel the walls closing in and hear the distant pulp trucks revving their engines. Then a voice.

"Stop, I want to hear this."

Nearly sobbing with relief, I turn back toward Jack.

"Jack—"

"I'm not Jack," the man snaps. "For Pete's sake, it's Taylor. Chad Taylor."

"Taylor? Okay, Taylor," I babble. "This is important. Seriously. I have a question, and I think I know the answer. But we need to settle this, so we can work something out."

"I'm listening."

"Mr. Taylor," I say, drawing myself up. "Are you telling me I didn't get the part?"

On the way out the door, as the officer exchanges a couple quiet words with Peggy, I have an opportunity to read the sign painted on the door. The printing is professionally done, but clearly several years old, cracking and peeling at the edges.

"Chad Taylor," I read out loud. "Assistant District Attorney."

"Best in the county," the officer says, leading me down the hall. "Picked the wrong guy to mess with, man."

I snort.

"If he's so good," I say, "how come he needs to work two jobs?"

△ △ △

Ben Hanstein *is a reporter for a small-town, digital newspaper, hidden away in the mountains of western Maine. When he's not lurking about courtrooms, alleyways and bloody crime scenes (actually, mostly street festivals, parades and the community theater), he writes, skis and fights a losing battle against his ancient house.*

Ring of Fire

Steve Liskow

Meredith almost dropped the plate of brownies when the dew reminded her she still wore sandals. She marched across the Davis' lawn and tripped over the sprinkler head; only the aluminum foil kept the brownies on the plate again.

She swept the shards of her dignity back together and looked toward the house, hoping Richard hadn't seen her stumble. Framed by the drapes, he sat on the couch in a white shirt and dark slacks, his tie loose and a glass in his hand. Meredith pushed the button and heard chimes echo behind the door.

"Yes?" Richard's voice sounded heavy as unbaked dough.

"Richard?" She tried not to chirp. "It's Meredith Tyler. From across the street? I've brought you some brownies."

"Meredith." She could picture him tightening his tie and hitching up his trousers.

"Are you all right?" Stupid question! "Well, I mean, of course you're . . . um, may I come in?"

The Nately kids rode their bikes up and down the sidewalk, screaming like birds of prey. Richard didn't even turn on the porch light.

"Um, I don't really feel up to seeing anyone right now." His voice sounded ancient, but Meredith knew he was only two or three years older than the twenty-nine she admitted to.

"Richard," she said. "You aren't alone. I know how you feel. And it's terrible." Terrible wasn't the word. Nicole, three months pregnant, had killed herself Monday. The door stayed closed and the light off.

"Richard?"

Meredith stood on his dark steps, the plate of brownies growing heavier by the minute. She had to make sure he was all right, that he remembered to eat. She rang the bell again, awkward in her T-shirt and cut-offs, especially because Richard still wore his suit from Nicole's funeral. He looked handsome in a suit. Well, she looked good in cut-offs. If men saw her legs first, they thought she was still in college. Maybe she shouldn't have changed out of her black dress, but who baked brownies in a dress besides June Cleaver?

The door swung open with a deep swoosh, and Meredith saw Richard's eyes sunk deep in his face. His chin seemed heavier than a week ago, and his hairline looked higher. He slumped against the doorframe.

"Richard," she said. "These are brownies. Just a snack, but I was afraid you wouldn't have anything in the house, you've been so busy with . . . I figured you wouldn't have time to shop. Do you need anything? Coffee? Can I heat something up?"

"Um."

He backed up, his breath at least forty proof. Meredith strode through the vestibule to the living room, dark leather and bright wood, but drab without Nicole, whose framed lopsided grin greeted her from the mantel. A half-empty glass rested on the coffee table. Meredith saw a plastic bag next to the flower arrangement on her way to the kitchen.

"Are you sure you don't need coffee or something?" She could feel Richard's eyes on her hip pockets.

"Um," he said again.

Johnny Walker stood at attention on the counter. Jack drank scotch, too. Or used to. He'd been so drunk after one of their fights that he'd missed the top step in the dark three months ago. Meredith tried not to think about it.

Richard's arm appeared at the edge of her vision and picked up the bottle. The counters were bare and the dish drainer empty, proof that he wasn't eating. He pulled a clean glass from the cupboard.

"Join me?" He scooped ice cubes from the freezer. They clinked like small kittens mewing in the glass. When he poured two fingers over them, the smell made Meredith's eyes water. The Natelys' cocker spaniel barked, shrill, like handclaps. One of the kids was probably throwing something for him to chase.

"No, no thank you, Richard. I just . . ."

"OK." He returned to the living room, and Meredith followed in his wake. He sank to the couch and saw the other glass. He put the fresh one on the coffee table and picked up the older one.

"Save myself a trip," he said.

"Richard," Meredith heard herself say. "Put something under that glass. It'll sweat on the table and ruin the finish. Leave a ring."

"A ring." He lifted the glass and Meredith wiped the table with her hand. Through the window, she saw her own house fading into the reflection of the lamplight. She lived alone in her house, just as Richard did now. She knew the whole neighborhood pitied her. Now, thanks to Nicole, the Nately kids had someone else to talk about in hushed voices after cutting the lawn.

"Do you mind if I close your drapes, Richard? It's getting dark enough so the neighbors can see in. They don't need to see you drinking."

"What? Oh. Sure, whatever." He finished the first glass and put it back on the magazines. Meredith drew the cord, and the drapes hissed closed. The room grew quiet.

"Do you have any idea why Nicole did it, Richard?" she asked. "I thought you two were so . . ."

He shook his head, the soft lamplight revealing what a handsome man he was even with grief-drawn wrinkles scoring his face. Meredith felt self-conscious, like she was watching a boy drive up for her first date. She lowered her hips to the chair opposite the couch.

"We were happy." Richard's voice had an edge like he had to convince himself, too. "And the baby was doing fine. Nikki was scared at first when she found out, but we'd been trying for three years."

His lip trembled before he hid it in the glass again. Children's voices screamed next door, and Mike Nately bellowed at them to pipe down.

"Then she waits until I'm out of town and just . . ."

"That should probably be your last drink, Richard." Meredith forced herself to watch the agony in his face. "Alcohol doesn't kill pain, it just delays it. And a hangover will only make it worse."

"One of us ought to suffer." Richard's black shoes needed polishing. "Nicole didn't. The doctor told me she didn't feel a thing. Just went into the garage, left the door closed, and started the car. The tank was empty and the ignition was still on when I found her Thursday. The police figure she'd been sitting there since Monday. That was when she filled up at the Quick Mart on Lincoln."

"But why, Richard?" Meredith wanted to touch him, but he looked fragile enough to crumble like spun sugar.

"I don't know. She didn't leave a note or anything. The police said she'd drunk a lot." He nodded at the bottle. "I didn't even know she liked scotch. She usually just had a glass of white wine."

"Is there any wine in the house?" Meredith asked. Richard shook his head.

"She only drank when we went out. And not at all since we knew about the baby."

He tore open the plastic bag, and a watch, ear studs, and a wedding band tinkled onto the coffee table.

"Her wedding ring," he said. "They gave me back her stuff after the autopsy. All she had, she didn't even have her purse, just took her car keys out to the garage and started the car. Nothing in her pockets."

His eyes each dripped one tear. Meredith heard a car rumble by outside. She didn't know much about cars, but it sounded like the muffler was shot. Richard picked up the ring, drawing all the light in the room to it, and she felt her heart lurch.

"I meant to bury her wearing the ring," he whispered. "I got so busy making all the arrangements, I forgot to take it to the funeral home. It just slipped my mind. Now Nicole's in the ground, and she doesn't have her . . . doesn't have . . ."

Meredith wanted to put her arms around him, but she felt cold and her feet didn't work. Richard looked like he wanted to throw the ring through the wall.

"May I see it, Richard?"

"It's just a plain gold band," he said. "Nothing fancy. I couldn't afford anything fancy, but she always said that didn't matter."

Meredith ran her fingers over it, smooth from years of wear. It was a little too large for her own small hand.

"God," Richard continued. "I remember when she lost it. She was heart-broken, worried sick. Then it turned up at the health club a few days later. I guess she'd taken it off and forgotten. She said someone turned it in. She looked so happy when she was wearing it again. Relieved, even."

"When was that?" Meredith asked.

"Um, a few months ago." Richard wobbled to his feet, the second empty glass in his hand. The setting sun threw a tiny gold line through a slit in the drapes.

"Sit down, Richard," Meredith said. "You don't need another drink."

"I think I do, Meredith."

"No," she said firmly. "Maybe later." She held up the wedding band. "Nicole's maiden name was Piper, wasn't it?"

Richard nodded. "Uh-huh. Nicole Cynthia Piper. Her mother was Cynthia, too."

"That's what I thought," Meredith said. "But the initials in this ring are 'D.V.T.'"

She handed the ring back to him and watched him hold it close to his face. He slid under the lamp at the end of the couch and looked again.

"Who the hell is D.V.T.?" His face wrinkled like an unmade bed.

"I don't know," she said. "Do you suppose she got another ring to replace the one she lost? The one she didn't really find again, to make you feel better?"

She let him escape to the kitchen.

"Richard? Could you make me one this time, too, please? Strong, with lots of ice."

She heard the cubes clink into two glasses and fumbled in her pocket for the tissue paper. She put it on the coffee table and stood to take the glass Richard offered her. He sat on the couch again before his eyes moved to the tiny package. He unwrapped the paper and stared at the plain gold band.

The scotch burned Meredith's tongue. "Look at the inside, Richard."

"'N. P. D.'" He stared at Meredith. "Where did you find this?"

Meredith sipped her scotch again. The room felt cold around her. "Between the cushions of our couch," she said. "The day before Jack fell down the stairs."

$$\triangle \quad \triangle \quad \triangle$$

Steve Liskow's *stories have appeared in the last four Level Best anthologies (Collect the whole set!). Two won Honorable Mention for the Al Blanchard Award.* Alfred Hitchcock's Mystery Magazine *published "Stranglehold" last summer, and* Who Wrote The Book of Death? *appeared last spring. He likes to think he's still learning.*

Tag, You're Dead

J.A. Hennrikus

Oh, Janet, hello. Isn't that sweet of you—what is it? A casserole? Sure, the refrigerator is over there. There are a few in there already, but I'll freeze some. Saves me from having to think about meal planning for a while. One less thing to worry about.

Kind of you to say—it means a lot. I know that Harry always thought a great deal of you. It still feels so funny—I keep waiting for him to walk through the door. Doesn't seem right, all of his friends were here yesterday, after the funeral, and not him. I suppose I'll get used to it at some point.

Sorry. No, please stay. I'll be all right. Maybe a glass of wine would help. Would you like one? I know it's early, but as Harry used to say, its five o'clock somewhere. My glass is right there. No, don't bother to rinse it. All reds taste the same after a while . . . at least the crap we always bought. I'm trying to use it all up, and restock. Oh, well, you won't mind if I have some, will you? How about some iced tea instead? Freshly brewed.

No, I don't mind talking about it. It was a heart attack. Well, you know that he had some heart troubles in the past. I guess it all caught up with him. He'd been burning the candle at both ends, poor darling. You know, working full time, taking a class at the community college.

Just one class, but he was there a lot. He really poured himself into college life, since he'd missed out on it the first time around. We'd gotten married so young, he dropped out . . . well, spilt milk. He started taking classes and, blam, he's wearing T-shirts and flip-flops, adding texting to his cell plan and running again. Talked about a marathon. At our age. Funny, last summer I'd wanted him to join Facebook to help watch over the kids, and he refused. Showed no interest in helping me make sure the boys were on track. But all of a sudden, he's a college man, talking about Facebook and tweeting and crap I've never heard about.

What? You were? You were his Facebook friend? Really? Hm. We aren't friends, are we? On Facebook, I mean. No, no, really, it's OK. I can hardly keep up with it as it is. Between me and the boys, there's a lot to look over every day. I'll have to look for you. Hidden? Why are you hidden? Isn't that beside the point?

Harry's profile is down? Well, I guess they do that when someone dies. I don't know how they found out. Does it really matter? It's a metaphor for life, isn't it? Someone was here, making connections, and now he's gone. In life and on-line.

What do you mean he isn't really gone? I thought when you . . . no, never mind. Oh, tagged photos. Yes, I know what they are. Just last week our oldest, Josh, was tagged at a party, and he'd told me he was studying. Constant vigilance, that's what you need these days.

Was Harry tagged? In some college photos? That's cute, isn't it? Were they good ones? No, we weren't Facebook friends. He didn't ask. No, no, it was fine. I trusted him. He said he wanted a separate persona, away from me and the kids. I got it. I would have loved a separate persona as well, but that wasn't feasible. Someone had to run the household, watch over the kids. Men, they compartmentalize so easily.

And besides, I trusted him. Implicitly. We were very happily married, right up until the end. No, no, you didn't upset me. It's fine. I'm glad you were Facebook friends. In his English Lit class? Really? I didn't know he was taking . . . well, I couldn't keep track.

He was a machine, just taking class after class. I know, the degree was something he really wanted. You, too? Good for you, Janet.

School just took so much time. Time away. Surely Tony must have felt the same way? Really, for how long? Jesus, Janet, I'm sorry. I had no idea.

It is different now that the kids are older. Still hard on them, no doubt. So you are going to school full time? That's terrific. No, I've never taken classes there. Haven't even been to the campus. No, that wasn't me. There are a lot of Pilots on the road these days. A POC sticker? No, it doesn't stand for Point of Care. I'd hardly advertise my work on my car. It means Pocasset. My folks have a summerhouse there. Well, I'll admit, there aren't many of those stickers around. Damn, I'm going to ground that kid. My son, Donny. He is only supposed to use the car for short rides, since his license is so new, but I can't always keep track. I don't know, maybe he wanted to see his father? Harry spent so much time at school, taking classes.

Not just taking classes? What do you mean? Janet, pull yourself together. What is the matter? Tell me what?

Who the hell is Charlotte? For how long? Was he even taking classes, for God sake? Or was tuition going to hotel rooms? Well I'm sorry, Janet. Finding out my husband was . . . of course it makes me a little upset. Understandable, don't you think? Or haven't you taken a psych class yet? Of course I didn't know. I never even heard of Charlotte. Well, maybe he mentioned it, but I thought he meant the city.

What do you mean I'm taking it well? That is a helluva thing to say. Really, Janet, I thought you were my friend . . . well, no, we're not that close, but still.

I know Harry was your friend. I can imagine that college is very expensive. Well, that's an odd thing to say. Yes, we will be saving on his tuition. But the boys will be going to school in a couple of . . . A loan? I really don't think . . .

No, I don't see. Harry thought I was cyber stalking him? How do you know? That's crazy. I can barely log on, never mind set up a different profile. Who did you say? Well, yes, Lorna is my middle name, but still? What does clearing your cache have to do with anything?

Seriously, you are way off base. OK, maybe it's the stress. It can't be easy, separated. On your own. Trying to make tuition payments. Listen, maybe I can look at our finances, float you a loan. No, really, happy to help. You're right, a cashier's check makes the most sense.

Do you really have to go? You look a little pale. No, no, really. It's fine. How about some more iced tea, for the road? Yes, it is good, isn't it? No, my special brew. It was Harry's favorite as well. They are lovely, aren't they? Oleander flowers. I picked them from the side of the road. They last a good long while, as long as you keep the stems trimmed and change the water.

Whoa, sit down for a second, Janet. You do look peaked. Hope you don't have that flu that's going around. I hear it can be deadly.

Oleander? Yes, the leaves are poisonous. So is the water they've been sitting in. I like to think it adds a little zest to the iced tea. Do you agree?

Janet? Janet?

Oh dear. Hitting your head like that had to hurt. Someone should really call 911. Oh, I guess that would be me. I'll get right to it.

After I finish my wine.

△ △ △

J.A. Hennrikus *teaches and works in arts administration at Emerson College, is a proud member of Red Sox Nation and a social media fanatic. She is also a member of the board of Sisters in Crime/New England and a Guppy.*

Communion

Ray Daniel

I sat in a cafe in the North End, drinking a double espresso, eating a biscotti, and waiting for a funeral. As I watched the snow fall onto Hanover Street, I thought, "What do I do with Joey?"

The cafe was empty except for three kids, teenagers, who sat against the front window, laughing and swearing, the way I once did with Marco and Joey. These kids looked just like we did, except we were always looking out the window in case Angie Morielli walked by in one of her tight dresses, while these kids were looking at their phones.

Shania Twain sang in the background: "Man, I feel like a woman." One of the kids sang along, replacing the word "woman" with "whore." His buddies laughed and joined in. I remembered when Pat Benatar was singing: "Hit me with your best shot."

Joey had said, "Oh yeah, baby, I'll give you my fuckin' best shot."

Marco said, "I hear she's tiny. She might like your best shot."

Joey stood and said, "Fuck you."

Marco stood and said, "Fuck you."

I stayed in my seat and said, "Why don't the two of you go fuck yourselves?"

Then I changed the subject, gloating about how it took an Italian like Mike Eruzione to finally beat the Russians in Olympic hockey. I didn't want to see Joey get another beating. Marco rode Joey all the time. When Joey couldn't take it anymore, they'd fight and Marco would kick his ass.

Those days were over.

I looked into my empty espresso cup and then at the three kids in front of me. In thirty years one of them would be dead, and the other two would go to his funeral. I threw down eight bucks for the guy behind the counter and left.

St. Stephen's Church was just a few hundred yards down Hanover, but I could barely see it through the heavy snow. The radio said that people were freaking out about the storm. In the suburbs, they might even have delayed the funeral. But, here in the North End, where we walked and took the T, nobody gave a shit about the weather. Marco was getting buried no matter what.

I walked down Hanover, past Mike's Pastry and the Peace Garden. When I reached the park across the street from the church, the Prado, I stopped and looked at Paul Revere's statue. It was the famous one from TV. There were already three inches of snow on his hat.

There were a lot of memories in the Prado. When it was too hot to sleep, Marco and I would ditch Joey and sit on a stone bench all night, smoking, drinking, bullshitting, and looking at Paul Revere. That's how you become best friends with a guy. You sit in a hot park on a summer night, drink beer, and talk about how you're gonna own the world. On those nights, we knew we'd live forever.

It was time to get into the church. I crossed Hanover and Victor Testa, the funeral director's son, held the door for me.

I said, "Hey Vic, shitty day for this, huh?"

"You know it, Sal."

Inside, I dipped my fingers in the holy water and made the cross. Then I walked halfway down the center aisle, genuflected, and sat in an empty row. I had been coming here all my life. I made first Communion in this church and got married here. I buried my dad here and then Ma. Now I was burying Marco.

There were only a few people in the church. Most of the mourners went to the funeral home, but I didn't because Marco's ma hated me. She thought that I got Marco in with the wrong people. That was a joke. Marco *was* the wrong people.

I turned and looked up at the organ and the soloist. Angie Morielli was standing up there in a black dress. She was practicing:

"For He is thy health and salvation . . ."

Her voice broke. She tried again.

"For He is thy health and salvation . . ."

I knew that she had been banging Marco. Marco called it being "friends with benefits." I didn't care. God bless 'em, they were adults. Too bad that Joey didn't see it that way. Now I was going to have to kill him.

While Angie sang, I looked around the church. St. Stephen's wasn't like other churches. It didn't have a big cross up front or a giant altar. It had two levels, with one set of columns holding up the balcony, and another holding up the roof. It had lots of windows and was bright even on a snowy day. I always wondered if the people who built it were really Catholic.

A couple of guys from the neighborhood came in wearing Red Sox warm-up jackets, and laughing. They were assholes who didn't know how to show respect. The assholes looked at me in my suit and waved. I didn't smile. I didn't wave. I gave them a look that said, *Sit down and shut the fuck up.* They took a hint and sat far away from me.

That was good, because I didn't want company. I was thinking about Marco in his coffin. Last night, at the wake, I'd knelt in front of Marco and looked at his dead face. He was my best friend. The tears had started to come. Marco would have been OK with me crying at his wake, but everyone else would say I was a pussy. I stuffed the tears down by thinking about what a great job Mr. Testa, the funeral director, had done with the hole in Marco's forehead. I couldn't find a trace of it, even though I knew it was there.

"Hey buddy, how you doing!" Joey bumped me as he sat in the pew. Melted snow splashed on my suit as he took off his coat.

I wiped at the melted snow and said, "Goddamn it, dry off before you come in here."

Joey didn't know that I saw him shoot Marco.

Marco had this little apartment he'd outfitted with an HDTV, a fridge, and a big bed. He called it his "man cave." I called it his "fuck pad" and he had laughed and said, "Yeah, that too." Marco and I were over there watching the Bruins. I had to take a piss and was in the bathroom when Joey knocked on the apartment door. I peeked out of the bathroom and saw Joey say, "I told you to stay the fuck away from Angie." He shot Marco twice in the chest and once more in the head. Then he ran. The moron had never checked for witnesses.

Now, in the pew, I leaned towards Joey and asked, "You go to the funeral home?"

"Yeah, you know, pay respects to his ma."

"His ma hates me."

"Oh, I know. She was bitchin' about how you got Marco killed."

How I got Marco killed?

I said, "With all due respect, fuck her."

Other wet mourners started coming into the church from their cars. The funeral lady, in her black dress, came down the aisle and stood in front of the altar. When she genuflected I looked at her good legs. I suppose I should have felt guilty. Jesus, it was a funeral. But, she had really good legs. Marco would have called them "dancer's legs." She turned and began directing people into rows.

When everyone was settled, the organ music started. We stood and turned to watch Marco's casket. They didn't use any pallbearers. One funeral guy pushed the casket from the back while old Mr. Testa directed it from the front. Angie sang from the balcony.

"For he is thy health and thy salvation."

Joey whispered, "Jesus, that Angie can sing, huh Sal?"

"Yeah, she sings great."

"I'll bet that's not all she does great."

"Shut the fuck up. You're in church."

A month ago I heard Joey tell Marco to stay away from Angie —that Marco had a wife and he should show respect to his marriage. That was bullshit. The truth was Joey had taken a shot at Angie, and she had laughed in his face. Told him he was no Marco. It was a fucking stupid thing to say. Joey had killed Marco over a wet dream.

The funeral Mass began. I stopped thinking about Joey and started listening to the priest. He was telling a story about how Jesus' cousin, Lazarus, was dead for four days before Jesus woke him up.

"Can you imagine that?" the priest asked, "After being dead for four days, Lazarus just walked out of that cave. Now, we know that Marco is not going to stand up and walk away . . ."

He had that right. Not with the back half of his head blown off. It would freak people out, especially Joey. I looked at him next to me. *What am I gonna do with you?*

I had figured I'd kill Joey after the funeral. But now that I was listening to the priest and feeling the peace of the Mass, I was having second thoughts. Killing him was the right thing to do. It was justice. But, Jesus wouldn't have done it. Jesus would have told the police and let them handle it.

I looked over my shoulder. Lou the cop was back there. He had been directing the traffic, helping the Testas get the cars parked. Now he had come in from the cold. It would be easy to go back there and tell him what I knew.

The priest said, "And now a reading from Marco's friend, Joey."

"Wish me luck," Joey said, and walked to the podium fishing a folded sheet of paper out of his jacket.

Marco's ma gave Joey a reading? Un-fucking-believable. Marco would have been pissed. Joey was always sucking up to our mothers. He'd give them his fake polite voice and then we'd hear, "That Joey's such a nice boy, why can't you be more like him?"

Because I don't want to be a loser, Ma.

Joey said, "A reading from the Book of Wisdom."

Yeah, wisdom from Joey. That's like getting salsa from a cannoli.

Joey put on his glasses and started reading some shit about how Marco had died too early. "For his soul was pleasing to the Lord, therefore he sped him out of the midst of wickedness."

Wickedness? What wickedness? Me?

If I popped Joey, would they read this at his funeral? Would they say that this asshole had been taken because he was too goddamn pure to live among us? What a load of bullshit. It would be better if he went to prison, where he'd get passed around like a bong. That would beat listening to this bullshit at his funeral.

Joey finished his reading. As he walked back to my row, he rested his hand on Marco's casket, like he was saying, "Goodbye, old pal." Fucking hypocrite.

Joey sat next to me and asked, "What did you think?"

I looked front and said, "You did good."

The Mass went like it always did. Marco's niece and nephew brought up the gifts for the communion and the priest said, "Let us ask our Father to forgive our sins and to bring us to forgive those who sin against us."

We prayed the Lord's Prayer. It was my favorite prayer, because it was the only one I could remember. The Hail Mary always gave me trouble after the word "thee." I hated when the priest made me say it as penance after confession.

Normally the prayer made me feel good inside. Peaceful. But with Joey standing next to me, it didn't work. My thinking wouldn't stop. We prayed:

"Our Father, who art in heaven, hallowed be thy name.

Thy kingdom come, thy will be done, on earth as it is in heaven."

I'll bet they don't shoot people in the face in Heaven.

"Give us this day our daily bread.

And forgive us our trespasses as we forgive those who trespass against us."

Really? Forgive? Forgive Joey for killing my best friend? Seriously?

"And lead us not into temptation, but deliver us from evil."

Deliver us from evil? What evil? Killing Joey? That wouldn't be evil. That would just be fucking justice. Joey shot Marco because Joey wanted to grab Angie Morielli's big tits. He was pretty evil, if you ask me.

The word "forgive" kept banging around in my head. "Forgive our trespasses" meant that I wanted God to forgive Marco, because he had some pretty good trespasses. He was married, and still he was banging Angie. He did it to spite Joey. It was his way of saying, "There ain't nothing you want that I can't take away." How much of that shit could Joey take? Maybe Marco brought it on himself.

I had some trespasses too. I had screwed Angie before either of them—just a year after she sang at my wedding. It was nothing serious, just a little change of pace, but I wasn't sure God would see it that way. Also, Marco and I did things like take care of scumbags who wouldn't pay their debts. Lou the cop couldn't prove it, but Jesus could. He's probably got a fucking videotape or something. Marco needed some forgiving in his box, and I'd need it when I was in mine. So maybe forgiving Joey was part of the deal. I forgive a little, and God forgives a little.

The priest said, "Let us offer each other a sign of peace."

Everyone started shaking hands. I shook hands with the guy in front of me, and the lady behind me. There was no one to my right. I looked to my left and Joey had his hand out, the one he used to shoot Marco.

Joey said, "Hey, peace be with you."

I took his hand, "Yeah. You too." I looked back at Lou the cop. I could tell him now.

The priest held up his giant communion wafer and said, "This is the Lamb of God who takes away the sins of the world. Happy are those who are called to his supper."

We all said, "Lord, I am not worthy to receive you, but only say the word and I shall be healed."

The funeral lady knelt and we all followed. Then she got up and started walking down the aisle, directing people up to take communion. When she got to us, I shook my head, but Joey stepped out into the aisle.

Joey asked, "You're not making communion?"

I didn't move. I just squeezed the back of the pew in front of me, my knuckles turning white. I remembered when I had made first communion with Marco and Joey. As we stood in line, wearing our white suits, Joey had whispered to me, "Sal, Frankie told me these things taste like shit. If mine tastes like shit, I'm gonna spit it out."

Eight-year old me had said, "That would be a disgrace. I'll kick the crap out of you. You keep your mouth shut and let it melt like Sister Angelina told us."

Now, Joey waited his turn in line. When he got to the front he opened his mouth. He was one of those guys who liked to let the priest do all the work. I always took the wafer in my hand and fed myself. The priest dropped the wafer into Joey's mouth, and then Joey followed the crowd down the side of the church and back into the pews. He stopped next to me, on my right, and knelt.

I leaned towards him and whispered, "Did you make fucking confession last night before taking communion?"

Joey kept his wafer-filled mouth shut and nodded.

"Yeah? Did you confess that you killed Marco?"

Joey's eyes widened, and he shook his head like he didn't do it.

I said, "Don't pull that shit with me. I was there. I saw you shoot Marco. Two in the chest," I tapped Joey's chest, "and one in the head." I tapped Joey's forehead. "It's lucky that Testa fixed up Marco, so his mother could have an open casket."

Joey went to speak, but I interrupted him.

"No, you just shut up and let the Body of Christ melt in your fucking mouth. You kill a guy and then take communion at his funeral? Do you think that wafer's gonna save you from Hell?"

Joey swallowed and put his hand on my arm, "Sal . . ."

I pulled my arm back and said, "Either you go to Lou and confess what you did, or you're not gonna live till Sunday."

The communion was ending, but I had had enough of church. I stood and stepped into the aisle. I pointed at Joey and said, "You got one day."

I genuflected, then turned and walked down the aisle past Lou.

Lou gave me a look, "You leaving already, Sal?"

"Yeah, Lou, I've done all I can."

I crossed Hanover Street into the Prado. It was still snowing. As I passed Paul Revere, I turned and looked at my church. I swore to myself. The Mass and all that talk of God and Jesus had confused me, made me stupid. Now, Joey knew I was coming for him. He would either hide or try to kill me. There was no way he'd confess to Lou.

The bell at the top of the church started tolling. They were rolling Marco towards his grave. I stood under the statue and paid my last respects. I knew there'd be another funeral before the snow melted.

△   △   △

Ray Daniel: *Raised in Revere, Massachusetts, Ray travelled beyond the 128 beltway into the wilderness of MetroWest to find his fortune., before settling down and raising a family in this new frontier. Today, he toils in the high-tech industry, writes crime fiction, and works the fertile soil of his lawn.*

The Book Signing

Kathy Chencharik

"Could I please have your autograph?"

Gretchen Garrity glanced up at the young man clutching a copy of her latest bestseller *Murder Is Only A State Of Maine*. She smiled when she realized he was the last of a steady stream of fans that had come this evening to the Maine Muse Bookstore for her signing.

"Sure," she said, taking the book from him. "How would you like it signed?"

"To Andy."

"As in Mayberry?"

"What?"

"Never mind. You're too young," Gretchen said, putting pen to book.

"I've read every one of your *Murder Is Only A State* series about a serial killer who murders someone in each state. If you keep it up, you'll have more books than Sue Grafton will. After all, there are only twenty-six letters in the alphabet."

Gretchen laughed as she handed the book back. She glanced at her watch. "It's getting late. I have to go. It was nice meeting you."

"I'm new to writing myself," Andy said, watching as Gretchen gathered her things. "And I've recently joined a writers group."

"Good for you."

"I have so many questions. Would you mind if I asked for a little advice?"

Gretchen grabbed her purse and stood up. "My car's parked out back. If you'd like to walk me out, I'd be happy to give you a few pointers."

Mist rising from the Penobscot River enveloped the only car parked behind the bookstore as they stopped beside it. Above, a light from a sodium vapor lamp winked through the mist. Gretchen opened her purse. As she pulled out her keys, a pen fell to the ground. Andy stooped down, picked it up, and handed it to her.

"Thanks," she said. "Now, what would you like to know?"

"One, how do you make your murder scenes so realistic? And two, what would be your best piece of advice for a novice writer like myself?"

"Those are simple." She unlocked her trunk, then turned toward Andy. "And I can answer both with one piece of advice."

"Really?"

"Yes." Gretchen pressed the button on her pen-like switchblade and said, "Write what you know."

△ △ △

Kathy Chencharik lives in North Central Massachusetts with her husband, dog and cat. She works part-time in an independent bookstore and loves every minute of it. This is her second story to appear in a Level Best anthology. The first appeared in Deadfall, *where she was also honored to have her photo chosen for the cover.*

Dead Man's Shoes

Leslie Wheeler

"Think I'll mosey over to the Calloways' and see about Jack's shoes," Herb Higbe announced at breakfast.

His wife Doris and daughter Hillary stared at him. "His *shoes*?" Hillary repeated.

"I'd like them," Herb said.

"Whatever for?" Hillary demanded.

"To wear. Jack was a friend, and we're exactly the same size."

"You'd actually wear the shoes of a man who's just died? That's so . . . so . . . creepy."

"Nonsense. People do it all the time. If I don't take the shoes, Amber'll donate them to the thrift shop or some other outfit. I'm saving her the trouble. Heck, I've waited a decent interval. Been two weeks now."

Hillary pushed her chair back from the kitchen table and started for the door. "I still say it's creepy. I'm going for a walk on the beach."

"Watch out for poison ivy on the path," Doris called after her. "You don't want another bad case."

Hillary slammed from the house. Herb exchanged glances with Doris. Time was, Hillary's departures had upset them. She was such a blonde-haired, blue-eyed beauty that they'd never quite believed she was their child. Rather, they thought of her as a fairy tale princess, whose real parents, the king and queen, would one day return to whisk her away from the lowly commoners who were raising her. But Herb had stopped worrying about that long ago.

"Maybe you shouldn't take the shoes," Doris said now.

"I *want* them."

Doris looked shocked by the bald declaration of desire. Herb was shocked, too. He sounded like a whiny child—like Hillary when she didn't get her way.

"I mean, I'm sure Jack would want me to have them," Herb backpedaled. "He had quite a collection. 'Member how we used to tease him about being a male what's-her-name?"

"If you say so," Doris replied. She gathered up the breakfast dishes and took them to the sink. Herb stared at the back of her blue terry cloth bathrobe. "That's a nice robe," he said more to appease her than anything else. "Is it new?"

"Mmmm," Doris said without turning around.

"I'll be going," Herb said.

A dense forest of oak and beech separated the modest Higbe cottage from the Calloways' sprawling, shingle-style McMansion. Both houses overlooked Lambert's Cove and had access to its stretch of private waterfront. Anxious to avoid Hillary on the beach, Herb followed the narrow, rutted driveway shared by the two houses, one fork leading to the Calloways', the other to the Higbes'.

As he walked along, visions of wing tips, tasseled and plain loafers, oxfords, lace-ups, slip-ons, boots, and sandals danced before his eyes. Shoes made of soft Italian calf, suede, and hard, shiny patent leather. Shoes by Bruno Maglia, Johnson & Murphy, Mephisto, and Gucci. Shoes he'd seen in the catalogs he kept stashed in his desk drawer at work, and coveted without being able to afford them. Not on his bookkeeper's salary with everything going to support Hillary in a style befitting a princess. Now, all this fancy footwear would be his for free.

Amber Calloway, trophy wife turned trophy widow, greeted him at the door. A tarnished trophy at that. Her long, auburn hair hung limp and lusterless around a pale, lined face with no make-up. Had grief done this to her? Or had he simply not noticed how she'd aged in the eight years she and Jack had been married? Once, she'd been the envy of the older wives. Not any more, Herb suspected.

"Thought I'd stop by and see how you're doing," he said.

"I'm okay," Amber replied.

"Good . . . Don't know if you've thought about what to do with Jack's things, but I'd be happy to take his shoes. Save you an extra trip to—"

"They went to the church bazaar last week," Amber interrupted.

"All?" Herb couldn't hide his disappointment.

"Every last pair." Amber smiled for the first time.

"Well, in that case . . . Let us know if there's anything Doris and I can do." As Herb turned to go, he spotted the stubbed, sand-caked toe of a boat shoe peeking out from underneath a bush by the side of the house. He pulled out the shoe and its mate and held them up. "Mind if I take these?"

"How did *they* get there?" Amber stared at the shoes like they were a pair of dead animals. "You don't want those old beat-up things. I'm putting them in the trash."

She tried to grab the shoes, but Herb stepped quickly away, holding his prize aloft and out of reach. "At least I don't have to worry about breaking them in."

Amber looked displeased, but didn't argue further.

When Herb was out of sight of the Calloways', he stopped and replaced his own newer boat shoes with Jack's. It didn't matter that the shoes were coming unstitched, that the leather was cracked and stained, or that the rawhide ties were frayed. What mattered was that they had belonged to Jack. Jack Calloway had been everything Herb wasn't. Wildly successful as a hedge fund manager, Jack was also movie-star handsome with wavy black hair and piercing blue eyes. So what if Jack's dazzling smile reminded Herb of a shark's? Jack had still oozed charm and money. Maybe, just maybe, a little of

Jack's glamour would rub off on him if he wore Jack's shoes.

Herb touched his thinning hair expectantly. But that wasn't where he felt a change. No. It was coming from his feet. They tingled, as if they'd been asleep and were just waking up. Then his feet began to move, not because he wanted them to, but because the shoes were making them. Herb could feel the worn leather pushing against his heels, tugging at his toes, urging him back toward the Calloways'. What was happening here? Were the shoes motorized and being guided by some unseen evil genius with a remote? Or maybe they were aliens disguised as shoes.

Whoa! Herb felt the same loss of control he'd experienced as a child when he'd put on roller skates for the first time and didn't know how to stop. At least he wasn't going as fast as he had on skates. But he was still scared. Especially when he realized he was on a collision course with the house. Herb reached out for something to grab onto. Nothing. Inches short of the house, the shoes swerved and carried him, arms flailing, down the stretch of lawn that led into the dunes. As he headed across the grass, Herb glanced over his shoulder to see if Amber was watching this bizarre performance. But there was no sign of her in the large, glassed-in living room that faced the Vineyard Sound.

The lawn gave way to a sandy path, which dipped into a hollow. Here, the path cut a swath through a thicket of scrub oak and cherry trees—some nearly six feet tall—along with beach plum and the ubiquitous poison ivy, before climbing over the dunes to the beach. Just before the ascent over the dunes, the shoes yanked Herb down a narrow side path leading into the thicket. Wary of poison ivy, Herb balked. The shoes yanked harder, leather chafing against his sockless feet.

Herb gave in and let them take him to a small clearing. Practically invisible from the main path, it was the perfect hiding place. Perhaps local children used it for that purpose. If so, there was no sign of their recent presence in the form of candy wrappers or forgotten toys. The sand looked as if it had been swept clean by tidy-minded little misses with pink plastic brooms like the one Hillary had had as a child.

Herb tried to leave the clearing, but the shoes wouldn't let him. They held him in place like cement. Well, he couldn't stay here all day. With difficulty he removed the shoes and put his own back on. The abandoned shoes ran in demented circles around him. Maybe that's what they were: demons. They certainly weren't angels. Herb had never known shoes to behave this way. Or any way, for that matter. But then he'd never worn a pair of Jack's shoes before.

Herb bent over and grabbed at the shoes as they whirled past. Finally, he managed to catch first one, then the other. They flapped frantically in his hands like wild geese struggling to get free. He carried them, still flapping, out of the dunes and back up the lawn in front of the Calloway house. Amber had come out on the deck and was watching him through binoculars. Herb waved sheepishly. Amber lowered the binoculars and disappeared into the house.

When Herb returned to his own home, Doris, now dressed for the day, was waiting for him with a puzzled expression. "Amber just called. She said you acted weird. First, you insisted on taking an old, worn-out pair of Jack's shoes. Then, you hurried across the lawn and into the dunes in them, waving your arms like a crazy person. Are you feeling all right?"

"I'm fine. Thought I heard something in the dunes and wanted to see what it was," Herb lied. If he told her it was the shoes' fault, she'd think he really was crazy. The shoes had calmed down on the walk home, but now they suddenly jiggled in his hands. Sole slapped against sole, sending a shower of sand onto the kitchen floor.

Doris frowned. "What're you doing? Put those outside immediately and leave yours there, too. I don't want sand all over the house."

"Naughty, naughty," Herb scolded as he put the shoes on the ground.

"I'm off to do some errands," Doris said when he came back

inside. "Going to work on your models today?"

"Thought I would."

From the kitchen window, Herb saw his wife hesitate by Jack's shoes. She stooped as if to pick them up. Then, realizing he was watching, she straightened and strode to the car. When Doris was gone, Herb went outside. He wasn't sure what to make of the shoes, but until he figured out what was going on, he had no intention of parting with them. He put them in a box for safekeeping. Otherwise, Doris might throw them out, as Amber had wanted to. Women were like that, always anxious to get rid of anything that might make a mess.

Herb took the shoebox into the shed he'd converted into a workshop. He'd loved ships and the sea ever since he was little. But being out on the water made him seasick. So he indulged his passion by building ship models. Now that he was retired and he and Doris lived on Martha's Vineyard full-time, he worked on them almost every day. At the moment, he was constructing a model of the *Shamrock IV*, an America's Cup challenger in 1920. Normally, the task absorbed his attention. Not today. His mind kept wandering back to his travels in Jack's shoes. Why had they taken him to the clearing in the thicket? It was almost as if they'd wanted to show him something. What? All he'd seen was an empty patch of sand.

Herb remembered a snippet of conversation he'd overheard in Cronig's Market right after Jack's death. "You hear about Jack Calloway? Dead of a heart attack at sixty-three?" one man said.

The other man chuckled. "Knowing Jack, there's probably a lot more to the story than—" Noticing Herb, he broke off.

A knock on the door brought Herb back to the present. Frank Nolan, the West Tisbury Chief of Police, stepped inside. "Just stopped by to see how you're doing with the *Shamrock*," said Nolan, who shared Herb's interest in model building.

"It's going well," Herb said. He worked in silence for a few minutes, then, on an impulse, he asked, "You went to the house the night Jack died, didn't you?"

"That's right."

"Did you notice anything . . . um . . . unusual?"

"Nope. Jack was slumped in a chair on the deck, dead. Amber said he'd had heart trouble for years. Guess it finally caught up with him."

"You guess?" Herb probed.

"I know. The coroner confirmed he died of a heart attack. Why do you ask?"

"Just curious. Anything else?"

Nolan thought a moment. "There was a lot of sand on him, but that's not unusual. There's sand everywhere. I figured he'd been for a walk on the beach. Also, he smelled of skunk, but that's not unusual either. Skunks come out on the beach at night. You get in their way, they'll spray you. Happened to me once."

"That's all?"

"No, wait a minute, there is something." Nolan frowned at the model.

"What?' Herb asked eagerly.

"The lazy jack on your model's not rigged right. The way you've got that line, the sail can't be lowered without some of it falling into the boat and conking someone on the head."

After Nolan left, Herb re-rigged the *Shamrock* and started on another model. Finally, he decided it was time to quit for the day. As he approached the house, he heard his wife and daughter's raised voices, but couldn't make out what they were saying. When he got close, the voices stopped.

Hillary looked like she'd been crying. Doris appeared upset, too. "I'm leaving on the eight-thirty ferry to Woods Hole," Hillary announced.

"You're welcome to stay as long as you like," Herb said. He didn't mean it, though. Hillary's departures were no longer cause for alarm. After thirty-one years, the king and queen still hadn't come for their princess. Herb suspected they never would. Instead, a string of princes had claimed Hillary. None of these relationships lasted very long. Hillary always returned home, tearful and unhappy, to await the arrival of the next prince. She was awful to be around during these times. When she wasn't bad-mouthing the last prince-turned-toad, she blamed Doris and him for letting another loser sweep her off her feet. No. Herb wasn't sorry to see her go. Now he and Doris could resume their quiet lives, free from Hillary's—what was that expression? Something about storm and drama.

"I've made up my mind," Hillary said.

□   □   □

Doris had often remarked that Herb could sleep through a hurricane, but tonight everything bothered him. The mattress was too hard, the pillow too soft. He was too hot, but after he'd thrown the covers off, too cold. Just when he was finally settling down, the rattling started. The noise sounded like it was coming from under the bed, but the only thing there was the box with Jack's shoes.

The rattling continued. Now, it sounded like whatever it was had moved out from under the bed. Herb reached for the flashlight he kept on the nightstand in case of a power outage. He aimed it downward, in time to see the shoes shove his slippers aside and take their place. They beat a rat-a-tat-tat on the floor as if raring to go.

"Shhh, you'll wake Doris," Herb whispered. When the shoes didn't stop their racket, Herb sat up in bed and swung his legs down, planning to remove them from the room. Before his toes even reached the ground, the shoes leaped up and clamped themselves onto his feet. Then they took off like race horses let out of the gate. Herb barely had a chance to grab his jacket as the shoes stampeded from the house.

A mix of terror and excitement filled Herb as he sped across the beach. A dark rounded object loomed ahead. "Watch where you're going!" he yelled at the shoes. At the last moment, they sidestepped the object. Herb felt something brush against his leg. He shone his flashlight on the plump, bushy rump of a retreating skunk. "That was a close call! What're you trying to do? Get me skunked like Jack?"

Ignoring him, the shoes continued their headlong rush. Over the dunes in front of the Calloway house. Down the narrow side path to the clearing in the thicket. Inside the clearing, they took him over to a beach plum bush and pranced up and down in front of it. Herb beamed his flashlight on the bush. "There's nothing here but a goddamn bush," he fumed. "Don't tell me you brought me all this way just to—"

A rustling sounded in the brush. The shoes pressed against his heels, tugged at his toes. Now, they seemed to want him to flee. "Oh no, you don't," Herb said. "I'm not leaving until I find out why you made me come here." When the shoes kept on insisting, he decided to take them off. Herb laid the flashlight on the ground while he removed the right shoe, balancing on the opposite foot as he did. He was in the midst of removing the left shoe when he heard more rustling in the brush, this time louder than before. Herb got the shoe off, but nearly lost his balance and fell. What was there? Another skunk, some larger animal, or . . .? The shoes raced to the entrance to the clearing. "Cowards!" Herb called after them. They returned to his side, nudging his bare feet like worried watchdogs.

Herb bent to pick up the flashlight. It illuminated the lower branches of the beach plum bush. A piece of nubby, white fabric was caught among them. He pulled the cloth free and slipped it into his jacket pocket. Before he could rise from his crouching position, something smashed into the back of his skull. A searing pain, then nothing.

□   □   □

Herb came to, dazed and hurting. He groaned and opened his eyes. Doris' anxious face hovered over him. "Where am I?" he murmured.

"In our living room."

"How did I get here? The last thing I remember was being hit on the head."

"Amber mistook you for an intruder," Doris said.

"Did she have to clobber me? Couldn't she have waited to find out who it was?"

"Amber hasn't been herself since Jack died. She panicked and let you have it. Then, when she realized it was you, she came to the house, all upset, to get me. We brought you back here."

"How? I gotta be too heavy even for the two of you to carry."

"We dragged you."

Herb put a hand to his throbbing head and felt grit. "That's why there's sand all over me?"

"Yes."

"Like Jack," Herb muttered.

"What about Jack?" Doris asked.

"Nolan said there was sand all over him the night he died."

"You've been talking to Nolan?"

The edge in her voice told Herb he might be on to something. "Yeah. Like some others I won't name, I've been wondering why Jack keeled over so suddenly. He was only sixty-three."

"Jack had a heart condition." Amber's strained voice came from a shadowy corner of the room.

"So I've heard. But . . ." Herb let the sentence hang, clueless how to finish it.

"What?" Amber prodded.

"I may not be the sharpest pencil in the box, but I know a thing or two," Herb declared with a confidence he didn't feel.

Amber came out of the shadows and stood over him. "What do you know?"

"That there's . . . um . . . more to the story of Jack's death than . . . um . . . meets the eye," Herb said. He wasn't sure whether this was true, but it sounded good.

"Oh, really?" Amber's tone was sarcastic, but Herb thought he detected a note of worry.

"Yes, really."

Amber and Doris looked at him expectantly, obviously waiting for him to continue, but again Herb faltered. What more could he say? He had a dim sense that the pieces to this particular puzzle—or ship model—were there in the back of his brain, if he could only figure out how they fit together. He'd just have to take a stab at it and hope he wasn't too far off base.

"Maybe Jack didn't die on the deck but someplace else," Herb said. "On the beach. Or in that clearing in the thicket, where I was tonight."

Amber and Doris exchanged anxious glances. They had never been friends, but now they almost seemed conspirators in some plot Herb didn't understand.

"And your point is?" Amber said.

"Well, if Jack didn't die where he was found, then someone must've moved him."

"That's ridiculous," Amber said. "Why would anyone go to that much trouble?"

"You tell me." Herb fixed what he hoped was a sufficiently steely gaze on her. He could tell he had Amber on the spot from the rapid rise and fall of her chest. She looked like she was about to explode. "It was Doris's idea to move Jack," she blurted.

So they *had* been in league with one another. Now, though, that league appeared to be falling apart. "Why did you do it?" Herb asked his wife.

Doris drew herself up to her full height, chin held high. "No one needed to know."

"Know what?" Herb asked softly, but Doris merely shook her head.

The answer came to Herb in a sickening flash. "About you and Jack?"

Doris gasped. "How did you guess?"

"I found this in the clearing just before I was knocked out." Herb removed the piece of white terry cloth from his pocket and held it out for her to see. "It's from your old bathrobe," he told Doris. "The one you replaced when it got ripped. Oh, sweetheart how could you?"

Doris bowed her head. "I'm sorry, Herb. You weren't supposed to find out."

Herb felt like he was going to be ill. He peered into Doris's familiar face with its wrinkles and the brown age spot the size of a penny on her left cheek. "But you and Jack? I thought he liked his women—" He broke off, for fear of offending her.

"Young and beautiful?" Amber said. "You're right. That's why the bastard was banging your daughter, not your wife."

"Hillary? Jack was having an affair with Hillary?" Herb stared at Amber, dumbfounded. "But Jack was twice her age."

"Welcome to Jack's world," Amber said bitterly.

Herb turned back to Doris. "Is this true?"

"I'm afraid so."

"Why didn't you tell me?"

"I had my suspicions, but I didn't find out for sure until that night when . . ." Doris hesitated and glanced at Amber.

"It's okay," Amber said. "You can tell him how I chased Hillary back to your house with one of Jack's golf clubs after we both realized he was dead."

"*What?*" Herb stared at her, alarmed.

"I was so mad, I wanted to kill someone. And because Jack was already gone, Hillary was the logical candidate. Fortunately, Doris intervened and got us both to calm down."

And he hadn't heard a peep—or rather a single shriek. No wonder Doris said he could sleep through anything.

"Then she came up with the idea to drag Jack from the clearing and put him in a chair on the deck," Amber went on. "She said that what'd gone on that night was nobody's business."

Herb wasn't surprised. Doris had always protected Hillary when she got into messes with men. Probably she always would.

"Hillary agreed, and so did I," Amber said. "I'm no fool. Think I wanted all the jealous bitches on this island pointing at me and saying, 'We knew it wouldn't be long before Jack replaced you with another trophy'? Not on your life!"

She said this with such rage that Herb shrank from her. What was that expression? Something about scorned women? Seeing Amber like this, he could easily imagine her killing Jack if he hadn't already been dead. Hell, when he thought of Jack with his filthy hands on Hillary, he wanted to kill him himself.

Herb's anger made his head throb more. He shifted on the couch, trying to find a comfortable position. The blanket covering him slipped off his ankles, revealing his bare feet.

"What did you do with my shoes?" Herb asked Doris.

Amber and Doris exchanged glances again. "You weren't wearing any when I found you," Amber said. "I assumed you walked to the clearing barefoot."

"I didn't see any shoes either when I came back with Amber," Doris said.

"But—" Herb heard a faint tapping at the window. Speak of the devil. The left boat shoe stood on its heel on the outside sill, peering in. Herb levered himself up with difficulty and staggered across the room. Doris and Amber tried to block his way, but he pushed past them to the window. The shoe hopped off the sill and joined its mate on the ground. Moonlight shone on the shoes as they started to slink off toward the dunes. Herb was tempted to go after them and throttle them, as he would've liked to throttle Jack.

Don't blame us, he imagined them saying. *We were only the messengers. You wanted to know what it was like to be Jack, and now you do.*

Just before they vanished from sight, Herb could swear he saw the rawhide tie on the left shoe stick straight up in the air. Waving good-bye? Or flipping him off, as a parting gesture from Jack?

△ △ △

Leslie Wheeler *is the author of three Miranda Lewis "living history"*
mysteries, most recently Murder at Spouters Point, *published in*
October 2010. Her short stories have appeared in four previous Level
Best anthologies. She is delighted to be published again in Thin Ice,
and also to join the Level Best team as a contributing editor.

Thin Ice
Crime Stories by New England Writers

edited by
Mark Ammons, Kat Fast,
Barbara Ross & Leslie Wheeler

Please send me ___ copies @ $15 per copy _____

Postage & handling ($2 per book) _____

Total $_____

Please make your check payable to Level Best Books.

If you wish to pay by credit card or PayPal, you may order through our website at www.levelbestbooks.com.

Send book(s) to:

Name _____

Address_____

City/State/Zip _____

Level Best Books
P.O. Box 371
Somerville, Massachusetts 02144